Praise for Teresa Hill's novels

Unbreak My Heart

"Teresa Hill has crafted a taut, intriguing story with memorable characters, plenty of heart—and more than a few chills. Enjoy! I did."   —Kay Hooper

"A compelling story about love, loyalty, and family secrets. . . . I couldn't put it down!"
—Barbara Freethy

"Proof positive that author Teresa Hill is a talent to be reckoned with. Her ability to paint stories that use vivid and complex emotions is a special talent that is sure to be an audience pleaser."
—*Romantic Times* (Top Pick)

"A moving family drama that touches the reader on several levels. . . . Fans will fully enjoy."
—*Affaire de Coeur*

"A poignant family drama . . . gut-wrenching."
—*The Midwest Book Review*

continued . . .

More Praise for *Unbreak My Heart*

"With the same unerring ability she displayed in *Twelve Days*, Teresa Hill finds the reader's heartstrings and isn't afraid to pull. . . . She had me in her grasp right from the prologue and didn't let go until the final page. . . . Make sure you have a few hours at your disposal before opening *Unbreak My Heart*. . . . Let this master storyteller pull you into her world."
—*The Romance Journal*

"A truly compelling novel of finding and letting go of the past so that the future can be lived to its fullest potential. Have a hanky handy." —*Rendezvous*

Twelve Days

"Take a leap of faith and read this book. *Twelve Days* will touch your heart, make you smile, and remind you that Christmas miracles really can happen, if only we reach out to others and believe. Teresa Hill spins a tale that is pure magic. *Twelve Days* is the best Christmas story I've read in ages."
—Catherine Anderson

ALSO BY TERESA HILL

Unbreak My Heart

and the story of how the McRaes became a family
Twelve Days

THE EDGE
of
HEAVEN

Teresa Hill

AN ONYX BOOK

ONYX
Published by New American Library, a division of
Penguin Putnam Inc., 375 Hudson Street,
New York, New York 10014, U.S.A.
Penguin Books Ltd, 80 Strand,
London WC2R 0RL, England
Penguin Books Australia Ltd, Ringwood,
Victoria, Australia
Penguin Books Canada Ltd, 10 Alcorn Avenue,
Toronto, Ontario, Canada M4V 3B2
Penguin Books (N.Z.) Ltd, 182–190 Wairau Road,
Auckland 10, New Zealand

Penguin Books Ltd, Registered Offices:
Harmondsworth, Middlesex, England

First published by Onyx, an imprint of New American Library,
a division of Penguin Putnam Inc.

First Printing, April 2002
10 9 8 7 6 5 4 3 2 1

Copyright © Teresa Hill, 2002

All rights reserved

 REGISTERED TRADEMARK—MARCA REGISTRADA

Printed in the United States of America

For my editor, Cecilia Oh,
because she makes time lines
so I can keep the dates straight in my own stories.
And because she wasn't afraid of Emma and Rye.

Chapter 1

He got into town just before dawn, having driven all night. Once he'd decided to go, he'd gotten into his truck and left, not wanting time to think about giving into this impulse one more time.

There was a note on the seat of the pickup with directions to the town and an address, but Rye didn't need to look at them. He'd memorized them long before he'd found the courage to come.

He wasn't sure what he was going to say once he got there. He usually played it by ear, and so far, it hadn't been too difficult to find out what he wanted to know. The hard part had been making himself keep searching.

It started snowing on I-75 in the mountains in Tennessee and kept it up the whole way to the tiny town of Baxter, Ohio, on the banks of the Ohio River just west of Cincinnati.

There were 8,436 people living here, according to the sign on the edge of town, which also bragged about being the home of an artist named Richard Landon, who made, of all things, snow globes.

Rye shook his head over that. A town would have to be pretty hard up for things to brag about to mention a man who made kids' toys.

But it was pretty here, like something out of a wintry postcard. The streets of downtown were wide, the sidewalks broad, many of the old brick storefronts preserved intact, everything neat and polished. There was an honest-to-goodness town square, an old courthouse behind it, a block of streets surrounding it with a parklike setting in the middle.

He turned into a neighborhood of Victorians, late 1800s, three stories, high-pitched roofs, stained-glass windows, wide porches. As someone who worked in construction, he couldn't help but admire the workmanship that had gone into restoring them.

He drove slower and slower, the closer he got. If he wasn't careful someone would call the law on him, and that was the last thing he needed.

.Finally, he saw it. No. 12. Maybe the prettiest house on the street. A soft gray with touches of blue on the trim and in the exquisitely beautiful stained glass in the windows and the panels of the front door.

There was money here. He frowned even more.

There was a pretty sign in stained glass hanging from the mailbox that said, McRae Construction, Props. Sam and Rachel McRae.

Yeah, this was it.

He parked on the opposite side of the street, cut the engine and the lights, and sat there, snow falling softly all around him, the neighborhood just starting to stir.

What now?

Knock on the door?

It was too early for that.

But soon lights started coming on inside the house, one by one, upstairs first and then down. A car came by, driving slowly, and the morning paper was hurled onto the front lawn. The front door of the house opened. A dark-haired man in worn jeans and a faded gray sweatshirt came outside and retrieved the paper. What was he? Early forties? Late thirties? That would be about right.

Not five minutes later, a taxi stopped in front of the house. Doors to the taxi and the house were thrown open. The man came back out. He must have been watching and waiting himself.

A woman climbed out of the taxi and ran to him, throwing her arms around him. He picked her up and spun her around in a circle before lowering her to her feet and giving her a quick kiss on the cheek. They were both laughing.

It looked like she'd been gone a while.

The man picked up her bag to go inside, but she stood there for a minute staring up at the house like she'd been absolutely aching to see it.

Someone was home.

Rye wondered if he ever would be again.

Emma sat hunched down in the backseat of the taxi, her cheek pressed against the cold of the window, careful the whole way not to make eye contact with the driver.

She'd done a hasty makeup job on the train ride home from Chicago, hoping to keep the worst of the last twenty-four hours from showing on her face—because she didn't want to talk about it. Not yet. It was still too raw. She was still shaking too much. Later, once she'd calmed down and had a chance to think it through, she'd tell.

She came down the snow-covered street to find the house waiting for her like the sanctuary it had proven to be. The people inside of it had opened up their arms to her and her brother and sister and given them what they'd desperately needed—a home, a place to belong.

She'd never been afraid here. Never. She was counting on that now.

The taxi parked by the curb. Emma grabbed her hastily packed bag, paid the driver, and climbed out. The front door of the house opened and Sam stood there. She ran across the snow to him. He caught her in his arms and lifted her off the ground, swinging her around like he used to do when she was younger.

It hurt. She tried not to let that show, then feared she'd start to cry. She pressed a hand to her mouth, somehow turning a near sob into laughter, which made the tears all right. Sam understood. She could see it in his face as he brushed a kiss across her cheek.

"God, Em, I didn't think you'd ever get home."

"I'm sorry. I should have come home for Thanksgiving. I missed you all so much."

"It's all right," Sam said.

They'd tried so hard to let her be on her own now that she was in college. The freedom had been heady at first, but on the back of that came the realization of how terribly hard it was to be so far away from all of them.

"I wish I'd come sooner," she said, fighting the urge to pour out the whole sad story to him. "It's felt like forever since I've been home."

"For us, too, Em."

She eased away from him, the side of her face throbbing. She was afraid she hadn't managed to hide the bruise, but Sam didn't say anything. Good. She'd bought herself some time.

Emma looked up at the house and forced herself to smile like nothing was wrong. "Where is everybody? Still asleep?"

"No. Not today. Let's get you and your bags inside, and I'll tell you what's going on."

Rye drove around town, had breakfast, killed some time thinking about his options.

This Sam McRae was in construction, probably a small contractor if his business was based out of the house. Rye could ask about a job. He had the experience. It would probably get him in the door, give him a chance to talk to the man. That's all it had taken before. A little conversation, a few subtle questions, and he'd known he was in the wrong place.

But as he drove back to the house, he saw the man come outside again, another suitcase in his hand. The man hugged the woman for a long time, then got into a big SUV and left.

Should he follow him? Or stay right here?

One thing about getting the urge to do this at Christmas—people tended to go away. This was the third time he'd gone looking for a man named Sam McRae, and he was surprised he hadn't found people leaving before this.

He sat drumming his fingers on the steering wheel, thinking about Christmas at some motel in this little town waiting for the man to come back. It wasn't a very pretty picture, but then Christmas hadn't been for years.

Why couldn't everyone just work through the holiday? He always found himself at loose ends, with time off and nothing to do. Then he'd pull out his list, think about trying to cross one more name off it.

What the hell? 'Tis the season.

It had become one of searching for him.

A phone call to every man on the list would probably have done the job. But what if the Sam McRae he was looking for didn't particularly want to be found? He didn't think he'd trust a voice on the other end of the phone who simply said, No, he wasn't *that* Sam McRae.

And hell, once Rye knew what the man was like, he might not want to have anything to do with him. So he came in person. It was safer this way, gave him some sense of control. He wanted to know a little about the man first. To know what he was getting into, whether it would be worth the trouble. Honestly, he didn't see how it could be, but still at Christmastime he kept climbing into his truck and taking off with his list.

Looking toward the house once again, he saw that the woman was still standing on the porch, her arms wrapped around herself to ward off the chill, and she was staring at him.

Well, hell, he thought. She'd seen him, and there was really no reason to put this off any longer. First steps were always the hardest. He'd take one right now. Obviously the woman and Sam McRae were very close. He'd see what he could find out from her.

He climbed out of the truck and slowly made his way up the walk. As he got closer, he realized she was younger than he thought. Early twenties, he'd guess, pretty in a quiet, clean-cut, good-girl kind of way, with dark green eyes and soft brown hair. It hung to the top of her shoulders, curling a bit at the ends. He liked the smoothness of her skin, the clean lines of her face. She seemed too young to be the man's wife, too old to be his daughter.

"Hi," she said as he stopped at the bottom of the three steps leading up to the porch. "Can I help you?"

"I hope so. That was Sam McRae, wasn't it?"

"Yes. You just missed him."

"Is he going to be back anytime soon?"

"Not for a week or so, I'm afraid. Something came

up unexpectedly. My Aunt Ann . . . Do you know Ann?"

"No. Don't think I do." But this one was a talker. It seemed she was going to make it easy for him.

"She lives near Cleveland, has for years."

"Oh." As if that explained it. He supposed in a town this small, most people who knew Sam probably knew Aunt Ann, too.

"She's having a baby. Hopefully not for another three months, but the baby's trying to come early. Rachel and the kids took the train up last night to help out with her other children. Sam left this morning to join them."

"Oh," he said. "And you must be . . ."

"Emma," she said helpfully.

He frowned. *Emma*? Was that supposed to mean something to him? Because it didn't. Truth was, he knew next to nothing about Sam McRae of Baxter, Ohio.

"Sam's my father," she said finally.

"Oh." It was impolite to ask, to even imply. . . . But curiosity was getting the better of him. He wondered how he might word the question. . . .

She rescued him by adding, "Let's say, my father in every way that counts."

He grinned. "Used to that reaction, huh?"

She nodded. "The women look disapproving. The men grin and wink."

"Yeah, I can see 'em doing that," he said, putting one foot on the bottom step and resting a hand on a column of the porch. "Sorry if I . . . Well . . . It's none of my business. I shouldn't have said anything."

"It's not a problem. Really. I introduce Sam and Rachel as my parents, and people know right away it's not a relationship based in biology. It's not something we've ever tried to hide."

And then he couldn't quite help himself one more time. "You don't mind? Being adopted, I mean?"

"No."

She gave him an open, honest look that said it would never occur to her to mind in the least. Good for her. Good for Sam McRae for making her feel that way.

"So, was Sam expecting you? He left me a list of appointments to cancel, but I haven't worked my way through them all yet. They were scrambling to get out of here, and he was afraid he'd forgotten some things."

"Not an appointment. Not really." He took a chance on lots of things having gotten lost in the shuffle and said, "We'd talked about me doing some work for him, and I thought I'd take a chance and stop by."

"You're not from here?"

"No."

"Well, we don't have to talk about this outside in the cold." She sized him up and must have decided he looked trustworthy. "Why don't you come inside and we'll have some coffee."

He was torn between taking advantage of the situation and giving her a lecture about how to keep herself safe. But he really wanted inside this house.

She turned toward the front door. He reached around her, intending to open it for her, but she jumped, startled, and then whirled around. They both stopped right there, a little too close for comfort. He was sure he'd blown the whole thing.

"Sorry, I was just going to get the door for you."

Once upon a time, in another life, he'd had a mother who'd taken great pains to instill some manners into him. He'd found they worked wonders with women, whether he was trying to impress them or just get them to talk to him. He still used them to this day, something he was sure would come as a surprise to the woman who'd taught him so much. He hadn't laid eyes on her in years.

"No, I'm the one who's sorry," Emma said. "You just startled me."

"Look, I can come back another time," he offered. "When Sam's here."

"Don't be silly. I'll make some coffee and take your name and number, and when Sam calls, I'll tell him you came by."

Great. He could just imagine how that would go. *Guess what, Sam? Guess who's here?* He wondered if the name even meant anything to the right Sam McRae anymore.

"I'll come back," he said. "It's almost Christmas, and—"

"No, really. Come in." She practically dragged him inside. "Sam said it's been crazy around here. He's got three projects going at once, and nothing coming together the way it should. He wouldn't have left, but Ann's husband wanted to be at the hospital with her and someone needed to take care of their kids. And if something did happen to the baby . . ." She stopped. "Sorry. More than you need to hear, I'm sure. But you know how much Sam hates letting a customer down."

"Sure," he said, as if he did know.

"I'd hate to let you get away when Sam needs help," Emma said, standing next to a little table in the hall that held a phone and a neat stack of papers. She had a list and she seemed to be working her way down it, much in the same way he was. She'd crossed six things off already. "He already warned me about Mrs. Wright, about the party she's having in January, when half her kitchen is still in pieces and her custom cabinets went somewhere out West instead of here,

the way they were supposed to. I don't suppose you
know anything about cabinets, do you?"

He shrugged as easily as he could. "I can lay tile
countertops with the best of 'em. Could probably hang
cabinets, if I had to. I'm better with brick, and I'm
great with rock."

"Rock?" Emma asked.

"You know, fireplaces, patios, sidewalks, walls, sid-
ing for houses, any kind of decorative stone."

"Oh. I don't know if Mrs. Wright has any of those
or not. We'll ask Sam when he calls."

"Okay." He figured he'd just have to talk her out
of that somehow, but that was for later. For now, he
just wanted her to talk.

He shrugged out of his coat, which she offered to
take and hang up. He used the time when her back
was turned to study what he could see of the house—
gleaming woodwork, polished wood floors, soft yellow
walls, and lots of windows draped in lace-panel curtains and floral-print swags.

It was neat and clean, and it smelled of something
he could never have identified by name but just
seemed to say "home." There was a big curving staircase to the right, rows of pictures in a pleasing, if
haphazard, arrangement up the stairway wall. He was
hungry to study each and every one, but she turned
around and caught him staring.

"Great house," he said.

"Isn't it?" She paused there in the hall in front of
the staircase and underneath a small, octagonal window of stained and beveled glass. Morning sun was
streaming inside. Dancing across the walls, it caught
in her hair and her eyes as she stepped to the right,
into the light. It was like she was standing in fairy
dust, he thought. Like he'd caught a fairy creature
come down to earth.

As if any creature like that would have anything to do with him.

He shook his head to dislodge the image, but it stubbornly remained, the dazzling young woman smiling up at him, too accepting and trusting for her own good.

"The house is more than a hundred years old," she said. "It belonged to Rachel's grandfather, although it was in bad shape when Sam and Rachel came here. You should see some of the pictures. They practically rebuilt it."

"Oh?" So maybe Sam McRae wasn't so rich, just lucky enough to have a wife who inherited a house like this and lucky enough to know what to do with it. Maybe he and Sam would have something in common after all. He'd have loved to get his hands on an old place like this. Not that he ever expected anyone to drop a house like this into his hands.

Emma led him into the front room. He ran a hand over the big, intricately carved, mahogany mantelpiece over the roaring fire, let himself glance at those photographs, trying not to be too obvious.

"That's your mother?" he asked, pointing to one of a pretty blonde woman with a baby in her arms. They looked sweet, both of them.

"Yes. And my sister, Grace. She'll be eight in a couple of weeks." Emma pointed to another picture of a boy, dark haired and mischievous looking. "That's Zach. He's twelve and almost as tall as Rachel and me. And, of course, that's Sam."

It was a casual shot, outdoors in front of a huge Christmas tree. They were all bundled up in coats and gloves, the kids in hats and scarves. Five people huddled together and grinning like crazy. The pretty blonde woman holding a much younger Zach in her arms, Emma leaning in close to her side, and the baby, a bundle of pink fluff, looking quite content in Sam's arms.

He studied the man, looking for something familiar in the shape of his face or the color of his eyes. He'd only had a glimpse so many years ago, when the man had been nothing but a stranger to him, maybe a hazy memory from so long ago when he was a little boy. He wasn't sure if he remembered Sam or if he'd conjured up an image in his mind, simply because he wanted so badly to remember.

This picture on the mantel screamed normal, happy family. His family had looked like that once upon a time. But it had all been an illusion, now faded away. Emma came to stand beside him, waiting quietly and letting him look.

"You have a lovely family," he said finally, and then had to turn away. Searching for anything to latch on to, his gaze caught on the intricate swirling pewter that made the base of a snow globe. "That's unusual."

"Recognize the house inside it?" Emma asked.

"Should I?"

He hadn't even looked, to be honest, but he did now. It was a Victorian, the same dove gray with light blue trim, lovingly rendered in such detail. He'd never seen such a beautifully made piece inside a ball of fake snow. Emma handed it to him.

"It's this house?" he guessed.

"Yes."

He flipped the heavy glass globe over in his hands, then flipped it back, making it snow, as it was outside right now.

"I had one of these when I was a kid. Used to love it."

"Me, too," she said. "I had a cheap version of this one, actually."

"This one?"

"Yes. That's a family heirloom, but copies are made here in town. You must not have come in from the east or you would have seen the factory. Rachel's grandfather was Richard Landon."

"The guy whose name's on all the signs?"

"Yes. This was his house. He used it as a model for this snow globe, which became his first well-known piece. He used a lot of the buildings in town as models."

"The Christmas town?" He'd seen all the signs, but had been too distracted by his mission to even try to figure out what they were talking about. Christmas town. Christmas festival. He wasn't big on Christmas.

But looking at the house inside the snow globe, he realized he did know it. He'd had a version of *The Night Before Christmas* illustrated with, among other things, pictures of this house. If he was a man who still believed in anything like magic or signs or things that were somehow meant to be, he'd have said that was significant. But he didn't believe in any of those things anymore, and that book was all over the place. Practically every kid had a copy.

"Yes, it's the Christmas town," Emma said. "If you're going to be here for the next week or so, you'll see. The festival's starting on Thursday."

He wasn't in the mood for any kind of festival, and he hadn't truly celebrated Christmas since maybe the last time he'd seen Sam. His life had gone steadily downhill from there. Handing the snow globe back to Emma, he said, "It's a beautiful piece."

"Come on." Emma put it back on the mantel, then steered him toward the kitchen. "The coffee's hot. I know it's closer to noon than morning, but I was on the train all night. I slept some this morning, and now I'm starving. I was about to make breakfast. Have you eaten?"

"No." he lied, not sure if he could choke down a single bite—but he wanted to stay.

Emma sat him down on a stool at the breakfast bar and poured him a cup of coffee, strong and black, just the way he liked it, then poured one for herself.

"How do you like your eggs?" she asked.

He took about two seconds to consider it, then said, "Any way you want to make 'em."

It would keep him here for a while longer, and he could probably keep her talking while she cooked.

She made great eggs, scrambled them with three kinds of cheese and some peppers, served them up with a toasted English muffin and blackberry jam she said one of her great-aunts made.

Great-aunts who made jam? It sounded so damned normal.

He'd grown up in a small town much like this. But now he lived in a big, anonymous place where hardly anyone knew his name or where he was from or what he'd done. He liked it that way. Emma seemed to fit right in here, in a pretty, old house with all her relatives out making jam and probably baking fresh bread. She seemed as wholesome a woman as he'd ever met in his entire life.

It was like a trip back in time to the childhood he'd left behind. He sat there for the longest time just watching her move through the kitchen and letting her chatter while she worked, mostly about Sam's business. It sounded like the man did well for himself, and the woman she called her mother did stained glass. Stonework couldn't quite compare, but it was construction and at the best of times a bit of artistry.

Under any other circumstances, he thought they all might have something in common.

"So, you think Sam won't be back for a week?" he asked, once he'd cleared his plate not once but twice and thanked her for the meal.

"I'm not really sure. It depends on what happens with Ann," she said, getting up and taking her plate to the sink. He followed her, doing the same. "Even if the baby doesn't come now, she might be in the hospital for weeks, and she has a three-year-old and a six-year-old. Sam and Rachel might bring them back here. I know that would be hard on Ann, but Rachel has tons of family here. Two other sisters, a sister-in-law, and two great-aunts. That way everyone could pitch in and help take care of the kids. Ann and Greg wouldn't have to worry about anything but the baby."

He nodded. Sam McRae seemed to have an abundance of family.

"I'm sure they'll be back in time for Christmas," Emma said, reaching for the dishwasher to load the plates and the silverware. "Can you wait that long?"

He thought about it. What else was he going to do? "I can wait."

"Well . . . Do you have a place to stay?"

He frowned. Surely she wouldn't invite him to stay here. Surely she knew better. He might have to stay just to make sure nothing happened to her.

"I'll find something," he said, as she pulled jam and salt and pepper off the table. He took them from her, put the jam in the refrigerator and the salt and pepper in the cabinet from which she'd taken them.

"Well . . . It's kind of hard with the festival and everything. The town just fills up, and it's not like we've got that many motels anyway."

"I'll be fine, Emma."

"You could head toward Cincinnati," she said, wiping off the breakfast bar with a hand towel. "It's not far."

"I'll do that," he said.

"Okay . . . If you're sure. But . . ."

Rye grinned as he figured it out. She thought he was down on his luck. Granted, his pickup looked beat-up. It probably needed to be washed after driving so long through all that wet, muddy snow. But it wasn't that old, and it was beat-up because it was a working man's truck. His clothes were nothing fancy. Jeans and a shirt were all he needed. But he supposed she could have taken those two things together with what he'd said and come to the conclusion that he needed a job so badly, he'd come here with nothing but a passing acquaintance with Sam McRae and the most casual mention of a job. Not that he didn't know what it felt like to be desperate for work. But he wasn't at the moment.

"I just wrapped up a big job in a suburb of Atlanta, and I guess you could say I've been thinking about heading this way for a while. It seemed like as good a time as any. And don't worry. I can afford a hotel room. I won't end up sleeping in the truck or anything like that."

"Sorry." She'd finished with the table and hung the towel on a hook by the sink, facing him reluctantly. "I didn't mean to pry."

"I know."

He leaned back against the counter, crossed his arms, and let himself take another long, slow look at her. She was sweet, he realized. Kind. Generous. And likely very, very soft. Where had all the women like her gone to? Probably they were all gathered in little towns like this one and the one he'd left behind as a boy. And somebody had to look out for them.

"Tell me you weren't going to invite me to stay in this house with you? Surely Sam taught you better than that. I'm a complete stranger to you."

"You said you know Sam."

"Anybody could walk up to your door and claim to know Sam. His name's on the sign on the mailbox."

"I know, but . . ."

"Emma, a woman's got to be careful these days."

"I know," she said, a little flush coming into her cheeks. "I wasn't going to invite you to stay in the house."

"Good."

"There's an old carriage house out back." She went to the back window and pulled the curtains aside. "See? Sam converted it into an office a long time ago. There's a cot and a bathroom, too. It's not much, but people have bunked there before, and I just thought . . . Just in case."

"Thank you," he said sincerely, grinning like he hadn't in years. "But I'll find a place on my own."

"Okay. The Baxter Inn on Main is nice and not too expensive. The diner next door has some of the best food in town, if you like home cooking. Nothing fancy, but filling."

"I like that just fine."

He stood up straight to leave, thinking it had been an altogether pleasant time here with her. It had been a while since he'd enjoyed something as simple as a meal shared with a nice woman. He thanked her once more, and all too soon found himself at the front door oddly reluctant to leave.

"What are you doing here all by yourself at Christmas?" he asked as he shrugged into his coat. "Why didn't you take off with the rest of them?"

"I was just finishing up at college . . ." she began.

Which made her . . . What? Twenty-two? Maybe twenty-three?

He felt ancient beside her.

"I'd planned to spend this week with a friend." She paused, for a moment looking uneasy, then pasted on a smile and continued. "But something came up at the last minute. I just left them a message on the answering machine and got on the train to come home early, while Rachel and the kids were already heading north. Sam sent them ahead in case the weather got bad today, and then he waited here for me. But I decided to stay."

"All by yourself?"

"Yes. A few days of peace and quiet sounds good to me." She took a breath. "Things have been hectic lately."

He nodded, thinking she seemed uneasy about something, thinking it was really none of his business, even if she was.

"Well, I guess I should go," he said, reaching for the door.

"Wait. You forgot something."

"What?" He turned back to her.

"Your name. I can't tell Sam who you are if I don't know your name."

"Sorry," he said, but it was no accident that he hadn't told her. "Emma, maybe it would be better if I just wait and talk to him when he gets back."

"But you came all this way," she said. "It must be important."

"It is, but . . ." He took a chance and admitted, "Look, it's more personal than business, okay?"

"Okay." She put her hand on his arm, ever so lightly, the touch thoroughly unsettling him. "Are you in some kind of trouble?"

"No." He stepped back. Her arm fell to her side, and he found himself missing her touch in a way he had no right to do.

"Sam's good when it comes to trouble, and he takes care of people."

He shook his head and tried not to think of the irony of that. One of those Sams had sure done a number on him. Not that he was going to explain it to her. He'd hang around town for a few days, see what he could find out, figure out what to do next.

"Look, it's nothing for you to worry about," he said finally. "Okay?"

"Do I at least get to know your name?"

He stared at her, not sure what to say to something as simple as that.

She laughed a bit. "It's such a hard question? Your name?"

"These days it is." But he'd gone and done it then. She was even more curious, and, he suspected, even more likely to go talking about him to Sam. Finally, he said, "It's Rye."

"Do you have a last name, Rye?" she asked, sticking out her hand for him to shake.

"I've got a couple," he said, forcing himself to grin.

"Aliases?" she teased.

"Not exactly." He took her hand. It was very, very soft and very smooth, small and slight. He liked holding that hand.

"You're just a mysterious kind of guy?"

"Ryan's the last name. John Ryan, but most everybody calls me Rye."

"Okay, Rye. I won't tell Sam. Not if you don't want me to."

"Thank you. And thanks for the meal."

She smiled again. "Any friend of Sam's . . ."

"I told you, anybody could walk off the streets and claim to know Sam."

"Okay. No more breakfasts with men claiming to be friends of Sam's."

Chapter 2

Emma felt better having him in the house.

She'd thought she'd feel perfectly safe here. Once she'd found out Rachel and the kids were gone and that Sam was leaving, she'd actually been relieved. Although she'd never wish for any kind of trouble for Ann or the baby, it meant Emma's secret was still intact. She hadn't had to explain anything.

But once Sam had left, she hadn't liked being here alone. She wasn't looking forward to trying to get to sleep by herself tonight, as ridiculous as that was, and she was reluctant to let Rye go.

Who in the world was he?

She puzzled over it as he buttoned up his jacket, one that wasn't going to keep him warm in this climate. She heard a touch of the South in his voice. He probably wasn't used to this kind of weather.

She was reaching for the front door to let him out when the phone rang.

They both froze, just looking at each other. She wished it was Sam, and he looked like he hoped it wasn't.

"I won't tell," she said.

One more secret she would keep from Sam, when there had been so few things she'd ever kept from him. She picked up the phone, thinking it was probably Rachel or one of her aunts wanting news about Ann. They were all on her list of people to call. She pressed the receiver to her ear and said "Hello."

"Emma," he said, his voice sounding smooth and easy, as if this were just any other old day. "I thought I'd find you there."

"Mark," she whispered, stunned.

"I wish you hadn't gone and left like that, Emma. My parents will be here any minute. What am I going to tell them? That we had some silly little fight?"

"What?" she asked. *Silly? Little?*

"Oh, hell. Never mind. Just come back, Emma. I'll tell them you're going to be late. We'll still have the rest of the week in the city with them. They've been waiting for months to meet you."

As if she'd just turn around and go back up there? As if she were going to forget what he'd done?

"No," she said. She didn't need to explain, didn't owe him anything.

"Emma, don't be like this."

"Like what?" she whispered.

"So silly."

"I don't think I am," she said, with a near-death grip on the phone.

"All couples have their little spats," he said.

Yeah, she knew all about little spats. "I'm going to hang up now."

"What?" The word positively exploded out of him.

"I'm going to hang up," she said firmly.

"Don't you dare."

"And I don't want you calling here. I don't have anything to say to you."

"Emma, this is crazy. You and me . . . You know what you mean to me. And this . . . I know I lost my temper, but . . . Surely you're not going to let something as silly as this—"

"I'm going to hang up now," she said again.

"Why, you little—"

She hit the button on the phone to disconnect the call, cutting off whatever else he might have said. But he'd been yelling, and the words carried through the air, the tone unmistakable.

She looked up and saw Rye watching her, his expression grim. She feared she was near tears, and her hands were shaking something awful.

He took the phone from her hand and set it down on the small table by the door, then said, "Come and sit down."

"I'm fine," she lied.

"No, you're not."

She went to turn away, thinking she didn't want to talk about this, and she didn't want him looking at her, didn't want him seeing. But he put his hands on her arm to stop her. For a moment, it just felt awful. Like she couldn't have gotten away from him if she'd wanted to.

She went a little crazy at that. For a second, it was like when Mark grabbed her and wouldn't let go.

Emma cried out, went to jerk herself away, and in the next minute her head cleared, and she realized this was Rye, not Mark. She was home, not at school, and then she felt so foolish.

"I'm sorry," she said softly, her eyes flooding with tears.

"No, I'm sorry." He waited, grim faced and fighting as hard as she was for breath, not moving a muscle, probably worried about scaring her again.

How had her life come to this?

"Will you come and sit down? Please?" he asked. "Because for a minute, you looked like the whole world was spinning, and I don't want you to fall down. That's the only reason I . . . I wouldn't try to hold you against your will, Emma. I promise."

"Okay."

She shivered. Rye hovered by her side, holding out a hand to her, ready to take her arm but not touching her this time, not without her permission. She took one step closer to him, and that was all he needed. His arm came around her waist, lightly, and she felt the warmth coming off his body.

For a moment, she let herself lean into him, not liking that little kick of fear that came from realizing how much bigger he was. The solidness of his body, the strength in it. She hadn't thought of those things in so very long—the things a man's strength could do to a woman. Or a child.

It had always seemed like another life entirely.

Until yesterday.

God, how in the world had this happened to her?

"Let's just sit down, okay?" He led her to the big, comfortable sofa in the living room, the one near the fireplace. Emma sat down in the corner, wanting the support, drawing her legs up beneath her, her head resting against the back.

"Want to tell me about it?"

"No, but I bet you can figure it out all by yourself."

He sat on the edge of the sofa facing her, one arm resting along the arm of the sofa, the other on the cushion behind her head. "Husband?"

"No. Thank goodness it never came to that." There had been hints that he wanted to give her a ring.

"Boyfriend?"

"He used to be." Emma shivered. She was still so cold.

Rye took the afghan off the back of a nearby chair and draped it ever so carefully around her. "And he's not happy about that?"

"No."

Rye took her chin in his hand and tilted her face up to his. He snapped on the lamp on the end table beside her. Leaning in close, he stared grimly at her right cheek, the tips of his fingers gently moving along the bruise she'd hoped so desperately didn't show.

Grim faced, he asked, "What else did he do?"

"Nothing."

"Emma?" he said harshly

"Please." She winced at his tone of voice. What was happening to her when nothing but an angry male voice could do this to her?

He leaned back, giving her some room, and when he spoke again, his voice was deliberately low and measured. "Did you tell Sam?"

"No," she admitted.

"Why not?"

"I will tell him. Just not now. I . . . It just happened yesterday. I'm still having trouble believing it actually did happen. It's all a big jumble in my head, and I need to sort it out, okay? Can you understand that?"

"As long as you don't start making excuses for him. Or listening to the pathetic little excuses he'll likely offer."

"No. I won't. I was on the train a few hours after it happened, and I'm not—" She started to say she wasn't like her mother. Not Rachel, but the woman who'd given birth to her. The one who'd made such disastrous choices in her life. A woman she'd mourned for so long.

She would have said she had nothing at all in common with her mother, but then her boyfriend had practically thrown her across the room. She shivered, hearing his voice once again, seeing his face. It was like all of a sudden, he'd turned into someone she didn't even know.

Rye took her cold hands between his warm ones. "Tell me?"

"I wouldn't even know where to start. It's a long, sad story, one I haven't talked about in years."

She didn't want him to know, either. She didn't want to see the pity in his eyes. Emma didn't think anyone had pitied her in years. Why would they? She had a terrific life. Two incredibly kind, loving parents. A brother and a sister she loved dearly. Relatives, friends, good grades. She was Miss Responsibility. Strong, capable, smart. She'd been so sure she was all of those things.

Until this.

"I just want to sleep," she said, if she could do that without dreaming.

"Did this jerk hit your head?" Rye asked. "Did you fall down or into something and hit your head?"

"I hit the floor," she admitted.

He put his hands on her head, coming close once again. It was okay, she told herself. She wasn't afraid. Not if she closed her eyes and thought of something else.

She ended up concentrating on the differences between Rye and Mark. Rye had a working man's body, a working man's hands. She's seen it in the subtle flex of muscles in his arms beneath the sleeves of his shirt and felt the slight roughness of his hands. He was warm, and he smelled very, very good. Something plain and strong and masculine, not fussy at all, just good. He moved like a man at ease with himself and his body, and he watched everything around him so carefully, seeming to miss nothing. Either that or he was looking for something. But what could he be looking for from Sam?

He found the bruise on her head. She winced as he traced the edges of it. "Did you lose consciousness?"

"No." She frowned. "Not really."

He tried again. "Everything went black for a moment?"

"Maybe. I don't know. My head hurts, and I'm tired. But even if I had a concussion, it's been more than twenty-four hours. If I was really hurt, something would have happened by now, right?"

"Probably, but you said it still hurts," he said, easing away.

"I sat up all night, shaking, on the train. Didn't sleep a wink. Which is probably why I have such a headache now."

"Okay. So, the guy's not here in town, right?"

"No, he's in Chicago."

"You think he'd come here?"

"I don't know." She didn't even want to think about that. "I would have sworn he never would have hit me, but he did."

"Sorry. I just . . . I don't like the idea of you being here all alone."

"And you're going to offer to stay with me? You're the one who told me I shouldn't have even let you in the door," she reminded him. "I'm supposed to trust you now?"

He looked over at the phone. "We could call Sam."

"You didn't want to call him, remember?"

"I remember, but . . . You're going to need someone."

"Rye, I know practically everyone in town. If I need help, I can find it."

"I'll help you," he said, which was just about the

kindest thing anyone had said to her in a long time.
He meant it. She was sure of it.

"Thank you."

"Look, what was the name of that inn you mentioned?" He asked, getting to his feet. "The Baxter
Inn? Let me call them and see if they've got a room.
That way, I'll at least be able to tell you where I am
in case you need me."

She told him where to find the phone book, in the
desk tucked under the stairs, and when he went to get
it, she wondered who he was. For a moment, he reminded her of Sam. Something about the way he was
so determined to take care of her, maybe. Sam was
like that.

She'd always known she could count on him and
was afraid she'd disappoint him when she told him
what had happened—as if it were her fault. She knew
that was silly, but dammit, that's how it felt. Like
something she'd allowed to happen to her, when she
should have been able to prevent it.

Rye came back and called the inn.

"Two nights. That's it. Then they're booked." He
hung up the phone, then started writing on the note-
pad. "I'm leaving the phone number just in case. Sure
you won't change your mind and call someone?"

"I'm not going to let him run me out of my own
house," she said.

"Okay. I want to check the locks on the doors and
the windows, just in case." He started in the living
room, pushing aside the pretty lace panel curtains and
jiggling the locks on the windows. "I still don't like
leaving you here alone."

"I'll be fine. It scared me, because I didn't see it
coming at all. But it really wasn't that bad."

"It looks like it must have been bad, Emma," he
said, heading for the dining room.

It held a wide mahogany table that seated twelve, an antique passed down from Rachel's great-great grandmother, an old-fashioned sideboard to match, a dainty lace tablecloth more for show than anything else, and silver candlestick holders. Emma thought about the familiar room. Home. She was home. So why was she still shaking? Why didn't she feel safe? Rye could see that, and she felt like she owed him some explanation.

"What you're seeing?" she began. "Me falling apart? It's not all about what happened yesterday. It's . . ." It was about what happened before. She was sure the extreme nature of her reaction was mostly about what happened before.

He didn't say anything, but came to stand in the wide opening between the living room and the dining room, watching her and waiting.

"Please don't ask me anymore."

"Okay," he said. "But even if it wasn't that bad, you're still scared to death, and I still don't like leaving you."

"The inn's not ten minutes away. The sheriff's department's even closer. If anything happens, I'll call." That should have made her feel better, shouldn't it? She wasn't sure if she was trying to convince herself or him.

It wasn't working on her, probably not on him, either, because he checked the kitchen. She heard him in the family room, in the sunroom.

He came back and pronounced the first level sound and locked up tight.

"You can check the upstairs if you like, but it's just the same way. Sam wouldn't have it any other way."

"Okay. If you're sure. How about some aspirin for your head before I go?"

"That would be great." She directed him to the cabinet above the refrigerator, where the medicine was stored, and he came back with two aspirin and a glass of water. "Thanks."

"Anything happens, you'll call? Promise me?" he said, standing over her and looking grim.

"I promise."

Well hell, he thought as he finally made himself walk out the door. Even if he'd wanted to leave now, he couldn't. Not after seeing the look on her face when her ex-boyfriend called.

He'd been up close and personal with men who made a pastime of beating up on women. It was like they thought they had a right; the woman was theirs, after all. What if Emma's ex was like that? If he didn't stay in Chicago? If he came here and hurt her again?

He really didn't need this.

Sam McRae couldn't possibly be worth it, even if he was the right Sam.

If Rye had any sense at all, he'd get in his truck and keep driving.

But as he stood there across from the house, thinking about Emma inside and all alone, he decided he could give it another day. See if her phone rang again, and if she had a better idea of when her family would be back.

A woman like her . . .

He thought again of the slight puffiness of her cheek, the bump on her head, thought of all the things that man might have done to her that she refused to admit. He thought of her being scared every time the phone rang or someone came to the door.

He could wait another day.

Emma lay on the sofa, wrapped up in her blanket, staring at the fire and afraid to go to sleep. But at some point, she must have drifted off because she jerked awake much later, when the room was dark and cold. The sun had gone down, the fire died down, too, and the phone was ringing.

For a minute, she wasn't sure she could pick it up, and then she decided she was being silly and melodramatic and snatched it up. "Hello."

"Hi, Em,"

It was Rachel. She was so glad to hear her voice. Rachel who was kindness incarnate, so supportive, so loving. Sometimes like an older sister to Emma and often the mother she needed so much.

"You okay?" Rachel asked. "You don't sound like yourself."

"I was napping. I couldn't sleep last night on the train, and I just crashed this afternoon," she said. "How's Ann and the baby?"

"Ann's scared, but hanging in there. They've got her on some medicine to try to stop the contractions, but they're just not sure if they'll be able to."

"And if they can't?"

"Then she'll have a very premature baby," Rachel said.

"But the baby will be okay?"

"Well . . . Honestly, they're not sure."

"Oh."

Neither one of them said anything for a moment. They didn't have to. Emma knew how hard this would be. She took her strength from them, had always thought they could get through anything together.

"Do you want me to come up there?" she asked, thinking maybe they'd take the decision out of her hands. It sounded so easy, just to go up there.

"No, sweetie. Not yet. Let's give it a day or two and see what happens. Besides, Sam said you looked all wiped out. Finals and all, huh?"

"Yes." She hated lying about it, but she was still thinking there might be a way to hide from it, maybe to pretend it never happened. How silly was that?

"What happened to Mark and his parents? You sounded so excited about meeting them," Rachel asked.

"Well . . ." And then she got all choked up. Darn. She had to say something. "We broke up."

There. That was easy. And true. It would have to be enough for now.

"Oh, sweetie. I'm sorry. Sam didn't tell me that."

"I didn't tell him," Emma confessed. "If I had, he would have felt like he had to stay, and I know he was worried about getting up there. I just told him things had been crazy and that I was looking forward to a little peace and quiet, which is true."

"Do you want to tell me what happened?"

"I will when you get home. I'll tell you everything."

"Okay, but . . . You sound a little shaky, Em. And I thought if you were going to meet his parents, things must be getting serious between you two."

"It wasn't like that. Really." At least, not on her part. "His parents were coming to Chicago on business at the end of the semester, and I haven't had nearly as much time as I'd like to see the city. We were going to catch a show, do some Christmas shopping, some tourist things. That's all."

"All right, but if you need us—"

"I'll call," she promised.

"Okay. We should have a better idea of what will happen with Ann and the baby tomorrow. I was going to ask you to make another round of calls—"

"I'll do it." She'd rather make the calls than have them call here looking for news. It would save her from worrying every time the phone rang. Rachel gave her the hospital phone number. Emma dutifully wrote it down. "Sam's at Ann and Greg's with all the kids. If you change your mind and want to come—"

"I'll just get on the train," Emma said.

It was a comforting thought. She could just leave and go be with her family, if that's what she needed. Maybe once the bruise on her face was gone. It would be bad enough to tell them, in time, in her own way. But to have them able to see it on her face the moment she arrived, and to have everyone see . . . Not just Sam and Rachel, but Zach and Grace. Her aunt and uncle. Her cousins. It sounded so humiliating, and right now she just wanted to hide.

Rachel said good-bye, and then Emma started calling relatives to fill them in on Ann's condition. By the time she was done, she had three invitations to dinner and two offers of places to sleep, in case she didn't want to be alone. But she put them all off with her same story—that she was wiped out after finals. Maybe she could buy a few days alone. Maybe she could just hide.

Women did this, she'd read. They wanted to hide, to pretend it never happened, that it never would again.

She would never have believed she could be one of those women. But inside her head, she heard all the familiar excuses. It wasn't like him to do this, not the man she knew. He must have been under a great deal of stress, because it wasn't something he'd normally do.

But he had. He'd done it to her.

Emma sat there trying to make all the images go away. She was thinking of building the fire back up, trying to go back to sleep when the phone rang one more time. She picked it up without even thinking, sure that it was one of her cousins or maybe a friend from high school.

"Emma." Mark sighed heavily. "I was hoping you'd

be on your way back by now. Don't you think this
has gone on long enough?"

Rye checked into the inn and had five different people ask if he was here for the Christmas festival. Obviously it was a big deal around here. That afternoon,
restless and with nothing to do, he started walking the
streets of downtown.

He found two discreet signs, one on a house under
construction and another being renovated, announcing
that the work was being done by McRae Construction.
The second time he saw one, there was a man out
front checking his mailbox. Rye struck up a conversation with him, telling him he'd been thinking of having
Sam do some work for him.

"You can't go wrong with Sam. He lives six blocks
over, in that house that was Rachel's grandfather's.
Been a part of this town for twenty years now."

"He's been here that long?" Rye asked.

"Longer, now that I think about it. He was a fresh-
man in high school when he came here. I graduated
a year or two before he did. I remember because his
grandfather had a house over on Sycamore Street, not
far from one of my uncles'."

"His grandfather lived here, too?"

"Yeah, and Sam did, once his parents died."

"That would have been rough. Losing both his parents like that."

"Oh, yeah. Life's just harder on some people."

What did that mean? That it had been for Sam?
Too bad.

The man he was looking for lost his parents at a
much younger age, then got passed from relative to
relative, foster home to foster home. He had no idea
where the man ended up. There was a birth certificate
supposedly showing the man to be thirty-nine now,

but none of the Sam McRaes he'd found had a birth-day that matched the one on the birth certificate. He had a feeling the Sam McRae he was looking for was older than that, anyway. Absolutely nothing fit.

"Guess Sam was lucky he had a grandfather to take him in," Rye said, remembering where he was, what he was supposed to be doing.

"I don't know if I'd go that far." The man shook his head. "Hate to speak ill of the dead, but Old Man McRae . . . I don't think anyone has fond memories of him. But somehow Sam turned out just fine. You don't have to worry. He'd do a good job for you."

Rye thanked the man and went on his way. The wind was picking up, and the sun was sinking fast. It was getting cold, and he was tired. Tired of looking for a man he sometimes thought he'd never find. What did he even think he had to gain by finding him? What could he ever say to Sam McRae?

Still, he kept going, finding himself in front of the diner Emma had mentioned. The food was indeed plain home cooking and very good. He sat at the counter, striking up a conversation with the waitress and two men who eventually came to sit on either side of him.

The story was always the same. Sam McRae came here as a teenager after his parents died. Which meant this couldn't be the Sam McRae he was looking for. He could cross one more name off his list.

It also meant there was no reason to stay here, except for Emma.

He sat in his room fighting the urge to call her. He had the number. He'd had it for months and never used it.

Finally, he convinced himself he was being ridicu-lous. If the woman needed help, she had plenty of people to call. If she needed him, she knew where he was. But she hadn't called him, so she must not need him.

He finally went to bed but slept badly. He got up the next morning and planned to leave, but decided to talk to her one more time. He needed to hear her say she was okay.

He called and called and called and never got an answer. No way he could leave like that. So he drove back to the house, managed to knock in a quite civilized way at first, and then, when she didn't answer, gave in to the urge to pound on the door and call out her name.

The phone finally stopped ringing shortly before ten the next morning.

She hadn't answered it, no matter how many times it rang. Not after the second time he'd called.

And then someone came pounding on the door.

She started shaking something fierce. Honestly, it was the most horrible thing. She felt absolutely powerless, in a way she hadn't felt in so very long. Almost enough to make her sick to her stomach.

Was that how her mother felt? This scared? This paralyzed?

Emma picked up the cordless phone, which she'd kept by her side all night and all morning, even though she wasn't answering it, and walked slowly to the door. Just in case, she hit the power button on the phone, carefully dialed nine-one and kept her finger on the one. If anything happened, all she'd have to do was press that button one more time.

As she stood by the door, willing her breathing to slow, she realized that over the pounding of her heart she could hear someone calling her name.

But it wasn't Mark.

Oh, thank God.

She flung open the door, and there was Rye.

Emma couldn't say who moved first. If she threw herself into his arms, or if he pulled her to him. Not that it mattered. Within seconds, she was there, held firmly against him, her face buried in the soft cotton of his shirt.

He was six feet or so of solid muscle, something she found thoroughly reassuring at the moment. His arms tightened around her. She sank against him, worried her legs might not hold her up much longer. But then, they didn't have to. Because he had her. He wouldn't let her fall.

She must have scared him as much as he'd scared her, because he kept asking if she was okay.

"Yes." The word was muffled against his shirt. She wasn't ready to relinquish an inch between them.

"He's not here?" Rye asked.

"No." Some of the tension in his body eased. His hold became one that was more about comfort than protection.

"You're shaking like you're scared to death, Emma."

"I was afraid you were him."

"That's it? That's all that happened?"

"No. He called again," she admitted, her face still buried in his shirt.

"Bastard. What did he say?"

"He's mad that I'm not back in Chicago. He thought I'd just go running back to him. Can you imagine that? He's mad because I'm not there asking him to forgive me for running away from him."

"He's an idiot," Rye said, practically growling.

"I know."

And then Emma felt better, fear receding and reality sneaking in.

She realized abruptly that she was clinging to him—

a man she'd just met the day before. She'd shown him
herself at her weakest and most vulnerable point, and
now she'd thrown herself into his arms.

Yes, she was fairly certain now that's what she'd
done.

And they were standing in the cold on the front
porch in broad daylight.

She eased back in his arms, looked up to find his
gaze running over her face and then her body, as if
he had to convince himself she was okay.

"Sorry," she said. She hadn't meant to scare him.

She stepped back, because she thought she had to.
But it was harder than she imagined it would be. She
was more shaken than she cared to admit, and he was
still right there.

She had her hands clasped to her chest one minute,
then reaching for him the next. She stopped to think
about what she was doing at the last moment, leaving
her hands hanging in the air, not sure what to do with
them anymore.

He knew. He covered her cold hands with his warm
ones and pressed them against the worn, smooth cotton of his shirt. His heart was thrumming heavily, and
she felt his chest rise and fall with the next breath he
took. It was cold enough that when he exhaled foglike
breath billowed out of his mouth and hung there between them, dissipating in the next seconds into
nothingness.

She kept waiting for the feelings that hovered awkwardly between them to do the same, but they didn't.
They seemed to be suspended there, frozen as the two
of them were. Strangers, too, and yet . . .

She had the strongest urge to ease herself back into
his arms. To raise her head and press her lips to his
cheek. It was a bit rough and dark. He hadn't taken
the time to shave, and she found herself wanting to

know what it would feel like to have him kiss her
with those soft, full lips and his rough cheeks. She
was fascinated by the idea, no matter how completely
inappropriate it might be.

Emma had been raised with all sorts of male relatives, young and old. They were a big, loud, affection-
ate bunch. This was just a hug. A kiss on the cheek.
Honestly, it was nothing at all.

She left her hands where they were, raised up on
her toes, and for a mere second, brushed her lips
against one of those cheeks that intrigued her so.

"Thank you."

Chapter 3

A shiver went down her spine at the light touch. Her lips tingled in the oddest of ways where they touched him. He smelled heavenly.

She figured out pretty quickly that treating him like a brother or a cousin wasn't going to work, and eased back, trying to figure out what to do next.

He stood there, his back ramrod straight and said, "I didn't do anything."

"You're here."

At the moment, that was all she needed. Him here with her.

He took a step back, a slight flush to his cheeks, and she thought she must have embarrassed him, something that made him absolutely adorable. Not that he wasn't that already. This just made him all the more so.

He had dark blond hair, almost brown, and the kind of dark eyes a woman thought she could drown in, thick, spiky lashes women tormented themselves with mascara to try to get. The stubble of whiskers gave

him a slightly rough look she found altogether appeal-
ing. And his body was all filled out, like a man's, not
a boy's.

She wondered how old he was. Late twenties,
maybe? That might be a problem, if anything were to
come of this. Not that she was looking to get involved
with anyone. Not after what she'd just been through.

But at the same time, she was suddenly completely
aware of him as a man. It was in the wide shoulders
and the rough cheeks, something about the way he
walked or maybe the way he filled out those smooth,
worn jeans.

There, she'd admit it.

The man was sexy.

Emma found herself frowning up at him and then
feeling completely bewildered about what had just
happened. She'd been scared half out of her mind,
and then grateful and then . . . Well, now she was
mostly breathless, the blood just humming through her
veins in the oddest of ways.

"I'm sorry. I . . ." And then she frowned once more.
"Come inside, okay? Just come inside."

He bent over and picked up the phone, which she
must have dropped, and handed it to her, then came
inside. She clicked off the phone and put it down on
the table by the door, then shut the door firmly behind
them and locked it.

He stood in the foyer staring at her. It was cold
outside. She just realized that, and they'd been out
there for a while, and now she was freezing. She was
also tired from lack of sleep and probably had her
hair sticking out every which way.

He leaned toward her, his hand against the side of
her face gently fingering the bruise on her cheek once
more. "The guy backhanded you, huh?"

"Yes." It looked worse this morning, redness and puffy giving way to a blackish/brownish swash of color she hadn't yet attempted to hide.

"I don't suppose you reported him?"

"No." His look told her he didn't think that was the smartest thing she'd ever done. "It's the first time anyone knocked me down. I wasn't quite up on the proper procedures. I just got the hell away from him."

Rye backed up once again, and she realized she'd been short with him, when all he'd done was try to help her.

"I'm sorry," she said again. "That was the last thing I should have said to you. You've done nothing but try to help."

It wasn't quite true that this was the first time something like this had happened to her, either. Did she really have to tell him about that? Every damned thing?

"It's all right," he said. "The guy's got you shaken and scared, but . . . Is that all he did, Emma? Knock you down and then start calling here wanting you back? Because if it's anything else . . . I know it's not easy to talk about things like this, but, did you see a doctor?"

"I didn't need a doctor." And then she realized what Rye was getting at. She sagged against the wall at her back, so very tired now, hating this. "He just hit me. I know I'm falling apart here. I know you're looking at me and thinking it must have been a lot more than one guy hitting me one time, but it's not so much about this as . . . My mother was a battered wife, okay?"

"You're mother?" He frowned. "You mean . . . ?"

"Not Rachel. Not Sam. My other mother. I . . . I don't even know what to call them all at times, and I really don't like calling him my father. But he beat up my mother. Quite often, I guess. It's not all that clear in my mind now. It's been so long. He beat her up, and when I was ten we left him, and then . . . It's a long story."

"Okay," he said gently.

"I think I'm reacting now as much to what happened in the past as I am with what really happened with Mark."

She studied his reaction, waiting for the way he looked at her to change. People tended to do that, look at her differently once they knew, and she hadn't told anyone about this in the longest time. But his gaze remained steady, reassuring, calming, as if he could handle whatever came along. Which was exactly what she needed now.

"Pretty ugly story, huh?" she said finally.

"I've heard ugly stories before."

Which actually made her smile. "Yeah, well . . . That's mine."

She'd told him, and it was okay. Maybe it was easier because he was a complete stranger. He didn't know the Ever-So-Capable Emma McRae, the one who tried so hard to do everything right, to never worry anyone, to never cause any trouble. This was so unlike her.

"So," he said matter-of-factly, "what are we going to do with you now, Emma?"

"I don't know." She smiled again, thinking the really hard part was over. He was here, and she wasn't so scared. "I was thinking maybe you'd stay awhile. I think I'd like it if you stayed."

"Then I'll stay," he agreed.

"Thank you."

And then she was back to shaking. It just wouldn't stop.

He must think she was a basket case, a crazy person

who let her boyfriend hit her. A wimp. Someone with lousy judgment in men. Someone who couldn't be trusted to look out for herself. There were so many things she'd always thought about women who let this happen to them.

Emma frowned. There it was again. *Let this happen.*

"Hey," he said, much too kindly. "I'm not bad in the kitchen myself. Since I'm staying anyway, why don't you let me feed you this morning, show you what I can do? You sit down and try to relax."

"I can't ask you to do that," she said, worried again about how she'd look in his eyes. Warm, brown, understanding eyes.

"You didn't. I offered."

"Oh. Okay. If you don't mind."

"I don't mind."

It felt absurdly like a date, except she had a bruised face and was wearing the clothes she'd had on yesterday, the ones she'd slept in. She was all rumpled and worn out.

"You know, what I'd really like is to take a shower and get dressed."

"Whatever you want," he said.

She nodded again. His kindness might be more than she could bear this morning. Tears stung her eyes, and she turned her head away once again. "I should show you to the kitchen."

"I know where the kitchen is," he said softly.

And he knew how close she was to weeping all of a sudden.

She'd just felt so alone, so completely and terrifyingly alone all night, and now she was so happy he was here.

"Go ahead," he said. "Take a bath, nice and hot. Trust me on this. I've been on the losing end of a fight before. Soak some of the soreness out. I'll take my time down here. We'll eat whenever you're ready."

"Thank you," she said, still not looking at him as she turned and headed for the stairs.

Rye stood there and watched her go, thinking he never should have left her alone last night. That Sam McRae, whoever the hell he was, for damned sure shouldn't have.

They'd call him. That was all there was to it.

If he was any kind of a father, he'd come home and take care of this.

If he didn't, Rye would have a thing or two to say to the man. He didn't care if it was any of his business or not. He was the one who'd seen how damned scared she was.

He moved slowly through the house and into the kitchen, putting his arms on the counter and leaning into it, staring at but not really seeing the cream-colored tile.

Life seemed immensely complicated at the moment, when until two days ago, it had been dreadfully simple. There'd been no one for him to worry about but himself. It had been that way for so long, and why he had to go and try to change that, he couldn't understand.

This was what happened when people got tangled up in other people's lives. There were always all sorts of complications, nasty little feelings of obligation, responsibilities.

Not that he regretted in any way helping Emma. He hated the idea of men beating up on women. One of the nastiest men he'd ever met had been like that, thinking he was somehow entitled to use other people as his own personal punching bag. No way he was going to leave Emma to face someone like that alone. He didn't care if he had just met her.

She was sweet and kind and lost right now. Somewhere in the back of his head was the nagging idea that he really couldn't afford to risk getting involved in a potentially volatile situation like this, but he couldn't walk away, either.

Rye walked into the kitchen and opened up the refrigerator, thinking that if he couldn't impress Emma with his cooking, maybe he could at least distract her from her worries.

A hot bath and a good meal, on top of a second sleepless night, would likely send her right off to sleep. He didn't like seeing the dark circles under her eyes, any more than that bruise on her cheek.

So he cooked, and when he'd gotten things started, he shoved his hands into his pockets and wandered restlessly around the downstairs he'd only let himself glance at the day before. There was a sunroom off the right side in back, full of greenery and white wicker, a generous backyard with a basketball hoop on a square of concrete at the back of the driveway, and a tree house in the big sycamore in back.

There was a video game system hooked up to the TV in the den, a half-dozen games spilling out of a nearby cabinet, children's artwork neatly framed and hung beside the big fireplace there.

There were a few nicely preserved antiques, a comfortable-looking afghan thrown over the back of the sofa, one big enough for a man to be comfortable on, and in a quiet spot in the back hall were a series of awards.

Sam McRae had been president of the Chamber of Commerce a few years back and the Jaycees' Man of the Year. The mayor had given him a commendation for his work in beautifying the town and starting some sort of festival. That Christmas thing Emma had talked about. He built playgrounds for underprivileged kids and started the local chapter of Habitat for Humanity.

Rye laughed at that. Not at the work. He wasn't that much of a cynic. But at the idea that this man could have been the one he was looking for. His Sam McRae had been a juvenile delinquent by all accounts, an angry, out-of-control kid who'd lost his parents young, someone nobody had wanted. What were the odds he'd have ever ended up like this?

No, this wasn't the man he was trying to find.

He went back into the kitchen, fiddling with the meal in progress, trying not to think about what his search had gotten him into.

He tried not to wonder about all the other Sam McRaes on his list, about how much longer he could stand to do this and if he would ever find the man he was looking for.

Emma finally came back downstairs. Rye frowned at the cloud of tempting fragrances that seemed to hover around her.

He'd been trying really hard to ignore those odd moments on the porch when she'd clung to him, then eased up on her tiptoes to thank him so sweetly. Damned if the muscles in his abdomen didn't go all tight, either at the memory or the sight of her or that smell. It settled deep in his lungs, warm and languid, making him hungry in ways he didn't want to think about.

"Hi," she said, looking better, more at ease, not like she might collapse any minute or break down into tears. "You were right. About the bath and sore muscles. It helped."

"Good."

She smiled shyly and drifted a bit closer, the smell coming along with her.

Vanilla, he decided a moment later. She smelled like vanilla. It made him think of warm cream dribbled over something sweet and sinful.

Emma and warm, smooth vanilla cream.

Not a good image for him to have in his head.

Sam's daughter in warm, smooth vanilla cream.

Even worse.

He'd think that would be enough to cure him of any lust-like thoughts where Emma was concerned. He'd think of her as Sam's daughter. The *right* Sam's. The man might well have one, and Rye would never have a single lust-filled thought about her. It was a completely logical, practical argument, and it wasn't working worth a damn at the moment.

If the smell of her wasn't dangerous enough, the sight of her was even harder to take. Her skin was still flushed from the heat and slightly damp in places, as if she'd toweled off in a hurry. Her hair was piled carelessly on her head and the pieces of it that had escaped were damp, too. Her cheeks were flushed, and he could see that she'd taken pains to cover that bruise again. But it was worse today than it had been yesterday.

Beneath all that, she looked all fresh faced and innocent and young. She was feeling shaky enough, as is, and he didn't mess around with nice women like her, not anymore.

"Something smells good," she said, coming closer, bringing that vanilla scent with her.

Rye bit back a reply, something that would likely have come out as, *Something certainly does.*

"Hungry?" he said instead, too late realizing that probably wasn't the best conversation opener, either.

"Yes." She came right up beside him, damp and

warm, and she might as well have doused herself in vanilla cream. Not that the scent was overwhelming. Just that it smelled so good he wanted to take a bite out of her.

Dessert, he thought. *Emma.*

"You made crepes?" she asked.

"Yes."

"Wow." She turned around and gave him a delighted and thoroughly speculative look. "I'm impressed."

So was he. In a very bad way.

"Let's eat," he said.

"Okay." She turned to the cabinets. Opening one, she raised up on her toes to reach the top shelf, giving him a perfect view of her tempting backside encased in a pair of jeans that fit like a glove and hugged every enticing curve.

He practically growled, "How old are you?"

"How old do you think I am?" She eased down off her toes, two plates in hand, seeming to take delight in throwing it right back at him.

But at least she was smiling. He liked seeing Emma smile. Trying not to growl at her or take a bite of her, he said, "Twenty-three? Maybe twenty-five?"

Please, let her be twenty-five.

"Close enough," she said.

"Emma?" He took a plate from her and filled one for her, cheese crepes topped with a sauce he'd made using some of her aunt's blackberry jam and some whipped cream.

"It's just a number, right?" she said, taking her plate and smiling mischievously.

"No, it's not just a number."

Not when he was thinking he might easily be ten years older than she was. Not that he was going to let anything happen between them. Still . . .

"I'm starving," Emma said. "Can we eat? And I was thinking . . . If you don't have anything to do today, maybe you could help me with the Christmas lights. I need to get them up soon."

He frowned. "You didn't tell me how old you are."

"Old enough," she claimed, seating herself on one side of the breakfast bar and waiting for him to do the same.

He made a plate for himself, sat down across from her, a good bit of pretty tile countertop stretching between them, which had seemed like a good idea at the time. But it meant he got a front-row seat as every spoonful went into her delectable-looking mouth.

And he was supposed to be figuring out how old she was, dammit.

He had a nagging sense that he wasn't going to like her answer, once he got one out of her. But honestly, how young could she possibly be? She'd said she was finishing college. So she had to be twenty-one or twenty-two.

Twenty-one?

He frowned.

Twenty-one-year-olds were practically infants, weren't they? Didn't they still giggle and flirt shamelessly and guzzle beer at parties with frat boys?

She probably went to parties with frat boys.

Rye sat there while she moaned and groaned in appreciation over bite after bite. He tried to block out the sound, because it made him think of Emma in her bath, in her vanilla-scented water with her now vanilla-scented skin.

If she was a day over twenty-three and he was anyone but who he was, he would have let himself imagine feeding her crepes in the bathtub, getting her out, and eating her up. Yeah, that would have worked for him.

"What's wrong?" she asked.

He looked up at her, finding her chewing slowly, her pretty mouth pursed into something that looked like a kiss at the moment. "Nothing."

"Headache?" she tried cheerfully.

"No."

"Bad news?"

"No."

Her cheer faded. "Mark didn't call again?"

"No. Nothing like that," he promised, putting down his fork and staring out the window into the backyard, anywhere but at her. "I'm just thinking about you and your little situation."

"Oh. You'll stay here today?"

"I don't know if that's such a good idea, Emma. Anyway, that just addresses today. You can't stay here by yourself worrying that any minute he's going to show up at the door."

"Do you think he would?" She looked so worried. "Because I thought of that, and I've been trying to tell myself I'm just being silly to be so scared."

"I don't know. You know the guy better than I do."

"No, I don't." She put her fork down, pushed the plate away, all enjoyment she might have taken in the meal gone. "I thought I did, but I didn't ever think . . ."

He was sorry he'd brought this up. "You didn't think he'd hit you?"

"No. He never came close to losing his temper like that." She stared at her plate. Her face tilted forward. Her hair fell across her bruised cheek.

"Okay." He forced himself to go on. She needed to hear this if she was going to be safe. "So the guy's got a temper, and you don't know what he might do. I think, to be safe, you shouldn't be here by yourself. Call Sam."

"I can't," she insisted.

"Why not? If your aunt needs help, Rachel could stay there and Sam could be here with you."

"I don't want to ask him to come. I don't want to ask him to leave Rachel."

"Why not?"

She sighed and pushed a stray strand of hair back from her face. "It's a difficult situation—"

"So's the one you're in," he said.

"How well do you know Sam?" she asked instead.

He frowned, thinking that had to come up sooner or later. "I . . . It's—"

"Complicated?" she suggested.

"Yes."

"Thought so."

Rye sighed and looked down at her hand, curled against the side of her plate. Her hand was trembling. "You have to do something."

"I know. I just . . . I don't know what to do," she said finally, getting to her feet and walking over to the window. It just about broke his heart. She sounded overwhelmed and so damned lost.

He pushed back his plate and stood up, fighting the urge to go to her.

"You don't understand," she said. "This is not who I am. This scared, indecisive woman. That's not me. I'm not like that."

"I believe you. You're just caught up in a bad situation. It happens. I understand about bad things happening, Emma. How they can throw you, make you feel like a completely different person."

"That's it." She turned back around, staring at him, as if she wanted to ask more—how he knew, what had happened to him to make him understand. Thankfully, she didn't ask. "I feel like this couldn't possibly be my life, and I want mine back. How do I get mine back?"

"A little bit at a time. First, you have to figure out how to handle the situation you're in. Take care of today."

"Well, I was thinking I would spend today with you."

"Emma, you don't even know me." He'd never hurt her, but hell, she didn't know that. "You let me in this house again."

Went upstairs and took off all her clothes and climbed into the bathtub. He groaned, shutting out the image that insisted on invading his head.

"You're going back to trying to convince me not to trust you?"

"Hey, a little skepticism is a great thing, especially when you're a young, beautiful woman."

"I'm not—"

She broke off, her cheeks flushed all the more, not looking at him now. He closed his eyes and bit back a curse. She was getting to him. That sweet, fresh-faced, innocent look of hers was killing him.

"I just want you to be safe, Emma, and I want both of us to be able to sleep tonight." Not that he had a prayer of that, not after smelling that Emma-after-her-bath smell and seeing her all flushed and fresh faced, her tight little jeans, and innocent eyes.

"And someone who was out to hurt me would say things like that?"

"He would if he was smart. It sure seems to be working for me. After all, I'm right here with you," he said, frustration getting the better of him.

"You think I'm an idiot, don't you?" She went from flattered to mad in about half a second.

"I think you can't be too careful. Look at what this jerk did to you."

"I know." She touched a hand to her bruised cheek, as if to test and see if it were still there, still as bad as she remembered. "I'm sorry. I didn't mean to drag you into my problems."

"You haven't dragged me anywhere, Emma," he admitted, taking those inevitable steps closer. He could rest his hands on her shoulders or maybe hold her hands. That seemed safe. He did that, just took both her hands in his. "I've come quite willingly. I'm afraid I'm just not that good at taking care of anyone. I've been on my own for a long time now."

"I think you're doing just fine at taking care of me. And . . . Well . . ."

She eased up on her tiptoes and placed a frustratingly brief, soft kiss on his lips this time:

"And I appreciate it. Thank you."

He just stood there. There was something so innocent about that little kiss. It might as well have been another peck on the cheek, like the one she'd given him earlier when she'd been so scared and he'd held her in his arms.

Except it rocked him all the way down to his toes again.

"Emma," he warned, holding himself absolutely still and straight.

"Hmm?" She brought her hands up to rest ever so lightly against his chest. The delicate touch burned right through the fabric of his shirt. She still smelled so good and the world was spinning oddly around him.

He hadn't had anyone to hang on to in so long, and how her mere presence could be so comforting and so unsettling at the same time, he could not understand. But he couldn't pry his hands off her.

"Things are crazy right now," he said.

"I know. For me, too."

And yet she stayed stubbornly right there, her face maybe an inch from his. He wanted to tell her she really shouldn't go around kissing men she barely knew, even those little pecks on the cheek. They gave a man ideas.

But this wasn't him getting ideas. She was inviting something entirely different now. A taste of her. All that sweetness, that innocence.

"I think I like you," she said. "Is that such a bad thing?"

"Yes. It's a very bad thing." A complicating thing. A pointless thing. Nothing could ever come of this.

He still stood here hanging on to her. Her eyes were a smoky green and there was a little gleam in them that told him she thought she was being quite forward and was delighted with herself for it. Her cheeks were flushed, and her lips were right in front of his.

In the end, it was the sweet softness of her that got to him. He hadn't held a woman like that in years. There hadn't been any like her, not where he'd been. Surely he could have a little bit of that. Just a taste.

He touched the tip of her nose with his, nuzzling closer. He heard her catch her breath and thought long and hard about the skin of her cheek, about her mouth, her neck. With her hair piled high, Emma had an absolutely delectable-looking neck.

Who's to say what he would have done in the end, given the chance. Probably gotten into the same kind of trouble she started. But she lifted her face that last fraction of an inch, and one more time, her lips settled against his.

They were so very soft. He teased at them with his tongue, at the opening there, thinking, *Let me in, Emma.* Just like this. It would be enough. He'd make it enough.

Her mouth opened to his. His entire body tensed at the possibilities. He gave himself up to the wonders of kissing Emma, put his hand to the back of her head, tangled within her hair, which he wanted down. Now.

His other hand went to the small of her back, arching her against him. Her breasts pressed against his chest. He let his hand slide down to her bottom, cupping it, pressing her against him.

He could devour her right here in the kitchen.

"Damn," he said, pulling back.

He had to remember who he was, what he'd done, what he was here for. This wasn't his place, just some side road he'd taken and found her. She was just a woman in trouble, and he would be moving on before too long.

"This is a bad idea, Emma."

She gazed up at him, looking dazed and confused. "What is?"

"You and me," he admitted. Might as well get it right out there in the open. This was impossible.

"How do you know?"

Because it felt too good, and since when did life get to feel this good to him? Since when did anything really good ever last for him?

"You don't know who I am. You don't know anything about me."

"So tell me. Tell me who you are and why you came here. Tell me why this is such a bad idea."

He was still trying to figure out what to say when the phone rang.

The blood drained from Emma's face at the sound. Poor Emma. She was so scared.

"I'll get that," he offered.

Even if it was Sam McRae. They'd settle this once and for all, and he could move on to the next name on his list.

"No," she said. "I will."

Chapter 4

Emma snatched it up and said, "Hello."

"Em? What's wrong?"

She let out the breath she'd been holding and said, "Sam. Hi."

Rye sat down in his chair, not exactly looking relieved.

"What's wrong?" Sam asked again. "You don't sound like yourself. Is it that boy? Rachel said the two of you broke up."

"We did."

"Is that all?" Sam asked.

"No." Emma hadn't meant to say that. It had just come tumbling out. She'd always told Sam everything. Well, practically everything.

"Tell me," he insisted.

"I didn't want to say anything. Not with everything that's going on with Ann and the baby, but . . ." Emma looked for some fine line she could walk here without spilling the whole thing. "He isn't taking this well, Sam. He's mad, and he's been calling here, even though I've asked him to stop."

"What happened between the two of you?" Sam asked, steel in his voice.

"I'll . . . Can we do this when you and Rachel get here, please? I'm fine, and I'll tell you everything. I promise. Just . . . not now. Not on the phone, okay?"

"You're fine?"

"I am. I promise."

"Okay, but what did he say?"

"I think I've embarrassed him, more than anything," she said, thinking how odd to find herself interested in one man while explaining to her father on the phone about the one she'd just left who was stalking her. Her humiliation just went on and on. "His parents were expecting to meet me, and I guess he doesn't want to tell them we broke up. So he's making excuses and waiting for me to get back there, even though I've made it clear I'm not coming."

Sam started firing off questions. "So he's not listening?"

"No."

"Has he threatened you?"

"No."

"I think you should come up here. Right now. You don't need to be in that house by yourself. Or you could go to Rachel's sister's or her brother's, her father's. Take your pick."

It made sense. She knew that, and it was so tempting.

But it felt like running away. It felt cowardly, and she already felt like such a coward. She already resented the way Mark seemed to have invaded her whole life, making her second-guess everything she'd ever believed about herself and her ability to take care of herself. She didn't want to be anyone's victim, not ever again, and running felt like admitting that she was.

"I really just want to stay here," Emma said.

"No," Sam said.

She frowned, knowing that tone well. Sam didn't use it often and certainly not arbitrarily. But he'd made up his mind. She'd never flat-out refused him anything, because she loved him and trusted him. She knew he loved her.

Emma looked across the room at Rye, who'd given her the same argument in much the same way. He'd even sounded like Sam when he did it.

"What did he say?" Rye asked.

Sam had just said the same thing. It echoed in her head. *What did he say?* Not just the words or the tone. The voice.

They *sounded* alike.

Looking up at Rye now, the color and shape of his eyes, that little notch in his chin, the way he simply held himself, he even looked like Sam.

And he'd come here looking for Sam. . . .

Not about business, but something personal, and seemed oddly reluctant to even let Sam know it. Why in the world would he do that?

"Emma?"

They both said it at once, Sam's voice coming through the phone, Rye's from across the room. It was just the same. She forgot all about Mark and the phone calls, the threats, and the bruise on her face.

The voices were the same.

Could it be?

She thought . . . just maybe, she was standing here with Sam's long-lost brother.

It just hit her out of the blue.

Sam had a brother she'd never seen. One Sam hadn't seen himself in ages. For the longest time, she thought he didn't have anyone at all, and she'd wondered how he'd stood that. She couldn't imagine a

world without her siblings, particularly after they'd
lost their mother. She'd said something about that one
day, and Sam had told her he had a brother but not
much else. It had obviously been so hard for him to
talk about.

But she'd always been curious. Where had his
brother gone? What had happened to him? Why
didn't Sam ever see him? Why did it still hurt Sam
so much?

Emma stared up at Rye. Rye who'd looked so troubled and so reluctant all along. She thought of the
way he was so reluctant for Sam to even know he was
here, almost like he was testing the situation first, before deciding whether he was willing to reveal his
true identity.

But why? If he really was Sam's brother. . .

Emma put her hand over the receiver and faced
Rye. "Who are you?"

He stared for a second, then turned and looked
away, up toward the ceiling and through the window
and off the back porch, anywhere but at her.

Wow.

He looked so uncomfortable, she thought he might
head for the door and not come back. She couldn't
let that happen.

"Sam?" she said into the phone. "I'll do something
tonight. I'll go somewhere or have someone come stay
at the house. Promise."

"I wish you'd come here," he said.

"I know . . . I just . . . I have some things to figure
out on my own. I'll talk to you, tomorrow, okay?"

"No, it's not okay."

"Sam—"

"I know. You're not a little girl anymore."

He sounded like such a father then, like such a great
father. He was having a really hard time with the idea

that she was growing up. Not that she seemed to be doing a good job of taking care of herself at the moment.

But if this was his brother . . .

She looked back at Rye, pacing the length of the kitchen. Sam would be so surprised. What a wonderful Christmas present that would be.

"I love you, Sam. I'll talk to you tomorrow."

She felt so much better, so excited, and she might just have to pull out her helpless female act again. Might as well have something good come from it. Because she had to get Rye to stay. Maybe between now and when Sam came home, she could figure out why he was so reluctant to tell anyone who he was.

"He's not coming?" Rye asked when she hung up the phone.

"No. I told him not to."

"And he agreed to that?"

"You think he should ignore what I want?" she asked.

"If it doesn't make any sense, yes."

Oh, that was Sam, all right. In truth, she was surprised he'd given in so easily. But there had been those very earnest conversations about her growing up and their faith in her ability to take care of herself, them wanting her to have the chance to make decisions on her own. They were both trying so hard. Sam just wasn't any good at letting go of people. He'd lost too many people.

"What?" Rye asked.

He sounded nearly as gruff and out of sorts as Sam could at times, when he felt too much and tried to hide it. It reminded her of the Sam of the old days, the man he'd been when she and her brother and sister had first come here. A man who was afraid to care too much, but did anyway. She liked to think they'd given as much back to him as he'd given to them.

"Nothing," she said. "I was just . . . You never told me how you felt about Christmas decorations."

"Christmas decorations?" He looked incredulous at the change of topic.

"You know, lights, wreaths, ribbons, bows? I'm all for them, myself." Especially if they'd keep him here for a while. No way was she letting him go.

He tilted his head to the side and frowned. "You want my philosophical take on Christmas?"

"No," she admitted. "I just want you to stay. Just for today?"

"Emma," he protested.

"Please. I have to get the Christmas lights up, one way or another. I'd have to be outside for hours, and you were so worried about me being locked up safe and sound yesterday that I just thought, you might . . ."

"You're going to blackmail me now?" he asked.

"Would it work?"

She was up to something. Rye knew it. But at least she didn't look so scared anymore. Her hand had shook as she picked up the phone when Sam called, and he hated the idea of Emma so scared her hands were shaking.

There'd been something odd about that phone call, too. For a minute, he could have sworn she knew everything. But she couldn't, because he was once again in the wrong place, checking out the wrong man.

She couldn't know. Something else was going on.

"You look guilty, Emma." She was no good at hiding her feelings behind that pretty face of hers. "What are you up to?"

"Well . . . I may not have told you the whole truth about what you're getting into, decorating and all."

"A few lights?" He shrugged. "How hard could it be?"

"Okay, you've been warned. I gave you a chance to get out of this, and you didn't take it."

She must have taken that as his agreement, because she took him by the hand, touching him once more. It still felt good. He started to pull his hand from hers, but she tugged until he turned around and followed her.

"Boxes are in the basement," she said. "Far left corner, marked Christmas decorations—Outside. I think there are twelve."

"Twelve?"

"We'll leave the inside boxes down there for now." She plowed ahead to what must be the basement door. "They'd only get in the way."

He stopped, crossing his arms in front of his chest. "No one could have twelve boxes of decorations just for the outside of their house."

"Bet me," she said. "Loser fixes dinner."

So, he was staying for dinner, huh?

He knew that wasn't such a good idea.

She frowned. "You can't run out on me now."

"Pretty sure of yourself, aren't you?"

"I know you," she said, her index finger tapping against his chest. "I know you wouldn't leave me alone, and I'm grateful for that. Thank you."

This time—thankfully—there was no kiss accompanying the words.

God, he'd kissed her.

Bad, bad idea.

And he'd liked it.

A lot.

An even worse idea.

Life was getting more complicated by the moment.

"All right. Boxes," he said. Twelve. That should keep his hands off her for a while, maybe his mind, too.

"Right down there." She opened the door, flipping on the light above the wide, well-maintained stairway, then pointing to the far-left corner of the basement. "And the extension ladder's in the garage."

He paused on the top step to turn back to her. "Extension ladder?"

"It's a long way to the top of the house," she said.

He remembered. It was. "What do you plan to contribute to this effort?"

"I'll tell you what to do. Every step of the way." She looked like she'd enjoy it, too.

"Gee, thanks." Her smile, he couldn't help but notice, was enough to light up a room. It came slowly across her face, seeming to warm him as it did. There was chilly air coming from the basement and drifting past them, but he was very, very warm.

"I'll hold things," she said. "Hand them to you. You'll need that."

"That's it?" As long as she wasn't holding him, he might be okay.

"And I'll cook for you tonight."

"Emma . . ." He hadn't been fishing for an invitation.

"We're both here," she reasoned. "We both have to eat. And once all the decorations are up, you'll need food."

"Yeah, but—"

"And I'll try to keep my hands off you."

She said it lightly, teasingly, a twinkle in her eyes.

He responded the same way. "You do that."

"I'm not usually . . . Well, I don't make a habit

of . . ." He just stood there, one step down, which brought him near to eye level with her. He watched her struggle for the right words, her embarrassment growing. "I'm sorry."

"Emma, it's not that I didn't like it. Not at all."

"Oh," she said.

It would be much easier if it was all coming from her, if he didn't like it or want more of her. "Look, I'm not staying here," he said. "I'm just passing through. A day or two. That's it."

"Okay."

But he didn't seem to have changed her mind about anything.

"I'm going to get busy," he said, making a full retreat when nothing else seemed to be working.

There were indeed twelve boxes marked CHRISTMAS DECORATIONS—OUTSIDE. He didn't count the ones labeled CHRISTMAS DECORATIONS—INSIDE. He just carted the outside ones up the stairs and to the front porch. She came outside, all bundled up, and handed him a small key on a crowded ring. He got the extension ladder from the garage, took her advice in beginning at the tip-top corner of the house, three stories up and dead center. It seems they were going to outline the whole front face of the house.

He took a strand of lights in hand and climbed to the very top. It was a long way to the ground. Thank goodness he wasn't afraid of heights. He looked down at her and said, "This is nuts."

"This is Christmas," she insisted.

"It's nuts." He worked from the center of the strand, down the angled roofline on either side, until he couldn't reach anymore, than climbed all the way back down in order to move the ladder all of six feet to the left.

"It's tradition," she argued. "Surely you have some Christmas traditions."

"None that involve ten thousand friggin' lights."
Not much of any kind of tradition anymore, but that
wasn't something she needed to know.

He climbed back up. The lights were tiny and it
looked like they were all clear. Little bitty, blinking
lights. He did as much as he could to either side of
the ladder without risking falling off, then climbed
back down.

"You don't know what you're missing." Emma un-
raveled the next strand of lights. "But on Thursday,
you'll see. We all turn on the lights on Thursday."

He leaned against the ladder for a moment. He'd
built houses that were easier than this job was going
to be. "What, you all made a pact or something?"

"It's part of the festival. Lights come on the first
day, which is Thursday. Just wait. It's beautiful."

No, she was beautiful. He'd been trying hard not to
look at her, bundled up in red: a long, red coat; red
hat; red mittens; and a little red nose from the cold.
She hadn't been moving around as much as he had,
and he knew she was cold. He was fighting the urge
to warm her up.

Damn.

He climbed back up. They outlined the entire front
face of the house, up and down the angled roofline,
across the second story and each of its windows, and
across the first story.

Climbing the ladder about a thousand times had
helped take his mind off her. Attaching lights to the
house until he thought his arms would drop off from
sheer exhaustion had helped.

He climbed down for what he hoped was the last
time. Emma, he saw, had been working on the first-
story windows, and she was done with those. That left
just the porch. She started at one end. He decided it
was best to start at the other, although working his

way to her didn't seem like a good idea at all, once he thought of it. He did it anyway, winding lights around each individual post.

"No more lights after this?" he asked hopefully. "Not that I can imagine an empty surface to which we might attach any more lights."

"Bushes. We have lots of bushes. But we can leave those until tomorrow." She was on her knees at the far end of the porch. "Thanks for this. I'd have been forced to call in reinforcements if you hadn't volunteered."

"Reinforcements?" Guys, he was thinking. Guy friends. More boyfriends. He hoped the rest of them treated her well.

"Cousins, most likely. I have lots of cousins."

He came to a column and wound his way up, remembering he'd come here to find someone, not to save her from her crazy ex-boyfriend. And he was fairly sure he was in the wrong place, but how hard could it be just to ask?

"Big family?"

"Yes." She rattled off lists of aunts, uncles, cousins, great-aunts, great-uncles, a grandfather, most of whom lived right here, all of whom were from Sam's wife's side of the family.

He concentrated on the task at hand, careful to space the swirls of lights at precise intervals so they would all match. As if that mattered at all. He was using her. Her and her too-trusting soul. She made it incredibly easy for him. All he had to say was, "Sam doesn't have any relatives here?"

"A grandfather, but he passed away a long time ago. They weren't close."

There'd been no mention of a grandfather in any records he'd seen. The Sam McRae he was looking for wasn't supposed to have one.

"What about his parents?"

"They died when Sam was young."

"Really?" He worked his way up another column with lights, thinking it had to be a coincidence. "Must have been tough. How young was he?"

"I'm not sure. I don't think he's ever said."

"Somebody told me Sam's been here since he was fourteen or fifteen?"

"That's right." Emma frowned at the third column on her side, making minute adjustments to the lights, seemingly concentrating on nothing but that. "Rachel talks about the first time she ever saw him, when she was thirteen, and he's two years older than she is. So he would have been fifteen. Why?"

He shrugged. "It's a long time to stay in one town."

"Not really. Rachel was born here. Her father. Her aunts. And they're all still here. I know it sounds odd to a lot of people these days, but they've all stayed close to home. All except my Aunt Ann. What about you? Your family doesn't know how to stay in one place?"

"Last I heard, they were right where I left 'em," he said.

"And when was that? The last time you heard from them?"

He tucked the end of the last strand on his side into place and suddenly wished he weren't done. "Almost eight years ago."

She paused and looked at him. "Rye? How can you not speak to your family for eight years?"

"We're not exactly close," he said evasively.

"Siblings?" She went back to fiddling with her lights, but he thought one more time that she knew.

"I was an only child," he said. He'd been raised that way, hadn't been told otherwise until he was fifteen.

"Oh. I can't imagine that. I can't imagine being without my family."

"Well, you didn't have a family like mine," he said, hoping he didn't sound as bitter as he still felt at times.

"Mine's not exactly your typical American family, either," she said, still working diligently, still not looking at him.

"I know. Sorry. I didn't mean to imply that everything's been easy for you." Hell, no way it could have been. She said her father had beat on her mother, and somehow she'd come to be adopted by the people she now called her parents.

"We all need people we can count on," she said.

"Do we?"

"Yes," she insisted, getting to her feet and handing him what was left of her strand of lights to put up the last column.

He could reach the top much easier than she could. She wasn't that tall, and she might be strong, but if anyone wanted to hurt her . . . It made him mad all of a sudden. All this talk about family, but look at the shape she was in, counting on someone like him to take care of her.

"Who exactly are you counting on right now, Emma? Where is this wonderful family of yours when you need them?"

"You don't know what you're talking about."

"What's to know? Look at you." He did, finally. Her cheeks were flushed from the cold, but he knew where the bruise was. "Your ex-boyfriend hit you and now he's calling here and scaring you half to death. If Sam McRae's such a fabulous father, where the hell is he?"

"He doesn't know Mark hit me. If he did, he'd be here in a second."

"So why haven't you told him? He's your family now. He's supposed to be the one you can count on when things get tough."

"I do." She crossed her arms, looking like she was stubborn enough that it would take a bulldozer to move her. "He's always been here for me."

"But not now? Come on? I know how scared you are." And he knew about needing people and having them turn their backs on you. He knew about how ugly life could get.

"He needs to be there right now."

"Because your aunt's having trouble with her baby?" He finished with the damned lights. What was he supposed to do now?

"No, because if her baby comes now, it may well die."

"Which would be bad," he admitted. "But you're his daughter, and you need him."

"I happen to think there are other people who need him more."

"How can that possibly be?"

She rolled her eyes and groaned, then said, "Where are your keys?"

"What?"

"The keys to your truck? Do you have them with you?"

"Yes." He pulled them out of his pocket and held them up. "So?"

"So, we're going somewhere. You can drive. Just let me get my purse and lock up the house."

"Where are we going?"

"I'm through trying to tell you about why Sam isn't here. I'm going to show you."

"Show me what?" What could there be for him to see?

"You'll see," she insisted, disappearing into the house.

He put the ladder and the empty boxes away, and ten minutes later they climbed into his truck. She directed him to a shop at the edge of downtown, a pretty, dainty-looking place called Nanette's Buds and Blossoms.

"Flowers?" he asked.

She frowned at him. "We could go back and string lights around the bushes in the front yard, if you'd rather."

"No, flower shops are fine," he said.

Emma reached into her purse and pulled out some money. "I called in an order. Would you mind picking them up? I'm thinking if I can hide from anyone who knows me for another two days, the whole town won't have to know my ex-boyfriend's taken up hitting me."

"Sure," he said.

He went in and asked the woman behind the counter, whom he soon learned was Nanette herself, a nosy-looking woman in her forties, for Emma's order. She came back with a simple spray of baby pink roses, tiny and delicate looking against the dark green leaves and the green tissue paper.

"Sam and Rachel still in Cleveland with Ann and her baby?"

"Yes," Sam said, extending the bill Emma had given him.

"And the baby still hasn't come?" She made change without a break in conversation.

"Not yet," he said, taking the flowers and Emma's money.

The woman shook her head. "You tell them we'll be thinking of them. All of them and that baby."

Small-town living, huh? Even the floral shop owner knew them and was worried about Ann's baby. Rye went back to the truck, climbed in, and gave Emma the flowers and her change.

"Is that what you wanted?"

"Yes. Perfect."

"What's going on, Emma? Where are we going?"

She gave him directions, little by little, until he realized she was taking him to the cemetery. They drove past row after row of graves, until she told him to park and got out of the truck, her steps getting slower and slower the closer she got to one particular spot under a big willow tree on the hill.

He followed two steps behind her. She knelt down to clear away a few stray leaves, then tucked the flowers against the tiny white gravestone with a lamb carved on the top.

The colors had his throat going tight, the stone so white, the flowers oh-so-soft pink.

He didn't really want to know this.

"Sam and Rachel had a baby once, a long time ago," she said.

He stared down at the grave. They'd named her Hope. She would have been nineteen in the spring. The gravestone showed that she died on the same day she was born, a long time ago.

Damn.

He couldn't say anything at first, and when he could speak without sounding like he was choking, all he could think of was, "They must have been young."

"Teenagers," Emma said quietly.

"What happened?"

"Car accident. Icy roads. The baby was born too soon. Sam was driving, and he blames himself. They did a hysterectomy to keep Rachel from bleeding to death, so there were no more children after that, something Rachel blames herself for. They've been through a lot, and they're both very strong, but . . . If something happens to Ann's baby, they need to be together. They need each other more than I need them right now, and I don't want you to think badly of them because of that."

Rye nodded, not sure what to say.

He and Emma had drifted together once more, her arm against his, her hand slipping into his.

He just stared down at the gravestone, and a split second before he would have turned away, he went back to the date again. It happened nearly nineteen years ago.

March 12.

What happened in March nineteen years ago?

He counted back in his head, looking for some kind of way to mark the time. . . .

It was when Sam came to see him. A stranger, he'd thought then. A stranger who was supposed to be his brother.

So this Sam had just lost his baby girl, when Rye's brother had come to find him. Both things would have happened within the same week.

Would a man do that? Lose a daughter, then try to find a long-lost brother? Did that make sense?

It felt like one big sign clicking irrevocably into place, and he found that the closer he thought he was coming to answers, the more afraid he was of what he was going to find.

This seemed like too odd a coincidence to ignore. It made him want to hope. It made him want to think the man he was looking for was right here. Or at least, he would be in a day or two.

Don't do this, he told himself. *Don't.*

"What?" Emma asked.

"Nothing," he lied.

But she knew it wasn't.

She still had that look on her face, like someone who understood. Someone who could see right through him. What would that be like? Having someone who saw it all and somehow understood?

He didn't know what to do or what to say. He felt

like something inside of him was just crumbling, piles of rubble falling down and lying in ruins. He felt vulnerable in a way he simply hated, open and completely without any kind of defenses, and he wanted to reach for her and just hang on.

He had the most absurd notion about leaning on her, not just in a physical way but an emotional one. That beneath that slender build of hers, beneath the fear and the tears, beneath the bruise that now had the power to make him murderously angry, she was a very strong woman.

She had old eyes, he realized. As young as she was, she looked out at the world with eyes that had seen too much. He thought as much as he would be staying here to help her and to keep her safe, she was likely going to help him, as well, if he could find the courage to let her in just a little bit.

She'd said everybody needed somebody, and he sure seemed to need her. It was Christmas. He'd been so sure he was in the wrong place once again, and there just weren't that many more names on his list. But now, he thought maybe he was in the right place after all.

He'd never understood how frightening that would be.

He stood there thinking, *Hold me, Emma. Don't let me fall.*

She slipped her arm through his and with great trepidation, he turned to face her. She put her other hand to the side of his face and smiled up at him through those old eyes of hers, now wet with tears.

"If you think you've cornered the market on hard times, think again," she said. "We've all been there. Whatever it is you've been through, we'll understand."

He caught her hand and held it against the side of his face. She'd taken off her gloves and it was cold, and he wanted to warm it, wanted not to have to give up the kindness of her touch just yet.

And then he leaned down and sought the comfort of her mouth, ever so softly, thinking the woman had a way of reaching right down to his soul in ways he just didn't understand. She dug down inside of him, finding things he didn't want anyone to find, and giving back things he didn't quite understand in return.

He just knew that whatever it was she offered, he needed.

So he kissed her cold lips, soaking up the strength, the kindness, and the comfort of her, things he'd never sought from a woman before, things she gave so generously.

Emma, he thought. Quiet kisses and soft hands, old eyes and a seductively gentle touch.

Letting her go was one of the hardest things he ever did. Pulling his mouth from hers, drawing his body away. Life was just too hard some days.

And if he had found the right Sam McRae . . . This was *Sam's* daughter.

"Emma, I . . ." He had no idea what to say. "What is this?"

"I told you. I like you. And you like me, too. It's not really that complicated, is it?"

He held her with his hands on her upper arms, telling himself it was because he had to hold her away from him, but maybe it was because he simply couldn't let go.

He cupped her poor bruised cheek in his hand and ran his thumb over her lower lip. She made him want so much on so many different levels he couldn't even quantify it. He seemed to want her in absolutely all ways, all at the same time. It was bewildering, surprising, even frightening.

"Yes," he insisted. "It is."

"Why? You don't like women?"

"I like women just fine."

"But not me?"

He didn't say anything at first. What could he say to that? He liked her very much, he just couldn't let himself.

The silence stretched awkwardly between them. She looked confused, then doubtful, then hurt. "Oh." She stepped back. "And I was supposed to keep my hands off you, wasn't I? Sorry."

"Oh, hell. I wish I was sorry about all of this," he said. "I don't know what to do with this, Emma. Aren't things complicated enough?"

"My life's more complicated than I'd like at the moment, but I still think you and I—"

He pressed his fingertips against her lips, stopping the words. "Don't say it. Please. It's just not going to happen."

He would hate himself if he let anything happen. Sam would, too.

"Why?" she asked.

"There are things you don't know, Emma." He felt like he owed her that. "Things I've done, places I've been."

"Long, sad stories. I remember."

"Not things that have happened to me. Things *I've* done. It's different when it's a bad place you take yourself to, not ones you end up in because of what the people around you do. I'm talking about who I am."

"Who are you?" she asked.

"I'm a mess. Have been forever, it seems. And you . . ." He still had her by the arms, his hands rubbing at the long, smooth lines of her shoulders. "Look at you. You know the first thing I thought when I saw you? I thought you looked like a schoolgirl for a minute. All soft and sweet and innocent, and I still think you're all those things. A very good girl. The kind a man protects. The kind who shouldn't give someone like me the time of day."

"Because you're just so bad?"

"And you're just about the most tempting thing I've ever seen. Must have awakened every good-girl fantasy I never even knew I had," he said, trying desperately to lighten the mood.

"So you go for the bad girls, do you?"

"Oh, yeah." He made himself grin.

"I don't think I believe that."

"Okay, mostly I've just been trying to get myself together and stay out of trouble the past few years. It's not a bad plan."

"So maybe you're not so bad, after all?"

"I'm trying," he said. "Not sure how well I'm succeeding."

"And I'm not helping matters. I did promise to keep my hands off you. Sorry."

"Yeah, well . . . Who's got their hands on whom right now?" But he let them drop to his side and stepped back, his head still kind of spinning. How did he keep ending up with his hands on her, anyway?

And what was he going to do with her now?

Chapter 5

He drove her home without saying a word, which was fine with her. She was perfectly content to think about him kissing her.

No one had ever kissed Emma like that, so sweetly, so softly, and yet with so much need. A lonely, weary, save-me kind of need. She wondered what he might need and how she might give it to him, because she found herself wanting to give him anything she had to give.

If only she knew what he needed.

They pulled into the driveway. He walked her inside, carefully checking the entire first floor once again, finding nothing out of place.

"Emma," he said, standing in the living room, hands on his hips, shooting her a look that was vintage Sam, that don't-even-think-about-arguing-with-me-now look. "You know you can't stay here by yourself."

Amused, her chin came up. "I can't?"

"You promised Sam. I heard you. And even if you hadn't promised him, I won't let you stay here by yourself."

"You won't let me?" she repeated.

"Okay, maybe that's not the best choice of words. I couldn't. How about that? I won't be able to sleep at night for worrying about you. Do you really want to keep me up all night, Emma?"

"Well . . ." She grinned, letting the word trail off.

He looked completely dismayed, probably thought she was going to throw herself at him again. She never did that. If anything, she was usually a bit shy. He'd probably never believe her if she told him that.

"Emma, this is serious. Don't make me park my truck in the driveway and sleep there all night. Go somewhere where you'll be safe."

"You could stay with me," she suggested.

"Yeah." He nodded, not looking happy. "Me and every other guy claiming to be Sam's friend. We've been through this."

"I'm not issuing invitations far and wide," she pointed out. "Just to you. You're the one who won't be able to sleep anyway."

"Neither will you," he insisted.

She grinned, wanting to kiss him again, as a thank-you for caring and for being here. Kiss him out of that bad mood, or maybe out of his frustrations with her. She wanted to tell him everything was going to be okay, because she was starting to believe it.

"Okay," she admitted. "You're right. I won't, not here by myself. And I really do have some common sense, not that I've shown any of it to you. I told you about the carriage house the other day. There's a bed and a bathroom. We've had people stay there from time to time. I was hoping you'd stay. It's nothing fancy, but . . ."

"I don't need anything fancy," he said.

"I'd be locked up nice and safe, inside the house," she reasoned. "There's an intercom system connecting the two, so if anything happened, all I'd have to do is press a button. You could be right here in seconds."

"Emma?" He was still frowning, still obviously uneasy about something. "These people? Your family? They're good to you, right?"

"Yes."

"Then why can't you bring yourself to even tell them what's going on? Why won't you tell them about this problem with Mark? I understand about the baby, about you wanting them to be together now, but what about you, Emma?"

Emma closed her eyes. *Damn.*

Helluva time to fall for someone, wasn't it? When her ex-boyfriend had turned nuts on her. Now she was making Rye think there was something wrong with her family.

His family, too.

When he already seemed so reluctant to have anything to do with them.

Which meant it was time for more of that painful kind of honesty and openness she was hoping to escape for just a bit longer, until maybe it didn't sting so much and maybe she wouldn't look so bad in his eyes.

His family, too, she reminded herself.

"It's not about them," she said. "It's about me. About who I am and how I want other people—especially my family—to see me. Have you ever done anything you were ashamed of? Deeply, deeply ashamed?"

"Yes," he said, the word positively wrenched from him. "More than I'll ever be able to explain."

What in the world? She'd blown off every attempt he'd made to tell her how bad he was. She didn't believe it for a minute, still didn't, but there were obviously things he deeply regretted.

Hanging by his sides, his hands were clenched

tightly into fists, as if he might pour every bit of tension in his body into them, making her want to touch him once more, something she'd promised herself she would not do.

"Rye—"

"We were talking about you, Emma, and you seem to misunderstand a basic fact about your situation. You didn't do this. Someone did it to you."

"I know that, and I'm not saying it makes a whole lot of sense, but that's how I feel—ashamed. I'm not used to feeling that way, and I guess I'm not handling it well."

"You don't have to handle it well," he said, looking like he might take her in his arms again and just hang on to her.

Come to me, Rye, she thought. *Just come to me.*

Whatever it was, she'd help him. There was a fine sense of give and take to a relationship. She'd seen it in Sam and Rachel's marriage. The way they depended on each other, propped each other up when things got bad.

She'd never imagined finding anyone she could depend on like that, but now, here he was. She wanted him to be able to depend on her, too.

"Do you always handle everything well?" he asked.

"Believe it or not, normally, I do."

"Well you don't have to do that now. It's time to let all those supposedly wonderful people you call your family take care of you."

"I was hoping you would," she said. "Just for another day? Please?"

He frowned at her, obviously torn.

"Let me get something in the hall." She went, hoping he'd follow, and he did. There was a desk tucked under the stairs, keys hanging on a neat row of hooks. "I'm going to pull myself together, I promise, and then

I'll tell Sam, and everything will be fine. But I just need a day or two to figure things out."

And she needed to keep him here. She needed to know what was wrong. Emma found the spare key to the carriage house and held it out to him.

"Sam's not going to think any less of you," Rye said, making no move to take it. "Not if he's the man you claim he is. No one's going to think any less of you because you made a mistake about a guy, Emma."

"I hope not."

"We all makes mistakes," he said.

"You could tell me about yours," she offered, key still in hand. "I'd understand."

"My mistakes are in a whole different league from yours."

"Give it up, Rye. You're not going to convince me that you're not a nice man. You've been so kind to me, so helpful, so understanding."

"That's not who I am," he insisted, shaking his head.

"It's exactly who you are, and I'm grateful for all those things."

"Don't thank me again, Emma. Please. I don't think I could stand it."

Don't touch me, he meant. *Don't kiss me. Don't get that close.*

He sighed and closed his eyes. She thought for a moment he was at war with himself, that she could feel him swaying toward her, catching himself just in time and then pulling back.

The room seemed charged with energy, want, and need, excitement and fear. Every little gesture, every word seemed to mean so much. She had a feeling that one misstep could ruin everything. It made her think every relationship in her life to this point had been nothing, that this was the first one that mattered.

She'd always thought it would happen someday, and she'd thought it would be fairly simple—she'd see him and she'd just know, and that would be it. She'd thought her heart would never truly steer her wrong.

It had told her all along that Mark wasn't the one. Just like she thought perhaps the man standing in front of her was the right one.

"All right, I'll stay," he said, finally taking the key. "I'll give you one more day, and then you call Sam."

Well then, that would have to be enough.

"I'll take you to the carriage house and make sure you have everything you need."

"I'll take myself. You lock the door behind me and go to bed."

"All right. Thanks for staying."

He waited until he heard the dead bolt on the back door click into place. He'd checked the place. It was sound. She should be fine, and he would feel better being close. Thankfully not in the same house as her. Emma curled up in a bed right upstairs or right down the hall was too much to even think about.

Emma with her wandering hands and sweet mouth.

Emma, Sam's daughter?

He hadn't begged the universe for anything in years, but he was ready to beg now. Please don't let him have come here, found his brother, only to be lusting after his brother's adopted daughter.

It was laughable really.

What an introduction that would be.

Hi. I'm your long-lost brother, and you really wouldn't mind if I drool over your daughter, would you?

Rye walked through the backyard and let himself into the carriage house with the key Emma had given

him. What more could a man intent on snooping ask
for than this—a damned key and hours alone with
which to search.

As soon as he found something that told him he
was in the wrong place, he'd stop and soon after that,
he'd leave.

As soon as he knew Emma was okay.

This was all some odd coincidence, anyway.

His brother wasn't supposed to have a grandfather,
for one thing. And he hadn't lost his parents at fourteen or fifteen. He'd been much younger, if Rye could
trust the records he'd found. But honestly, how could
that be? In those hazy images in his head, his brother
had always seemed so much older than Rye. So even
the ages didn't make sense.

Hell, he might not even have the right man's name
on his list, but he could cross them off one by one,
because there was nothing else to do.

He locked the door behind him and pocketed the
key, then flipped on the lights and found himself in a
big room. The carriage house was indeed very, very
old, but it was solid. A neatly restored structure that
now housed a large, well-organized, well-equipped
workshop. From the looks of it, he suspected Sam
McRae was very good with wood.

He ran his hands along a very old piece of crown
molding, intricately carved, chipped in places, broken
in others. Someone was painstakingly restoring it. It
was nice work. He couldn't have done it himself, but
he appreciated the skill and patience it took to do
it right.

Passing through the workshop, he came to what had
to be Sam's office. There were papers piled everywhere, but again, things were orderly, organized.
Along the back wall, he saw a cot and through a door-

way to the left, he suspected he'd find a bathroom. Everything he needed.

He reached for the top middle drawer in the desk and slid it open. It was that easy. Slide open drawers one by one.

"God," he muttered, sitting down and staring at the wall.

It was an awful thing to want so very much and be scared to have it.

He'd been living scared for a very long time, living like everything he had might be ripped away from him at any moment, and it seemed safer just to never have that much in his life.

But surely he could have something. Surely it was safe now.

He started digging through the drawer. Almost everything here was work-related, he realized an hour later. Sam McRae had a very prosperous business. He wasn't a wealthy man, but he was clearly comfortable. His customers sure seemed happy with him. They wrote him letters thanking him, sent pictures of their newly renovated houses, everyone beaming at the camera.

There were few personal bits of information. His social security number on a few of the forms Rye found. If he had the social security number for the man he was looking for, that might prove quite helpful. Unfortunately he didn't.

Other than that, the personal papers must be in the house.

If he wanted to search, that wouldn't be a problem. All he had to do was get Emma back into the bathtub. He could probably get through the whole downstairs in the time she was up there soaking, if he could keep his mind on what he was supposed to be doing.

Sam's daughter, he told himself.

No more kissing her. No more hanging on to her. No more sweet lips or sad, understanding eyes. Not for him.

He glanced out the window one more time, finding everything just as it had been. Nothing moving in the yard. No sounds of any kind, except for a dog barking a few houses away.

The light was still on.

He didn't blame her. If he was scared someone was coming after him, he might sleep with the light on, too. It was so much easier to get lost in your fears in the dark, so easy to get lost completely.

He paced the narrow confines of the office for the longest time, and he thought about going outside and walking around the backyard. But Emma might hear him, and she might be afraid. Someone might see him and call the cops. He really didn't need that. So he forced himself to calm down and not to think of this little room as a cell. Narrow spaces tended to do that to him—make him just a little bit crazy and even break out into a cold sweat sometimes.

He could go outside at any time, he told himself. No one had locked him inside.

Finally, he unfolded the linens and the blanket stacked neatly on the end of the cot, clicked off the lights, took off his shoes and socks, and lay down.

He'd figure this out and go. He didn't have to say anything to anybody about why he'd come. Rye slept fitfully, dreaming of things best forgotten, came awake with a start, gasping for breath as an old, familiar nightmare took hold.

It took him a minute to figure out where he was.

The cot was small, the space nearly as tiny, and there didn't seem to be enough air. It was pitch-black, save for a stream of light shining through a tiny window far above him.

But he was okay.

He stood up and looked out the window, finding everything just as he'd last seen it—quiet, still, undisturbed.

Good.

Everything was fine.

Except him.

He was coming apart.

He kept thinking about the date on the baby's grave, the date when he'd last seen Sam. Through sheer force of will alone, he'd managed not to let himself think about it so far. But now, his will was gone. He really didn't believe in coincidence. He believed in lousy luck, lousy decisions, black holes people dropped into and seemed to never quite crawl out of.

Those two things had happened within the same seven days. What did that mean?

And what did he think he was ever going to find, even if he did stumble upon the right Sam McRae one day?

Rye got up, took a quick shower, shaved, dressed quickly, then stalked off across the yard in a lousy mood. Emma was up herself, although it was still early. She unlocked the back door and welcomed him inside, asking how he'd slept.

"About as well as you, it looks like," he said, because there were still dark circles under her brown eyes. Then he winced at how unkind that was.

"What's wrong?"

"Nothing," he said, wishing so badly that he could just go. It was a refrain pounding through his brain, *Go, go, go. Before anybody catches you and anything really bad happens.*

"You're just always this happy in the mornings?" she asked, wearing another pair of snug jeans and a little blue sweater, smelling like she'd come straight from a vat of vanilla.

Her mouth looked eminently kissable. There was a sparkle in her eyes that made him nervous, a hint of either mischief or sheer delight—he couldn't say which one—in her entire manner.

"Put me to work," he demanded.

If he could wear himself out, give himself something to occupy his hands and his mind, he might last another day. And then he'd go. It made no damned sense for her to be here by herself, and he wasn't going to listen to any excuses or rationalizations about why she should be.

"Okay," she said. "More lights?"

"Every damned light you can find," he said.

She seemed to know this wasn't the time to talk to him. It wasn't the time to try to soothe him or to put her hands on him. God only knew what he might do if she did. Grab her and just never let go, probably.

He was crazy today. Just crazy. Too damned close to the past, too close to answers. He wanted too much and he just wanted to run.

He worked tirelessly that day. She watched him, wondering what kind of demons were eating away at him. All she'd figured out was that he wanted to be busy, so she kept him busy.

Once they'd strung lights around bushes and trees, they went to work inside. He hauled more boxes of decorations upstairs, and they moved furniture, making room for the tree that would come later, draped garlands of greenery everywhere, put up red ribbons, wall hangings, and strings of lights made to look like stars. He didn't complain once, just set himself grimly to the task with complete concentration. He didn't smile, didn't laugh, hardly spoke.

She thought he'd gone through some of the papers on the old rolltop desk in the living room while she'd been upstairs, but she hadn't said anything.

Whatever he needed to see was fine with her.

More than once she thought about going to the phone, calling Sàm, and telling him everything, telling him he had to come home now. But if that's what Rye wanted, why hadn't he said anything? Why was he so uneasy? Something was dreadfully wrong.

They worked straight through lunch. It was mid-afternoon before they stopped.

"I have to go to the inn and check out of my room," he said, when the last of the boxes was empty, the house transformed. "They said I could only have it through last night, and . . ."

"No need to keep it. Not if you're going to be here," she said.

Except she was afraid he wasn't.

She rode with him into town, sat in his truck while he checked out of the room, and then directed him to the town's sole Chinese restaurant where she'd ordered take-out by phone. He went inside and picked it up, because she was still hiding her bruised face.

When they got back to the house, it was crisp and cold. There was a fine layer of snow on the ground. Soon it would be Christmas, a time that was both joyous and bittersweet for her. She and her brother and sister had come here for the first time at Christmas, but lost their mother soon after. It was a time when she was grateful for all she had, yet conscious of all she'd lost. She wondered what the man sitting beside her had lost and how he coped. By running away, it seemed.

"You're leaving, aren't you?" she asked as they pulled into the driveway and he cut the engine.

"You asked for another day, and I gave it to you."

"I know. Can you just tell me why you think you have to go?"

"It was a mistake to come in the first place," he said, looking out the window toward the house.

"Why?"

"Long story," he said, drumming his fingers on the steering wheel.

"I've got time."

"Well, I don't know if I could get through it," he said. "You need to find a place to stay. Pack whatever you need. I'll take you wherever you want to go."

"Rye, you can't go."

"I am," he said, climbing out of the truck.

She scrambled after him, practically chasing him across the lawn. "Wait."

"There's nothing left to talk about."

"There is." There must be. "Rye—"

"It's between me and Sam," he said, not slowing down at all. He charged toward the house. "I'll take it up with him."

"Will you?"

"Yes."

He'd gotten to the porch, to the front door, but he couldn't go anywhere else. She had the key. "At least tell me what's wrong. Tell me why you came here in the first place."

"I came to find someone," he admitted as he stood at the door.

"Sam," she said, following more slowly.

He turned around. "No. I thought maybe . . . But it's a mistake, that's all."

"I don't think so," she said, finally reaching his side.

"I'm looking for a man named Sam McRae, but not your Sam."

"How do you know he's not the one?"

"I know," he said, tension radiating from him.

"Tell me. Tell me about the man you're looking for."

He took a breath and said, "He was born in Chicago."

"Sam was born in Chicago."

"Him and millions of other people, I'm sure."

"Millions of other men named Sam McRae? Rye, listen to me, please—"

"Emma! Emma, is that you?"

She froze, the voice coming from behind her.

Shocked, she turned to Rye and whispered, "It's him."

Chapter 6

She'd almost forgotten about him.

Rye shoved her behind him. Like a coward, nearly paralyzed with fear, she hid there, his body between hers and Mark's.

Waves of fear rolled through her. Time slowed to a crawl. She saw the porch, wide and shadowed, saw the pretty wicker furnishings and the cushions with the wild, bright floral print Grace had picked out.

She saw the hooks that in the summer held baskets of wide, bushy ferns and the Christmas lights she and Rye had strung up yesterday.

It was her house.

How could he come to her house and scare her this way?

And she was so damned scared. It was the worst feeling, to find that nothing but a man's voice could reduce her to this. Could make her think about crouching in the corner and trying to make herself invisible, because if he couldn't see her, he couldn't hurt her. She'd tried long, long ago, to make herself invisible.

"Emma?" Mark began.

She peered over Rye's shoulder to see him standing there looking confused and very angry. His dark hair was disheveled, his clothes wrinkled, the white shirt nearly untucked on one side. He was normally so careful about his appearance, about everything. Calm, mature, insistent, but not unreasonable. Now he looked wild. She glanced down at his hands, clenched into fists, and shuddered.

"She doesn't want to talk to you," Rye said firmly.

"You know that, do you?" Mark yelled.

"Emma, tell him one more time that you don't want to talk to him," Rye said, his voice perfectly steady. He wasn't afraid. Thank goodness he wasn't.

"I don't want to talk to you, Mark," she said in a mousy, breathless voice she despised.

"She doesn't want to have to tell you that again. Neither do I."

"Emma, this is crazy," Mark said. "A big misunderstanding that's gotten all blown out of proportion. If we could just talk."

"She is talking," Rye said. "The problem is that you aren't listening."

"What are you doing here, Mark?" she asked, holding on to Rye's shoulders and peeking from behind them now and then, like she might at a bloody scene from a horror flick. "What do you want?"

"You wouldn't talk to me on the phone. I had to come."

"Again, she is talking. What part of this do you not understand?" Rye asked, towering between her and Mark. "She doesn't want to talk to you. That's her right. She doesn't want to see you. Also, her right. And if you ever lay your hands on her again, I will make you sorry for it."

"Emma?"

"He's right, Mark. I don't want you calling me. I don't want you here."

"Emma, we can fix this. You love me. You know you do."

"No. I don't." There'd been a time when she thought they might be headed in that direction, but obviously she was wrong. So horribly wrong. "I don't ever want to see you again."

"Want me to repeat that part?" Rye asked.

"Who the hell are you, anyway?" Mark yelled, coming closer.

"Emma, go inside." Rye gave her a little push in that direction.

"I . . ." She wanted to. She wanted to run, but she wasn't sure she could even move. Surely she could still move.

"Go," Rye said.

"She doesn't want to go," Mark said.

He'd gotten close enough to try to reach around Rye to her.

The next thing she knew, Rye grabbed him, swung him around, and slammed him up against the side of the house. She heard his head crack against the wood.

Rye got right up in his face. "Don't you dare touch her again."

His forearm was pressed against Mark's throat. Mark gagged a bit and pulled at Rye's arm.

"Not a lot of fun to be on the receiving end of something like this, is it?" Rye asked. "Having someone who's bigger than you and stronger than you shoving you around."

"Come on," Mark choked out, still pulling at Rye's arm.

Rye merely pressed harder with the arm. "If you

touch her again, you will answer to me. Do you understand?"

Mark nodded. Rye let him go. Mark slid down the side of the house until he collapsed in a heap on the porch. He was coughing and clutching his throat.

"Emma go inside, now."

"But—"

"Don't worry. I'm not going to kill him. Not this time."

Mark's head came up at that. She thought she saw both fear and fury in his eyes. "I'll get you for this."

Rye loomed over him. "Please, try it."

Mark got to his feet and turned back to Emma. "And you . . ."

"Come on," Rye said. "Give me an excuse."

They glared at each other for a long moment. Mark finally headed down the porch steps. He was halfway across the yard before he turned around once again.

"This is what you've been doing here behind my back?" he screamed. "Fooling around with him? This is how you treat me?"

Emma slid back behind Rye, closing her eyes and wishing she could block out the words as well as the sight of him. It was so humiliating. She'd welcomed this man into her life, trusted him.

"It's not over, Emma. I'm not done with you, you little slut."

Rye practically growled, the sound coming from deep within him. She thought for a minute he was going to go after Mark. It seemed every muscle in his body was hard as a rock right then.

"Let him go," she said. "Please. I just want him to go."

Rye turned halfway around. She slipped in under his arm and anchored herself to him. He felt like a mountain right then, strong and every bit as unyielding. She tucked her face against his chest. Mark kept yelling foul things, and Rye put his hand over her face, her ears, trying to muffle the sound.

Finally, the commotion ceased. She heard a car door open and close. Heard the engine start, the car screech away.

She stayed where she was, shaking so badly.

It had been so awful.

He was here in her town, and she was so afraid he was going to hurt her again.

"I'm sorry," she said again and again.

Rye brought her inside. He tucked an afghan around her once again, as he had that first day, and built up the fire, but she just couldn't get warm.

He brought hot tea, which he made her sip. She held it with hands that trembled so badly, the cup rattled against the saucer. It was a miracle she didn't spill it all over herself.

"I was so scared," she said finally, after she'd drunk half the cup. "And I hate being scared."

"Well, I don't know anybody who enjoys it," Rye said easily.

He settled himself on the floor in front of the fire, his back against the sofa. His arm was stretched along the cushions, his hand closing around her ankle. Just that made things a little better. As long as he was touching her.

She wanted to slip into that spot at his side. Maybe then she would feel safe again. Maybe she'd stop shaking. She was nearly there—to the point where she could have stopped shaking—when the phone rang.

She nearly jumped out of her skin, took a breath trying to calm herself, and then it rang again.

Rye picked it up and said hello. A moment later,

he covered the mouthpiece with his hand and said, "It's your neighbor. Mrs. Wells. She heard some of that outside, and now she's worried about you. You need to tell her you're okay."

Emma did that and only that, then gave the phone back to Rye. He told Mrs. Wells that he was a friend of Sam's and that he'd look out for Emma, and then he hung up. They got another call just like it not five minutes later.

"Small-town living," Emma said, thoroughly ashamed. Rye hadn't really told them anything, but if they'd heard Mark yelling, they knew enough.

"They're looking out for you. That's good. I told them if they see anything suspicious to call the sheriff. You know, it's not a bad idea for you to tell him what's going on, Emma."

"You think so?"

"Cops don't always take trouble between a man and a woman seriously," he said softly, his thumb lightly rubbing the bottom of one of her feet. "If they know ahead of time there's been trouble . . . Well, if you need to call them, I want them here fast and to know what they're getting into."

"You don't think he'll leave, do you? Not after tonight?"

"We can hope. I was rough with him. Not just because I was so mad. I was trying to scare him. I want him to think twice about what might happen to him if he comes back. I hope I didn't just make him madder," Rye said. "He thinks there's something going on between you and me, which might also make him madder."

"I thought it was all over," she said. "I mean, I was scared, but I didn't really think he'd come here."

On the porch of her house, screaming at her and trying to grab her.

She started to cry again. Rye pulled her down onto the floor beside him and then into his arms, into that spot she'd wanted. She pressed her face into his shoulder, into that warm, dark place that was so comforting and smelled of him.

She'd spent another lifetime, up until she was not quite twelve, being scared. It was like living with a time bomb, except there was no face on this particular clock. She knew it was ticking, but never knew when it would go off.

Mark was like that now. She didn't know where he was or what he would do. She didn't know if he was coming back.

"I hate this. I hate it so much," she said, weeping into the hollow between Rye's shoulder and his chin, wishing she could just crawl inside of his skin, because she knew she'd be safe there.

All these things she thought she'd forgotten . . . They were still inside of her. She remembered what it sounded like when her father hit her mother. She remembered the sounds her mother made, awful, pitiful sounds. She remembered hiding from him and trying to make herself as small as possible, trying not to even breathe.

"Your father?" Rye asked. "He didn't just hit your mother, did he?"

"No," she said.

He dipped his head to hear the whispered confession, kissed her softly on the cheek and then stayed there, his lips next to her right ear. "Tell me."

"It was just that once. I'd always been scared it would happen, but it only did once, and then we left. Not that we were done with him. The damage had been done to my mother's body then, and she was pregnant with Grace when we left. He found her one more time, after Grace was born, and that time, she never recovered. He's in prison now, and I promised myself I'd never be that scared again. That no one would ever make me feel like that again."

"Good for you," he said.

"I feel that way now, Rye. My father made me feel that way and now Mark has, and I'm so mad at myself for being in this position again. I'm falling apart, too, and I hate that even more."

"Shh." His breath brushed past her cheeks, her lips. He kissed her closed eyelids, kissed a tear from her cheek. "Emma. It's all right. It's done."

She sobbed, clinging to him even harder. "What makes a man think he can do that? That he has the right?"

"I don't know. But you're not going to let anyone treat you like this. This is going to be over, and you'll put it behind you."

"I don't feel fine right now. I feel like Mark could come barging in here any minute."

"Hey." He took her face in the palm of his hand and tilted it up to his. "I've got you. I'll stay right here."

"You said you had to leave."

"Well, now I've got to stay, as long as you need me." His forehead came down to rest against hers. He kissed the tip of her nose. "Promise."

"You must think I'm awful," she said, not quite able to meet his gaze. "That I'm such a mess."

"No. Just scared. You're caught up in something crazy. It happens. Life can just explode around you, and all of a sudden, nothing makes sense. You really can't do anything except hang on and try to ride it out."

"You know that?" she asked, the tears running down her face faster than he could catch them and wipe them away. "It's happened to you?"

"Yes."

"But you made it," she said. "You're okay."

"I think I'm still caught up in it, too. That really crazy time. That maybe I'm just starting to come out on the other side of it."

"Then you can hang on to me," she said.

"Emma—"

"I feel safe with you. I feel perfectly safe right here with you."

She felt the tension coming into his body. They'd been close, still were, and he'd been kind and so very tender, gentle and heartbreakingly sweet. It had been intimate without being sexual at all, and now it seemed she'd crossed that line, as she kept doing with him, and made it something else.

"I need you," she said. "I forget to be afraid when I'm this close to you. I forget how bad things are and how stupid I must have been. I can lose everything . . . all the bad things. In you."

And then, despite all his protests, she leaned over once again and pressed her mouth to his.

He didn't mean to let her draw him in one more time, but dammit, the woman had the sweetest-tasting mouth he'd ever known.

She was so soft, so good. Sometimes she felt like everything good in the world, all wrapped up in a tiny package and handed to him.

He'd warned her about himself every way he knew how—except to blurt out the brutal truth of who he was and what he'd done. That would solve all of this. She'd run so fast in the other direction, he'd never have to worry about her being this close to him again.

But he didn't tell her, because he wanted her hands on him and her mouth. God, how he wanted it.

He tried telling himself he could have just a little

bit of her, took that innocent, thank-you kiss and tried very hard to keep it light.

Necking in front of the fire with Emma.

He could do that.

Rye angled her body around until she was facing him and leaning into him, until he had her pressed securely against his body, and he could drink from her mouth, long, sweet, drugging kisses. Taste after taste after taste.

It started a slow burn deep inside of him, but he could handle slow burn. He'd wanted her right from the start and been just as determined he wouldn't ever have her. But he could have a taste of her.

"Emma." He pulled away long before he was satisfied.

She blinked up at him, looking like a woman drugged into the kind of lazy, soothing happiness that came from pure sexual pleasure. "Yes."

"Stop that," he said. "Stop tempting me."

"How do I do that?" she asked.

"God," he muttered. "You'd have to be in another state to stop."

"Well, I'm not leaving, and you promised you wouldn't, either."

"No, I won't," he reassured her. He could suffer through a little sexual frustration for the sake of keeping her safe. No problem. He knew all about sexual frustration.

And then he kissed her again. Her mouth was moist and warm, her lips the same, from all the kisses they'd already shared. Her arms slid around his rib cage and pressed against his back. It wouldn't take much to lift her onto his lap and enjoy sexual frustration at a whole new level, or maybe go to work on the buttons of her blouse. He started to sweat just thinking about it.

Long, satisfying, frustrating moments later, he lifted his head once more. "I don't think I'm going to be spending the night in the carriage house."

"I don't want you to. I want you right here."

It was probably the only place he could be where he'd know she was safe.

"Nothing's going to happen," he insisted. They'd neck in front of the fire. She could crawl all over him, if she had to, and he'd hang on tight, but nothing else.

"Okay," she agreed.

Yes, the woman needed a keeper.

"You know, you never did tell me how old you are," he said. "I'm wondering more and more just how bad that's going to be."

"It's not like I'm jailbait," she insisted.

"So we've got that going for us," he said. "But it's bad. I know it. Otherwise, you'd have told me already."

"Does it really matter? You keep insisting nothing's going to happen."

"And I keep ending up right back here. You're hard to resist, Emma."

"I think you're doing a fine job of it, myself."

"No, I'm not." He kissed her as softly and leisurely as he could manage. "Give me this, Em. Just your mouth. Wrap your arms around me and lie here in my arms and kiss me until we can't stand it anymore, until you aren't so afraid."

"You're doing this because I'm afraid?" she asked.

"No, I'm doing this because I want to. Because it's going to be a long night, and you're probably going to spend it right here in my arms. You haven't slept since the day that jerk hit you, have you?"

"No," she admitted.

"Well, you'll sleep tonight. Right here."

"I don't know what I'd have done without you."

She raised her face once again to his, so trusting, so needy. Just a kiss, he told himself. Sweet, soft Emma kisses. He'd draw them inside of him, and they'd be all the softness he knew. If a woman could ever change him, ease the hurt, squeeze out all the bad times, it would be her.

For tonight, he'd hold her close. He'd kiss her until he couldn't stand to anymore, and he'd make sure she was safe.

Chapter 7

Emma slept in his arms. They made out in front of the fire and slept and talked and then made out some more. It was an interesting way to spend the night.

At some point, they spread out on the floor beneath the afghan, Emma curled up against his side, her head on his shoulder, his arms still around her. She woke to find the fire had died down and weak sunlight was shining through the front windows. His hair was all mussed, stubble dotted his jaw, and he looked like so much trouble and so much joy all rolled into one.

"Good morning." She eased back to get a better look at him.

"Good morning." He took his hand and tucked a strand of hair behind her ear. "Sleep well?"

"Yes."

He grinned then. "Emma, do me a favor, okay?"

"Anything," she offered.

"Get upstairs before we end up rolling around on the floor this morning."

"Do I have to?" She reached for him. How could she help it?

He caught her hands and held them away. "I'm doing my best here."

"I know. I wish you weren't."

He got to his feet. She laughed and did the same. She was perfectly safe with him. He was only going to let things go so far, and while she hoped to change his mind about that in time, for now, she was enjoying every minute of it. He kissed like a man who had all the time in the world to savor the taste of her, to explore every nuance, every sensation, and he was wonderfully touchable.

"Last night was wonderful," she said.

He groaned. "God, don't say that. If you say that to anybody, they're going to think—"

"I won't tell anyone." She laughed, feeling on top of the world this morning, which was amazing after feeling so horrible the night before when . . .

When Mark showed up.

Rye touched her chin, then ran a finger over the tip of her nose. "Hey, don't go back there, okay? I worked hard to cheer you up, to make you forget."

"And I did," she said, the worst of what the day before had brought coming back to her in a rush. "It's just . . ."

"Yeah, yeah," he said, folding her into his arms once more. "And don't think you're fooling me. This is just some new bit to get your hands on me, right? Drum up a few tears and hang your head, and look what happens?"

She did manage to laugh then. "It worked, didn't it?"

"You are a shameless woman, Emma."

She lifted her head from his shoulders and stared

up into his beautiful dark eyes. His mouth was right there, stretched into something of a smile now, and there were little laugh lines crinkling together at the corners of his mouth. She wanted his mouth, all of his heat, all the need.

"I'm only shameless where you're concerned," she said.

The smile disappeared. Heat flared in his eyes, and he went tense.

"You do want me," she said, because she needed to believe that.

"What man wouldn't want you?" he said. "Emma, you can't be that innocent. Please, tell me you're not."

"I'm not," she lied quickly and, she hoped, well. She couldn't let him guess how innocent she was. He'd back away for sure.

Truth was, she'd never quite managed to lose herself completely in a man. Sometimes she thought she was cautious, sometimes reserved. Sometimes she wondered if there were something wrong with her, that maybe she was waiting for something she'd never find.

Mark had . . .

Oh, she didn't want to think about Mark. But he'd never pushed for anything more than she was willing to give. He'd told her more than once that he was glad she was such an old-fashioned girl.

Emma shivered, coming back to the present, the good with the bad.

Deal with it, Emma.

"I'm just a little shaky right now and not trusting myself," she said. "But I trust you."

Emma eased up on her toes and tilted her face to his. He groaned and dipped his head again. It was a scathing kiss, a fire starter. The man certainly knew how to start a blaze. Maybe he truly had been holding

back the entire time with her. Maybe he had the kind
of control she'd never even guessed at, if this was how
he'd really been wanting to kiss her.

She found herself plastered against him, his hands
slipping down to cup her hips and pull her into the
cradle of his thighs, hard, throbbing heat waiting for
her there.

Oh, my.

She wrapped her arms around his shoulders and
held on tight as he backed her up against the wall and
leaned into her in a way that had her thinking about
a scene in a movie that had made her blush.

She thought about hands sliding up her bare thighs,
beneath her dress, if she'd been wearing a dress.
About bare hands on her hips, sliding beneath her
panties and lifting her into him. Hands working franti-
cally to free her and him, and about him having her
right here against the wall.

She made a little whimpering sound, and that was
enough to break the spell. He lifted his head, his eyes
darker and more dangerous than she'd ever seen him,
and then he shuddered and backed carefully away. His
hands came to rest against the wall on either side of
her head, and he leaned into it, so that his face wasn't
so far from hers but the rest of his body was.

"Good God," he muttered. "Emma . . ."

"It was my fault. . . ." Oh, her cheeks were burning
now. "I'm sorry."

He winced and threw his head back to groan. When
he faced her again, it was with something of a smile.
He touched her face so softly and said, "That takes
two. And we really need to get the hell out of here.
If you and I stay here together much longer . . . You
know what's going to happen."

Did she? Emma leaned against the wall on trembling
legs and tried to breathe. She supposed she did, and

she didn't have any objections, but he would. He'd
never take her to bed with him once he found out
how old she was. Which was really a shame, because
this was honestly the first time she'd ever really
wanted to go to bed with a man out of anything other
than curiosity.

This went way past that into honest, deep-down
need and greed. Did good girls like her feel like this?
Because if they did, how did they ever manage to stay
good girls?

"Do not dare look at me like that," he growled.

"Sorry."

She couldn't quite look him in the eye then and
made the mistake of letting her gaze drift lower and
lower until she hit the waistband of his jeans and then
went ever so slightly lower to . . .

Oh, my.

If she thought her face was red before, it was surely
flaming now. Heat flooded her cheeks, and she
couldn't quite look away from the unmistakable ridge
straining against the fly of his jeans.

Her first thought was, *That has to hurt, doesn't it?*

And then she wanted to touch it, to run her hands
over it through the fabric of his jeans and then with
nothing between them. She wanted to be pressed up
against the wall again with that rubbing sensuously
against her and then he could put it inside her.

Her. Emma. *The good girl.*

What would that be like?

"Emma, I swear to God . . ." He stood there, no
doubt ready to growl some more, but before he could,
the doorbell rang.

At first, they both froze.

"Oh, no. Not again." She scrambled to the front
window to look out.

"Is it him?" Rye asked, following her.

She looked across the street, where Mark's car had been parked the day before. It wasn't there. She looked in the driveway, wondering if it was a neighbor or a relative. Which would be worse?

Both would be bad, she thought, until she saw the sheriff's car there.

"Oh, hell," Rye muttered behind her. "I really don't need this."

"It's just Joe. He's a friend of Sam's. He probably heard about the shouting match on the porch yesterday." He could have had better timing. She wasn't crazy about explaining this to anyone, but as choices went, the sheriff wasn't a bad one. She reminded Rye, "You wanted him to know what was going on."

"That's not why he's here, Emma." The doorbell rang again, and then Joe rapped on the door, calling Emma's name. "Go on. Let him in. You'll see."

"I'm telling you, Joe's a friend."

"Well, he's going to love this." Rye looked from her to the makeshift bed on the floor by the fire. "He's going to be on the phone to Sam so fast—"

"Emma!" Joe rapped on the door even harder.

"Let him in before he knocks down the door."

Rye brushed his hair down as best he could and grabbed the afghan and the pillows off the floor. Emma tried to smooth down her own hair and wished she didn't look and feel so rumpled.

She pulled open the front door and smiled up at Joe. "Hi."

He frowned. "You okay?"

Her cheeks were flushed, and she wondered how that might blend in with her bruise this morning. Hoping for the best, she angled her head to the right and didn't bother turning on the light in the hallway. It was light enough outside to make do.

"I'm fine," she said.

Joe looked around at what he could see of the room. "Sam still gone?"

"Yes."

"I need to come in, Emma."

"Oh, sure. Sorry. Please, come in."

She stepped back and gave him some room, then shut the door behind him. When she turned around, the sheriff was staring into the living room at Rye, who did indeed have that rumpled, straight-out-of-bed look to him. Oh, well. What did it matter? Nothing happened. She'd tell Sam, and he'd believe her. No big deal.

Except for the way Rye and Joe Mitchell were sizing each other up. She sensed trouble and hurried to get between them.

"Joe, this is Rye . . . John Ryan, actually. But he goes by Rye. Rye, this is Joe Mitchell, the sheriff."

They stood their ground, nodding in each other's direction.

"Sure you're all right?" Joe asked, as if he might need to rescue her from Rye.

"Yes."

"Someone came to see me about a problem here yesterday," he said, not taking his gaze off Rye. "You and I need to talk, Emma, and then I suspect I'll need to talk to your friend."

"Of course. Why don't we all go into the kitchen. I'll make some coffee."

"Okay," Joe agreed.

She went first, the men parading behind her, no letup that she could see in the open hostilities. She made Joe sit on one of the stools at the breakfast bar, Rye, too, and then dared turn her back to them to start a pot of coffee. She was going to have to tell Joe everything. She could see that from how worried he was and how suspicious he was of Rye.

"Which one of the neighbors called?" she asked, keeping her back to them as she filled the coffeepot with water. "Mrs. Wells?"

"The neighbors saw this?" Joe asked.

"Heard it, at least," Emma said. "I'm not sure if they actually saw it."

"Which ones? I might need to talk to them, too," Joe said.

Emma turned around, still not getting it. Rye looked just about as angry as he had been when Mark showed up. "What's going on?"

"Your ex filed a complaint," Rye said, then looked at Joe. "Right?"

Joe nodded. "He claims your friend tried to kill him."

"What?" Emma was so mad, she was sputtering.

"That's what he said."

"Are we going to talk about it first?" Rye said, in a voice she scarcely recognized. "Or do you want to go ahead and arrest me now?"

"I thought we'd talk first," Joe said.

Rye just nodded and eased back on his chair, looking not at all surprised.

Emma was outraged. "That snake! That dirty, rotten snake. I can't believe he'd do that."

"He claims he's your boyfriend," Joe said.

"Not anymore. Not since . . ." She faltered then. Damn.

"Emma," Rye said. "We talked about this. I'm sorry, but he's got to know, so he'll watch out for you."

"Know what?" Joe asked.

Emma sat down and closed her eyes. It was as hard as she'd imagined it would be. "He hit me."

"Your ex-boyfriend?" Joe asked.

"Yes. We met at school this fall, and we've been

going out. As Christmas break started, we got into a fight. He hit me, and I came running back here."

"Hit you?" Joe asked. "How? I need to know, Emma. Tell me exactly what happened."

"He slapped me."

"He hit her hard enough to knock her down," Rye said. "Come over here in the light and show him the other side of your face, Emma."

She'd done her best to stay on Joe's right side, to hide the bruise from him. But she couldn't anymore. Rye flipped on the bright light that hung over the serving bar in the kitchen, and she showed off her bruise to Joe.

He swore and asked, "Anything else?"

"No," Emma said.

"Yes," Rye insisted at the same time. "I suspect there's some bruising on her arms where he grabbed her. And her ribs are sore. What did he do? Kick you while you were down, Em?"

Shame had her cheeks burning all the more. Oh, she hated this.

She finally lifted her head to look at Rye. "Sorry," he mouthed. "He needs to know."

She looked away again. "Yes, that's what happened."

"That's all? You're sure?"

"Isn't that enough?" Rye asked.

"Just want to get it straight," Joe said, pulling a small notebook out of his pocket and reaching for a pen. "Did you file a complaint there?"

"No," she said.

"Emma—"

"I know. I know, okay? I just wanted to come home."

Joe had started to write, but he gave up and said, "Sam left, after hearing this?"

"She didn't tell him," Rye said.

Emma glared at him. Joe scratched his head and frowned at her.

"Why the hell not?" he asked.

"I don't know, Joe. Why don't women complain about things like this? You tell me. I bet you've heard it all over the years."

"Not from you," he said.

Rye jumped in at that. "Hey. She's had a hard time, okay? She's doing the best she can."

"I know that. I just . . ." Joe swore once again, his voice trailing off.

Emma put her hand on Rye's arm, to let her know she didn't need him defending her at this moment. "Rye, he didn't mean it like that. Joe and I go way back, too. He was a deputy here when my mother left me and my brother and sister in a motel on the edge of town. He helped arrest my father, in fact."

"Shit," Rye said.

"Yeah, that's about the size of it," Joe agreed.

"I'm sorry, Joe." Emma sat down, feeling older by the minute and very, very tired. "I should have reported it. I should know better. But I guess I was embarrassed."

"Emma, you didn't do anything wrong," Joe began.

"So I've been told." She glanced over at Rye.

"Okay, so the two of you got into a fight, and he hit you, and you came back here." Joe started scribbling again. "Then what?"

"He's been calling her," Rye said. "And scaring her."

"When?"

"Ever since I got back here. He called the first day and acted like this was a silly misunderstanding. Can you believe that?"

"Yeah. It's what guys like him do," Joe said. "Manipulate, intimidate, isolate, somehow convince a woman everything's her fault. Don't fall into his trap of thinking you're the one with the problem. He is."

"Thanks," Emma said.

"Okay, so he's been calling, and you told him . . . What?"

"To stop. That I didn't want to talk to him. That I wanted him to leave me alone. But he wouldn't."

"Well." Joe sat back and considered. "I'd say to put a block on the phone, but unless you know the number he's calling from . . ."

"He's not home," she said. "It's no telling where he is now."

"A motel just across the county line in Wilmont. At least, that's what he told me this morning when he came to see me." Joe looked utterly disgusted. "So, he called, and when that didn't work he just showed up here?"

"Yes. Yesterday. Rye and I had been out. We were about to come inside and there he was, standing on the lawn yelling at me."

"Did he threaten you?"

"I . . . I don't know exactly. He scared me."

"Did he have a weapon?"

"Not that we saw," Rye said, coming to stand beside Emma. She eased into his side, his arm coming around her.

"Tell me exactly what happened, Emma."

"He was mad and yelling. I told him again—or Rye told him for me—and then I told him—that I didn't want to see him anymore, and then . . ."

"And then your friend nearly strangled him?" Joe asked.

"It wasn't like that," Emma insisted.

"What was it like? Tell me?"

"Rye was standing between us, and when Mark tried to grab me—"

"I grabbed him," Rye said. "Shoved him up against the side of the house and pinned him there with my forearm against his throat."

Joe just looked at him, seeming to take the measure of the man. Rye didn't sugarcoat it at all, and he didn't look particularly sorry. In fact, he looked like he was daring Joe to make something of it, maybe expecting it.

"That's it," Emma said. "That's what happened. Exactly like that."

"Did you threaten to kill him?" Joe asked Rye.

"No."

"He said you did."

"I said I wasn't going to kill him. Not this time. But that if he ever tried to hurt Emma again, he'd answer to me. Now, if you want to call that a threat, then yeah, I threatened him. What am I supposed to do? Stand by and watch him hurt her?"

"No," Joe said. "I wouldn't ask anybody to do that. But . . ."

"Yeah, I know. He said I attacked him. He's got the bruises to prove it."

"Well, so do I," Emma said.

"He came to me and complained Emma, which I wish you'd done."

"So, because he went running to you first, Rye's in trouble?"

"Look," Joe said. "I got a complaint. I had to follow up on it. Obviously, I didn't have the whole story from Mr. Jacobson."

"So, now what?"

"I'll tell him what I've learned. I'm assuming if he intends to press charges against your friend—"

Rye stiffened. Emma said, "You can't let him do that."

"Wait a minute," Joe said. "If that's what Jacobson

wants to do, I'm assuming you'll be interested in pressing charges against him?"

"Yes, I will."

"Okay. We'll see what he says. I suspect he'll yell and call me a few names, and then he'll back down. We could forget this whole thing then. But if you want Mark arrested, I'll do it. I'll arrest them both, and they can both tell their stories to Judge Williams. Your choice, Emma."

"I don't want anybody arrested," she said.

"Emma, think about this," Rye began, looking more serious than she'd ever seen him. "This guy's scared you, and he's hurt you, and we don't know what he's going to do next."

"I'm not letting you end up in jail for trying to protect me," she said.

"I can take care of myself," he insisted.

"And I can't?"

"That's not what I meant," Rye said. "He's bigger than you, and stronger than you, and a whole lot meaner. He needs to go to jail, but I suspect if the sheriff arrested us both, he'd get out a hell of a lot faster than I would, and then you'd be here alone. And that worries me."

"Because I can't be trusted to take care of myself?"

"Let me lock him, up, Emma," Joe began. "I'll put the fear of God in him while I've got him."

"Oh, please. Think about my father. You know how many times he got thrown in jail. It's not like it did any good in the end."

"I know," Joe said. "I'm sorry."

She'd heard all about it. Her mother hadn't been willing to press charges, but her father's next girlfriend had, several times. He never stayed in jail for long, and it just seemed to make him madder. She couldn't see having Mark thrown in jail helping her situation.

"I just want this to be over," she said.

"I know." Joe got to his feet. "I'll do anything I can to help. I'll talk to Jacobson, tell him what I think of men who hit women. Maybe that'll be enough, and he'll pack up and leave. I'll call the clerk at the motel tonight to see. If he stays . . . When's Sam coming home?"

"I don't know."

"He's going to hear about this sooner or later," Joe said. "If Mrs. Wells heard this, you know he's going to find out."

"I know. I just . . ."

"Emma, he's your father. This is what fathers do. If anything happened to you, and he wasn't here to protect you . . ."

"I know."

"All right. I'm going to see if I can run my friend Mr. Jacobson out of town. I'll tell him we're recording all your incoming calls, in case he has any ideas about calling again, and it's not a bad idea to do that. You can buy a little machine at almost any electronics store."

"We'll get one," Rye said.

"Okay. I'll tell the guy if I find him anywhere near your house again, he'll answer to me." Joe looked at Rye when he said that last part. "In the meantime," he looked back at Emma, "you gonna be all right?"

She nodded. "Rye's staying here."

Joe looked worried again. It seemed the sleeping arrangements hadn't escaped his notice.

"I told Sam I'd broken up with Mark and that he wasn't taking it well, and Sam made me promise not to stay here alone," she explained.

"Okay." Joe looked to Rye once again. "Why don't you walk me out, and we'll have a little talk."

*   *   *

Rye was surprised he wasn't already in handcuffs on his way to jail. He had no doubt he'd left marks on the little weasel's neck, and he could just imagine the story the guy told.

He got to his feet to head outside. Emma started to protest, but he stopped that. "Let it go, Emma. I'll talk to the man."

Rye grabbed his jacket off a hook by the door, and they stepped outside onto the porch. Joe Mitchell looked him up one side and down the other.

He figured he had about a fifty-fifty chance the sheriff would run his name through the department's nifty little computer and pull up his record. Once that happened, the sheriff would either be on the phone to Sam or heading over here with his siren blazing, worried about what Rye might have done to Emma. And probably rethinking everything about that mess with Emma's ex-boyfriend.

Rye kept thinking about that safe, uncomplicated existence of his, the one he was blowing all to hell. But there was Emma to think about. No way was he leaving her now.

"So"—Rye palmed his hip pocket reaching for his wallet—"what do you want? Full name? Address? Social security number? Driver's license number?"

"What is that going to find me?" Joe asked.

"Everything you need to know about me."

"Social security number works for me. And an address."

Rye slid the wallet back into place and gave the information. "That's it?"

Joe shrugged. "You want me to arrest you?"

"Not particularly. I'm just surprised."

"The guy had some holes in his story. He tried to tell me how much Emma means to him, but to hear him tell it, he was attacked for no reason by a half-crazy man who scared him to death, then left her here all night with the guy while he got a good night's sleep. Then he came to my office this morning to report it. It didn't seem like the kind of thing a guy does to his girlfriend."

"I wouldn't," Rye said, more relieved than he could say. "You going to call Sam and tell him what's going on here?"

"Maybe," Joe said.

"And if you do that, he'll be back here? He'll take care of her?"

Joe nodded.

"Okay," Rye said.

One way or the other, whether Rye was here or not, she'd be okay.

Chapter 8

Emma stood in the front hall under the little window of beveled glass, the one that made the pretty designs that danced across the floor as the sun moved from east to west every day.

Grace used to chase those sparkles of light. She used to dance inside of them. She'd pat them with her little baby hands and try to capture them in her fists. It had been the source of endless fascination, like a little touch of magic inside this house.

For the longest time, Emma had honestly believed nothing could ever hurt her as long as she was within these walls and the people here were safe. And now she'd brought trouble to the front door.

She couldn't believe the mess she'd made of things.

It was like she'd taken one wrong step and sent her life into a downward spiral, sinking faster and faster. It was no telling what Mark would do next. Everything was so crazy.

And yet Rye was here. Rye who was so reluctant to be here, so troubled by something, and yet had been so wonderful to her last night, so sexy.

He came back inside, looking grim after his little conversation on the porch with the sheriff.

"I'm so sorry," she said. What he must think of her . . . "I dragged you into this whole mess."

"Emma, I showed up at your front door." He shrugged out of his coat.

"And walked into the middle of this."

"The way I remember it," he said, hanging up the coat, "I came here quite willingly, and I sure wouldn't want you going through this alone."

Which was about the nicest thing he could have said to her at the moment. It brought tears to her eyes. "I wouldn't have wished this kind of trouble on anyone."

"Hey." He shrugged, facing her again. "I can handle a little trouble."

"Like having the sheriff come and want to arrest you?"

"Wouldn't be the first time that's happened."

"Oh, right." He was just trying to make her feel better, as he always did.

"Emma, I've been taking care of myself for a long time."

"Still—"

"Enough." He leaned back against the wall and folded his arms across his chest. "Let's talk about you. You know what you have to do, don't you?"

She nodded. "I have to call Sam."

"Now would be a really good time."

"What am I going to tell him?"

"To get the hell home. Surely you don't have any doubts about the fact that you have to do that now."

"No . . . It's just . . ."

"What?"

"It's not because of me. Because of you. You and Sam."

"Emma . . ." He turned away and stared up at the

ceiling. He was dangerously close to the front door, if
he wanted to take off. Not that she'd let him. Not
now. But what in the world was he running from?

"How can you not want to tell him?" she asked.

"Tell him what?"

"Rye, this is me. I've told you the worst parts of
my life. You've had a front-row seat for a performance
of the Stupidest Things Emma's Ever Done."

"We've been over this," he reminded her, facing
her again. "This was not your fault. The guy is nuts."

"And I went out with him for months."

"So? Guys like him are good at hiding who they
really are. That's how they get nice girls like you in
the first place."

"Okay. You're right, but—"

"No. No buts. You're not getting that part of it,
Emma, because you still want to blame yourself." He
sighed and then looked worried. "Is there more to it?
Were you in a lot deeper than you told me? You
didn't think you were in love with him, did you?"

"No. Not really . . . I mean, you're always wondering, aren't you? You meet someone, and isn't there
always some part of you that thinks, maybe he's the
one? I did in the very beginning with Mark, and then,
mostly, I tried to figure out why I didn't feel more for
him. Everything he showed me about himself seemed
so right, and yet . . . It wasn't there. I thought about
Sam and Rachel, about what I believe they feel for
each other, and I . . ." She stared down at the floor,
the little shimmering bits of light from the window she
loved. "Don't laugh, okay?"

"Okay," he said softly.

"I thought about this floor."

"The floor?"

"Yes." She stepped back, out of the pattern of light,
and he did the same. "See how pretty it is? How it

shimmers and dances? See all the colors? I used to think that's what love was like. That it shimmered and sparkled and danced inside of you. That it was alive and had an energy all its own. I kept waiting, thinking I might feel that way with Mark, but I never did."

And now she was here with Rye.

The light beamed in through the window and danced between them.

She'd felt it from the first time she touched him, that little spark and sizzle. He'd been so wonderful last night, so kind, so tender. She'd felt closer to him than she'd ever been to another human being. She'd felt absolutely and completely safe, and this morning, she'd just wanted to drag him upstairs to her bed. This was everything that had been missing, and he was as different from Mark as night and day.

And she thought he was Sam's brother. . . .

"You're sure?" Rye asked. "You just looked so sad for a minute."

It took her a minute to realize where they'd left off in the conversation. Rye asking about Mark and her thinking about Rye.

"I wasn't thinking about Mark," she said.

Rye looked at her and just as quickly looked away.

She was afraid of losing him, of never having him.

Did they really have to give this up because he might be her adoptive father's long-lost brother? Did that have anything to do with what they might feel for each other? And why was he so reluctant to admit to any relationship with Sam?

"So, when I call Sam," she began, "do I just tell him to come home, that I need him? Or do I tell him about you?"

"Emma, I don't know if there's anything to tell."

"You want to take him by surprise?" she asked. "It's fine with me. Just as long as . . . Rye, you came all this way. You're going to give him a chance, right?"

"I don't know what you think you know, but—"

"Of course, you do. You're Sam's brother."

He froze, his gaze locked on her. "Why would you say that?"

"Come on, Rye." She took her hand and slipped it into his, as if she couldn't stand the idea of him being all alone in this for another moment.

He stood there staring down at her hand. He felt like his entire body had been waiting for her to touch him. She had the power to steady him, reassure him, calm him, and at times, she just plain turned him on.

Please don't be Sam's daughter, he thought. *Please don't let me be desperate for the touch of Sam's daughter.* That was disaster in the making, almost as bad as thinking he'd struck out once again and would likely find himself on the road again next Christmas on a search as pointless as this one.

He just kept wanting things he didn't think he'd ever have, and he was afraid she was fast becoming one of those things he'd regret not having the most.

"Just tell me," she said, her voice as soft and inviting as any he'd ever known. "Or if you can't do that, I'll tell you. His name is Sam McRae. He was born in Chicago. His parents died when he was young. He came here to live with his paternal grandfather."

"The Sam McRae I'm looking for didn't have a grandfather," he said, forcing the words out. "The records show no listing for a paternal grandfather."

"What records?"

"Social services' records. When the parents died, social services went looking for relatives. There weren't a lot to be found. No grandfather."

"Maybe he and Sam's parents weren't speaking. He

was supposed to have been an awful man. Sam was miserable here with him," she said. "What about you? What do you say when people ask about your next of kin?"

"I don't say anything," he admitted. *Damn.*

"The people who raised you? Do you give their names?"

"They're not my parents. Andrew and Gail McRae were my parents."

"Okay." She looked so damned understanding and so worried about him, he could hardly stand to face her. "I don't know Sam's parents' names. But I'm sure we can find out. We'll just ask him. Why is it so hard for you to just ask?"

"Because I've been through this before." Frustrating as it was, he couldn't believe he was putting himself through it again. "I might as well be chasing a shadow. At first, someone tried to tell me he'd been adopted by a cousin in Minneapolis. I chased down a guy named Greg Hammond, but he wasn't my brother. The Hammonds had Sam and they adopted a kid out of foster care at one point, but not Sam. And later, from what I could piece together, there just isn't anybody who fits what I know about . . . about . . ."

"About your brother," Emma said softly.

That word again. It rolled through him every bit as heavily as it had the first time. He looked up and found tears in her eyes, the kindest look on her face. Sometimes kindness was harder to take than anything else. Because it implied understanding, which meant the other person knew how you felt.

Eighteen years he'd been alone and so lost, he thought sometimes it would simply choke him, that it would crush the air from his lungs.

He'd never really thought it would end.

But everything inside of him said that maybe, just maybe, she understood it all. It was that come-through-the-fire look in her eyes. She had to have been lost at one point if she'd come here and been found.

"Sam has a brother," she said. "A brother he hasn't seen in years."

Rye tensed all over, and it wasn't until she gasped that he realized he had a near-death grip on her hand. "Sorry," he said, loosening his grip but not letting go. "What's his brother's name?"

"I don't know. I'm sorry. I don't think I ever heard his name."

Rye shook his head and swore. "He never talked about me?"

"Not really."

He nodded, clamping his mouth shut, trying hard not to make a sound.

That hurt.

"I'm sorry," she said.

"Not that it comes as a big surprise," he said, wincing at the bitterness coming through in his voice. "He sure never tried to find me."

"What do you mean, he never tried to find you?"

"Okay, once in all these years. He found me, then just walked away."

"Sam wouldn't," Emma insisted.

"You're the one who's telling me I'm his brother, and I'm telling you, that's what my brother did," Rye said, feeling raw and exposed, every emotion right on the surface. "I know this part of it, Emma. I was there. It's one of the few things I know for sure."

"So . . . You think he won't want to see you now?"

"I think that's a distinct possibility, and I'm not sure I want to know him. I mean, we're strangers. I have no idea what kind of man he is. He doesn't know what kind of man I am. Who's to say whether we'll ever have any kind of relationship? Hell, I might not even want him knowing who I am or how to find me. I might not want him in my life at all."

"Rye, you want it so bad you can hardly stand it."

Shit, she did know.

"And what if I want something I just can't have?" he asked. "Surely you know what that's like. To want something so badly that you just can't have."

"You can have Sam. He's right here, and he's the best. All you have to do is tell him who you are. You'll never regret letting him into your life."

"You don't know that. There's no way you can know that."

"I know because I know Sam, and I know you," she said. "Tell him who you are. Give him a chance."

Emma finally talked him into it, offering to make the call herself to break the news. Rye was pacing back and forth in the living room. He simply couldn't stand still. She got Sam on the phone.

"I have some news for you, and you might want to sit down," she said. "Someone came to the house looking for you the other day."

"Who?" Sam asked cautiously.

"His name is Rye." Sam didn't say anything. She thought he might not know the nickname. "John, I mean. John Ryan."

The silence coming from the other end of the phone was deafening. She could feel the tension coming across the phone line. Sam made an odd, choking sound, and then he called out, "Rachel," like she was his lifeline and he needed her desperately right that instant.

"Say the name," Sam said urgently. "One more time."

"John Ryan," she repeated.

"God," Sam said.

She looked at Rye. Every muscle in his body seemed to tighten. "The name doesn't mean anything to him?"

"Yes, it does," Emma reassured Rye.

"Wait. Tell him it"—Rye took a breath—"tell him it's Robbie."

"Robbie," she said into the phone, thinking of the first day when she'd asked his name and joked about how hard a question that could possibly be. But maybe it was. "Sam, he says he's Robbie."

Sam called out to Rachel again, more urgently than before. Emma heard them whispering urgently. Rye was holding himself rigidly, so tall and so still, a world of hurt evident in the way he stood there.

Finally, Sam came back on the line. "He's still there?"

"Yes, he's standing in the living room right now."

"I should talk to him," Sam said, making a choking sound. "I . . . God, I don't know if I can."

She'd never heard Sam like this. Never heard him admit to being unable to do anything in the entire time she'd known him.

"I . . . I need a minute," Sam said.

"Okay. I understand."

"Does he?"

No, she could see that Rye didn't. He'd held out his hand for the phone, and now it hung in the air for an awkward moment, then dropped to his side.

"I'll explain," she said. "I'll make him understand."

"I need to come home," Sam said. "He's not going to go anywhere, is he? It's been so long. . . . Ask him to promise that he won't leave until I get back."

Emma thought about how simple it would be just

to give the phone to Rye so they could talk to each other, thought about Sam saying he couldn't. Whatever happened to tear them apart, it must have been terrible.

"He asked you to promise to stay until he gets back," Emma said. Rye nodded, his eyes glistening with moisture, his jaw impossibly tight. She told Sam, "He will."

"Okay. Tell him I said thank you, and that I'll be there as soon as I can. Emma, is he okay?"

"Yes." As okay as Sam was at the moment.

"Are you okay?"

"Yes. There's some stuff I need to explain to you, but I'm okay, and Rye's looking out for me."

"Ask him if I can count on him to make sure nothing happens to you."

She did. Rye nodded, still looking wary, still looking like a man who wanted very much to be anywhere but there.

"He will, Sam."

"Emma, I can't . . ." Sam's voice broke.

Rachel came on the line. "Emma, I need to talk to Sam now, but I'll explain everything. Later, okay?"

"Okay," Emma said.

"Just don't let that man go anywhere."

Rye had heard enough. He headed out, thinking to get as far away from here as he could. He was in the backyard when he remembered Emma's crazy ex-boyfriend.

He couldn't go anywhere.

He'd promised his brother.

God, his brother . . .

He was still standing there in the middle of the yard a moment later when Emma came out. She stayed there on the porch, as if she were afraid coming at him right now might send him running in the other direction.

He just turned and looked away.

"You said your name is Rye," she said finally.

"It is."

"But I don't understand." To which he said nothing. He didn't understand, either. "Is that what I'm supposed to call you? Rye?"

"It's what everybody calls me."

Except for the parents who weren't his parents, whom he didn't talk to anymore at all. He didn't recall ever being Robert Jordan McRae, and even when he'd found out that was the name he'd been born with or that they'd called him Robbie, that person seemed like a stranger to him. As much of a stranger as John Ryan had become.

What did a man do when neither name seemed to fit anymore? He'd stuck with what he'd always been called and left it at that. Whoever had actually given birth to him and Sam had died long ago, and the only person who even remembered Robbie, as far as he'd been able to figure out, was Sam.

Emma walked up to him. He heard her coming. Tried to brace himself for what would inevitably happen, but what could he really do?

There it was. She put her hand on his arm and asked, "Are you okay?"

He stared down at that hand. Her touch, as always, was light and somehow comforting. He just wanted to hang on to her, to lean on her a little, but he didn't lean on anyone. He hardly trusted anyone. He lived a solitary life, and some might say it wasn't much of a life at all, that it hadn't been for the longest time. But she made him want to let her in just a little bit.

And if Sam really was his brother . . .

Oh, hell. She was Sam's adopted daughter, and that would make him an uncle of sorts. . . .

Rye felt oddly like he'd taken a blow to the chest, like something huge and solid had connected solidly, dead center to his chest.

He felt oddly like he'd lost something very precious, like it had been torn from him before he'd even known what he had.

"Rye?" she asked again, still touching him.

He couldn't have her doing that. He stepped back for real this time, turning to his side, not quite facing her, but not looking away, either.

Her hand fell to her side, and he told himself he did not miss having her touch him, that he wouldn't really miss her. They'd be some kind of distant relatives. He might never see her again. He might never see Sam again. What did he really expect to come of this anyway?

"How is it that you and Sam were raised apart?" she asked.

"I'm not sure." How in the world had he ever even gotten here? To this point in his life?

"Then why are you so angry at him? You don't even know him."

"Which is probably a big part of why I'm angry, Emma." And he wasn't very proud of that, because he knew it wasn't quite fair. But that's the way he felt.

"You think it's his fault that the two of you were raised apart?"

"I know that he knew about me, when I didn't know about him for the longest time." And Sam had been right here in this town the whole time, this house, even. He looked up at it, bathed in late-afternoon shadows from the tall, broad trees. It looked tall and proud and so very solid, a vast amount of space, the kind to shelter a man all the days of his life.

So different from where he'd been.

"You don't have any memory of him?" Emma tried again.

"Just that one time when he walked away without saying anything. It's been years now. Maybe he forgot he ever had a brother. Maybe that's the way he wants it."

"It's not that." Emma slid closer. She was going to touch him again. "You didn't hear his voice on the phone—"

"Emma, he wouldn't even talk to me. You caught that part, right? I was right there, and he wouldn't even talk to me."

"He could hardly talk. I think it was hard for him to even breathe, Rye. I asked him about you once. It seemed like it hurt him too much to even talk about it and all he said was that he'd lost you."

"Lost? Like he put me down someplace and forgot where he left me?" He scowled. "You don't lose a human being."

"How did you lose him?" she asked, her head resting against his arm.

"I was two or three. Hell, I don't even know, and I can't do this anymore, Emma. Not now. I'm sorry. I have to get out of here." Oh, hell, but he couldn't go anywhere. He'd promised his brother. "I'm just going to take a walk. Up and down the street in front of the house. I won't go any farther than that. I'll keep the house in sight the whole time."

"Okay," she said.

So understanding.

It was killing him.

He had to get away from her before he did anything else he'd regret. Like beg her to hold him for another minute.

He'd kissed her, he remembered again. More than

once. His brain was so scrambled, he'd actually forgotten that for a moment when he started to believe he'd finally found his brother.

Sam, he told himself over and over again. Sam's daughter. Sam's little girl. Maybe if he could make it sound remotely incestuous, he would be okay.

"About what happened this morning . . ." he began, withdrawing completely, leaving her standing in the middle of the yard alone.

"When I kissed you?" Her chin came up. "And you kissed me back?"

Yeah, that.

"You know that can't happen again, right?"

"Because you're Sam's brother?"

"Yes," he said.

"But you're not my uncle," she said. "Sam hasn't seen you in years. I've never seen you in my life. There are absolutely no blood ties between us."

"It doesn't matter. And I just came here to find Sam. I told you, Emma." But that wasn't fair at all. He'd told her one thing with words, and then somehow he kept ending up with her in his arms. "I'm sorry. I can't do this. Sam is . . . There's no way he'd understand or even begin to approve, and even if he did . . ."

He let the words trail off, wincing when he realized what he'd said, when he thought of how she'd take it.

"I told you, there are things you just don't know about me."

"I remember." She nodded. "A long, sad story. So's mine."

"Your father treated your mother like a punching bag. That's not anything you've done."

"I grew up that way. With the arguments and the yelling and the hitting."

"It's not who you are," he insisted. "It's what you

came from. We all have bad times. We all have choices. Some people handle whatever comes along. Some people run away. Some people feel sorry for themselves. Some people hit. Some of 'em do worse than that."

"And what did you do?"

"Worse than that," he said.

"Oh, please. Look at me. I thought I was falling in love with a man who hits me when he gets mad."

"We're not even talking about the same things. Not even close."

He could tell her. He figured he owed her that. But if he told her the truth about the last eighteen years of his life, she'd probably kick him out right now, and he couldn't take that kind of chance with her safety. He wasn't leaving her alone now.

"Is that what you're so worried about with Sam?" she asked. "Telling him what you've been through? What you've done?"

"I'm not looking forward to it." Maybe that was why he'd never heard from Sam. Maybe Sam knew exactly where Rye had been.

"Sam is the kindest, most generous man I know. He'll give you a chance."

"I guess we'll see about that," Rye said.

"And I . . . Rye, I—"

He put his thumb to her lips, not letting her say it, wishing he could have found a way to stop the words without touching her again, because damned if he didn't still like touching her.

"I'm sorry. It's not going to happen," he said, and then made himself walk away.

Chapter 9

Emma let him go because she could see how torn he was. Not just about her and him, but him and Sam.

It's going to be all right, she wanted to tell him. *You're in the right place. You've found your way home.*

She wanted to take him in her arms and just hang on to him. Nothing felt quite as good as that to someone who was lost.

Except he didn't want her anywhere near him.

Was that from the shock of what he'd found out? That Sam was his brother. Would anyone really care? And they hadn't even addressed the whole age thing. Sam had just turned thirty-nine. Emma wasn't sure how old he'd been when his parents had been killed in an auto accident. If he'd been ten and Rye was just a baby . . . What did that make Rye now? Twenty-nine? Thirty? At the youngest?

Perfect, Emma.

She watched as he stalked across the yard, heading down the driveway to the front of the house. She knew he wouldn't leave her. Even as upset as he was, he was still taking care of her. She wanted to take care of him, too.

Emma went inside, carefully locking the door behind her. Upstairs in Sam and Rachel's room was an old cedar chest. A newer one in the family room held pictures and some of Grace's baby clothes, things Zach and Grace had made at school, certificates Emma had won, but the chest upstairs had much older things. She went to that chest, pulled off the framed photos and a delicate piece of lace used as a drape, opened the chest, and carefully pulled things out.

Somewhere, there was an album with a very few photos of Sam as a child and his parents. It was all she knew to do for Rye now—show him his past, help him to understand what he could have here in the present with Sam.

The two of them, she'd worry about later. Let him settle in, feel like a part of them. She knew what it was like to need a place to belong, and she wanted him to have that.

He wouldn't leave now.

Sam wouldn't let him.

Calm down, Emma, she told herself quite sternly.

This was not disaster in the making.

He'd found them. They wouldn't give him up.

She sat down on the floor by the chest and paged carefully through the photos. There were ones Rachel had taken of Sam, a few when he was fifteen or so and more after that. There were heartbreaking ones of Rachel pregnant and then nothing for a long time. A couple of her grandfather, who'd died not long after that, some of the house as they slowly restored it.

She moved farther back.

There was Sam at . . . She couldn't tell how old he

was. Certainly not ten. He was with a pretty young woman who had to be his mother. A tall, serious-looking young man stood by her side, and she was pregnant, too.

With Rye?

So there weren't that many years between them?

Emma had to tell herself to calm down once again. She wasn't losing him.

She dug through the photos, finding a handful by the time the phone rang. Emma closed her eyes and took a breath, thinking again about the crazy state of her life—scared to pick up a phone—and then, determined to see it through, she grabbed it from the nightstand by Sam and Rachel's bed.

"Hi." It was Rachel. "Sam wanted me to call and make sure . . . He's really there? Still? Robbie, I mean?"

"Yes." Emma settled in on the floor by the bed, ready to talk. "But he says everyone calls him Rye. It seems like he thinks of Robbie as someone else completely."

"Now that I think about it, I can see why he would," Rachel said. "He was about three when Sam left, and the Ryans changed his name."

Three? Emma thought about Zach. He'd been five when they'd come here. It had been so scary, even for Emma, and she'd been almost twelve. But what would it have been like for Zach if he'd been all alone?

And then, there was no hiding from the rest of it. She really had to know how old Rye was now. How to even ask? "How old was Sam then?"

"He thinks he was eight, maybe nine," Rachel said.

Sam had just turned thirty-nine.

Which made Rye thirty-four? Thirty-three at best?

All the breath left Emma in a rush.

She felt like she had when she'd looked up and seen Mark on the porch, when she realized everything was so much worse than she'd feared.

Rye certainly didn't look thirty-three. Not even thirty, but then what did she know? She didn't run around with thirty-year-old men.

"What is it, Em?"

"Nothing. I was just . . . trying to understand what happened to them."

And what would happen to her and him.

Nothing if he really was in his early thirties. Sam would have a fit. It was likely that most everyone she knew would raise an eyebrow at that.

Emma sat there on the floor ready to cry.

It was so odd. Most all her life, she'd felt old already. People had always said that about her. *That child was born old.* And that's how she'd always felt.

She'd never been too young for anything.

"I don't know much about it," Rachel said. "Even after all this time, it's hard for Sam. Their parents died when Robbie was just a baby and Sam was five or six. They went from relative to relative, until the Ryans took them. I'm sure it would have been much easier for a baby to adjust. We know it is."

Because of Grace. She'd been a year old when they'd come here, and she didn't remember anything of life except being here. She'd missed all the bad times. Rye could have, too. But Sam would have always known.

"Sam wasn't doing well there," Rachel said. "He'd been through so much at that point, and he thought they wanted to get rid of him and keep Robbie, to pretend Robbie hadn't ever had any other parents or a brother, and that's what they did. They adopted Robbie, but not Sam. It was probably harder on Sam than even losing his parents. Robbie was all he had left then."

"He thinks Sam abandoned him," Emma said.

"Sam was eight or nine. What could he have done?"

"Oh. Of course. How awful for them both. But Rye doesn't understand that part."

"Then we'll have to explain it to him. Sam is . . . Oh, Em. He's wanted his brother back for so long."

"Rye wants that, too." Emma was sure of it.

"He said that?"

"No, but it's what he wants."

"Then everything will be fine," Rachel said, and she started crying then. "I can't believe he just showed up at the house. I've tried to talk to Sam over the years about going to find him again, about telling him the truth. I even thought about doing it myself and just bringing him here."

"Why didn't Sam want to find him?"

"Because the Ryans never told Rye anything. Sam went looking for him one day. He introduced himself to Robbie when Robbie was fifteen or so, and Robbie said his name was John Ryan. He acted like he'd never heard of Sam."

"Still, all Sam had to do was—"

"Tell him he'd been lied to his whole life? Can you imagine what that would have done to someone? Sam said he seemed like a perfectly normal, happy kid, and Sam thought it would tear his life apart to tell him the truth. Sam couldn't do it. Even if he could have, he was afraid his brother would hate him for it. So he just walked away and didn't say anything."

"Well, something must have happened. Rye doesn't have anything good to say about the Ryans, and when he talks about Sam . . . It comes off looking like anger, but it's hurt. I know, because he's like Sam that way."

"Well, they'll just have to get past all that," Rachel said. "I'm so happy for Sam. He's scared, but so happy. He's picked up the phone a half-dozen times to call, and then he puts it back down again. He says it's something that needs to be done in person. We called Ellen and told her what was going on. She'll be here late tonight, and Sam and I will leave first thing in the morning. I'm dying to meet him. What's he like?"

"A lot like Sam," Emma said. "I didn't see it at first, but I knew there was something familiar about him, and he's . . . He's great. He's kind and funny and considerate. He's very strong and very protective of me. Like Sam."

"Em, I feel awful that we weren't there after you and Mark broke up."

"Well, don't. I know what's going on there. I know how worried you all are about Ann and the baby. They're hanging in there?"

"So far. But I worry about you, too."

"I'll be fine. I'm not heartbroken over Mark."

"He's still upset? Still bothering you?"

"I don't know what he's doing right now. I'm hoping I won't hear anything from him again. But I'm okay, and if I need anything, Rye's here."

"And we'll be there soon," Rachel promised. "I love you, Em."

"I love you, too."

Emma hung up the phone and thought, *One more day.* That was it. She had one day left alone with Rye.

When she hadn't been able to keep herself from thinking . . .

Oh, it was crazy.

Crazy.

She'd been thinking she wanted a lifetime with him. That maybe even a lifetime wouldn't be enough.

This morning when he had her pressed against the wall, she'd wanted to take him by the hand and lead him upstairs to her bedroom.

She probably wouldn't have done it, probably wouldn't have had the nerve. But she'd wanted to.

But he was thirty-three or thirty-four years old.

And she was six weeks shy of her nineteenth birthday.

He walked up and down the block again and again. He walked for what seemed like forever in the cold, the wind biting into every inch of exposed skin, stinging his eyes and his cheeks. When he thought he was surely frozen through and through, he went back inside.

Emma was standing by the front window staring at him. He glanced at her for maybe half a second and then looked away, stomping the last of the snow off his shoes on the mat by the door and toeing them off. He pulled off his coat and hung it on a hook by the door, shoved his hands into the pockets of his jeans, and then dared come two steps closer.

"You okay?" he asked, because she looked like something was definitely wrong.

Emma nodded, still not looking at him. "Rachel called. Her sister's leaving today to go up there and help out with Ann's kids. Sam and Rachel are leaving first thing in the morning. They'll be here tomorrow night."

"So you finally told them what's going on?"

"I didn't have to. Sam wants to see you." He glanced up at that, then just as quickly away. "He does, Rye."

"Whatever you say."

"Whatever you think happened . . ." she began. "You don't remember him at all from when you were little?"

"I . . . I'm not sure," he said, trying to keep his distance from her. "Sometimes I think I might, and at other times, I don't know. The scene's all murky, almost like a dream. Sometimes I think I just dreamed about him a few times, and that's what I'm remembering, not anything that really happened. But there are times when I think I'm standing next to someone, and he's so much bigger than I am, and . . ."

He wasn't going to talk about this. Truth was, he was huddled by someone's side shaking and the next thing he knew, he was hanging on to someone's leg, his arms wrapped around someone's knee. He was screaming and hands were grabbing on to him, pulling him this way and that, until someone else had him and wouldn't let go.

"Sam was eight or nine, he thinks," Emma said.

"What?" Rye asked.

"Sam. He was eight or nine when he left the Ryans, and he thinks you were three."

Rye frowned. Could that possibly be the truth? "How old is he now?"

"He just turned thirty-nine," Emma said.

Rye was thirty-three. He'd be thirty-four in the spring. They were only five-and-a-half years apart.

"I always thought he was so much older than me," he said. "We found a birth certificate, but I thought the date of birth had to be wrong, because he seemed too young and I never found anyone named Sam McRae with that birth date. We checked a driver's license data base. Nothing was right. What's Sam's birthday?"

"May twelfth," she said.

"The database shows it's August twelfth."

"He makes fives that look like eights. We laugh about it all the time. Phone numbers, addresses, appointment times, dates. You don't ever want to count on your reading of his writing for anything like that. Come to think of it, I remember one year he got his license renewed and the date was wrong. I bet someone couldn't read his handwriting."

Which meant Sam really had been nine when they were separated.

Nine-year-olds didn't exactly leave on their own, did they?

Rye eased into the chair in the corner by the window. Emma sat down in a matching one a few feet away. It was one of those odd moments when the world seemed to shift.

"I thought Sam just walked away." It was one thing he'd believed when his so-called parents had explained it all to him. "I thought he left me there."

"Tell me what you remember."

"Nothing really, except being with the Ryans. Then one day when I was fourteen, almost fifteen, I was shooting baskets at a park near our house, and there was a guy watching me. I didn't know who he was, but there was something about the way he was watching me. . . . He came over to me and introduced himself—Sam McRae—like that was supposed to mean something to me, and I told him my name was John Ryan. He looked like somebody had knocked the wind out of him."

"Because you didn't recognize him."

"I didn't. I'd never heard of Sam McRae. Hell, I didn't even know I was adopted," Rye said. "We talked for a few minutes. He shook my hand and left. That was it. It was so odd, I went home and told my parents about it, and they . . . I didn't know what I was seeing in them at the time, guess I didn't really want to know. It scared me, because they looked terrified."

"That Sam was going to tell you the truth?"

"Probably." Rye nodded. "But he didn't tell me."

"Would you have told him, under the circumstances?"

Rye closed his eyes and thought about it. A year later when the truth came out, it had rocked his world. Not so much the fact that he was adopted, but the fact that they'd lied to him about everything forever.

"It changed things between me and my parents," he admitted. "They'd never been the most easygoing people in the world, but they were downright paranoid after Sam's little visit. It was like they didn't trust me all of a sudden. Like they were watching me all the time, just waiting for me to screw up. I never screwed up back then. I was a great kid. They told me what they expected of me, and I made sure I did that and more. But after Sam came, I couldn't do anything right as far as they were concerned. And I hadn't changed. They had."

"Then what happened?"

"It just all went to hell. It was like they tried to grab on to me and hold tighter and tighter. Always wanted to know who I was with and what we were doing. I didn't understand, didn't think it was fair. Pretty soon, I figured why behave at all. They were still all over me. I figured if they were going to treat me that way, I might as well give 'em a reason."

"What did you do?"

"Stupid kid stuff at first. Just stupid, little things. Which made them even more uptight. One night a year later, when I'd stayed out way too late just to piss them off, they told me. Just blurted it out. I wasn't their son. Not their blood. They'd taken a chance on me, thinking their day-to-day influence should be enough, that I'd turn out okay. But obviously, it hadn't worked. Somewhere in the middle of that, they started talking about Sam, that it seemed I was turning out to be just like my troublemaking brother, Sam." He shook his head and tried to play it off with a grin. "There it was. That's how I found out."

And how he came to wonder why in the hell Sam had just left him there, why he'd just walked away. He wondered where Sam had gone, what his life had been like. Couldn't he have taken Rye along? Surely it had to be better than leaving him with the Ryans. He'd never thought about Sam being a kid himself.

"He wouldn't have forgotten you," Emma said. "Not ever. If he left you there that day after he found you again, he must have thought you were better off where you were, maybe better off not knowing."

"Maybe," Rye said. He certainly had to entertain the possibility.

And what would have happened if he'd gone looking for Sam then? When Rye was fifteen and before he'd really fallen down the rabbit hole, into that other world? What might his life have been like then?

It seemed he'd taken an irrevocably wrong turn. Sometimes it still didn't feel like this could possibly be what was left of his life. But he'd never know what might have happened, because he couldn't go back. He had to deal with what was real, what had happened. He had to stay and talk to Sam, he supposed. See what they could make of this mess.

"So what happened to you after that? After Sam came and your parents finally told you the truth?" Emma asked.

"Lots of things." He looked over at her, curled up in that chair. Things a good girl like her just wouldn't understand.

"Rye, I don't know what you think you can't tell me—"

"It's all going to come out, but I'd like to have the chance to explain it to Sam first, if that's all right with you."

"Sure." She looked away, and he thought again that something was wrong, something she wasn't telling him.

Was this about them rolling around on the floor this morning? About her sleeping in his arms last night?

He'd apologized for that, hadn't he? He'd explained. Not that he thought there was a particularly good explanation, but it had happened. He couldn't change it now, and he was the world's expert on regrets. There was nothing left to do, except to stay away.

Yes, he decided, looking at her again. Something was wrong.

Emma slid a stack of papers toward him. "I found some things. Photographs of Sam and your parents, I think, and a couple of them with you."

It was the last thing he expected.

Her generosity, her kindness overwhelmed him.

She was giving him back his past, whatever there was of it.

"Thank you," he said.

"You're welcome. I'll leave you to . . . I'll just be in the other room."

He didn't even reach for the photographs, just looked from them to her, then back again, as if he couldn't quite bring himself to look at them, as if someone might come snatch them away.

She stepped outside for a moment to give him some privacy. It was the first day of Christmas, at least according to the town's festival schedule, so she turned on the Christmas lights she and Rye had put up. It was tradition here that on the first day, all the lights came on.

Emma stood on the porch once she was done, staring up and down the street, remembering that she'd thought it was a winter wonderland the first time she'd seen it. She'd been sure it was all going to disappear into thin air, had felt the same way about Sam and Rachel and the way they'd opened their home to her and her brother and sister. She'd been so afraid it wouldn't last.

What kind of demons had made Rye feel that way? No doubt what had happened with his adoptive parents, but what else?

Emma wondered what it would have been like if she'd lived her life in reverse. If it had been completely stable and normal until she was twelve or fourteen and then someone had taken it all away.

Instead, hers had been chaos and terror for nearly twelve years, and then she'd come here. Other than losing her mother shortly after that, life had been a cakewalk.

Of course, the difference was in what the person was left with in the end. This was her family now. There was stability, dependability, and so much love. Rye, it seemed, had nothing. She'd take her life over his any day.

Except, he wasn't alone anymore. He had all of them now.

She went back inside a few minutes later and found him still sitting in the chair by the window, looking dazed and overwhelmed. She wanted to draw him into her wonderful, strong, generous, loving family, and at the same time, she wanted so much more.

"Thanks for these," he said, holding up one of the photos.

She didn't say anything, just nodded.

"Emma, has something happened that you haven't told me about?"

"No." She stared intently at a spot on the wall three feet to the left of his head, trying not to think of what she'd learned. He was fourteen or fifteen years older than she was.

Would it matter to him that she was the oldest almost-nineteen-year-old on earth? She doubted it.

Which meant this was likely her last chance to be with him. Sam would be home. Rye would find out how old she was. It hurt just to think about it.

She crossed the room to where he sat, sank down to the floor, her back to his chair, circled her arm around his leg, and rested her head on his knee.

"What's wrong with you?" he asked, ever so softly as one of his hands slowly stroked her hair.

She thought maybe if she didn't move an inch closer, he'd let her stay, and she needed to be here right now for as long as he'd let her.

"Sometimes, it just seems like everything's gone all wrong," she said.

"I know, Em."

He still had his hand in her hair, and it felt so good. *Touch me, Rye,* she thought, her tears starting to fall. *Touch me anywhere, and just don't stop.*

It seemed like he was meant to be a part of her life—maybe the most important part—but it also seemed absolutely impossible that they'd ever be together. How could that be?

Emma cried even harder.

He went still. She heard him swear softly, and a moment later, he slid to the floor and pulled her to him. She wrapped her arms around his chest and pressed her face to his shoulder. He wasn't happy about this, but he held on to her while she cried. His arms were so strong, so reassuring. She felt perfectly safe here, felt cherished in a way that she'd never felt before.

This was her spot. Her one safe, special place. In his arms, where he was so determined that she should not be. He'd be running her off any second.

"I'm sorry."

She tried to pull herself together, tried to stop crying, but she found herself burrowing closer. She thought of what she would say to him once he knew, if she could explain that from the time she was born, it seemed, she'd been taking care of everyone around her. Herself, Zach, her mother, Grace. By the time she'd come here, it was too late. She'd forgotten how to be young.

Rye didn't seem too old to her at all. He seemed just right. A bit lost and lonely and obviously searching for something, but Emma knew all about being lost and lonely. She thought he was her reward for growing up too fast and having the weight of the world on her shoulders for too long.

"Have you ever been in love before?" she asked, when the worst of her tears had abated. Because it was hard to let yourself love anyone when you'd lived through the kind of chaos she imagined they both had.

"What kind of a question is that?" he murmured.

"Just a question," she insisted.

"No, I don't think I've ever been in love before."

"Me, either. But I think it's out there, and I think it's real. When you see Sam and Rachel, you'll know."

"Demonstrative, are they?"

"Yes, but that's not what I'm talking about. It's strength, Rye. Faith. Patience. Generosity. Hope. Kindness. Understanding. Staying power. All those things. It's enduring, and it's real."

"I've never seen anything like that," he admitted,

still stroking her hair. It felt so good. Every time he touched her, it was so good.

"But you came to find Sam. You have to have some hope. . . ."

"It was a mistake. It's not going to work, Em."

She lifted her head just enough to look at him. He looked so sad, like it was torture just to be there. "Why would you say that?"

"Because things just don't work. Not long-term."

"You can't believe that. You can't be completely without hope. Otherwise you wouldn't have come here." She put her hand to the side of his face, and heat flared between them, just like that. "And if you hadn't come, you would never have met me. Do you regret that so much?"

"No, but I will before we're through."

"I don't regret it," she said. "I never will."

"How can you not? Look at where it's taken us."

"Right here," she said, her mouth about a centimeter from his.

"Emma, I am trying so hard not to hurt you. Not to touch you."

"Doesn't that tell you something? How hard you have to fight to stay away from me?"

"It tells me that once again, I want something I just can't have."

"Rye, you can have me. I'm right here."

He groaned and closed his eyes. She truly had no shame where he was concerned, because all she saw was that she was losing him, and if there was anything she could have of him, she wanted it. Anything at all.

She kissed him softly on his cheek, his closed eyes, the corner of his mouth. She kissed him until he took her mouth once again with the kind of fierce, rolling hunger she'd never known.

He was a little bit rough and dangerous, impatient

and needy, strong and moving very fast. He hauled
her into his lap, and she wound her arms around his
neck, curling her body into his. His mouth was hot
and eager, and she was burning up deep down inside,
her body practically singing with pleasure.

He did want her. She hadn't been quite sure of that.
So often, he was pushing her away, as if it might be
nice to have her, but he could certainly do without
her. But he must have been fighting himself every bit
as hard as she had, and they were both failing marvel-
ously at the moment.

Touch me, she thought. *Anywhere. Everywhere.
Touch me, now.*

His hand came to the side of her face, angling her
mouth against his so he could go deeper, harder. He
was thrusting against her with his tongue and doing
this little rolling thing with his hips that had her
squirming to get closer. There was a spot way down
deep inside of her where she just ached for him.

"Rye," she said, thinking she'd hang on to him.

This would bind them together, and when the truth
came out later, they'd deal with it. Which made what
she wanted now blatantly unfair to him, but she'd
never wanted like this.

He dragged her down to the floor, first with her
sprawled out on top of him and then he rolled her,
until he was lying on top of her, six feet of gloriously
hard, sexy male smothering her a very good way.

Oh, my, Emma thought, nerves hitting her hard in
that moment.

"Tell me you've done this before."

"I've done this before." If rolling around on the
floor counted, she'd been here, but it hadn't felt like
this.

"How old are you, Emma?" he growled the next
time he lifted his mouth from hers.

Damn. "Does it really matter?"

"Yeah, right now, it matters."

It wasn't right of her not to tell him. It was one of the only times in her life she'd knowingly, willfully done the absolute wrong thing.

The only answer she gave him was a kiss, a very wicked kiss. She wriggled her body against his. He swore and pressed her harder into the floor. He was so big, big everywhere, and he was crushing her, and she liked it.

"You make me crazy," he groaned. "You make me forget everything. Everything but you and how much I want you."

"For me, too. It's just like that."

Emma opened her eyes, wanting to see him then, wanting to know everything there was to know about him and about love.

When she looked up, happiness turned to terror.

She opened her mouth to scream, to warn him, to save him.

Mark was there, standing over them with the little shovel they kept by the fireplace. Before Emma could utter a word of warning, Mark raised the shovel over his head and smashed it into Rye's head.

It made a sickening thump.

Rye jerked back for a moment, flinching from the pain.

The look on his face was one of surprise at first and at the last minute, before he collapsed on top of her, sheer terror.

Because he knew.

He knew Mark was there, and that he wasn't going to be able to save Emma from him.

Chapter 10

Emma finally screamed.

Too late to do any good, but finally, she screamed.

Mark stood over her, shovel in hand and the ugliest look she'd ever seen on his face. Rye was out cold, sprawled on top of her.

At least, she hoped he was only unconscious.

She put her hands against his head, looking for the bruise, and they came away with blood on them.

"Oh, my God," she said. "Rye."

Had Mark killed him? Had Emma gotten him killed with her own stupidity?

"Get up," Mark growled.

Emma whimpered. She'd been reduced to a shaking, whimpering mess.

"I said, get up!"

"I can't," she tried.

"Sure you can." He took Rye by one arm, dragged him off her, and dumped him on the floor. Rye didn't make a sound. He felt like dead weight.

Please, God, she prayed, *don't let him be dead.*

"For the last time. Get up."

Mark hauled her to her feet, nearly pulling her arm out of its socket, then kept a brutal, biting hold on her arm, the one he'd bruised four days ago.

Had it only been four days? Had her life sunk into sheer chaos in just four days?

Mark finally let her go. He backed up one step, then two, the shovel still held in his right hand. He swung it aimlessly back and forth like a kid might swing a bat to warm up before a big hit, as if he couldn't quite decide what to smash next. He looked dazed and a little bit crazy, so different from the person she'd thought she'd known.

"Dammit, it didn't have to be like this," he said finally.

"What?"

"This," he said, gesturing between them and vaguely toward Rye.

He hadn't moved. Emma tried not to think about that, because she had to concentrate on handling Mark. Her wits were all she had to help them both.

"What do you mean?" she asked, trying to calm down, to calm her voice. *Let him talk*, she thought. *Find out what he plans to do.*

"Things just get so messed up sometimes." He was pacing back and forth now, his movements faster and jerkier, increasingly agitated. "That idiot chemistry professor of mine . . ."

He wanted to talk about a class? Standing here swinging a fireplace shovel in her face after breaking into her house?

Okay. Talk. "What did he do?" Emma asked, her eyes following him warily.

"He flunked me. I'm premed. I can't flunk chemistry."

She'd had no idea he was flunking chemistry. She

didn't care in the least, but she could pretend. "I thought you were doing fine."

"I was, and then . . . Oh, hell, I don't know what happened. I got a little behind, that's all. Everything would have been fine, except for that one test. No way I did as bad as he said."

"Well, he must have made a mistake," Emma said, turning with him slowly as he circled her. "That's all. We'll talk to him. We'll straighten it out."

"You have no idea how hard it is to get into a good med school, and it's got to be the best for me," he said, still pacing. "It's always been that way. The best. All along. I can't flunk chemistry."

"Of course not."

"My dad . . . You didn't get to meet my dad." He glared at her.

"I know. I'm sorry."

"They're still there. They're waiting for you. I told them something came up, some family thing, and that you'd be back, because you really wanted to meet them. They're counting on meeting you. I was counting on that."

"I was, too," Emma lied.

"They would have liked you." He kept going, round and round. She did, too, not wanting her back to him. "I could have straightened out that idiot professor, and I just dropped the other class. I was doing fine, but I dropped it. Things just got so hectic. But I can hold them together. I always have. People just don't listen to me sometimes, that's all. If they'd all just listen to me, everything would be fine."

"I know," Emma said. She knew his father could be a real jerk, and he set the bar high. This was the first she'd heard about any problems at school.

"You should have listened." He pointed the shovel like a scolding finger.

"You're right. I should have. I don't know what came over me. I was just nervous about meeting your parents, I guess. I wanted everything to be perfect."

"I told them all about you, about how well everything was going. When you weren't there, they had all kinds of questions for me. About everything."

So, it was all her fault, was it?

"Well, then . . . If they're still in Chicago, let's go," Emma said. "I'll tell them it was all my fault. Family emergency. We'll fix everything."

Mark stopped and looked down at Rye. God, he still hadn't moved.

"I saw you rolling around on the floor with him when I came in," Mark said. "You're not supposed to do that, Emma."

"I know," she said, thinking she had to get him out of here. Rye was unconscious. He didn't have a prayer of defending himself. She just had to get Mark away from him, and then she'd think about herself.

"You're mine," Mark said.

"I am. I know that now." He swung the shovel in front of Emma. She felt the whish of air as it passed and imagined what it would feel like if it hit her. "I'm sorry, Mark. I'm so sorry. I won't ever do anything like that again."

"No," he said. "You won't."

She was thinking he meant she wouldn't be around to do anything like that again, that maybe he was going to kill her and be done with it.

Emma had never really thought about dying before. She'd always thought about surviving. When her father hit her mother, that one time when he had hit her. When her mother died. Emma went right on. She had no idea what to do now.

"Please, Mark, let's just go. Now. I want to see your

parents. I want to tell them all about us and all that we have planned."

"You'd be a good doctor's wife," he said, coming a step closer. "You'd be perfect. They want things to be just perfect for me, and I don't know what happened. That idiot in chemistry . . ."

"We'll straighten it out. All of it. But we have to go to Chicago."

"We could," he said. "If you were there, we could make it work."

"Of course." So she was part of the image he thought he had to maintain, the best grades, the best school, and a perfect little moldable woman as wife material. "Let's just go."

Mark had a sick look on his face as he looked down at Rye. "He hasn't moved. Do you think . . . He's not dead, is he? Because, if he is . . . How would we fix that?"

"He's not." Emma refused to believe he could be.

"We can't just leave him here."

"We can. I want to. I knew it was a mistake to go, the minute I left."

"You did?" Mark looked hopeful at that.

"Yes."

"But you wouldn't come back," he said, swinging that shovel once again and advancing one step toward her. "I begged you, Emma. I begged you to come back."

"And I should have." If she'd gone, this wouldn't have happened.

"You're going to have to learn to listen to me," Mark said, closer still. "I can take care of you, but you have to listen."

"I will," she said, tears pouring down her cheeks.

"I don't know if I believe you, Emma," he said, a

breath away. "You let him touch you. I can't just let something like that go. You can't let anyone else ever touch you like that again."

"I won't," she said, wanting to back up, but there was nowhere else to go. She tried to look contrite and not so afraid. He was sweating and breathing hard, his face bloodred, close enough to hurt her now.

"You have to learn, Emma."

He drew back his hand and smacked her across the face. The blow propelled her backward. She fell and fell and fell. It seemed to go on forever. And then her head smashed into something and everything went black.

When she came to, she was whimpering. What a pathetic sound. She couldn't believe it was coming out of her. She lay there, frozen, and he was standing over her, the shovel still in his hand.

Hide, she thought, as she had when she was little. *Just hide, Emma. Make yourself invisible.* How had she done it back then?

He grabbed her and jerked her to her feet. She shrank back from his touch, still thinking that if she could somehow just make herself as small as possible it would be okay.

"Look at that." He pointed to her face. "You made me do that. Do you understand. You made me. And your face . . . Jesus, Emma, what are you doing? I can't take you to Chicago looking like that. How am I going to explain that?"

He blamed her for it? Her head felt like it was about to fall off it hurt so bad. What was he going to do now?

"No," Mark said. "There's no way now. We can't hide that."

She watched, seemingly in slow motion, as his hand drew back and then started swinging forward, toward her.

He was going to hit her again, and she hated him. Absolutely hated him.

And she had to stop him.

She dropped to the floor, thinking that was the fastest way out of the path of that fist, and still she braced herself for the blow.

But it never came.

Mark fell instead, his legs coming out from under him.

They both went down together.

Emma didn't understand at first. They both landed on the floor side by side. She stared at him, waiting for him to come after her, and then she looked up and saw Rye standing over them.

It happened so fast from that point, a blur of fists and harsh, angry voices. The sound of fists hitting flesh, bodies hitting the furniture and the floor.

Emma just scrambled to stay out of the way, and was too dazed at first to think about anything other than the fact that she wasn't going to die today and that Rye hadn't either. She made it behind the side of the couch, shaking and rocking back and forth, and when she found the courage to peek around the arm of the sofa, she saw Mark lying on the floor, Rye on top of him, fists flying.

Mark wasn't doing anything to even try to defend himself now, just rolling with the blows.

Emma wondered if she'd looked like that, when she'd been too scared to even move. Finally, she realized what was happening had gone long past stopping Mark from hurting anyone.

"Rye," she said, her voice hoarse and tight.

He didn't even look up.

"You bastard," Rye said to him. "Want to pick on women? Want to hurt them? How does it feel?"

"Rye?" She didn't think Mark could have made a

sound now. His head was rolling back and forth. And still Rye didn't let up.

"Hey. It's over." Emma walked toward them both, got too close in fact.

She came up on Rye's blind side, and the next thing she knew, he grabbed her hard, something absolutely wild and fierce in his eyes.

"Rye," she whispered. "It's me."

"Emma?" His grip tightened on her for a minute.

She winced. "Rye, my arms. Let go. You're hurting me."

There was a sick look on his face, as he stared at her as if he just then realized who she was. He stared at his hands, still on her arms, then down to the floor to Mark. His face was a mess. Emma knew what a man's fists could do. She'd seen her mother's face when it was a mess, but this . . . His lips were swollen and bleeding, his eyes red and swelling, too, his nose bleeding, his jaw lying at an awkward angle, and he was moaning and making a choking sound.

"Are you okay?" Rye asked.

"Yes. Are you?"

He nodded.

"Your head . . . You're bleeding. We have to call someone. We have to call for help."

Rye's arms finally dropped to his side, and he sat down hard on the arm of the sofa, his eyes closing. "Did I kill him?"

"I don't think so," she said, still afraid to get any closer to Mark.

"I'm sorry, Emma," Rye said in a voice devoid of all emotion. "I'm so sorry."

"So am I." Sorry she'd gotten him into this and sorry for the way Mark looked right now, sorry for everything she feared would happen next.

She called the sheriff, talked to him herself and told

him what had happened, and he said he'd radio for an ambulance. Then she sat down on the sofa, her on one end, Rye on the other.

They didn't say anything.

Mark was scaring her now with the sounds he was making, the rough, rumbling, wheezing sounds like all of his insides were broken and scrambled.

She couldn't make herself go to him. She was afraid of everything.

It seemed to take forever for help to come. She seemed to live a lifetime in those few minutes. It reminded her of when she was a child and her father beat her mother. It had been hard to know for sure when it was over, when it was safe. She'd sit huddled in a corner, and after a while, the blows would cease. Her mother might be moaning or crying, but she'd try to be quiet. Emma would, too. Her father would keep swearing and yelling. It wasn't really over until he got quiet, too. Until he passed out.

Once he did, none of them knew what to do. Mostly, they tried not to look at each other and not to talk about it.

Emma was thinking now that she needed to straighten the chair in the corner. It had gotten turned over onto its side, and the lamp on the table was in pieces on the floor.

Someone could get cut on that.

She should sweep it up.

She went to the chair first, her head protesting the movement. She turned it carefully and gently onto its side and then lifted it with her trembling hands into its place by the window. There. It looked just the way it was supposed to.

The lamp was more of a problem. She stared at all the pieces, too many to ever put back together. She couldn't make that right again.

The frosted white glass of the lamp had been hand painted with dainty blue flowers to match the blue in the stained-glass windows. Rachel had done this herself. It had been so pretty. Emma loved this lamp.

She picked up some of the biggest pieces. They clinked together as she stacked them on one of her hands.

"Emma?" Rye asked. "What are you doing?"

"Picking up the pieces."

"Why?"

She frowned, her hand trembling, the glass clinking from that alone.

It made perfect sense to her. You couldn't pretend everything was okay until you swept up the mess and put everything back in its place.

"It's what I do," she told him.

Her job had been picking up the pieces. She was ready to get the broom when she first heard the sirens and decided to sit down again.

It was odd having strangers in the house picking over the wreckage. They'd never called the police or the ambulance for her father and mother.

Joe came roaring into the house, another of his deputies behind him, and he stood there speechless for a moment. She looked up at him, thinking he could fix things. He could put all the pieces back together. But he looked dazed and kind of sick, too.

"Get the paramedics in here," he called over his shoulder, then looked back at Emma. Very, very gently, he said, "Are you okay?"

She nodded.

The paramedics came in a rush, with all sorts of equipment and a stretcher. "Jesus," one of them said. "Look at what's left of his face."

"What happened, Emma?" Joe said, trying to put his body between her and Mark to block her view.

"Mark came to get me," she said, then made the mistake of looking down at her hands. There was blood on her hands. She closed her eyes and remembered how Mark looked, what was left of his face.

And then everything went black.

Rye sat on the arm of the couch, wiping a trail of blood from the side of his face, looking at the end of life as he'd known it. He'd almost made it. Eight years. The magic mark. The end of his probation. When something like this would cease to have the power to send him back to prison.

He was two months and four days shy of that, and why the hell he hadn't just waited until then to come here . . .

And then he looked over at Emma and knew why.

She'd told him she was okay. Scared, shocked, but okay.

Of course, she'd never look at him in the same way again. He'd known that when he whirled around in a flash and grabbed her.

Rye heard the sheriff ask Emma what happened, heard her say, "Mark came to get me," and then she pitched sideways in a dead faint.

"Emma?" He caught her before she fell over and leaned her gently back against the sofa cushions. "Dammit, she said she was okay."

The sheriff was right there, looking like he didn't want Rye even touching her, not that Rye could blame him. He'd obviously found out all there was to know about Rye's past.

"Did you hurt her?" the sheriff asked.

"No," Rye lied. He could see the discolored flesh on her arms where he'd grabbed her.

"Did he?" The sheriff gestured to the man on the floor.

"I don't know."

"You don't know? Where the hell were you?"

"He bashed me over the head with something, and I blacked out. I don't know for how long." Rye felt sick just thinking about it, him lying here while that guy had Emma. "I don't know what he did to her."

The sheriff called one of the paramedics over to look at Emma. He listened to her heart and lungs quickly, checked her pupils.

"Did he have a weapon?" the sheriff asked.

"Just that shovel from the fireplace, as far as I know," Rye said. "Did she hit her head? He knocked her down the other day. Maybe he did it again."

The paramedic checked quickly. "There's a knot on her head, but I don't think it's that bad. What about you?"

"I'm fine," Rye insisted. There was hardly any blood. "What about her?"

"Give me a minute with this guy, and I'll make sure she's okay."

"Is he going to make it?" the sheriff asked.

"Who knows? We cleared the airway, but I can't see inside of him. Who knows what kind of damage might have been done."

Rye kept his gaze locked on Emma. If he never saw her again, Sam had damned well better take good care of her.

"Emma? Come on. Wake up for me. Tell me you're okay."

"You tell me what happened here," the sheriff said.

"You know what happened," Rye said. "The guy got in here—"

"How? Did he break in?"

"I don't know," Rye admitted, hating himself for that, too. He'd been rolling around on the floor with Emma when it happened. "Emma and I were here, and the next thing I know, somebody hit me over the head. I was lying on the floor when I came to, and I could hear him talking to her. He wanted her to come back to Chicago with him, and he was mad that she hadn't. He said she'd have to learn how to behave. He drew back his hand to hit her, and I stopped him."

"You stopped him all right," the sheriff said.

"I had to make sure he didn't hurt Emma anymore," Rye said. "I couldn't let him have another chance to hurt her."

"Last guy you got into a fight with didn't ever hurt anybody again, did he?"

Rye just looked away.

What was there to say?

"And you're still on probation for that?" the sheriff asked.

"Yeah, I am," Rye said.

He started thinking that if the sheriff had hauled him off to jail the day before . . . But no. He looked down at Emma, still lying on the sofa between them. She would have been here by herself, then.

She started to stir. Rye could tell when she remembered everything. She jerked upright, and he grabbed on to her. "It's all right. The sheriff's here. Mark's . . . He's not going to hurt you anymore, Emma."

She looked up at him, still half out of it, and he could tell when she remembered what he'd done, because she looked scared of him then.

He eased her back against the sofa cushion once more and let her go, probably for the last time, then got up and walked to the other side of the room, waiting for the sheriff to haul him off to jail.

Sam got the call that evening, but couldn't make sense of it at first.

Emma was at the hospital? So was her ex-boyfriend,

who'd broken into the house, and his brother was in jail?

It wasn't the first time, either. The last time, his brother had killed a man.

Sam covered the mouthpiece of the phone and yelled, "Rachel," in much the same way he had the day before when he found out his brother had come to find him. His brother who was in jail, not for the first time.

"Sam, I'm sorry," said his friend Joe Mitchell. "I feel terrible. I just didn't see it coming. And Emma—"

"She's okay?"

"She may have a concussion, but other than that, I think she's just shaken up. She claims the guy hit her once, and that was it. I had one of my guys call Rachel's Aunt Miriam. I thought Emma might want someone with her, until you and Rachel can get here."

"Thanks, Joe," he said, then just stood there, a thousand conflicting emotions rushing through him. Finally, one came to the forefront. "What's going to happen to my brother?"

"I don't know, Sam."

Rye sat in one of the county's four jail cells, which was actually nothing more than a holding area. They normally took people right away to the regional jail thirty minutes away. It wasn't anything more than two cells on either side of the room, a narrow hallway between them. He didn't know how long he'd been here, and he really didn't care.

The door to the cell block opened. The sheriff walked in, unlocking the door to Rye's cell and holding out a cordless phone to him.

"I don't think we got around to offering you your one phone call."

"You call Sam?" He wanted to make sure Sam was on his way to Emma.

"Yeah."

"There's nobody else to call."

"You sure?"

"You could call the hospital and check on Emma," he said. That was really the only other thing he needed that could come from a phone.

"I did that already. Mild concussion. That's it, except for . . . Well, she's pretty upset. When they finish checking her over, if they think it's safe, they're going to give her a sedative to help her relax. Sounds like when Sam gets there, they'll let her go home."

Rye nodded, the invisible band gripping his chest easing a bit. He could almost breathe again, then found the courage to ask, "The ex-boyfriend still alive?"

The sheriff nodded. "You broke about every bone in his face, compromised his airway, broke a couple of ribs."

Rye shrugged. "Yeah, well, the guy pissed me off."

"Me, too," the sheriff said.

That surprised Rye. He hadn't expected any kind of understanding.

"But you didn't nearly kill him," Rye said, wondering if the fact that the guy wasn't dead would be of any great help to him. Not that he was expecting any miracles. He was going back to prison.

"Look, I should have done more," the sheriff said. "I thought the guy was annoying as hell, but not really dangerous. I wish I'd done more."

That surprised Rye even more. A cop who really cared? One who could admit to making a mistake? Not that he thought it would do him any good.

"Am I going back to Georgia? Or do we settle this

mess here first?" he asked. To this point, he'd confined his crime spree to one state. He wasn't sure what
the process would be like from here. "I just want to
be sure Emma's okay, and if I go back to Georgia
right away—"

"You're not going anywhere fast," the sheriff said.
"Except maybe to get that cut on your head looked
at. I didn't think it was that bad, but . . . Maybe you
and I should take a ride over to the hospital."

Rye looked up, surprised once again. They'd offered
to take him to the hospital earlier, and he'd refused.
Emma had been so upset, and he'd thought it would
be better for her if he just got the hell away from her.
So he'd turned down their offer of further medical
attention.

But if the sheriff was saying what Rye thought he
was saying . . . Emma was there. He'd cut off his right
arm for the chance to see her one more time.

"Hurts, huh?" the sheriff asked, nodding toward
Rye's head.

"Yeah, it hurts," he agreed.

Fifteen minutes later, Rye was in the emergency
room of the small-town hospital, which was actually
not much more than a clinic. He was in handcuffs.
The sheriff had caught hell about that from at least a
half-dozen people who knew Emma and knew that no
matter what else Rye had done, he'd saved her. He
guessed they hadn't seen what was left of Emma's ex-
boyfriend's face yet.

Ten stitches later, he and the sheriff were out in the
hall. The sheriff said, "I'm thinking I should check on
Emma. Guess you'll have to come with me."

Rye shook his head as they headed down the hall.
"I've never met a cop like you."

"Yeah, well . . . Me and Sam go way back. Doesn't
seem like that long ago I was hauling him off to jail."

"Sam? The way Emma talks, the man's a saint."

"Not when he was fifteen or sixteen. He's straightened out pretty well since then," the sheriff said. "You got locked up when you were sixteen?"

"Yeah." He and a buddy of his had stolen a car, just for the hell of it, just to piss off their parents. It had worked really well.

Rye and the sheriff walked down the corridor to room 104. The sheriff pushed open the door. "They said she'd probably be sleeping, that it's what she needs now. Other than a bump on the head, she's fine."

Rye walked over to the bed. She didn't stir, just lay there so still and so pale against the stark white sheets, her hair falling across her face. He wanted to push it back out of her eyes. But the thought of touching her with hands bound together by handcuffs was enough to make him feel sick.

So he just stood there with so many regrets it seemed they should have choked him by now. If he didn't watch it, he might damned well cry.

He'd have given anything to be able to come to her as anyone except who he was, but that was impossible. He was chained to the past, as securely as his hands were chained together in front of him.

So he bent over and kissed her forehead, ever so softly, and said good-bye, then turned and walked away.

Chapter 11

Night came and went. Rye sat in his cell. One of the deputies brought him dinner from the diner on the corner. The sheriff brought him breakfast the next morning, along with the news that Sam had gotten into town early that morning and that Emma was home, shaken but fine. Mark was in Cincinnati, a surgeon trying to save his face. He was a bloody mess.

Rye was waiting for his brother to pay him a visit. He didn't think it would be long now. He'd have to face him with a set of bars in between them.

He laughed a bit at that. Hell, if he'd known it would be like this, he wouldn't have had to wait all these years.

He thought about talking to the sheriff, who seemed like a really decent guy. If Rye said, "Please don't make me see my brother for the first time in almost twenty years from behind bars," the sheriff might let him talk to Sam somewhere else.

But the next time the door to the cell block opened, he looked up and there was Sam.

Damn.

He looked like a man who'd driven like a maniac all night to come rescue his daughter from disaster, like a man hell-bent on getting some answers, answers he didn't think he was going to like.

Rye took all that in within seconds, looked the man up one side and down the other, and then looked away. He couldn't even look his own brother in the eye.

Sam just stood there, maybe a foot and a half away, rows of metal in between them. Finally, he said, "What the hell happened, Robbie?"

The Robbie part just about did him in. Robbie was a little kid who'd disappeared a long time ago. He wondered if he'd driven Sam crazy all those years ago with stupid kid stuff, wondered what kind of life they'd had and how things might have been different if they'd ever been together.

Not that it really mattered now.

"You mean with Emma?" Rye asked.

"I mean everything. How did you . . ."

"How did I end up here? Your friend the sheriff didn't tell you?"

"I'd like to hear it from you."

Rye shrugged and tried to look like it didn't matter in the least. What a crock. "It's a long story."

"I've got time, and it sure looks like you do, too."

Well, there was that. He was completely without the luxury of walking away. For as long as Sam wanted to stay, he supposed they'd talk.

"Is Emma okay?" he asked instead.

"Yeah. She's got a bruise on her head. She's shaken, but fine. Except for being worried about you."

Rye's head finally came up at that, and there they were, face-to-face.

It wasn't like looking in a mirror. Not exactly. Like looking at one that subtly distorted the image. Him but not him. Sam's hair was darker. He was a bit taller, a bit broader, a bit older, sterner, angrier, but then he had a right to be.

"She is worried about you," Sam said, as if that really had him going.

Rye couldn't imagine why Emma would care, unless . . . "She has this crazy idea that all of this is her fault. That she should have known her ex was crazy, and . . . You'll tell her what a crock that is, won't you?"

Sam nodded, not giving an inch.

"I tried to tell her, but she wouldn't listen to me."

"And she couldn't even tell me what was going on?" Sam asked.

That part seemed to be eating away at him, and if Rye had any doubts about the way Sam McRae felt about his daughter, they were gone right then. The anguish on his face, in thinking he'd disappointed her or failed her in some way, was enough to ease Rye's mind on that score.

There wasn't much else that really mattered now. Except maybe trying to help his brother.

"She was afraid you'd be disappointed in her."

Sam gaped at him. "She couldn't disappoint me if she tried."

Yeah, Rye thought. Good for Emma. He wanted her to have a father who thought about her that way. He wanted her to have everything. And the way he saw it, he owed his brother an apology, too.

"I'm sorry," Rye said. "I didn't . . . I should have taken better care of her."

"Oh, hell, I should have," Sam said, as if he didn't have any patience for anything resembling an apology in this.

"I told you I'd make sure she was safe."

"And she says you did, until the guy bashed you over the head."

"Still . . ." Rye began.

Sam held up a hand, waved off the words. It was his turn to look away. In a voice that shook, he asked, "Did you really kill that kid sixteen years ago?"

"Yeah, I did."

Sam took that about like he might a blow with a shovel. He backed up two steps, staggered almost, and shook his head. "Robbie—"

"Don't call me that," Rye said, more harshly than he should have.

And then Sam looked at him one more time, and it wasn't with anger that Rye had ended up this way. It wasn't disgust or embarrassment. It looked a lot like hurt, disappointment, disbelief, the need to understand struggling with the need to say there had to be a mistake. It was a where-did-you-go-so-wrong look, and it nearly sent Rye stumbling to his knees.

He hadn't really expected his brother to care, and he was coming to understand the depths of Emma's need not to let this man down. Because Rye found that he really hated the idea of disappointing Sam or hurting him.

"I'm sorry," he said.

And then, he didn't think there was much they could possibly have left to say, but Sam was still there, still waiting.

"Will you do something for me?" Rye asked.

"Name it." As if that was all it would take. He asked and Sam provided.

"Tell Emma I'm sorry."

Sam nodded, then looked thunderous all of a sudden. "That's another thing. She has this crazy idea that the two of you . . . That . . ."

Oh, hell, Rye thought. Things had been going so well, relatively speaking.

"Tell me nothing happened between you and Emma," Sam insisted, in full outraged-father mode.

"Nothing happened," Rye said. "I mean—"

"What? What do you mean?"

"When the guy broke into the house . . . I should have known, but . . . I was kissing her."

Which obviously had Sam wanting to break him in two. "What do you mean, you were kissing her?"

"Look, I kissed her, okay?" Rye wasn't about to get into the rolling around on the floor part. Not if kissing went over this badly. "I knew you wouldn't be too crazy about the idea, and I doubt she is, either, at the moment. But it didn't go any farther than that."

Sam still looked murderous.

Lost, Rye said, "I'm sorry. Obviously, it won't happen again."

Not with a set of bars and his past between them. Not when she was scared of him. Emma was slipping away into that good-girl-dream territory he'd always known she belonged in.

"You really don't know?" Sam roared. "You didn't think to wonder? To ask, maybe?"

"Ask what?"

"How old she is." Sam glared. "She's eighteen, asshole."

"Eihhh . . ." He felt like he'd been hit with the shovel again and started to say something, but got no more than that out before words completely failed him. He backed up a step, not sure the bars were enough at the moment to keep Sam from wringing his neck.

Eighteen?

"No way," Rye said.

"Do I look like I'm kidding?"

No, Sam did not.

Rye had an awful image of schoolgirls, ponytails, and shy grins. Of indecently young girls. This felt even more bizarre than the whole scene with Emma's ex. If she'd been just a year younger, he might well have gone to jail for what he'd been *wanting* to do to her.

"Jesus," he muttered.

"Yeah. She's my daughter. Keep your filthy hands off her."

His hands felt filthy at the moment. His mind.

Shit.

"Wait a minute. She's in college," he said, not as a way of defending himself, but trying to understand. Surely he hadn't been lusting after an eighteen-year-old girl. "She said she was finishing college."

"Which would have made her what? Twenty-one? Twenty-two?"

Which wasn't much better. Rye got that. But it was a lot better than eighteen. He stood there waiting for lightning to strike him dead right then, and when that didn't happen, he realized he still had to face Sam. Lightning didn't sound so bad.

"She said she was finishing college," he insisted.

"She's finishing her *first semester* of college," Sam said, very slowly and carefully, as if he might be talking to a dunce. "You make a habit of dating college freshmen?"

"No," Rye insisted.

Shit.

He couldn't believe this.

He was behind bars, seeing his brother for the first time in almost twenty years, and feeling like he was practically on the same level as a child molester. He really knew how to make an impression on someone.

And his brain was still stuck on the idea of Emma, so soft and so sweet, so understanding of him and so hard on herself. Emma scared and clinging to him. Emma whom he'd obviously let down so badly. Even worse were the things he'd wanted to do to her. . . .

"How the hell could she be eighteen?" Rye asked.

One look at Sam's face told him it wasn't the thing to say. It would never be the right moment to say that.

"I'm sorry," Rye said. He thought about saying he'd asked, more than once, how old she was, and she hadn't told him. But Emma had enough to worry about. He certainly wasn't going to add to her troubles.

Besides, he was supposed to be the grown-up here.

Not the dirty old man.

Jesus.

"I kissed her. That was it."

"You spent the night at my house with her, and not in the carriage house."

"She was scared," Rye said. "Her ex-boyfriend kept calling, and he'd already shown up at the house once. And nothing happened. I guess this isn't the time to ask you to believe me about anything, but . . ."

And Rye just gave up then. What was the point? He'd screwed things up as badly as he possibly could here in this town and with this man.

With this man's little girl.

"I'm sorry," he said again.

"Yeah, me, too."

And with that, his brother walked away.

Emma lay in her bed staring at the ceiling, just about as miserable as she'd ever been in her life. The past twenty-four hours seemed like a blur. Her and Rye sitting in front of the fire, her lying on the floor with him on top of her, kissing her. Mark scaring her half to death; Rye doing the same.

Now he was behind bars. Mark was in the hospital,

and she was here, bewildered. How in the world had this happened?

She'd never forget the look on Sam's face when he'd burst into her room at the hospital early that morning. He'd been so scared, so worried, and so very hurt. She hadn't thought she'd ever hurt him and hoped to go her entire life without ever doing that again.

He'd started asking her what happened, and she'd just burst into tears, not remembering half of what she'd said, just happy to have him close.

He and Rachel had brought her home. She'd slept for a few hours. Now she needed to go downstairs and face them. She was trying to find the courage to do just that when the door to her room opened slowly and Rachel looked in.

"Hi. Feeling better?"

Emma started to say she was. She was in her own house, in her own bed, Sam and Rachel here, too, and Mark wasn't going to drop by anytime soon.

Nightmare over.

Except it wasn't.

She was going to cry yet again.

"Oh, Em." Rachel came and sat on the bed beside her. "I'm sorry."

"No, I'm sorry. About everything. I don't know how it happened. I don't know why. Everything just went crazy all of a sudden."

Rachel bunched all the pillows up against the headboard and sat down beside Emma, Emma's head on her shoulder, the way they used to do when Emma was much, much younger.

"And you couldn't tell us?" Rachel asked. "Did you think we wouldn't understand? That we wouldn't help you? Emma, we would do anything for you. Absolutely anything."

"I know," she said, tears falling faster. "I know that."

"Sam is so upset. He thinks he's failed you in some way—"

"No." Emma shook her head. "I did this. This is my life, my decisions."

"And you're growing up and making decisions on your own. I know that, and Sam does, too. But in our hearts, you're still ours. Our daughter. You always will be. And he's a man. A father. He thinks he's supposed to be able to keep all of us safe and happy, that it's his job."

"I'm sorry."

Emma stared around her room, which was painted in the softest, creamiest yellow. She had a gauzy and puffy rose-colored comforter that looked like a cloud and a fabulous old bed made of intricately swirling iron. They'd done this just for her, and it was so pretty. Zach and Sam had been at an auction looking for things Sam might salvage from an old house and use in his construction business when they'd found the bed. She and Rachel had sanded it and painted it a grayish white that made her think of clouds, too. Sam and Zach had painted the room. Grace had picked out the curtains.

This was her room, her family, her place. How could she have forgotten that?

"Right after it happened, I got on the train to run back here. I thought I'd pour out the whole story to you both. But that night on the train I kept thinking about my mother. About how crazy everything was back then. Mark hit me, and it all came rushing back." Emma wiped away tears with a trembling hand. "It was so ugly. All of it. I didn't want to bring it into this house, or to have it anywhere near Zach or Grace. She doesn't know what it's like to be afraid like that, and I didn't want her to know. I didn't want her to ever think of anyone hitting her or me. I guess I thought if I never brought it here, I could pretend it never happened. Look how well that turned out."

"Emma, listen to me." Rachel gave her a squeeze. "This is not your fault. Mark obviously has problems. But those are his problems. Not yours."

"I brought him here."

"He brought himself here."

"To find me, and now he's Rye's problem," Emma cried. *Rye.* "He was just trying to protect me. That's all. I thought Mark had killed him yesterday. He was so still for so long, I thought he was dead and that maybe I would be, too."

"You're not," Rachel said. "Rye's not, either."

"He's in jail," she cried. "He must hate me. He was so worried about what Sam would think of him, and now look at this mess. All because of me."

"Emma, we talked to Joe. He said you both saw what Mark looked like when Rye got done with him. It went long past subduing him. It was brutal."

"He did it to protect me," Emma insisted.

"Did he?"

What else could it have been? She knew him, after all. Not the way she'd thought she'd known Mark. This was Rye. She knew what he was, deep down inside.

Oh, God, Rye.

She wanted him here with her, had to talk to him, try to make him understand, and she had to understand him.

"What happened between the two of you?" Rachel asked. "Joe said . . . He said Rye spent the night here with you, that it looked like . . ."

"It was nothing like that," Emma said. Surely Rachel would understand, Rachel who'd been so in love with Sam for so long. "Mark had been here, and I was scared. I hadn't slept much at all. Having him in the carriage house didn't seem like enough. But nothing happened. He wouldn't let anything happen."

"*He* wouldn't?"

"That's right. I admit it. I wanted something to happen. He's special, Rachel. He's so kind, so understanding, so gentle." Not anything like the man she'd seen yesterday tearing into Mark. Not really. Was he?

"Emma, he's thirty-three."

"I know," she said, turning into a girl who just needed her mother. "I didn't when he first came here, and by the time I did, it was too late."

"Too late for what?"

"I think, maybe . . . I'm in love with him."

"Oh, Emma. No." Rachel sat up and turned to look at her, dismay on her face.

"Yes, I am. And I know what you're going to try to say. That he's too old for me. And that I'm too young, but you and Sam were married by the time you were my age." They'd snuck around behind Rachel's father's back, because he'd disapproved of Sam so much, and then Rachel had gotten pregnant. "You're really not going to try to tell me I can't be in love with him, are you? That I can't possibly know what's in my own heart?"

"I guess I can't. But, Emma, you've only known him for a few days."

"How long did it take for you to know you loved Sam?" she tried. "You said you always knew."

"Maybe I did. But, as much as we loved each other, it was still so hard. We were so young, and we almost didn't make it. I don't know if you ever really understood how close Sam and I came to losing each other."

"But you made it," she said.

Rachel covered her face with her hands and used

her fingertips to rub at her forehead as if it ached, then switched tactics. "What about him? Is he in love with you? Did he tell you that?"

"No," Emma admitted. "He didn't want to have anything to do with me. He didn't think Sam would like it, and he really wants to get to know Sam. I don't think he has anybody else left."

"Doesn't sound like it," Rachel said.

"I know it's all a mess right now. I can't imagine what he must think of me, but it won't always be this way, will it? Things are bound to settle down, and then . . ." He'd forgive her for this mess, and he wanted to get to know Sam, which meant he'd be here, a part of their lives, and as long as he was here . . . "There has to be a way."

"Emma, did he tell you where he's been? What his life has been like?"

"He told me about his problems with his parents, and he tried to make it sound like he'd done awful things I wouldn't understand—"

"He has," Rachel said softly. "It's not the first time he's beaten up someone. Badly. He's been in prison, Emma. Joe has the records. Rye told him what he needed to find the records. It's no mistake. He was arrested for the first time when he was sixteen."

"When he stole the car. He told me about that. Rachel, he was sixteen."

"And they sent him to a juvenile detention center, and while he was there, he got into a fight with another boy and killed him. He spent the next eight years in prison for manslaughter."

Emma wouldn't believe it until she heard it straight from Rye. She waited until Rachel finally left, then slipped out the back door, walking the eight blocks to the jail in a daze.

Joe took one look at her and said, "Sam know you're here?"

He didn't want to let her in to see Rye, but she simply refused to leave. Joe finally gave in. He took her back into the office, unlocked a door, and there was Rye, locked up in an awful little cell in the back corner.

It was a colorless place, washed-out gray with gunmetal bars. He stood in back by a tiny window—covered with more bars—and he didn't turn around.

She stared at his back, at muscles bunched in his shoulders and his arms, strength that had never frightened her until yesterday, when she'd tried to pull him off Mark, and he'd turned around like a wild thing ready to attack.

He had scared her then.

But he'd saved her from Mark, and she'd been scared enough that she couldn't regret the manner in which he'd done that. Except for the way he was suffering now because of it. She remembered how her mother looked after her father had taken his fists to her. Mark could easily have done that to her. If she'd let him, he might have done it again and again and again.

Some men were just like that.

She'd have sworn Rye wasn't.

"Sure you want to do this?" Joe asked softly.

"Yes."

Rye turned around at the sound of her voice. Clearly, she'd surprised him. He put his back to her again just as quickly, shoving his hands into the pockets of his jeans. His head dropped back until he was staring up at the ceiling and probably swearing, if she was any judge of the situation.

"You yell if you need me," Joe said, obviously not liking this.

He left, not quite shutting the door behind him.

Emma walked over to the bars. She hated the idea of him being caged up this way, of having these bars between them. She hated dragging him into a situation blind and having him end up here because he wanted to protect her.

Didn't they know that? None of this would have happened if he hadn't simply been trying to protect her.

Rye finally turned around again. He looked like he wanted to strangle her at first, and then he just looked so tired. "You okay?"

She nodded, tears threatening already.

"What are you doing here, Em?"

She cleared her throat and managed to say, "You're here."

"And believe me, this is a lousy place to be."

"I know. I'm sorry."

"Emma, don't even start with that."

"I know you must be angry. . . ."

"Not at you," he said.

She blinked back tears. "But you're here because of me."

"No, I'm here because of me. My choices. My actions. We talked about this. Remember?"

"You saved me from him," she said.

"And then practically beat him to death. If I'd pulled him off you and called the sheriff, I wouldn't be here. I know that. You do, too."

"I know that it was my problem. All of this has been my problem."

"Come on, Emma. You're smarter than that." She flinched at the tone, but he kept on going. "Guys like Mark want you to believe it's all your fault. That's how they get girls like you and how they keep them. Don't buy into that crap. Not with him and not with me."

So he was being cruel to be kind. Fine. And maybe he had a point, but she had one, too. "Look at this." She threw her hands out toward the bars. "Look at where you are."

"It's not anyplace I haven't been before," he said. "I told you it was ugly. I told you that you wouldn't understand."

"Make me understand," she begged. She wanted him to make excuses, to tell her it was all a mistake.

"What is there to understand? This is who I am. This is what my life has been like."

She came to the heart of it, then, to the hardest part. She whispered, "They said you killed someone, years ago."

He looked her in the eye and said softly, "I did."

Emma took a step back at that.

He wasn't anywhere near her. It wasn't like she was afraid of him. It was the truth. She thought maybe if she could get away from it, it wouldn't hurt this badly and that maybe it wouldn't be true.

"How could you do that?"

The look he gave her then left her nearly completely undone. He took a ragged breath and stepped back himself. One minute, he was looking at her. The next he was staring off into the corner of the room behind her. He was lost, gone back so many years. She thought she was seeing the boy he'd once been.

Seventeen, she thought. Not far from the age she was now.

He'd taken someone's life at seventeen?

She felt like she could see it all, the horror, the bewilderment, the sorrow, and she wondered what he'd been like before that, what he might have been.

"I just did it, okay? We got into a fight, and by the time they pulled me off the other guy, he was dead," he said, finally looking her in the eye. "If you were expecting some pretty story, you're not going to get it. I told you, dammit. I told you what it was like. I told you that you didn't know me, and you just wouldn't listen."

"I'm sorry," she said.

"Yeah, well, so am I."

"What's going to happen to you?" she asked.

"I don't know, and I don't want you to even think about it. I want you to forget about this. Go back to that pretty little life of yours. Find some boy and . . ." He was pacing then, fuming. "God, Emma. You're really eighteen?"

"I'll be nineteen in February," she said.

He laughed then, a disgusted sound. "And you think that makes a damned bit of difference?"

"You care about me," she said. "I know you do."

"Emma, you're a child. Sam is ready to kill me for ever laying a hand on you, and honestly, if I were in his place, I'd feel the same way."

"I am not a child," she insisted.

"Well I'm thirty-three. It's indecent."

"You didn't think so a day and a half ago," she reminded him.

"Okay, so you don't look eighteen and I sure didn't think you were. Believe me, if I'd known, I never would have laid a hand on you."

He was fuming then, and he looked a lot like Sam. If her heart wasn't breaking, she might tell him so. But her heart was breaking. She hardly had any words left, hardly had anything left inside of her at all.

"I'm sorry," she said, in complete and utter despair.

"Oh, God, Emma." It was a ragged sound, the sound of a man dragging the bottom, every bit of energy and hope gone, which was exactly how she felt.

Empty.

Spent.

Lost.

She walked up to the bars then and hung on to them, leaning her forehead against them. In the short time they'd had together, she'd come to crave his touch. Not just his lips, but his hands, his arms, the curve of his shoulder, the shelter of his embrace.

He came to her, just stood there for the longest time, then bent his head, too, so that, if not for the bars, their foreheads would be touching. He slipped his hands through the bars. They slid along her forearms and cupped her elbows in as much of an embrace as this place would allow, and it was just as she remembered it, every bit as powerful, every bit as necessary as breathing.

"You do care about me."

"Not the way you're thinking," he insisted.

Was that true? She didn't want to believe it. So what if she was not quite nineteen and he was thirty-three. She was still the same person he'd met six days ago, a girl who'd never really been young in her whole life, and he was . . .

He'd killed someone.

How could that be?

"Go on," he said. "Get out of here."

"I can't just forget about you."

"You will, in time. You have to. I want you to be happy, Emma."

"I want you to be happy, too."

"Well I just don't see how that's going to happen for me. But that's my problem. Not yours." He kissed her forehead and then backed away. "Go home. And don't come back."

Chapter 12

Emma stayed stubbornly right there, but Rye wouldn't say another word.

Fine, she thought. It wasn't like he was going anywhere.

Emma went back to find Joe, who took one look at her face and swore. "What did he do to you?"

"Told me to go away and forget about him," she said.

"Good for him."

"Joe—"

"You know what he did. He killed someone."

"I spent six days with him, Joe. He's not—"

"What? Not your idea of a killer? An ex-con?"

"Don't call him that," she insisted.

"That's what he is."

"Surely he's more than that," she argued.

"Come on." Joe took her by the arm and steered her down the hall. "You need to understand some things about this."

"No, you do. He's Sam's brother, and he was kind to me. He was gentle and considerate, and he protected me. And as for what happened when he was seventeen . . . Do you know what happened?"

"A fight in a juvenile detention center. What's there to know?"

"There has to be something more. It's not . . . I don't want people to look at him and see just that." She wanted them to know the man she'd spent those six days with. "Can you look into it, Joe?"

"I guess I could," he said, pushing open the door to his office.

"Thank you." She followed him inside and then got to the really hard question. "What's going to happen to him?"

"I don't know. It's up to the county attorney to decide what to charge him with, and from there, it's up to a jury. But he's still on probation from the manslaughter conviction, Emma."

She sat down, afraid of what was coming. "What does that mean?"

"They sentenced him to sixteen years. He served a little more than half before he was paroled on the condition that he stays out of trouble. A conviction for assault, and he may well go back to prison to serve the rest of those sixteen years."

"Oh, my God." Emma sat back, feeling winded. "Does he know?"

"Oh, yeah. He knows."

And there he was, calm as could be, telling her it wasn't her fault. Telling her to forget about him.

"We can't let that happen to him, Joe."

"I told you, it's not up to me."

"Do you think he deserves to go back to prison for this?"

"I think it's hard to know what's inside of a man, what he's capable of, and I've misjudged people before, Emma. I know you think you know him. But you saw what your ex-boyfriend looked like when Rye was done with him."

"And if Rye hadn't been there?"

Joe frowned. "If you'd had to depend on the law and not an ex-con to protect you?"

"That's not what I meant, Joe."

"I know, but it's what I'm thinking. I'm sorry. I should have done more. Couldn't have stood it if that guy hurt you. Either one of 'em."

"Rye wouldn't hurt me," she said.

"So you say. I'm still sorry."

"Then make it up to me. Do it by helping Rye now."

Sam felt sick, literally.

He stood in the cold on the back porch of his house because he wasn't sure what he could say to either Rachel or Emma, and when he couldn't stand it any longer, he reached for the door to go in.

There'd been a time when his little brother had been all he had left in the world, and losing him had felt like the last straw, like losing everything. He'd wanted Robbie back in his life so badly, and now here he was.

Sam pulled open the door, coming in through the combination utility room/laundry room in the back of the house.

Rachel was there pulling a load of clothes out of the dryer. She stood up straight, a bundle of clothes in her arms, frowning. "It was bad?"

"Worse than I ever imagined," he admitted, toeing off his boots on the mat by the door. "I should have listened to you. I should have found him and told him everything. I could have brought him back here to stay with us, before anything happened."

"You know why you didn't." She dropped the bundle of clothes onto the top of the washer. "You didn't want to tear his life apart. You said he was happy then, that everything seemed fine with him."

"It did."

"So what happened?"

"I don't know." He watched as she started to fold the clothes, then went to help her, pulling an old, worn sweatshirt from the pile of laundry. It was still warm, and he shook it out and folded it. They'd had a million conversations right here in this room, her folding clothes and him helping her. He'd never thought they'd have this particular one.

"Emma might know what happened to him," Rachel said.

Sam took a breath and let it out very, very slowly. *Emma.*

Emma and my brother.

He was torn completely, between bone-deep sorrow over the mess that was his brother's life and fatherly outrage over anything that might have happened between Rye and his daughter.

"I told him she was eighteen, and if I hadn't been so damned mad at him, it might have been funny," he admitted. "The look on his face . . ."

Rachel shook out a shirt and held it against her chest to fold. "He really didn't know?"

Sam shook his head, then got mad again. "Hell, he could have asked."

"Do you know that he didn't?"

"I know that he's a grown man, and he damned well shouldn't be putting his hands all over a girl without knowing how old she is."

"Sam"—Rachel left the laundry alone and turned to face him—"I hate telling you this, but Emma thinks she's in love with him."

"Shit," he said, staring down into the face of the

woman he'd loved since she was even younger than Emma. Of course, he'd been nearly as young himself. He'd fought and lost a long, raging battle with himself to try to keep his hands off Rachel for years. So he knew what that was like. But he hadn't been nearly fifteen years older than she was.

"What the hell happened between them?" he growled.

"Nothing." As always, Rachel soothed him. She put her hands on his arm, running them up and down for a moment. "She said nothing happened."

"She doesn't think she's in love with him over nothing."

Rachel's mouth twitched at that, the corners curling, and then her soft lips stretching into a smile.

"What is so funny?" Sam asked, putting his arms around her and hauling her to him.

"You, like this. Better be careful. You might remind me of my own father when he was so mad about you and me."

"I wasn't thirty-three when you and I got together."

"No, but you can't tell her she's too young to know what love is. She knows I was married to you and pregnant with your child before I was eighteen."

Sam choked back what he'd been about to say: *Hell, yes, she's too young.* Instead, he said, "How did she get to be eighteen anyway?"

Rachel kissed his cheek, whispered, "I don't know. One of those mysterious things. You turn your back, and they're grown."

They hadn't had enough time with her. She'd been almost twelve when she came to them, and a little grown-up even then.

"She has her whole life ahead of her. We'll start there," he reasoned, then remembered something else. "Oh, hell, it's not like Emma's going to have a choice.

He's still on probation for the manslaughter conviction years ago. If he gets convicted of assault here, he's going back to prison for a long time. That'll keep him away from Emma."

"And away from you," Rachel reminded him.

"Shit."

"I know." Rachel held on tighter.

Sam stood there, still stunned sometimes by how very much he needed her. He'd always believed she had saved him. He'd been as lost and as angry as he thought his brother must have been, and who was to say what might have happened to Sam if not for Rachel. She was every bit of softness and love he'd ever known, except for those very early years with his parents and the last seven years they'd had with the kids.

He thought of all he had now, Rachel and the kids, his work and the home they'd built here. It was more than he'd ever imagined having, more than he thought he deserved. Life had been very, very good to Sam McRae and just lousy to his brother.

"I could have been just like him," Sam said, holding her tighter, pushing her face to his chest and kissing the top of her head. "It would have been so easy. I could be sitting right where he is now."

"I'm not sure I believe that."

"I do. Emma probably thinks she can save him from himself."

Her head came up at that. "Maybe she can."

Sam let her go. "Don't tell me you're okay with this."

"I'm not crazy about the idea of Emma growing up, but I think parents have been trying to stop it from happening for thousands of years, and as far as I know, it's never worked."

"She's eighteen," he said, totally unable to connect his daughter now with the age his wife had once been when they'd gotten together.

"And she's not foolish or reckless. She's careful and smart."

"And the last guy she got involved with smacked her around." Sam groaned. "How the hell can I condemn my brother for doing something I'd really like to have done myself. I'd like to tear that little bastard who hurt her apart limb by limb."

"I know that, too." She understood him better than he did himself.

He took her hands in his, holding on. "I don't know what to do," he confessed. "I have absolutely no idea what to do."

"Sure you do. We'll try to help your brother. There's no reason to get crazy about him and Emma, especially when he's in jail. Nothing's going to happen between them as long as he's there."

"Okay." He could do that. Sam was just afraid it wouldn't be enough. That nothing he could do at this point would be enough. But Rachel was here. They were in this together. He could do anything as long as he had her, couldn't he?

"I love you," he said.

"I love you, too."

"How's Emma?"

"She went to see him this afternoon. I think she had to hear it from him before she could believe he'd killed someone."

Sam braced himself to hear. "What did he tell her?"

"That he did it. What did he tell you?"

"Just that. I meant to ask, but we never got around to the details. We didn't get around to much except me jumping down his throat about Emma, and . . ." He swore softly and looked up at the ceiling, defeated. "Oh, hell, Rachel, he saved her."

"I know."

"I didn't even thank him for that. *Rye.* I can't get

used to thinking of him that way. I look at him, and I see a little kid. . . . But I didn't even thank him for saving Emma."

"So, the next time you see him, you'll thank him."

"I don't want to lose him. Not again. And I'm so mad at him. How the hell did he screw up his life like this?"

"Ask him." Rachel said. "Give him a chance to tell you himself what happened."

"I should have told him about the two of us. All those years ago, he should have known that if he ever needed anything, he could have come to me. I would have done anything for him." Sam was nearly choking. "He must have needed someone so badly."

"He did come to you," Rachel said. "He came to you six days ago."

"And what if it's too late?"

That was about to burn a hole in his gut. *Too late.*

"He's still here, Sam. You're here."

"He's in jail. He could be going back for a long time." Sam wasn't sure what was worse—thinking about his brother in jail or thinking about him deserving to be there. "He really killed someone. How could he do that?"

"Ask him, Sam. And then listen to what he has to say. Let him know that whatever happens, we'll be here for him."

Emma went to bed sick at heart and woke up nearly screaming.

She sat up, shaking and freezing, trying to breathe normally and push the nightmare out of her head. A glance at the clock by her bedside showed it was shortly after three in the morning, too early to get up and stay up, but she wasn't willing to risk going back to sleep yet.

She got out of bed, pulled on a pair of sweats and socks, because it was cold. Padding to the window, she saw the tiniest bits of snow falling from the sky. It hardly made a dusting on the ground below.

Behind her, the door to her room gave the slightest creak. She turned toward the sound. Sam stood in the doorway, one of the saddest looks she'd ever seen on his face.

"You okay?"

She nodded, feeling just awful. She hadn't just hurt Rye. She'd hurt Sam, and left the two of them to start over together in the worst possible way.

Sam leaned against the doorjamb. "Can't sleep?"

"No."

"Me, either. Nightmare?"

He knew her too well. "Yes."

"Come on." He nodded to the right. "Let's go downstairs. We'll build up the fire. Pull out the chessboard, if it comes to that."

"Okay," she said, nearly choking on the word.

She followed him, conscious of the fact that he'd come into her life when there hadn't been a single shred of anything resembling security or predictability, and he'd given her and her brother and sister all of those things.

She thanked God for him every day.

It hit her a moment later that she was going to grow up someday and leave this precious house and these people. She had faith that they would always be here. She'd always be able to come home, but it wouldn't be quite the same. She wouldn't always be right down the hall from him when she needed him.

"I'm going to miss you, Sam," she said, tears threatening once more.

He paused at the top of the stairs, looking uneasy. "Are you going somewhere, Em?"

"Not now. But someday I will." God, she didn't even want to think about going back to college. It was so far from here, so much closer to Mark.

"You don't have to. You could just stay here with us forever."

She wiped away tears then. It was scary how much you could love someone, how deep it went, how people could grab on to a piece of your heart and it would simply always be theirs, no escaping it, no changing it. Sam had a big piece of hers. She never wanted to hurt him.

"Come on," he said. "Downstairs."

She followed him down and into the family room. He knelt by the banked fire, and she knelt beside him, because there was still some warmth left there, and she was cold.

"I'm sorry I made things harder for you and Rye," she said as she stared into the faintly glowing coals.

"Emma, no."

"I did. I know it." She might just cry again. *Damn.* "He just wanted to come here and find you. He wanted that so badly. I'm not sure if he's even admitted that to himself, but that's what he wants. Sam, please don't let me mess that up for the two of you."

"You haven't messed anything up," he insisted as he started stacking logs on the fire.

"You're mad at him."

"I'm mad at just about the whole world right now, except for you."

Which made it even harder. He loved her so much.

Emma sat there in utter misery as he tended the fire, finally reaching for one of the tools to rearrange the wood. There was a little metal stand to the right of the fireplace that held the set of black metal tools. Emma's gaze hit on the shovel.

There was a different set of tools by the fireplace

in the living room. The shovel was missing. The sheriff had it for evidence in her nightmare come to life. Just like that, Emma started shaking again.

And she owed Sam an explanation. A big one.

"I'm sorry I didn't tell you about what was going on with Mark," she began. "I know you don't understand—"

"No, I really don't."

He looked over at the stand with the tools himself, no doubt thinking the same thing she was. She had been in so much trouble. Anything could have happened to her, things even worse than what had happened.

"Emma, I thought you knew you could come to me with anything, and that I would help you. I would do anything for you."

"I know that," she cried. "I never had any doubts about that."

"Then what?" He sat there with his head bowed, defeat in every line of his body. "Make me understand. Because right now, I feel like I failed you. I must have."

"No, Sam. It was me." She put her hand on his arm and then slipped her hand into his and held on tight. "I knew you'd be shocked and so disappointed. I kept thinking there had to be some way to tell you to make it not seem so bad. And my face was bruised. I didn't want you to see me like that, with a big bruise on my face. Isn't that the stupidest thing?"

"Hey." He reached out and brushed away one of her tears. "You're eighteen. Comes with the territory."

"Almost nineteen," she said.

"You want to hear about all the bad decisions I made when I was fifteen, seventeen, nineteen? It would take weeks for me to recite just the ones I can still remember."

"I'm sorry," she said again.

"Come on." He got to his feet. "Hot chocolate time."

He took her hand and pulled her to her feet. Together, they walked into the darkened kitchen. He bent to dig a pan out of the cabinet. She grabbed the milk for him to heat. They'd done this before.

He pulled out the pan. She poured milk, then put the rest back in the refrigerator. He was setting the burner on low when he said, "Promise me the next time you can't handle something on your own, you'll come to me or Rachel."

"I've got a problem like that now. With Rye. I don't know how to fix things for him."

Sam turned around, looking like he was going to say one thing, then changing his mind. He took a breath, reconsidered, and finally said, "I don't know if anybody can fix that, Em."

"But you'll try, right? Don't be so mad at him because of me that you don't try. Please, Sam. It's not his fault."

Frowning even more, he said, "What's not his fault?"

"The way I feel about him," she whispered.

Sam took on that look that said he could cheerfully chew nails at the moment without flinching. It was as bad as she'd feared it would be.

"He said nothing happened."

"Because he wouldn't let anything happen," she admitted. "Not because I didn't want it to."

Oh, that made it worse. "Emma—"

"It's true. He didn't know how old I was. He asked, but I didn't tell him, because I didn't want him to know, because . . . Sam, he's special."

Sam swore softly. "He'll be thirty-four in the spring. He's fifteen years older than you."

"I know. I didn't at first, and then when I did . . .
It was too late. I've never felt this way about anyone before."

"Give it some time. You will."

"Did you? Did you ever love anyone else the way
you love Rachel?"

He frowned at her then. "Emma, you barely know
him."

"I know." She couldn't look at him then. She was
too worried about what was going to happen, about
whether she'd ever get a chance with Rye.

Wanting something to do, Emma found a spoon and
stirred the milk. She knew to heat it slowly, so that it
never boiled, just warmed through and through.

She'd always been so careful about everything,
would never have thought she could fall for someone
so quickly and so completely. Everything inside of her
said that he was the one, the one man in this whole
world she could love.

Sam watched her, seeming to grow more tense with
each passing moment. Finally, he said, "You have so
much ahead of you. College and—"

"I don't know if I can go back there," she blurted
out. "Not because of Rye. Because of Mark. He lives
two hours from there, Sam."

"Well, it doesn't have to be Chicago. You can go
somewhere else, if you want. But you're going back
to school, Emma."

Was she? She'd never imagined not going. Now the
thought terrified her. But she wasn't worried about
herself. She wasn't the one in jail.

"You're going to help Rye?"

"I'll do what I can for him," Sam said grudgingly.

"He needs you. He needs all of us."

"He needs to keep his hands off you."

"Oh, Sam." She laughed, embarrassed but not about

to let that stop her from setting the record straight. "It wasn't like that. Not at all. I know you don't want to hear this, but he was the one begging me to keep my hands off him."

Sam looked like he could cheerfully throw something then, but he wouldn't. She knew it. She knew him.

"I could lock you up until you're thirty," he said finally.

"You could. I'd still love you."

She thought she'd still love Rye then, too.

Emma drifted through the next day and a half, sitting in her room staring at the walls, afraid to sleep in the night. She dozed off and on through the days, jerking awake at the sight of Mark's face in her dreams.

And she spent a lot of time missing Rye.

Joe Mitchell stopped by that afternoon and went into Sam's office to talk to him, and then he and Sam came into the house.

"I asked him to find out what he could about my brother's troubles with the law," Sam told Emma. "You want to hear this, too?"

"Yes," she said.

Joe took a seat by the fire, Sam opposite him, and Emma went to the couch and sat beside Rachel. The three of them looked to Joe.

"I talked to the officer who arrested him for stealing the car, who said he seemed like a pretty good kid. Never been in trouble with the law before, although it seemed like there were problems at home, pretty normal teenage kid stuff. He was with a buddy of his, another sixteen-year-old. They wrecked the car, did a few thousand dollars' damage to it, and the owner pushed to have them punished. The other kids' parents were both lawyers, determined to get their son out of it with a clean record. They pointed the finger at your brother as the instigator of the whole thing, made sure their kid had the best legal representation, and Rye's parents basically washed their hands of him."

"Those—" Sam bit back whatever else he might have wanted to add. "They just had to have him. A dozen years before that, they had to have him."

"Yeah. I'd say if they'd stood by him right there, stood up to everybody on his behalf, he'd have never been sent to the juvenile facility. Probation, community service, restitution. That would have been it."

"His whole life would have been different," Emma said.

"Maybe," Joe said.

"What about the kid he killed?" Sam asked.

"I found an officer at the juvenile facility who was there when Rye was. Said he seemed like he was going to come through it okay. I mean, it's a bad place to be, and if you're not tough when you go in, you either get tough inside or they'll eat you alive. So, I'm not saying he was a saint, but . . . Well, who's to say what he would have been like? But there was a fight one day. Rye didn't start it. A troublemaker named Morgan did. They weren't happy about having him in a juvenile facility and were trying to get him moved. He and Rye had been in some spats. Nobody's sure why. But the day the kid died, everybody said Morgan's the one who jumped your brother, and Morgan had a knife."

"So he was just defending himself?" Emma asked.

Joe hesitated. "I don't know, Emma. I wasn't there. The jury convicted him of manslaughter."

"The other guy had a knife and jumped him." Surely that meant something.

"Yeah. Who's to say? I could see it going either way, from what the guy at the juvenile facility told me. They'd had some trouble before. The place was getting a bad reputation. Lots of fights. Lots of kids getting hurt. It may have been that they wanted to make an example of him."

"This is his life we're talking about, Joe," Emma said, then turned to Sam. "He's not a bad person."

"I want to believe that," Sam said. "But you saw what he did to Mark."

"And what would you have done to Mark, if you had been here when he broke into this house and you'd found him getting ready to smack me with a fireplace shovel?"

"I don't know," Sam admitted, then turned to Joe.

"I feel bad about this," Joe said. "I wish I'd done more to head this off before it ever got ugly. Emma, I'm sorry."

"Joe, I'm not the one who got hurt. If you want to make it up to somebody, make it up to Rye. Can you do that?"

"I'll try," he said.

"What's happening now?" Rachel asked.

"Well, Mark's parents showed up, screaming about their precious little boy being attacked. They didn't want to believe anything I told them, but we got the fingerprint evidence back today. His fingerprints are all over your back door, the frame of the broken windowpane, the lock, and the fireplace shovel. Emma saw him hit Rye with that shovel. He waved it in her face and talked about needing to punish her. So we're looking at breaking and entering, assault and battery . . . His parents sure aren't going to like that. Apparently, they think he's downright perfect, and they want Rye locked up for a long time."

"Is that going to happen?" Emma asked.

"I'm not sure," Joe said. "If we charge him with a felony, he may have to serve out the rest of the time on the manslaughter conviction. But it's not really up to me. I'll make a recommendation, and from there, it's up to the county attorney, a judge, and a jury."

"What about Mark?" Rachel asked.

"I sure don't want him to do this to anybody ever again. Which reminds me . . ." He turned to Emma. "Has he hurt anyone else? Did he mention any old girlfriends? Any of them ever give you any kind of warning about him?"

"You know . . . One of them did say something." Emma felt sick just thinking about it. "I didn't think much of it at the time. It sounded more like someone who was jealous because he'd broken up with her. And . . . Oh, no."

"Em, it's okay." Rachel put her arm around her.

"She tried to tell me. She said something like, he wasn't what he seemed." She leaned into Rachel, thinking that this whole thing could have been avoided, thinking about Rye and all the trouble she'd drawn him into.

"What was her name?" Joe asked. "If there's a pattern of behavior here, I need to know about it."

Emma gave him the name. "That will help?"

"We'll see," Joe said. "Give it a few days. We'll see how it plays out."

Chapter 13

It took two days. She had to go to the county attorney's office and give a statement. They took one from Rye, one from Mark, conferred with the attorney Mark's parents hired, and finally called Emma back in. Sam and Rachel were with her. She sat in the thickly padded leather chair in front of a massive, gleaming wooden desk and felt like her whole future was on the line.

Joe was there, along with the county attorney, Jim Dixon. She knew him. She'd gone to high school with his daughter.

"Emma, I'm sorry about all of this." Jim opened up a file on his desk and frowned. "I know it's been difficult, and I hate putting you in this position, but it's time for us to make some decisions."

"About Rye?" she asked.

"About the whole thing. The Jacobsons are screaming, but there's no doubt their kid was the instigator. We've got his fingerprints. But you and Sam's brother came out of this relatively unscathed. Mark's still in the hospital, and we've got Sam's brother's own statement that he basically beat the hell out of the guy. He never tried to deny that. Although I have a feeling if I put Emma on the witness stand in court, she'd say he was just trying to defend her."

"He was," Emma said.

"Emma," Sam began.

"No," she insisted. "He was."

"Okay." Jim jumped in. "I can see where this is going. The Jacobsons' attorney seems to understand it, too. Bottom line is, they have high hopes for their son, and it doesn't include a criminal record. At the moment, they're more interested in making this go away than seeing Sam's brother punished."

"What?" Sam asked.

"Yeah, I'm not crazy about any of it, but you know what the courts are like these days. We plea-bargain most everything. The Jacobsons' attorney asked us to consider a misdemeanor battery charge against their son, a year of probation, and court-ordered counseling. Maybe he can work through that little problem he has in controlling his anger and wanting to hit women."

"No," Sam said. "He hit Emma. He harassed her, scared her, chased her here from Chicago, and for that, you're going to send him to a shrink?"

"I know, Sam. I'm sorry. It's not what I want, either, although I have to tell you, the courts have never been too concerned about a guy hitting his wife or his girlfriend. Not the way they should be. I think you know that."

"Shit," Sam said.

"We can add a restraining order against him, make sure he doesn't go anywhere near Emma," he said.

"I'm sure she'll sleep better at night. I'm sure we all will," Sam said.

"I'm sorry," Jim said again.

Emma didn't know what to say. She'd tried not to think about how she would feel when Mark was out of the hospital. It had seemed very far away.

"I want him in jail," Sam said.

"Even if we pressed, I'm not sure what we could do," Jim said. "He slapped her a couple of times. I know it was a lot more than that to you and to her, and I'm sorry. But I've gone into court with women with broken bones and bruises like you wouldn't believe all over them, and . . . Well, it doesn't often amount to much jail time."

"So you can't do anything?" Sam roared.

"I'm not saying that. We can get him on breaking and entering. If you want me to, I'll go at him as hard as I can on both. I'm just telling you about an offer the Jacobsons' made."

"What offer?" Sam asked. "To get their kid off?"

"No. Not just that. They've gotten wind of the family connection here, and are thinking you and Emma might not want your brother in jail, Sam. In exchange for us offering probation to their son, they'll agree not to press for charges against your brother."

"You'll let him go?" Emma asked, stunned and hopeful.

"I can't prosecute one without prosecuting the other. It's not like Sam's brother jumped this guy on the street and beat him up. I can't ask a jury to punish Sam's brother for his part in it and ignore what Jacobson did. I'd never win that kind of a case."

Emma smiled for what felt like the first time in days. "So what would happen to Rye?"

"Same thing. Misdemeanor battery and probation. He may have to face a parole hearing in Georgia over it, but basically, if he stays out of trouble from here on out, this is likely all over."

"You'd do that?" Emma asked.

He wouldn't go back to jail then.

Maybe she hadn't ruined his life, after all.

"I'm trying to decide what to do, and as part of that, I'm asking you how you'd feel about that kind of plea bargain for both of them. I know Jacobson hurt you, and I know the idea of him going unpunished would make me furious if I were you or your father."

"Yes," Sam said. "It does."

"But, as I said, I won't prosecute one without the other, and I'll need your testimony to do that. If you get up on the stand and say Sam's brother was just trying to protect you from Jacobson . . . Even if the jury's looking at the damage done to Jacobson's face, the guy broke into your house. You said you thought he might well kill you."

"I did," Emma said.

"I can't see getting a lot of jail time for Jacobson, even if we go breaking and entering and assault. The jury's going to look at pictures of his face after the beating and say the guy's been punished. End of story. But Sam's brother is going to pay big-time if the Jacobsons push this and Georgia decides this is a violation of his parole." Jim threw up his hands. "It doesn't seem fair, but that's where we are. I'm asking you, as the victim here, what you'd like me to do."

"I want it to be over," Emma said.

"Emma, think about this. Mark is going to get away with what he did."

"I don't care," she said, although, honestly, that was a lie. It scared her. But if the price was Rye going free, she'd pay it. "Rye was just trying to help me."

"That's not all he did," Jim argued.

"But he never would have been in that position if it hadn't been for me," she said. "I want you to do it. Let them both go."

*   *   *

Sam was still in shock a few minutes later. He'd sent Emma and Rachel home. Jim sat at his desk watching Sam warily, and Sam was torn, not knowing whether to thank the man or rant and rave at him.

"Look," said Joe, who'd kept quiet through everything so far, "if it helps, I think the Jacobsons know their kid needs help. I found his old girlfriend and the one who came before her. They all tell the same story. He roughed them all up. They're all scared of him. I made a point of telling the Jacobsons they're damned lucky nobody pressed charges before now, and I think they see that. I don't think they'll let this go without getting him some help."

"Emma can't even sleep at night, and you know what it takes to scare Emma." Joe put a hand on Sam's shoulder. Sam shook his head and tried to breathe. "And would somebody tell me there is something fundamentally different about my brother and what he's done, and this kid who's hitting my daughter."

"Your brother doesn't hit women," Joe said. "In fact, he doesn't seem to hit anybody who doesn't hit him first."

"Yeah, but what happens when he gets mad, Joe?"

"Sam, I checked him out. He's been living in the same town in Georgia for almost eight years. The sheriff there hasn't heard so much as a peep out of him."

"He was locked up for almost ten years," Sam said. "That changes someone. And even you were shocked by what Emma's boyfriend looked like when my brother got done with him."

"I was," Joe admitted.

"So as long as nobody jumps him, maybe he'll be okay?"

"I wouldn't turn him loose on my town if I thought he was a walking time bomb," Jim said.

"And another thing," Joe added. "He knew what was happening here. He knew Emma's ex-boyfriend was going to cause trouble, and he knew what trouble could do to him. I was ready to arrest him after Jacobson did that little song and dance and showed off the bruises on his neck, and you know what your brother did? He stayed right here. Told me everything I needed to know to find out all about his record, knowing I probably could have arrested him right then for what he'd already done and that it might well send him back to prison on a parole violation. You know the only thing he asked me?"

"What?" Sam asked.

"He wanted to know whether Emma would be okay if you came back here. Which was him wondering, if he got locked up, who would look out for her? He knew the risk he was taking, and he stayed anyway, Sam. Now to me, that says something about the kind of man he is."

"I hope so," Sam said. "Don't get me wrong. I appreciate what you're trying to do for him. I don't want him in jail for the rest of his life."

"Let's give him a chance," Joe said.

It was more than he'd thought his brother would ever have when he came back here and found his brother in jail. Maybe they could make something of this yet. Maybe everything would be okay.

"Have you talked to Rye about this?"

"Not yet," Jim said. "I wanted to know how you and Emma felt first. I figured there was no sense in getting his hopes up, in case it didn't work."

And then Sam had to ask for one more thing. "Can you make him stay here, as part of the probation deal?"

Joe nodded. "As long as they don't want him back in Georgia, sure."

Sam thanked both of them, staggered by the sense of relief that washed over him. His little brother . . .

"So, that's what we'll do," Jim said, closing the file in front of him. "You want to tell him the news yourself?"

"Yeah, I could do that."

Rye was staring at the walls, wondering if he could take another stint behind bars. He'd thought he was going to die at first, and that he might be happy to do it, given the alternative of life on the inside. He'd railed against everything, the unfairness of it, the shock, the shame.

Then that guy jumped him, and things had gotten so much worse.

If they sent him back . . .

Rye started to sweat. Inside, he was screaming and outwardly, he just shook.

In the midst of that, the door to the cell block opened and in walked his brother.

Rye made himself stand up straight and look the man in the eye, still getting used to the idea that there was someone else who was so like him, so familiar and yet such a stranger. He had about a million questions about their parents, about what life had been like before they died, questions he'd probably never ask. And he felt the need to make a lot of excuses and apologies for the way he'd ended up. How ridiculous was that? None of it would do any good.

He also really didn't want any more scenes like this one, him on this side of the bars, Sam on the other.

Maybe this would be it—the big good-bye, nice-knowing-you, please-stay-the-hell-out-of-my-town speech before they shipped Rye out of here. They should have taken him to the regional jail days ago, not that it really mattered. He knew where it was going to end—with him behind another set of bars.

"What's wrong now?" he asked finally, when Sam didn't say a word.

"I was just wondering if you're ready to get out of here."

"Sure." He was up for anything, as long as it put some miles between him and Sam. "Where am I going? County jail? Or back to prison in Georgia?"

"Neither one. Joe and the county attorney are about to make you an offer you can't refuse. They're going to let you go."

"Yeah, right." He laughed at the idea.

Sam didn't. "They are. Misdemeanor and a year's probation."

Rye couldn't quite breathe for a moment. He had a flash of how it had felt that day when the prison doctor had gotten done stitching up his side, and one of the guards had walked in and told him the guy who attacked him, the one Rye had beaten senseless, was dead.

For a long time, it was like Rye was, too. Even after he'd gotten out, he couldn't quite believe the nightmare was over, that he was free. Maybe he'd always known it wouldn't last, that nothing ever really did. Maybe he'd been preparing himself all along for the day he went back inside. He hadn't been all that surprised to find himself back here.

And he couldn't quite believe what he was hearing now.

They were letting him go?

Finally, he managed one word. "Why?"

"Plea bargain," Sam said.

"What does that mean?"

"You know . . . where they cut a deal—"

"I know what a plea bargain is," he cut in. "I just can't imagine anybody offering me one like that."

Sam shrugged. "Joe's a friend."

"Of yours, not of mine."

"You're my little brother," he said.

As if that mattered? He wasn't sure if the relationship meant anything to Sam, and why it might mean anything to the sheriff or anyone else in this town, he didn't understand. He and his brother had seen each other three times now in the past thirty years or so. They didn't know shit about each other.

"You must have some serious pull in this town if you can make something like this go away," Rye said. "I thought you just restored houses."

"I do, and I didn't pull any strings. I would have tried, if I thought it would do any good. But I never expected anything like this, either."

It was still too much to take in. He kept looking for reasons this would never work. "Sure you want me loose on your town?"

"I don't want you locked up, Robbie."

Rye just looked at him. Hearing Sam call him Robbie like that was like taking a kick in the gut every time. Who the hell was Robbie? He really didn't know. He never would.

"Sorry," Sam said. "It's going to take some time for me to get used to the new name."

"It's not like I'm in a position to complain about anything right now." Rye took a breath and let it out slow. "So, these friends of yours . . . They're just doing you a favor?"

"They're trying to be fair. They know what's at stake for you. A felony conviction, and you'll probably go back to prison on the manslaughter charge. I suspect they're thinking of Emma, too. She told you about how she and Zach and Grace came to me and Rachel?''

"She said her father liked to hit her mother."

"He did. She'd left him but a couple of years later, she was sick and desperate to find someone to take care of her kids. She was going back to her hometown to ask a relative for help, but was scared to take the kids anywhere near her ex, so she left them in a motel here. They'd been there for three days before anybody found them. Grace was a year old, Zach was five, Emma was not quite twelve. It was right before Christmas seven years ago. Rachel and I have had them ever since. We finally found their mother two weeks later in a hospital in Indiana. Her ex-husband had beaten her up and left her for dead. She'd been in a coma the whole time. Three months later, she *was* dead."

Not a very pretty story, Emma had told Rye. He remembered thinking she had old eyes, that she understood him so well. All those dark places . . . She'd been there, too.

"Anyway," Sam said, clearing his throat. "People in this town know what Emma's been through. I don't think the county attorney liked his chances of getting a jury in this town to convict you of anything to do with keeping that guy from hurting Emma. So they're letting you go. Hopefully this won't mess up the parole situation in Georgia."

"I can't believe it." It was starting to sink in. The room started spinning for a moment. He leaned back against the wall, needing the support.

"I know." Sam dug into his pockets and came up with a key, which he fit into the lock on Rye's cell door. "Maybe this'll help."

Honestly, it didn't. Sam pulled open the door, but Rye couldn't bring himself to step through the opening.

Then he thought of something else. "What about Emma's ex-boyfriend?"

Sam looked wary. "He's gonna walk, too."

"No. No way."

"It's part of the deal."

"You mean, if I walk, he walks, too?"

Sam nodded, his mouth stretched into a grim line.

"What about Emma? She's scared to death of the guy."

"She's already agreed to it."

"Shit. For me? She did this so that I can get out of here?"

"Yeah."

Rye threw back his head and wanted to scream. At her and his brother. The sheriff and the county attorney and the whole friggin' world. "You can't let them do this. She shouldn't have to put up with that bastard being loose on the streets."

"I'm not crazy about it, either, but it's already done."

"Well, undo it."

"Look," Sam said. "The only reason the Jacobson kid isn't pressing for assault charges against you is because he wants to save his own butt."

"I'm sure he does, but I can't ask Emma to do this for me."

"You didn't. Joe, the county attorney, and the Jacobsons' attorney did."

"Well it's dead wrong," he said.

"Yeah, it is. But the truth is, Emma couldn't stand it if you went to prison for this. You said it yourself—she feels guilty about drawing you into this."

"It's not her fault. I told her that."

"So did I, but I know her. There's nothing either one of us could say to make her feel any differently," Sam argued. "It's who she is. She feels responsible for people, and she takes care of them. It started with her brother and sister, probably even before that with her own mother. She even tries to take care of Rachel and me. Now she thinks this mess with you and her ex-boyfriend is her fault. It would haunt her, every day you spent behind bars. She won't be able to let it go until you're free."

"But her crazy boyfriend will still be on the streets. I saw her when he was out. She was afraid to pick up the phone, afraid to open the front door."

"He'll stay away from her or he'll go to jail. There's a restraining order as part of the deal, and Joe will enforce it."

"She couldn't even sleep at night for dreaming about him coming to get her," he argued.

"Robbie, she's my daughter. I'll take care of her now."

Robbie.

There it was again. It stopped him cold. He had to convince Sam that Robbie was gone, and he wasn't coming back.

But this wasn't about that lost kid. This was about Emma. Rye couldn't tell if Sam resented him because Emma, when she'd needed help, had turned to him, or if Sam was just mad because Rye had screwed up the situation so badly.

He still worried about her, even if he didn't have the right. Sam, the father, was clearly telling him that if Emma needed taking care of in the future, *he* would handle it. Rye barely stopped himself from telling Sam he'd damned well better handle it.

"Come on," Sam said. "You've spent enough time here. Let's go."

The sheriff and the county attorney outlined the deal for him. He was fine with everything, except that he had to stay here during his year's probation. Not that he was in a position to argue. They explained that there would be court papers to sign, and an appearance before a judge to finalize everything. But basically, they were letting him go.

"We'll need to know where you'll be staying," Joe said, as Rye stood up.

"He'll stay with Rachel and me," Sam said.

Rye just looked at him. He had no intention of doing that. Sam took a breath. His jaw went tight. Did he think they were going to be one big, happy family now?

"Didn't Tim Davison move in with Mollie Grainger a couple of weeks ago?" Joe asked.

"Yeah, I think I heard something about that," Sam said. "His ex sure wasn't happy about that."

"He was living in that room over Rick Stephenson's garage. Why don't you give him a call? It's not much, but . . ."

"It doesn't have to be," Rye said.

"Just let us know where you end up," Jim said. "You'll need a job, too."

"That's it?" Rye asked.

"Until we have a court date. We'll let you know."

Rye held out his hand to both the county attorney and the sheriff. "Thanks. For everything."

Joe said, "Just don't make us sorry about this."

"I won't."

He and Sam walked out the door together.

It was the middle of the afternoon, clear and cold, the sun glinting off the thin layer of snow on the ground. The air was crisp and cold. It stung his cheeks, burned a bit as he drew it deeply into his lungs.

It was hard for him to breathe indoors sometimes, even when he wasn't inside a cell. Just an enclosed room could do that to him, just the idea that he was trapped inside, unable to get out. It had taken him years to get over that sick, claustrophobic feeling.

Right then, he felt weak and dizzy with relief at the thought of standing at the top of the steps, outside in the bright December sunshine.

"You okay?" Sam called out from the sidewalk below.

"Yeah," Rye said, wondering how long he'd been standing there, how long Sam had been staring at him.

"You're welcome to stay at the house for as long as you like, or in the carriage house, if that's what you want," Sam said.

Rye shook his head. "I can get my own place."

"Okay." Sam nodded in the direction of a big red Suburban parked by the curb. "I've got a cell phone in the truck. We can call Rick, see if he's rented that room, if you like."

Rye walked down the steps and couldn't quite look at his brother once again. "You know, you don't have to do this."

"Help you find a place to stay?"

"Any of this."

Sam looked honestly surprised. "Did you think I'd just walk away?"

"I didn't know what you'd do." Not when he'd come here to find Sam and certainly not now. He'd been kind of hoping they could get to know each other a little before he sprung the whole ugly picture of his past on Sam.

"Robbie . . ." Sam's voice trailed off. He looked like it was pulling teeth to get the words out. "Sorry. I didn't want to leave you there with the Ryans. Nobody gave me a choice in the matter. But I've never forgotten you. I've asked myself a million times whether I was right or wrong to walk away without telling you who I was eighteen years ago, and I still don't know the answer to that. But there's not a day that's gone by since then, that I haven't wondered where you were or what you were doing. When I haven't thought about going to find you again."

"But you didn't," Rye said.

"Neither did you," Sam pointed out. "Not until now. You've known for what? Almost eighteen years? Look, I just didn't want to screw up your life, okay?"

Rye laughed at that. "I sure didn't need any help doing that."

"Mine hasn't exactly been a prime example to follow."

"Ever kill anybody? Ever been to prison?" Sam just stared at him. "Look, I'm ᐟsorry I can't just leave, okay? We're both stuck in the same town for a while. I can't change that. But you don't owe me anything, and I sure don't expect anything from you."

"Then why'd you come here in the first place?" Sam asked.

Shit. "I don't know."

What was there to say after that?

He couldn't change a damned thing.

"Come on," Sam said. "We'll call Rick. I'll take you over to meet him, if you like. We'll get your truck and your things from the house, and then you can do whatever you want."

Rick did indeed have a room to rent. It wasn't much, a place to sleep, place to wash up. But then, it was bigger than any cell Rye had ever been in. It looked just fine to him. He struck a deal with Rick on the rent, and Rick said he could move in that day. Then they drove to Sam's house to pick up his truck and his things.

They got there, and a pretty blonde woman came out onto the front porch. She gave Sam a beautiful smile. Tears glistened in her eyes as Sam introduced them. Rye nodded politely and couldn't quite imagine his stern-faced big brother with someone as open and gentle as her.

She ignored the hand Rye extended to her and wrapped her arms around him tightly instead, squeezing hard and reminding him of Emma.

"I can't believe I finally get to meet you." She stepped back, beaming up at him. "We moved your things into the back bedroom. It's as out of the way as things get around here, so it should be fairly quiet, even once the kids get back."

"Rachel, he's not going to stay here," Sam said.

"Oh . . ." She looked from one man to the other, obviously wanting to protest, but fighting the impulse. "Well . . . whatever you want."

"I appreciate the offer," he said.

"And I'm so thankful that you were here when Emma needed you." She did start to cry then. "I can't help but think of what might have happened, and . . . Well, we couldn't bear to lose her."

Rye wasn't quite sure how he was going to manage without her himself.

"She's a great kid," he said, because she was as lost to him as any female possibly could be. He had to both remind himself of that and reassure Sam and Rachel that he was very much aware of the fact that Emma was just a kid.

"Where is she?" Sam asked.

"Dozing on the sofa in the family room." Rachel looked to Rye and explained, "She hasn't been sleeping well at night."

Rye certainly knew that.

"I should get going," he said, wanting to be gone before she woke up. "If you don't mind, I'll just get my things."

Rachel looked like she might well argue about him going. Could she really want him to stay? In her house? With her kids? Surely the past few days had proven that they really didn't know him. What did a blood tie really amount to when two people were strangers?

"Come on," Sam said, leading Rye into the house.

Rachel followed, offering to pack his things for him, but he declined her offer. So she directed him to a bedroom upstairs at the far end of the hall.

He scarcely let himself glance into the rooms. It all looked so ordinary, much like the place where he'd grown up. Grace's room was hot pink and filled with stuffed animals and what looked to be leftovers from the seventies, a decade he understood was in the middle of a comeback. Zach's room was plainer, with none of that fuss, just about three-dozen sports trophies. Looked like he was a ball player, baseball and basketball.

Emma's room . . .

God, he thought, *don't even look into Emma's room.*

But this had to be it. Soft and romantic looking, the walls a rich, creamy, soft butter color and the bed . . . *Damn.* It was made of swirling iron, washed in that same creamy color, four posts nearly touching the ceiling and draped in gauzy fabric in the palest of lavenders that matched the sheer curtains.

He really didn't need to have a picture in his head of Emma in her bed, but damned if it wasn't right there now that he'd seen her room.

Rye walked into the last door on the right and saw that Rachel had indeed intended to make him feel at home. She'd put fresh flowers here, and the room smelled faintly of cinnamon, warm and inviting. Like he was an honored guest.

No way he was staying here.

He threw things into his bag, had very nearly made good his escape when he heard footsteps coming down the hallway.

He turned around and there was Emma.

Chapter 14

She stood in the doorway wearing a soft pink sweater and a pair of blue jeans that lovingly followed every curve of her eighteen-year-old derriere. Her whole face lit up with a smile, and then she threw herself into his arms.

Rye had no choice but to catch her.

"You're free." She wrapped her arms around him, buried her face against his neck.

For a minute, he couldn't do anything except breathe in the scent of her, the sweet hint of vanilla and warm woman-child. He hadn't thought to ever have her in his arms again, and he shouldn't even want that, not now that he knew her little secret. But she'd gotten under his skin.

He was dismayed to learn that it wasn't enough— knowing how impossibly young she was—to stop him from remembering the way it had been between them. How sweet it was, how soft she was, how good she smelled, the distinct pleasure of holding her close and kissing her soft lips.

Damn.

He really hadn't expected to have to fight this particular battle anymore, thought whatever was between them would have magically disappeared, like smoke dissipating into thin air.

"Emma?" He set her firmly away from him and stepped back.

Eighteen, he told himself, trying to construct a huge blinking, neon sign in his mind and superimposing it over her image. *Eighteen. Eighteen.*

It wasn't quite doing the job.

He was so happy to see her.

"You okay?" he asked.

Tears swirled up in her eyes, but she smiled and nodded. "Are you?"

He nodded, then wanted to growl at her. "They told me what you did. You shouldn't have, Emma."

"What? I should have let you go back to prison? I couldn't do that. I couldn't have stood it."

Sam was right about that part. She never would have been able to put this behind her if he was locked up. Still . . . "I know how much that guy scares you."

"He's in the hospital." she shrugged. "They're still trying to pretty up his face, and when they're done, he won't be anywhere near here."

"You're still going to be scared," he said.

"For a while." She was too honest to lie about something like that. "But I'll get over it, and I've got Sam and Rachel and . . . What about you? Do I still have you?"

"Emma," he protested.

She stared at the suitcase on the bed, nearly full of his things. All the light went out of her eyes. "You're not staying?"

"Not here, but I have to stay in town." *Away from you.* He'd have thought that wouldn't be hard at all, but saw now that he was wrong.

It wasn't that he wanted anything to do with an eighteen-year-old girl. He just wanted the woman he'd thought she was, all that hope and understanding, her all-knowing eyes. What had happened to that woman? Where had she gone?

Sometimes he thought he must have made the whole thing up, that the things he remembered couldn't possibly have happened between him and Sam's little girl. But here she was, looking so innocent and yet so hurt. God, he didn't want to hurt her or for anyone else to ever hurt her.

"I want you to be careful, Em. I don't care where you think that jerk is."

"I will. Rachel and I are going to take self-defense classes at the Y. Sam said if I knew where to hit and how, I could hurt just about anyone."

"You could." Rye could teach her a thing or two about how to hurt somebody in a fight. He'd learned the hard way. "Still, promise me you'll be careful."

She lifted her chin and smiled at him. "You do care about me."

Oh, hell. "I told you, I don't want anything to happen to you."

"That's part of it."

"No, that's it," he insisted, backing up a step.

"If you say so," she said, but by her tone, she might as well have come right out and called him a liar.

He decided retreat was his only answer. "I have to go."

He zipped up his bag, took one more look around the room, and when he turned around, she was right there, wrapping her arms around him once again. She just never learned, he thought. This really had to stop.

"Emma—"

She hung on tight. "I'll never forget what you did for me."

"Forget it, please."

"No, I won't."

He closed his eyes and hugged her close, in spite of himself. "Emma, I killed somebody. That's got to mean something to you. That you should stay the hell away from me, at the very least."

"No." She backed up enough to look him in the eye, looking as sure of herself as he'd ever seen her. "That's not what it means."

"I almost hit you," Rye said, firmly pushing her away. "You know that, don't you? It's like a fog comes over me in a fight like that. All I know is that someone's after me, and I've got to be tougher than they are, or I might end up dead. It was true when I was in prison, but I'm not in prison now. I was in your living room, and I nearly hurt you before I figured out who you were."

"But you didn't hurt me," she insisted. God, she had to be the most stubborn woman alive.

"I scared you half to death. I know that."

"Yes, it scared me. But you know what? Lots of things in my life have scared me. I've come through them all. And I'm not scared of you. I know you would never hurt me."

He wished he could believe that. Not that it mattered. He wouldn't be anywhere near her. "Just be careful, okay? Promise me that?"

"You sound like I'm never going to see you again."

He shrugged, carefully trying to keep his distance. "It's a small town. I'm sure we'll run into each other from time to time."

"But you and Sam . . . You're his brother."

"I know, Emma."

"Did you two have a fight?"

"No."

"Over me?" She drifted closer.

"No." What was there to fight about? She was eighteen.

"You promised me you'd give him a chance."

"I've got a whole year. I'm sure I'll run into him, too." Who knew what might happen then? He hadn't thought much about it. He hadn't had many second chances in his life.

"I'm glad you have to stay."

She reached out and put her hands on his shoulders, lightly. They fluttered against the muscles at the top of his arms, and before he could protest, she was coming closer still.

It wasn't such an inappropriate kiss, just a feather-soft touch. It was everything that had come before that made it decidedly inappropriate. It was him remembering and wanting her back, the Emma who couldn't possibly be eighteen. The good girl who made him wish he could be a good guy. The woman who constantly had her hands all over him.

Again, he thought, where exactly had she gone? That woman had been here with him just a few days ago. He knew what they'd shared, cursed himself for showing so little restraint in that time, yet was profoundly grateful for what restraint he'd mustered. When he thought of what might have happened . . .

Rye took her by the arms and pushed her firmly away.

She gave him a downright wicked grin that said she knew exactly what he'd been thinking.

There was a sound from the hallway. They both looked up in the same instant and saw Sam.

Emma went completely still, as did he. Sam glared at them both. Emma started to say something. Rye could have told her she was wasting her breath. Obviously, there was no reasoning with Sam at this moment.

A moment later, Sam sent her away. Rye gathered his bag, walked downstairs, and said good-bye to Rachel. He thanked her once again for the offer to let him stay and made a noncommittal reply to her assumption that as part of the family he would of course spend Christmas with them.

Sam followed him every step of the way. Outside, in the driveway, as far as they could get from the house, Rye turned around and waited, thinking it would be a fine thing to get into a fight on the day he got out of jail. He might be going right back. Not that he had any intention of fighting Sam. But he wasn't sure what Sam was going to do, and as he'd told Emma, he wasn't quite rational when it came to people hitting him. A man in prison learned to fight back or else.

"We've got a problem," Sam said. "She thinks she's in love with you."

Rye tried not to think about that. *Emma loving him.* About how that might feel under any other circumstances. The circumstances were what they were. She was much too young. She didn't really know him. She was never really going to know him, because they were done.

"I don't want to hurt her feelings," Rye said.

"You may have to, because she can't go on thinking there's going to be anything between the two of you."

Rye swore softly. "Okay, I'll do it."

He'd hurt her.

Dammit.

"Soon," Sam said. "And I don't want you alone with her."

"Fine," he said.

He'd break her heart in public, if that's the way it had to be.

*   *   *

Rye made a quick trip to Georgia, sublet his apartment, packed his things, and told the contractors he worked with regularly that he was leaving.

He was back in Baxter before Christmas, spent Christmas eve in blessed solitude, but let his brother's wife somehow convince him to come by Christmas day for what she said was an informal open house with family and friends dropping by all day.

Rye parked a block away, found cars practically crawling all over the house, men standing on the front porch smoking, kids all bundled up in their coats and hats, playing in the snow. It looked like half the town was there, and he had second thoughts about coming. How was this supposed to work exactly? Him being part of this family but staying away from Emma? It was more her family than his.

He made his way down the front walk and onto the porch, where a white-haired man in his fifties with a noticeable limp came forward to shake his hand.

"You must be Sam's brother. I'm George Phelps. I own the drug store on Main," he said. "Merry Christmas. Welcome to Baxter."

"Thank you," Rye said.

He shook four more hands, then rang the doorbell. Rachel answered it, looking festive and very happy. She pulled him inside and gave him a big hug and then a kiss on the cheek. Maybe this was where Emma picked up that particular habit.

"Merry Christmas," she said. "I was afraid you weren't coming."

"I almost didn't," he admitted.

She frowned at him. "We would have come looking for you, you know."

"Then I guess it's a good thing I came on my own."

"Yes, it is. Come meet my family."

She slipped her arm through his and led him from

person to person, neighbors and relatives alike. He couldn't begin to keep all the names straight, just smiled and nodded. It seemed any brother of Sam's or defender of Emma's was welcome, regardless of his checkered past.

The house glowed with the light of dozens of candles, fires blazing in the fireplaces. Christmas music was piped in from the stereo in the family room in back. Food was everywhere, as was laughter and conversation.

"I know it's a bit overwhelming at first," Rachel said, when they stopped in the kitchen long enough for her to check on something in the oven.

It was. He wasn't planning on staying long.

"The last time I saw Sam he was in the backyard with my father, but this . . ." She snagged the arm of a teenage boy passing by. "Hey, wait a minute. What about me?"

"Sorry, Mom," the boy said, grinning as he turned to face Rye, seeming perfectly at ease having his mother with her arm around him, even in public, surprising for a kid who looked to be twelve or thirteen.

"This is our son, Zach. Zach, this is Rye."

"Hi," the overgrown boy said. He was taller than Rachel, with long, lanky arms and legs, baggy pants, and huge feet. Around the eyes, he looked a little like Emma.

"Hi," Rye said.

"Thanks for taking care of my sister."

"Sure."

"Guess I'll be seein' you around."

Rye nodded. Zach sauntered off into the midst of the chaos in the dining room, sliding up next to another overgrown boy with the same baggy pants, a big T-shirt with a peace symbol on the back of it, his hair mussed and sticking up every which way.

Rachel rolled her eyes and grinned. "I feel ancient these days. Emma and I went through boxes of things in the attic last year trying to find my old bell-bottoms and tie-dyed T-shirts. They're in again."

"Yeah, I noticed." Emma's generation was wearing them. If that was a subtle way of pointing out the age difference between them, Rye could tell her it wasn't necessary. He was very much aware of it.

The back door opened, and someone shrieked. He turned around to find his brother standing there with a little girl flung over his shoulders. She was laughing as he set her on her feet. Sam stood up straight, smiling. Rye hadn't seen him do that before.

"This is our daughter, Grace," Rachel said.

The girl leaned in close to Sam's side. Her cheeks were pink from the cold. She had the biggest blue eyes he'd ever seen, thick soot-colored lashes, and long, blonde hair. She had on a bright red sweater and a Santa hat, which she'd somehow managed to hang on to while she'd been hanging over Sam's shoulder.

Sam put an arm around her and said, "Grace, this is my brother."

"Hi." She beamed up at Rye.

"Hi," he said, deciding this must be like looking at Emma so long ago. He felt a little hitch in the region of his gut that he didn't like at all. Maybe Emma before all the bad things, or Emma if none of the bad things had ever happened.

What had she said? That her brother hardly remembered any of the bad times and her sister had escaped them altogether? Yeah, he could see that. There was an openness and a sheer joy to this girl he didn't think Emma had ever known, and he wished she had.

"We've been waiting for you," Grace confided.

"You have?"

"Yes. For the ornaments."

"Ornaments?"

"Tradition," Rachel said, taking him by the arm again. "You guys round everyone up for me, okay? We have to do this now, because Ellen and Bill have to get to Bill's parents' house soon."

"Do what?" Rye asked.

"Finish the tree."

She took him into the living room next to the big tree, where the decorations did seem a bit scarce. Still, it was nearly two o'clock Christmas day. It seemed a bit late to be decorating.

"Don't go anywhere," Rachel said. "I just need to make sure we have everyone."

Everyone turned out to be about fifty people who eventually gathered around the tree. Two older women pulled out stacks of thin, rectangular white boxes, which he thought he remembered from foraging in the basement himself.

"Hi." Emma came up beside him, slipped her hand through his, letting it rest in the crook of his elbow, and kissed his cheek. "Merry Christmas."

Rye looked up just in time to see Sam frown at them. He let himself glance at her ever so briefly, just long enough to take in the cream-colored sweater she wore and the tiny little skirt. He didn't dare so much as glance at the expanse of legs showing beneath it.

Maybe he really was a dirty old man in the making.

She had her hair pulled back in a neat little twist, diamond studs in her ears. Her bruises were all gone, and there was a hint of color in her cheeks, a pretty smile on her lips.

"Merry Christmas, Em," he said, knowing he shouldn't even be this close.

"Did you meet everybody?"

"How would you ever know in this crowd?" he asked.

"I know. It's crazy, even when it's just family. Did you meet Zach and Grace, at least? Zach's right there in the corner. The tall one. And Grace is right there." Emma pointed to the spot next to the fireplace, Grace sitting on the floor with her knees drawn up to her chest and giggling with another little girl about her age. "Isn't she beautiful?"

"She looks like you," Rye said, without even stopping to think that was a bad idea. But the child was beautiful, and Emma was, too.

Emma looked up at him, a faint sheen of tears in her eyes. "Thank you."

He didn't think she'd ever cried because she was happy, at least not around him, and hell, she had to know she was beautiful. No way she could be unaware of that. He was merely stating the obvious.

And this was all such a bad idea.

"Brace yourself," she said. "This always gets to me."

"What does?" he asked, as a man who looked to be in his sixties took center stage beside the tree, everyone gathering around him.

"You'll see," she said, still holding on to his arm, still too close.

The man turned out to be Rachel's father. Her aunts gathered around him holding the boxes, which contained the ornaments, three-dimensional stars made of beveled glass. He held the first one out to one of Rachel's aunts. It spun around on its string, the bevels in the glass catching the light from the candles, glints of light coming off the little star.

With great reverence, he called names one by one, family member after family member, each of them coming forward to put his or her ornament on the tree. There was laughter and lots of hugging going on, tears shed over family members who weren't with them and those who'd passed away.

Rye stood there with a huge lump in his throat as he watched Sam and Rachel put their ornaments on the tree, then Emma slipped away from him long enough to hang hers. Zach and Grace were next, and then Rachel's father looked at Rye and held out one to him.

He felt all eyes turn to him, couldn't have begun to figure out what the man said. Emma squeezed his arm, urging him on. He looked from Sam to her then back to his brother once again.

Sam took the little star himself and brought it to Rye. He turned it this way and that in his hand, seeing his name etched into the side and the year.

They were welcoming him into the family.

He felt his throat close up, felt like he couldn't breathe.

"Go on." Emma squeezed his arm. "Put it on the tree."

He did it, somehow without dropping the thing and breaking it, somehow hanging on to the merest threads of his composure. No one had welcomed him anywhere in the longest of times. He'd never expected this here. Not now. Not once they all knew . . .

Surely they knew. It was a small town. No way to keep anything quiet, especially a thing so public as what had happened to Emma. Hell, they'd thanked him for taking care of her. They knew.

Rachel gave him another hug, beaming at him. Her father shook his hand. Her aunts hugged him. For a while, they passed him down a line of waiting relatives, smiling, hugging, kissing, slapping him on the back.

Grace was at the end of the line. She tugged on his hand until he leaned down far enough that she could give him a little butterfly kiss, so light it felt like a whisper against his cheek.

When he stood up, Emma was standing in front of him, tears streaming down her cheeks.

"She always cries when we do this," Grace confided, slipping her hand into Rye's and looking up at the tree. "Isn't it beautiful?"

Rye nodded.

If he could have moved a muscle, he'd have fled long ago. But they'd floored him with this. He fought for every breath he took, his chest all tight, and he looked at Emma, begging her with his eyes to save him.

She took him by his other hand, telling Grace, "Can I borrow him for a minute? I need to show him something outside."

"Okay." Grace frowned but let him go.

He let Emma lead him through the crowd, desperate to get away. They went through the kitchen and into a little utility room where there were dozens of coats piled on the washer and dryer.

"Just grab one," she said. "We'll come back in a minute."

He did, shoving his arms into a dark blue coat.

She opened up the door, and he followed her outside to the porch, where he leaned against one of the support columns and took in great gulps of the crisp, cold air.

Jesus, what was that?

What did they think they were doing?

He'd had this, years ago, had a family that looked much like this. Except it had all been an illusion, blown away like so much dust on a hot summer's day. He fished in his pocket for his keys, thinking he'd just get in his truck and go. But this wasn't his coat, dammit, and he didn't have his keys.

Emma slipped her hand into the pocket, her fingers curling around his, her touch calming him down a little bit, making him not so desperate to run.

"I remember the first year we came here," she said, wiping away tears with her other hand. "It was Christmas, seemed like ages since I'd seen my mother, and I'd told myself if we could just hang on until Christmas day, she'd be back. I was counting on a Christmas miracle."

"And you found her, right?" he said.

"Sam found her, just not quite the way we expected. She was dying. She didn't tell us until a week later, but I knew it when I saw her that Christmas day. I think I knew it before we even came here. There's an ornament on the tree for her. We put it up on Christmas eve, when it's just the five of us, so it's like she's here in a way, and she knows Zach and Grace and I are fine. I believe that."

"No doubts?" Rye asked, amazed at that kind of faith.

"None, but I had a lot that first Christmas. It wasn't until late in the afternoon that they found her. Christmas eve, Christmas morning, most of the day, I spent thinking that was it. If she wasn't back by then, she wasn't coming back. I didn't know what would happen to us. Sam and Rachel said we could stay with them for as long as it took, but we really didn't know them, and it was hard to believe after everything we'd been through that anything could ever work out for us."

"What happened, Emma?"

"We had a Christmas like this, in this house, decked out in all twelve boxes of decorations, just for the outside, and as many or more for the inside. It smelled like Christmas and looked like Christmas. We were warm and had plenty to eat and were safe. They had piles of presents under the tree, and all these people. I was starting to think this might be okay, and then they pulled out those ornaments, sprung them on us just like they sprung them on you."

"And what did you do?" She would have faced this at twelve. Even then, she'd probably handled it better than he had.

"I just wanted to run away, as far and as fast as I could. Because I knew what it meant. They'd already opened up their home to us, and now they were making us a part of them in a way we'd never been a part of anything before. I wanted that almost as much as I wanted my mother back. But when security is something you've never had, it's hard to trust that anything will ever really last."

Yeah, she knows all right.

"Part of me wanted them to grab me and hold on to me until I felt safe again, and part of me just wanted to run. I wanted to yell at them, to tell them they'd better not offer me anything unless they were sure they meant it. That they'd better not ever try to take it back, because I'd lost too much already. I didn't think I could stand to lose one more thing."

She still had tears in her eyes. They were running down her cheeks. He turned to her and brushed them away. "Emma."

"They mean it. You're one of them now. They're not going to forget. They're not going to change their minds, and you can't run away, Rye. Sam couldn't stand that."

"Sam's not too happy with me right now," he said.

"Because of me. I know, and I'm sorry. I know he told you to stay away from me—"

"Wait a minute. I don't need Sam to tell me what I already know, Emma. I know what's right and what's wrong, even if I don't always do the right thing. And this is wrong."

"Is it? What's age anyway? It's a number, that's all."

"No, it's years and years of living," he said, drawing away from her. "Damn, I don't want to do this. Not today. Not when you've been . . . Emma . . ." She truly was amazing, and she did understand him, maybe better than anyone ever had. What was he supposed to do about that?

But he knew. Dammit, he knew.

He had to make it clear to her that he didn't want anything to do with her. Otherwise, she'd keep hoping. She'd keep putting her hands on him and kissing him and understanding way too much about him. Sam would be furious and Rye would be tempted, even knowing how young she was.

So this had to stop.

If it hurt for now, it just had to hurt. At least it would be over.

"Emma, I don't know how I would have gotten through today or any day since I came here without you, and I mean that. I'm grateful for it. You're sweet and so kind, but . . . Emma"—he looked her right in the eye—"You're just a kid."

She blinked up at him, seeming frozen in time for a moment. She cocked her head to the right. Her mouth came open, but she didn't say anything, just looked at him, those old eyes of hers getting bigger and bigger, then flooding with tears.

"You don't mean that," she said.

"I do. You just got out of high school, Emma. You just went to the prom. I guess you've gotten some crazy idea that it doesn't matter, but it does. I don't run around with teenage girls."

"No, it's Sam. Sam made you say that."

"Sam doesn't tell me what to do. I'm a grown man. Nobody tells me what to do," he said, then thought to add, "except my parole officer."

"Don't be like this," she begged.

"I'm sorry," he said. "I really don't want to hurt you. But you've got to see the truth in this. It's part of growing up, Emma, and you've got a lot of growing up ahead of you."

"Me?" she scoffed. "Who do you think you're talking to? I've never been young. I never had the chance until I came here, and by then, honestly, it was just too late. I'm the oldest eighteen-year-old you'll ever meet."

"Maybe so. But you want things from me. I know you do. You've got this crazy idea that you and me . . . Emma, girls your age fall in love once a week. Believe me, you'll get over it."

She gaped at him. "And you don't feel anything for me?"

"I told you." He gritted his teeth and kept going. "You're a sweet kid."

She closed her eyes and hung her head for a moment. He heard her take one long, ragged breath, and when she lifted her head she somehow managed not to cry. He felt like he'd drop-kicked a kitten, and it had come running back to him, dammit, like it just hadn't understood the first time.

Well, he couldn't do it again.

"Emma, I never wanted to hurt you."

"Really?"

"No, I didn't."

She looked at him, her shoulders heaving, her expression crumbling for a moment before she took off through the backyard. He thought of going after her, thought of begging her to forgive him, even if that would just make things worse. But he had to tell her these things. It was the right damned thing to do.

So why did he feel like the lowest creature on earth?

Emma hid in her room. Sometimes she cried. Sometimes she stared at the ceiling. Sometimes she dreamed. Mark was back, swinging the shovel at her. Except in her dream, nobody stopped him. The shovel crashed into the side of her face. She fell to the floor, and when she looked up Rye was standing over her saying, "You're a sweet kid, Emma."

After days of this, she was disgusted with herself. Life went on, after all, and she was alive, though one would hardly know that by how she'd spent the past few days.

She went downstairs, congratulating herself for that monumental move from one floor of her own home to another, not looking at the living room, where *it* had happened. Not looking at the front door, because it made her think of going outside, which she did not want to do. How long could she stay inside before someone noticed and carted her off to a shrink? she wondered.

She looked out the front window. It wasn't quite daybreak and there looked to be a crisp, clear one on the way. She wandered through the downstairs, startled at first to hear voices coming from the kitchen. Really, it was ridiculous how much that scared her.

But it was just Sam and Rachel. Both of them were early risers.

She was afraid they might be talking about her, so she didn't say anything at first. Then she realized they were talking about Rye. She eavesdropped shamelessly.

"Did you ask him?" Rachel said.

"Yeah. He turned me down again."

"Keep after him. He'll come around."

"I hope so," Sam said.

So he was keeping himself away because she was here.

Emma stood there, slumped against the wall, her head leaning back against it. All he'd wanted when he came here was to find Sam, and she'd messed that all up. He might stay away as long as things were awkward between them, and she didn't see it getting better anytime soon.

Which meant this was her mess to fix once again.

It was time for her to get her life back together, time to start acting like the woman she was, not this scared, spineless mess she'd become.

She'd make a list. She was so good at that.

A Get Emma Out of This Mess List. Get on with her life. Grow up. That's what he'd said she had to do.

It really wasn't hard, now that she'd become so disgusted with her own behavior. Especially not since she knew what she had to do. Get her life back. Get out of the way of Sam and Rye. She made a list and started crossing things off one by one. By the next afternoon, things were falling into place in a way that told her she'd done the right thing, that this was all meant to be. There was only one more thing to take care of—facing him.

She had enough pride left that she dressed for the event, fussed with her hair, put on a short skirt that rode low on her waist and a skinny sweater that left a solid inch and a half of her midriff bare.

Let him think of her as a sweet kid, if he could.

She added her favorite boots that gave her an extra two-and-a-half inches, the pretty diamond earrings Sam and Rachel had given her for graduation, and told herself no one would guess that she spent the better part of three days crying in her room.

Fifteen minutes later, she was knocking on Rye's door.

He frowned when he opened it and found her there.

"Are you going to let me in? Or should I stand here a little bit longer until someone sees me going into your apartment?" she asked, not in the mood to have to argue about getting in the door.

"Emma, what is it?" He sounded more weary than he had in his jail cell.

"I just wanted you to know I'm leaving," she said, holding her head high.

He stepped back and let her inside. "Back to Chicago?"

"No. I can't do that," she admitted, looking around the place. It was tiny, clean but dingy, drab, colorless. She supposed it was better than a cell, but she hated the idea of him living like this. Not that her opinion mattered to him. And she had things to say to him. "Mark lives two hours from there. His parents told Sam he's skipping spring semester at least and may never go back, but I can't go, either. I guess I am a coward. But . . . It all started there, and it's a long way from home."

"You're not a coward." His poker face was gone for a moment, and he looked worried. "And you don't have to go back there. You don't have to do anything right now."

"Yes, I do." He hadn't asked her to sit down or even offered to take her coat. Fine. They could do it this way, get it over with. She really only came to talk. "I'm transferring to UC."

"Where?"

"The University of Cincinnati. I almost went there in the first place, but I got this idea in my head that

I wanted to be on my own and farther away. . . .
Chicago sounded so big and so different." What a
mistake that had turned out to be. "They still had my
transcripts, test scores, application, all that, which
made things easier. Some of the freshmen have already dropped out, so they have space. Sam and I
talked to the dean of admissions this morning. He
gave him an edited version of what happened, and
they've accepted me for the spring semester. Classes
start in ten days."

"Sure you're ready for that?"

"No, but I'm going to do it." She managed to smile
then. Life went on, didn't it? "It's close enough that,
if I need to, I can be here in an hour. But it's still
school. I can still be on my own. And I want to go. I
won't let myself stay here and be scared for the rest
of my life."

"Anybody who'd been through what you have
would be scared," Rye said.

For a minute, she thought he did really care about
her. Of course, that's what she wanted to think. "Besides," she said. "You and Sam . . . I know you've
been staying away, and I know why. I'm sorry I made
you feel like . . . That I made you uncomfortable."

"Emma, it's not that," he lied.

"Yes, it is. You came here to find Sam, and everything that happened afterward just messed that up,
and I feel bad about that."

"It's not—"

"I know. Not my fault." She even managed to smile.
"Everybody's said that. I'm working on believing it.
But things are going to be awkward for a while, and
I don't want to be the one standing between you
and Sam."

"There's a lot more than you standing between me
and Sam."

"Well, then I want to be one less thing."

Rye pushed an impatient hand through his hair and looked ready to argue. "I think you need them right now, Emma. They're your family. Much more yours than mine, and I'm just fine on my own."

"This is my time to be on my own. To head off into the world. My family's not going anywhere. I know that. I can always come back. This is your turn to become a part of them."

"No. Don't do this for me," he insisted.

"I'm doing it for me, and I'm doing it because I love—"

"Emma—"

"I love Sam." She rushed on. He'd looked so pained when he thought she was going to blurt out the fact that she loved him, but this was the truth of it. "I love Sam, and I know what it means to him to have you here now. Get to know them all. Learn to trust them. You promised you'd give Sam a chance."

"I know."

"So." She took a breath. There it was. She'd done it, and she hadn't even cried. But she had to get out of here. Now. "I really have to go. Classes start on the seventh. I have a million things to do. So, I guess I'll see you around. Easter dinner or the Fourth of July . . . Any of those major holidays."

They'd be surrounded by dozens of relatives. He'd stay on one side of the room, and she could stay on the other. They'd get through it just fine.

Emma walked back to the door and stood awkwardly in front of it, forcing herself to smile at him. "Go see Sam one day soon, okay?"

"I will." He hesitated then, looking torn. "Emma, I'm sorry."

"Me, too."

And then she turned and fled.

* * *

Someone came banging on his door an hour later. He promised himself that if it was Emma, he just wouldn't open the damned door. He'd had three beers, and it was no telling what he'd say to her if he did.

But it wasn't Emma.

Looking through the peephole, he saw his brother. He pulled open the door and frowned. "What is it now?"

"What the hell did you do to her?" Sam asked, looking ready to strangle someone.

"What do you mean, what did I do?" Rye asked. He was sick of this. He'd tried so hard to do the right thing, and it just felt like shit.

"I mean, when Emma came home, she'd been crying. I took a wild guess that she'd been here. Every time I've seen her miserable lately, it's because she's been talking to you."

"I did what you wanted me to do. I told her Christmas day that she was a sweet kid who had a lot of growing up to do."

"Shit," Sam said.

"You said to make it clear. I made it clear."

"So what the hell happened today?"

"She came to tell me she's going away, giving you and me some time to get to know each other." What a crock, like he and Sam wanted time together.

"She swore she wanted to go to school," Sam said.

"She said that, too. Scared or not, she's going."

"Dammit, I knew she was scared. She's hardly left the house until yesterday."

"Yeah, well she's not going to let something like being scared stop her."

And then they just glared at each other, Rye thinking he just had to come back here and find his brother. What a good idea that had turned out to be.

"I did my damnedest not to hurt her," he said. "When that didn't work, I did what you asked me to do. But I hope to hell you know what you're doing."

"I think I know a little more about her than you do."

But she was special, Rye thought.

Sweet and strong, and dammit, he needed her.

He couldn't even admit to himself how much he needed her.

"Oh, hell, she's eighteen," Sam said. "She'll get over you. She's going to college, and she's so smart. She could do anything she wants with her life."

"Good for her," Rye said. She could certainly do a lot better than him. "I just . . . It's hell seeing her like this."

Sam took a moment and really looked at him. Rye grew more uncomfortable every moment, until he had to look away.

"You really care about her?" Sam asked.

"How could anybody not care about her?" he roared. "Yeah, I care. But you told me to stay the hell away, and I will."

He wondered if he'd said too much, if Sam was really going to go nuts on him now. It took his breath away, thinking about what he'd just revealed. It was impossible. So what if she was the sweetest thing life had ever dangled in front of him? He couldn't have her.

Sam looked confused, then wary, then like he just didn't want to know, like he was afraid to ask. Good. Rye sure as hell didn't want to talk about it.

"She never really got to be young," Sam said finally. "To have time when she didn't have to take care of

anybody but herself. To relax, have fun, figure out
what she wants from life. You and I never had that,
but I want her to."

"So do I," Rye said. She could have anything she
wanted, as long as it made her happy.

"It's college. Three-and-a-half years. She doesn't
need to fall in love with anybody, to even think about
finding someone to spend her life with. Her whole life
is just beginning."

"I know." Rye glared right back at his brother.

Sam put his hands on his hips, his gaze locked on
Rye's. "Are you trying to tell me that you honestly
think you're in love with her?"

"No." No way Rye was saying anything like that.
But tension was tying his gut into knots, panic spreading through him at the thought of her hating him for
this, at the idea that shoving her away like this might
not be the right thing.

How could it not be the right thing? She was
eighteen.

"You said you'd take good care of her," Rye reminded Sam as he was leaving a few moments later.

"I will," Sam promised.

"And she'd better be happy."

If not, he was coming after Sam.

Chapter 15

Rye settled in easier than he would have expected in Baxter, Ohio. It was a nice little town. Quiet. Friendly, even to ex-cons like him. There was more work than he could do. Sam kept throwing jobs his way, which made him uncomfortable at first. He turned down more than he accepted, and then he just gave up and did those jobs, too.

Work helped. It helped him get so tired, he could almost forget everything. His past. What there was to his present and whatever might come to him in the future.

There were women who were happy to go out with him, and he went with one after another, telling himself he did not miss Emma at all.

He didn't let himself ask Sam about her, not wanting to see the look his brother would give him. But Rachel must have known how badly he wanted to hear about her, because she didn't make him ask. She volunteered the information. He'd started going to their house for dinner every now and then just so he could hear about Emma. Her grades were great, as always.

She'd moved into the dorm. Good. She'd probably feel safer with lots of people around her. She liked her roommate, and she might take some extra classes in the summer instead of coming home.

She'd been here for her birthday in February—an event he'd skipped. He didn't think she'd been home since, and this was April. He felt bad about that and needed to tell her it really wasn't necessary for her to remove herself so completely from her family.

Which was why he was so surprised to show up for dinner there a few weeks later and find her there. Grace let him in that night and jumped up into his arms. He lifted her off the floor and spun around with her while she giggled, her hair flying. She was the sweetest child, pure joy to behold. With her, he felt like an uncle, and it was a nice feeling.

"We've got a secret," she said, giving him a big squeeze before he set her down on the floor.

"You and I?"

"No. Me and everybody here." She stuck a pert little nose up in the air and practically dared him to figure it out.

"I could tickle it out of you, you know." He reached for her rib cage.

"No, you can't," she insisted, horrified.

"All right, I won't."

"Grace?" Rachel called from upstairs. "What are you doing?"

"Rye's here. I let him in."

"And didn't brush your teeth, did you?"

She frowned. "I thought about it."

"But you didn't. Come and do it now."

"Come on in." Grace tugged on his hand.

He followed her to the bottom of the stairs. Rachel stood at the top.

"We'll be right down," she said. "Make yourself at home. Beer's on ice in the cooler by the refrigerator."

"Thanks," Rye said. "Take your time."

He strolled into the kitchen and there was Emma. His first thought was that he'd been set up—given a minute with no prying eyes to prepare himself for her being here. And he supposed he needed that.

She stood in front of the stove, wearing a soft, butter-colored sweater and a pair of snug jeans. Her hair was longer, brushing her shoulders, and she was intently stirring something on the stove.

Finally, she turned, glanced at him, and just as quickly turned back. "Hi."

"Em," he said. "How are you?"

"Good. You?"

"I can't complain," he said, except for the little kick in the gut that came from seeing her and the urge he had to walk across the room and . . .

And what? Grab her? Hang on to her? Make sure she really was okay?

He walked into the kitchen, picking a spot in the corner that gave him a view of her from the side, so he could see her face and she couldn't turn away. He leaned as casually as he could against the counter and crossed his arms in front of him. She looked tired, he thought, but he probably wasn't supposed to notice or to ask.

He wanted to make this as easy as possible for her. So he took a whiff of that dish she was stirring and said, "Chili?"

"Of course."

He gave her a blank look. *Of course?*

"Rachel said it's your favorite."

"It is."

Emma laughed. "You have no idea why you're here, do you?"

"Dinner?" he tried.

"Well, there is that. What day is it, Rye?"

"April third." It was starting to get warm. Birds were singing in the morning as he woke up. Trees were budding, and he missed her, dammit.

"And next week? Monday? What happens then?"

Again, there was nothing but a blank look. He didn't know.

"It's your birthday," Emma said, smiling and shaking her head.

So, it was. Honestly, he hadn't given it much thought. It was just another day, and now he saw it as something that removed himself even more completely from her. He was turning thirty-four.

"Try to look surprised when they pull out the cake, okay?" she said "And it wouldn't hurt to admire it profusely. Grace helped make it. It has lime green icing and pink blobs that are supposed to be roses. She was sure you needed pink roses. In case you haven't noticed, she worships you."

He just stood there, thinking about a cake made with the help of Grace's two tiny hands. He could imagine her working so diligently over it and with so much excitement. He was enchanted with her. He'd start doing his hibernating, grumpy-bear thing, hole up in his dark cave of a room, and Grace would call and charm him. She'd make him laugh, make him feel guilty for ever turning down an invitation to her house. How could he ever let her believe he didn't want to see her? And sometimes he couldn't look at her and not imagine Emma at Grace's age, trying so hard to hold her little family together. He delighted in her, and yet he reminded her of too many things he was trying to forget.

Like his birthday.

It seemed it wasn't going to be just another day.

Emma laughed again. "If you could see your face right now . . ."

He shook his head. "They keep surprising me."

Although this really shouldn't. He knew about this family now. They never passed up an opportunity to celebrate or to get together.

"I told you they'd make you one of us," Emma said.

She put the lid back on the pot and put down the spoon she'd been using to stir, then walked up to him, close enough that he could smell her, that sweet-vanilla-Emma smell. She stopped all of a foot away, thank goodness, and he didn't move any closer.

"I've been thinking about you," he admitted. "Worrying about you. How are you, really?"

"I'm fine. I've been thinking about you, too."

"Nothing from Mark?"

She shook her head. "I think it's really over. I don't wake up shaking anymore."

"And you feel safe there?" That was important.

"Yes. I've been taking some psych courses, figuring some things out. It's helping," she said. "Rachel said she manages to drag you over here every now and then."

"Her and Grace."

"Grace can't stop talking about you."

"She's amazing," he said.

"I know. Always has been."

"Emma, they all miss you. Don't stay away on my account, okay?"

"I've just been busy," she insisted, smiling when for a moment she'd looked so sad.

He reached out, grazing his fingertips to the bottom of her chin, just for a second. Her gaze shot up to his, and she went still, not even breathing, it seemed. His heart was hammering out her name. *Emma, Emma, Emma.*

Nineteen now. Not nearly enough.

Damn. He'd gotten too close. Even after more than three months, he couldn't be this close to her for five minutes without those old feelings rearing up and making him do things he regretted.

"I've missed you," she said softly, sadly.

"Emma." He stepped back, his hand falling to his side.

Yeah, he'd gotten way too close.

Emma declared a major that spring—counseling—thinking she could help people whose lives were as screwed up as hers. How could people with really together lives ever understand half-crazy people, anyway? She figured they needed someone like her, and she needed them.

She made it through the summer mostly by staying away from home, trying to shore up her resolve and soothe her hurt feelings. She couldn't decide if she was being foolish or whether she was truly in love with Rye, but she just couldn't forget about him.

Girls did this, didn't they? Little girls. They took the smallest hint of interest from a man and blew it all out of proportion. They replayed every word, every look, every touch. They daydreamed. They fantasized. They held on, even in the face of overwhelming evidence that the man in question scarcely knew they existed.

It seemed as mature as she might be in most ways, she was woefully inexperienced when it came to relationships. She worried she was acting like the child Rye had accused her of being.

He'd been seen all over town with half a dozen women in the past few months. Grace, who was insanely jealous of anyone who took his attention away from her, told Emma all about it. Grace didn't care if she was only eight, she thought he was hers, just like Emma didn't care that she was only nineteen.

Was she any less foolish than her baby sister when it came to Rye?

Maybe not, but surely she could hide her feelings a little better than Grace, who pouted prettily and batted her eyelashes at him. She grabbed him by the arm and tugged him away from his current woman— Janeen Wilkes—something Emma would really like to do herself.

She couldn't believe she was standing here at her grandfather's annual Labor Day cookout shooting daggers at a woman whose kids she used to baby-sit, because Rye happened to bring the woman to a family party. She could just picture Janeen turning around and seeing Emma and going, *Oh, yes. What a sweet kid. She used to baby-sit for my children.*

Rye would just love hearing that.

Emma, Grace, and Janeen could fight over him.

"Oh, that is a wicked look," her roommate Melanie said. "You're not going to hurt someone, are you?"

"I hope not."

"So . . ." Melanie moved in closer as they stood beside the picnic table laden with food and nodded in Rye's direction. "That's him?"

"Yes."

"God, he's gorgeous. Did I really tell you to give up on him?"

"Yes, you did."

"Well, I take it all back. I never knew men could look like that in their thirties. That nice, tight little butt and those dimples. You think he might take his shirt off later, if they play ball?"

Emma had seen him without his shirt on. She knew

just how impressive a sight it was. "I don't think we could take it if he did. Not with it being so hot already. We'd get dizzy and fall down."

Melanie pointed to Janeen. "And who is he with?"

"A different woman every few weeks, from what I hear."

"Oh, Em, I'm sorry."

"It's not getting any better," she confessed. "I'm trying. I'm trying so hard to forget about him."

"I know."

"Do me a favor, Mel. Don't let me make a fool of myself with him today. I did on his birthday, and I really don't want to do that again."

Sam asked Rye to meet him at an old house on Front Street a few weeks before Christmas, his second here. He liked this place. Amazingly, he felt at home here.

Sam was probably going to throw some more work his way. He hadn't figured out a way to tell his brother he really didn't need any help staying busy, and it sounded ungrateful, too, which he really didn't want to do.

Their relationship was . . . Hell, he didn't know what it was.

He loved Grace, shooting hoops and playing football with Zach, who worked with Rye sometimes on the weekends and after school. He adored Rachel, and he got along okay with Sam. They didn't really growl at each other anymore. There was still that thing with Emma, which he mostly tried not to think about.

He parked in front of a sadly neglected Victorian, porch sagging, a couple of the front windows broken, weeds all over the yard. Sam was standing on the sidewalk staring up at it.

Rye got out of his truck and walked to Sam's side. "Man, you've got your work cut out for you here."

"Somebody does," Sam said. "What do you think?"

Rye shrugged. "I guess if they've got the money and know what they're getting into . . . Who are you to try to talk 'em out of it?"

"I'm not. I was wondering if you were interested in it."

"Working here? Sam, I—"

"No, buying it. I know it's a mess, but for somebody who had the time and knew what to do with it . . . I could help you. Zach's always available, and he works cheap. What do you think?"

He thought with enough time and effort, it could be a great house. That's what he thought. What he asked was, "Why?"

"You don't really want to live over Rick's garage forever, do you?"

"I hadn't really thought about it." He wasn't there much, and he couldn't say he'd cared that much about where he lived. After years spent in a cell, a man developed very simple needs.

"It's time to start living, don't you think?" Sam said.

Maybe it was. Maybe he had been living for the last nine years like he might well get thrown back in jail at anytime. He'd caught himself lately, when he was working on a house, glancing at this and that, thinking about what he would have done with the hallway or the banister or the mantel, if it were his place.

"This little old lady named Marge lived here for about seventy years," Sam said. "She went into a nursing home fifteen years ago and refused to let anybody do anything with her house. Even though she knew she'd never be able to live here again, she just wanted to know it was still here. Made the kids absolutely crazy, and they refused to spend a dime on upkeep. She died last week, and they can't wait to put it on the market."

"Like this?" Rye asked.

"Maybe. One of them asked me to work up an estimate on repairs, which they didn't like at all. I told them they'd get a lot more out of it by getting some basic work done, but they're not inclined to wait. Then I thought about you." Sam turned and looked at him, looking uneasy and maybe hopeful at the same time. "Your year's almost up. You weren't planning on leaving, were you?"

It was probably as close as Sam would come to out-and-out asking him to stay. Rye grinned. "Hadn't planned on going anywhere."

"Good. Grace would cry for a month if you did, and then she'd probably blame me."

"You're just jealous 'cause she likes me more than you," Rye said.

"You spoil her rotten," Sam protested.

"And you don't?"

Sam couldn't say anything to that. Everybody spoiled Grace rotten, and yet she didn't seem spoiled at all. Just happy.

Which made him think about Emma. Was Emma happy yet?

No way he could ask Sam.

"So, what do you think about the house? You could buy it cheap, do the work as you could get to it. I could help you with the down payment—"

"I don't need any help with the down payment." Rye hadn't done much of anything but work for the last nine years, and he hadn't had anything he really wanted to spend his money on. He could have this, if he wanted it.

It meant staying here, making a life here. How did he feel about that?

"I guess we might as well take a look since we're here," he said. "If the ceiling won't cave in on us or anything like that."

They walked through the house. It really was a mess, would need practically everything. A new roof, new electrical system, new plumbing, new heating system. The works. But what he didn't know how to do, Sam did.

A house, he thought.

It had four bedrooms, a fireplace in nearly every room, and a big yard.

What was he supposed to do with a house?

"Heard you bought a house," Emma said to him, as they helped pull down the Christmas decorations that year.

He was up on a ladder, pulling strands of lights off the second story, handing them down to her. "More like buying a headache," he said. "But yeah, I bought the place."

"So, you're not going anywhere?"

Rye came to the end of what he hoped was the last strand and climbed down. It was bitterly cold, the wind howling, and she was shivering. "No," he said, when they were face-to-face. "I'm not going anywhere."

"I guess Meg Reynolds is happy."

Meg Reynolds was the woman he'd been dating for about six weeks. "I didn't buy this house for Meg Reynolds."

"Does she know that?" Emma asked, rolling up a strand of lights.

That stopped him. Truthfully, he'd never thought about Meg when he decided to buy the house. She was a perfectly nice woman, late twenties, divorced with a couple of kids. He tried not to see them, be-

cause he didn't want them to get ideas. He'd never
said anything to Meg to indicate that he was interested
in any more than a little bit of fun on a Saturday night.
Rye was careful to never promise a woman more than
he was willing to give. Not that they always listened.
That baffled him. You tell them one thing, they start
thinking another. He thought sometimes he must be
speaking a foreign language, when he could have
sworn it was plain old English.

"I heard she's picking out wallpaper and studying
paint chips," Emma said.

"Not for me and her, she's not."

Emma shrugged. "You might want to make sure
she understands that."

Dammit. He would.

"Rye?" she said, putting her hand on his arm to
stop him when he would have walked away. "I just
wanted to say . . . I'm glad you're staying."

"Me, too," he said. "Come on. Let's get inside."

Get back into the middle of the crowd. Keep his
hands off her. Just try to think about anything but her.

Emma walked inside and headed upstairs. She
stripped off her coat and her gloves, planning to hide
in her room if it came down to that. But she ran into
Rachel in the hall.

"What's wrong?" Rachel asked.

Emma heard someone else coming upstairs. Rachel's sister Ann and her husband and children—including one adorable, perfectly healthy baby Ann had
managed to carry nearly to full term—were here for
another two days. The house was full of people. She
headed into her room and Rachel followed her.

"He didn't buy the house for Meg Reynolds, after
all." Emma sat down on the bed, trembling and so
relieved. "When he bought that big old house, I

thought that was it. He must have found someone he wanted to share it with. What does he need with a house that has four bedrooms?"

The only thing she could think of was that he intended to fill them up with Meg's boys and then children the two of them would have together.

"He didn't go looking for that house," Rachel said. "Sam found it for him. I think he wanted something to tie Rye to this area, and the house did it."

Emma had been afraid to ask if he was leaving, now that he could. Then she heard about the house. "I'm doing a lousy job of forgetting about him," she admitted. "And it's not that I haven't tried."

"I know you have."

"I thought he really cared about me. I know it made him uncomfortable, even before he knew about the age difference. But I thought he just never let anyone get that close, and he was worried about what Sam would think."

"Are you sure he doesn't care about you?"

"I want to believe he does. I told myself we'd get past the age thing. That Sam would get to know Rye, and then he wouldn't object. And I thought Rye wouldn't be able to stay away from me. Isn't that the stupidest thing? He's been out with most of the women in town between twenty-five and thirty-five."

"But I haven't seen a one last more than two months," Rachel said.

"So, he has a short attention span. Or he just likes variety."

"Maybe. Or maybe he really doesn't care about any of them."

It was a long year. Emma just worked and worked. She came home for Memorial Day, at which time Rye barely even looked at her. She was mad enough by

Labor Day that when she came home for her grand-father's annual cookout, she wore the tiniest excuse for a bikini she could find.

The family gathered at a small, sandy beach on the river for a cookout, swimming, sunning themselves, and fireworks.

Emma had the bikini on underneath her T-shirt and cutoffs. Her cousin Becky gawked at her when she finally worked up her nerve to pull off the T-shirt. "Gee, wonder who you're trying to impress."

"I've given up on impressing him," Emma said. "But he's not going to ignore me today."

The tiny string bikini was a flaming red, shimmering, reflective material that would not be overlooked, and the top was made of the narrowest triangles of mate-rial. She didn't have anything to write home about in the way of breasts, but this sure made the most of them.

"Chickening out?" Becky asked.

"No way."

Rye was playing volleyball, him and all the guys and some woman he'd brought with him. Not Meg. He seemed as happy as could be.

He was shirtless—God help her—and sweating, his muscles and all that glorious sun-browned skin gleam-ing. He attacked the ball and the net the entire game, and she had to admit, he looked perfectly at ease here and happy in a way that she didn't think she'd seen him before.

Maybe he'd finally settled in, figured out that he was a part of them, that he always would be. He just wouldn't be hers.

Emma took her beach towel and spread it out in the sand near the volleyball court, sat down, slipped off her shorts, and stretched out facedown on her towel. She was working up her nerve to reach behind her back and untie her top when Sam came along.

He nudged her with his toe. "Did you lose something?"

"No," she insisted, turning her head to look up at him.

"Emma, I've got socks with more material than that swimsuit. Tell me you don't normally go out in public in that thing."

"Only when I'm working on my tan."

"Very funny," he said.

"Sam, I'll be twenty-one in five months."

"You think I won't tell you what you can and can't do when you're twenty-one?"

"You don't do that now," she reminded him. He trusted her, little Miss Responsible. He'd never really played outraged father, except with her and Rye.

Emma wondered if he knew this was about that— her and Rye. She wondered suddenly if everyone knew, wondered if they just looked at her and everything she did or said when he was around, and knew.

She groaned and buried her head in her beach towel.

"You've made your point," she told Sam.

A glance out of the corner of her eye told her he'd accepted that and moved on. She flipped over onto her back and then her side, so she could look out at the family members and friends gathered here. Did they pity her? For everything she felt for a man who simply didn't feel the same way about her.

She was sick just thinking about it. This really had to stop. It had been more than a year and a half. How long was she going to hang on to any hope that he felt something for her?

Emma sat up, pulling on her shorts and grabbing

the towel and her shirt. She shook the sand off her
towel and draped it over one shoulder, had the shirt
in her hand as she took off for the trees that lined
the edge of the beach. She'd just made it into the
trees when she heard someone coming after her. Turning around, she saw Rye glaring at her.

"What the hell are you doing, Emma?"

"Enjoying the picnic," she claimed, though from the
way she'd snarled at him, there was no doubt that was
a lie.

"In that?" He nodded toward her practically non-
existent top.

She stuck her nose in the air, not about to back
down from him on anything today. "You have a problem with it? It's what all the little girls are wearing
this year."

"Emma, don't." He was breathing hard, sweat making little paths down the muscles of his chest, and he
looked like he wanted to grab her and shake some
sense into her.

Well, he didn't have the right.

"Don't you dare think you have the right to tell me
what to do. You're nothing to me, right? And I'm
nothing to you. Isn't that what you wanted?"

She thought he was going to grab her for a minute,
and maybe she thought he was going to deny it. That's
what she really wanted—to goad him into a reaction.
But he didn't do either of those things. He held his
temper somehow and held back anything he might
have said, turned, and walked away.

Story of her life. He was leaving once again, and
she'd made herself look like a fool.

Christmas was quiet that year, New Year's the
same. Rye was polite, a bit distant with her, like she

was nothing more than someone he saw on major holidays and didn't give a second thought to otherwise.

She no longer looked for little hidden signs that he cared, no longer read things into every glance, every word. She was done. It was over.

She came home for her twenty-first birthday in February in a bittersweet mood. Twenty-one was one of those landmarks. No one could say she wasn't an adult. The summers she'd spent at school and the extra courses she'd taken throughout the years were going to pay off in May, when she graduated after three years instead of the usual four. She'd be on her own then, get an apartment, get a job.

Get a life. She'd promised herself. It was long past time.

She wandered into the kitchen as Rachel was putting candles on her cake. It was grape colored, the icing looking a little rough, the orange and green roses a bit lopsided.

"Grace?" she guessed.

Rachel nodded. "She takes food coloring very seriously."

Emma started to cry then. She couldn't help it.

Rachel put down the cake and pulled Emma into her arms. "Oh, honey. I'm so sorry. Did Becky say something to you?"

"About what?"

"About Rye and Laine Wilson."

"What about Rye and Laine Wilson?" Emma asked.

"Oh, honey. I thought . . . Well, what is it?"

"Never mind what it is. Tell me about Rye. What? He's engaged to Laine Wilson?" Emma had baby-sat her kids, too, dammit.

"Becky said she's been in every jewelry store in

town, looking at rings. But nobody's seen Rye in one, and he hasn't said anything to me. I've been helping him with a pattern for the tile he's putting in his kitchen, something special."

"Something special for her? For when they get married?" Emma asked. God, she hadn't forgotten him. She hadn't forgotten anything.

"She drops by all the time, and she sure is interested in how the house is going to be finished out. But he's doing what he wants there. He asks me as often as he asks her about what should be done."

"But she's picking out a ring?"

"Maybe," Rachel admitted. "I don't know."

Emma shook her head miserably, telling herself it was bound to happen sooner or later. Just because he didn't care about her, that didn't mean he wouldn't ever come to love someone someday.

"I feel like such a fool. I actually thought that maybe now . . . I'm not eighteen anymore. I'm twenty-one. I actually thought that might matter to him."

"I'm sorry," Rachel said, hugging her close.

"Me, too."

Chapter 16

He didn't even come to her twenty-first birthday party.

She could have screamed at him, just for that, stupid girl that she was.

Everybody else came, tons of family members and half a dozen or so friends from high school, who happened to be home for the long weekend.

She hadn't seen some of them in years, including Brian Evans. She'd had something of a crush on him in tenth grade, and he still looked really cute. Not much different than he had then, actually.

"We're going to a little party later," he said. "A friend of mine—Todd Myers—remember him?"

"Two years behind us in school, right?"

"Yeah, that's him. We've got an apartment over on Seventh Street. Why don't you come over there with me? This is way too tame a party for anybody who's turning twenty-one."

Emma suddenly thought it was. What was she going to do anyway? Go back to school and hide in her

room, feeling sorry for herself and picturing Rye and
Laine together?

She really didn't need to do that.

Not anymore.

She thanked Sam and Rachel for the party, told
Rachel she thought she'd head back to school that
night, that Brian had offered to take her. It was one
of the few lies she'd ever told either of them.

Brian had a cooler full of beer on ice in his truck
and pulled out one for her. Emma wasn't much of a
drinker. Her birth father was an alcoholic, and while
she wasn't one to excuse his behavior because of it,
she knew it took his out-of-control personality up another notch into the danger zone. From what little
she'd experienced of it, alcohol deadened her sense of
self-control, and after the childhood she'd had, Emma
placed a great deal of value on control in any
situation.

But she was twenty-one, dammit. Rye hadn't even
come to her party. He hardly knew she was alive, and
he was probably going to marry Laine. She was going
to give up on him, once and for all.

If there was ever a night to get drunk, this was it.

She took the beer and tried not to grimace at the
taste.

"You're not really a beer drinker, are you?"
Brian said.

"Not really."

He stopped at a liquor store along the way and
came out with a bottle of champagne. "We'll try this.
It's your birthday, after all."

She finished the beer anyway, and by the time they
got to his friend's house, her head was spinning. She
was determined to enjoy it. Images of Rye were fad-
ing. It didn't quite hurt as much to think of him.
Maybe she could simply make her heart numb.

The party was a small one. Her and Brian, Todd and some girl Emma didn't know, and one other couple. They were crawling all over each other in one corner of the sofa.

"Hey." Todd nudged the guy. "Get a room, why don't you."

The guy grinned. "You've got one, right?"

"Yeah, sure." He nodded back toward what had to be the bedroom. "Make yourself at home."

That was that.

Emma caught Brian looking at her with a little smile that she knew probably should have made her nervous, but she really didn't care at the moment. He opened the champagne, which was sweet and bubbly, definitely much better than the beer. She had two glasses, and when she tried to stand up, she swayed on her feet.

"Careful." Brian slipped an arm around her waist. "We don't want you to fall down. You might want to hang on to me."

She might as well.

He steered her down the dark hallway, into what she finally realized was a bedroom. He closed the door, didn't turn on the lights, and then he kissed her.

Emma closed her eyes and tried to make herself feel something, anything.

The champagne helped. The darkness helped.

He put his hand on her breast. She thought about that, how it felt to have him touch her. It felt good, didn't it? She was a perfectly normal woman, a twenty-one-year-old woman, and she had the same basic need to be touched and kissed that any woman had.

It didn't have to be about love, did it? It didn't have to be about forever.

Why not just let him . . .

He worked on the buttons on her blouse, fumbling one and maybe snapping it off, but he got his hand inside, closing around her bare flesh.

Go ahead, she told herself. *Let go. Let it happen. Let him do whatever he wants.*

"Come on, Emma," he said.

It wasn't so bad like this. She wasn't sure if she was crazy about the way he kissed, and he sure seemed a bit impatient. She tensed up a bit and willed herself to relax, to feel, to like it.

Normal women did this. They liked it.

"What's wrong with you?" he asked.

What was wrong with her? She didn't know, but tears came to her eyes. She knew she couldn't go through with this.

"I'm sorry," she said, pulling away.

He didn't let go at first. He held on and ground his mouth against hers, his pelvis, too. It seemed he wasn't having any trouble getting into this.

"Brian, I'm sorry," she said, pushing him away.

"Sorry about what?" he asked, obviously angry.

"I thought this was what I wanted. I thought I could, but—"

"Just relax. Everything will be fine," he insisted. "Surely you're not still doing that little miss holier than thou thing you had going on in high school."

"What?" she asked.

"You know. Miss Untouchable."

She hadn't been. She'd had the same curiosity and the same interest in the opposite sex everyone else did. She was just more cautious than most people. Or maybe she was just a coward. Relationships between men and women could turn out so badly. Who knew what she really felt? She'd never been able to understand it, and maybe she never would.

She just knew now that he wasn't Rye, and that seemed to say it all.

"I have to go."

"Wait just a damned minute."

He grabbed for her, got mostly her blouse and hung on tight. She heard it rip, heard him swear. He'd been drinking, too. She pressed herself against the wall for support and held her hands up in front of her to keep him away. For a minute, she was thinking about Mark and how crazy guys could be.

"I'm not staying here. I'm not doing anything with you," she said, her voice shaking, her hands shaking, too.

"What? I'm not good enough for you or something?"

"No. It's not you. It's me. I'm sorry."

She found the doorknob, pulled it open, and slipped into the hallway, startling the couple in the living room. They looked at her like she was some kind of alien creature, her blouse torn, tears falling down her cheeks. She grabbed her coat and ran out the door and into the night.

Brian came after her. "Emma, wait a minute. I'm not some kind of monster, dammit. Emma, how are you even going to get home?"

She didn't care. She just wanted to get away. She ran down the street until she didn't hear anyone coming after her anymore, and then she leaned against a lamppost and cried. Her head was spinning. It was cold, and her blouse was torn. She pulled on her coat. In the deep pockets of her coat were her keys, her wallet, and her cell phone, thank goodness.

She pulled out the phone, calling three of her cousins and her roommate, but no one was home. Cell phones were either turned off or they were at a bar

somewhere with music blaring. Or maybe they were
in bed with their significant others, people with none
of the hang-ups she had.

She was miles from anyone she knew. She could try
to walk, but where would she go? After fifteen minutes of racking her brain for some alternative, she
called home. She'd just tell them she had a misunderstanding with Brian. If she could dry her tears and
keep her coat buttoned, they wouldn't know anything
different. Emma hoped Rachel would answer the
phone. The line cracked with static, but she could tell
right away she'd gotten Sam.

Damn.

"Sam, let me just tell you this, and try not to say
anything, okay? I'm all right, but I need you to come
and get me. Please?" Her voice broke there. He had
to hear that. She gave him the address, not telling him
she was outside in the cold, just telling the number of
the house closest by.

"What the hell are you doing in that part of town
at this hour?"

"Sam, please? Please just come and get me.
Please hurry."

"I'll be right there," he said.

It seemed like forever before she saw the Suburban
moving slowly down the street. She waited until it was
nearly even with her before she stepped out of the
shadows and onto the sidewalk.

Her stomach had turned queasy. She was afraid she
was going to be sick. It was one of the most miserable
nights in her life, and that was saying something.

Then she realized this wasn't Sam's Suburban.

It was a truck. A big, black truck.

It stopped in the middle of the deserted street, and

Rye climbed out. He walked over to her, his gaze raking over her from head to toe. "What happened?"

She just stood there for a minute, thinking if her humiliation weren't complete before, it surely was now. "What are you doing here?"

"Dammit, Emma—"

"I called Sam," she said, wanting to weep again.

"And you got me. Sam and I were watching a ball game. I happened to pick up the phone when he went to grab a beer. Now what the hell happened?"

He put one hand on the side of her face, tilting it this way and that in the light, making sure she was in once piece, she realized. The hand against her cheek was trembling, whether in anger or in fear, she couldn't tell.

"Nothing happened," she said, a totally ineffectual lie given the circumstances, but it was all that came to mind at the moment. No way was she telling him the truth.

"Tell me another one." He stepped closer, his gaze even harder. "You've been drinking?"

"What if I have?" she said. "It's my birthday. I'm celebrating."

"All by yourself? In the street in the middle of the night, in a bad part of town?"

"This is none of your business. Nothing I do is any of your business."

"I'm making it my business tonight. Get in the truck, Emma," he ordered, his voice growing danger-ously quiet.

"Rye—"

"Get in."

He wrenched open the door for her, and she climbed in. He got inside himself and closed the door, then cranked up the heat. She couldn't stop shaking, didn't say so much as a word, and thankfully, neither did he. She closed her eyes and leaned her head back against the seat, staying as far away from him as the confines of the truck would allow.

Could this night possibly get any worse? She didn't see how.

The truck finally turned into the driveway and stopped.

"Please, don't bother to get out. I can get myself inside." She scrambled out of the seat belt and out the door.

Rye didn't listen, dammit. He turned off the engine and climbed out, too. She was coming around the front of his truck, trying to figure out how to get rid of him, when she looked up and realized she wasn't home.

He'd brought her to his house.

She knew it was his because there were times when she knew he wasn't home that she'd driven by, parked in the driveway, gone up on the porch and peeked in the windows, walked through the backyard. She knew as much as she could about his house without ever having been inside, and she was such a fool for even wanting to know about it.

He took her by the arm, in a grip that was unbreakable. "We're going inside, and you're going to tell me what happened tonight."

She thought about fighting him, about screaming at him, at the whole entire world. But he was moving quickly, all but dragging her along. They were inside before she knew it. She scarcely even noticed her surroundings. She was just trying to figure out how to get away when her stomach lurched painfully.

Oh, damn.

"Rye," she began, clamping a hand over her mouth. "I think I'm—"

"Come on. Over here."

He dragged her into the bathroom. She made it with a split second to spare, falling to her knees in front of the toilet. Even then, she tried to get away from him, tried to shove him out of the tiny bathroom, but he wouldn't go, damn him. He just wouldn't go. When she was done, feeling as if she'd coughed up half her insides, she leaned, weak and miserable, against the wall by her side. He handed her a hand towel, damp on one end. She wiped her face, then pressed the towel against her forehead.

Of all the nights for him to pick to stop ignoring her . . . Could she just roll over and die right now? At least she wouldn't have to face him.

"How much did you have to drink?" he growled.

"What does it matter?" It was out of her system now, wasn't it?

"Emma—"

"I had a beer and three glasses of cheap champagne," she said.

He frowned down at her. "Not much of a drinker, are you?"

"I'm thinking about taking it up as a pastime. God, would you just leave me alone?"

"No," he said. "You think you're done in here?"

"With any luck at all."

"Then come on. We can try to sober you up. Then you can tell me what the hell you thought you were doing."

He dragged her upstairs and into a huge bathroom. The light hurt her eyes, and she started to protest at that, then realized she had a bigger problem. He was tugging her coat off her.

"Don't," she said.

"We're inside. You don't need the coat. Unless . . ."

His voice trailed off. Looking down, she saw that

her blouse was torn and gaping open. He swore softly. She went to pull the ends of her coat back together, but he wouldn't let her. He held it open and studied her once more, as he'd studied her face earlier. Looking for bruises, she realized.

"Nobody hit me," she said.

"No? Somebody just got you drunk and tried to rip your clothes off?"

"Not exactly," she said.

"Try again, Emma. Exactly what happened?"

"I got drunk and thought I'd go to bed with this guy, okay? That's what happened. And then I decided maybe that wasn't the best idea after all. He ripped my blouse, and I left."

Rye might as well have been carved of stone. He didn't so much as blink. Just stared down at her as if he couldn't believe what he was hearing. As if he might explode at any moment.

Finally, quietly, he said, "He didn't hurt you?"

"No."

Then he yelled again. "Why the hell would you do something like that? Get drunk. Climb into bed with some guy you barely knew."

"Why wouldn't I?" she said.

"Why wouldn't you?" The words blasted out of his mouth. They echoed back and forth in the small room. "What the hell is the matter with you?"

"You," she screamed right back. "You're what's wrong with me. You're everything that's wrong with my life, and I'm sick of it, do you hear me? I want you out of my head. I want to forget I ever met you. I want to do away with any hold you have over me."

"I'm not a part of your life anymore."

"I know," she cried.

He never would be. She saw that now. Nothing else seemed to matter.

He stood there for the longest time, started three different times to say something, and then changed his mind. What was there to say? This had been impossible from the very beginning.

Finally, he turned and pulled clean towels from the cabinet, then turned on the shower full blast. "Get in there," he said. "Keep the water as cold as you can stand it at first. It might help clear your head. I'll find you something to wear when you get out."

He walked out of the room, and Emma went to lock the door, but realized there was no lock. There wasn't even a doorknob. The floor was plywood only, the cabinets freshly sanded but without any stain or finishing. Obviously, his house wasn't quite done.

Which struck her as ridiculous to notice under the circumstances, but she was mad about the lock. Or the lack of one. Not that he was going to come in while she was in the shower. Why the hell would he do that? He didn't care about her. She just liked the idea of being able to put a locked door between him and her. She didn't want to ever have to face him again.

Her head was aching. She had a horrible taste in her mouth. Her stomach clenched and released, clenched and released, until she couldn't tell what it was going to do next. The room was still spinning, and the lights were horrible. Why had he used such hideously bright lights?

She finally stripped off her clothes and climbed into the shower. The cold seemed to blast right through her. She gasped, then swore, sat down in the corner, curled up into a ball, and cried once again.

If she ever got through this night, she would never

cry over this man again. Not ever. This was the end. She was done. There had to be a way to forget him. She promised herself she'd find it. So what if that's what had gotten her into this mess in the first place.

He was waiting for her when she finally came out of the bathroom. She'd stayed there in the cold water for as long as she could, and then switched to scalding hot water, to try to stop herself from shivering. She'd found a spare toothbrush in a drawer and used it. He would keep one on hand. He probably bought them in bulk for the parade of women he had coming through here.

He'd left her some clothes in the bathroom. A big white T-shirt of his that hung halfway down her thighs and a pair of sweatpants that were huge on her but had a drawstring waist.

She put those on and dried her hair as best she could, then stopped to say a little prayer that he wouldn't be right there on the other side of the door, but nothing was going her way tonight. He was there.

Her cheeks burned with shame, and there was no way she could even look at him. Not after what she'd admitted to him.

"Are Sam and Rachel expecting you home tonight?" he asked.

"No. I told them Brian was giving me a ride back to school."

"Brian?" he asked. "Just how well do you know Brian?"

"Well enough," she said.

"Well enough to climb into bed with him?"

"We didn't exactly make it that far."

"Dammit, Emma! He could have really hurt you. You know that, don't you? You know how stupid a thing that was to do? Do you have so little respect for yourself and your body that you'd just go off with some guy and—"

"And you're so picky about the women you take to your bed?" she yelled right back, then looked around the room, plain as can be and empty, except for the bed. "This bed, right? I'm surprised you haven't installed a revolving door to handle all the traffic."

"What the hell does that mean?" he yelled.

"You and all those women parading in and out of here. It's what people call a double standard, Rye. You can sleep with as many women as you want, and it's fine, but if I go to bed with a guy, there's something wrong with that?"

"I wasn't questioning your morals, Emma, just your incredible stupidity. You could have been hurt so badly. Do you know anything about this guy?"

"We went to high school together."

"And you were close?"

"Not exactly."

"Have you seen him at all since then?"

"No," she said.

"So you just thought, What the hell? Have a few drinks and hop in bed with him."

"That was my plan," she admitted.

"You make a habit of doing things like that?"

"No, I was thinking if I got drunk, I might be able to go through with it."

He just got madder. "Why would you ever want to force yourself to have sex with a guy you barely know?"

"Because he was there, okay? Because he poured champagne down my throat, and because it's my birthday."

"So this is some kind of ritual? You have sex with strangers on your birthday? Jesus, Emma, what the hell are you doing?"

"I don't have sex with anybody, you stupid man," she said. "I don't ever go to bed with anybody. I swear I'm the only virgin left on the entire campus of the University of Cincinnati. Maybe the only one over twenty-one in the whole state, if not the entire Midwest, and I'm sick of it. I'm sick of missing you and wanting you and wishing that everything could have been different between us."

"Emma—"

"It's you. How can you not know it's you? I've been so stupid. I've been waiting for you. Waiting for you to get over this hang-up you have about my age or to stop caring what Sam thinks or for me to grow up enough that it didn't matter anymore. And I guess some really stupid part of me held out some hope that today, when I turned twenty-one, that might be enough. That you might come to me and say, 'Okay, twenty-one I can handle. It's not eighteen. It's not nineteen. It's not twenty. And I just can't stay away any longer.' But that didn't happen. You didn't even come to my party."

He didn't say anything for the longest time, and Emma couldn't believe she'd said all that she had. God, could this night possibly get any worse? But she'd said it all, finally, and no matter what the consequences, she felt better getting it out. She was furious with him and herself and everything about his awful night.

He'd been just as angry himself, but as she watched, all the anger seemed to drain out of him, weariness and maybe resignation seeping in. He gave her a cautious glance and just as quickly looked away, no doubt trying to build those walls once again to keep her out.

"Emma, I'm sorry."

She believed he was, and it was the last thing she wanted from him.

"Why? For not caring about me? For thinking I'm

a sweet kid?" The words dripped with sarcasm. They'd been burnt into her brain, from that first day he'd called her that, when she'd sworn he'd been doing it just to push her away. She'd been so sure he hadn't meant it.

The years had taught her that he had.

"I'm sorry for hurting you," he said.

"It's not your fault. You can't help it if I don't even register on your radar. I know there isn't any lack of female companionship in your life."

"It's not like that, Emma."

"Oh, please. I've heard all about it."

"They're just women," he claimed. "No one special."

"Fine." She started seething again. He'd go out with anybody but her, and she'd gotten to the point where she'd do the same thing, if it helped her get over him. She closed her eyes and sank back against the wall. "I can't keep doing this, Rye. I can't keep living my life like someone in a deep freeze, waiting for something I'll never have. And I know it's not the smartest plan in the world—to fall into bed with someone. But I'm desperate. I have to forget about you. I have to break that hold somehow and move on."

"You were ready to sleep with the first guy who came along to do that?"

"No. I tried it with . . . I've been seeing this guy for months. He's been so patient, so understanding, and I kept hoping I would love him. Why can't I just love him?" she said, her voice breaking.

"I don't think we get to choose, Emma. I don't think we can will ourselves to love anyone, any more than we can will ourselves to stop loving someone we're not supposed to care about."

"Then I'm doomed? I'm going to be this miserable for the rest of my life? Because I won't let myself feel this way forever. I can't. It hurts too much."

She started to cry again, dammit. Miserably. Uncontrollably.

Rye picked her up and carried her to the bed. She didn't want to be there. Didn't want any part of the room where he'd brought all those other women, damn him.

"Let me go," she said.

"No." He pulled back the covers and put her between them.

"Rye—"

He sat down on the bed beside her, bunched the pillows against the headboard, and then climbed in, clothes and all. He settled himself against the pillows and then pulled her to him, her head to his chest and her arms going around his waist.

"I can't let you go on like this." His arm came around her, his hand stroking her hair. "It's no telling what you might do. Grab the next man you see?"

"I didn't mean to do that," she said miserably. "I had a perfectly reasonable plan."

"Sex with someone you don't even like is not a reasonable plan, Emma."

"I didn't plan that. That just happened," she said, closing her eyes and letting her tears fall. She had a feeling she'd hate herself in the morning for telling him these things. She had just been so mad at him, so mad at the whole situation. "I had a good plan. With . . . the guy I told you about. The one I've been seeing. I do know him, and I like him. Really, I do."

He thought she had some odd sexual hang-up when she wouldn't sleep with him, even more so after she'd finally told him she'd never slept with anyone. And she let him go on thinking that, unable to tell him the truth. That she was stupidly in love with a man who didn't care about her at all and had never been able to give herself to anyone else.

"I was going to just make myself do it with him," she said. "I even went to a doctor and got one of those shots—like the pill, except you get one and you're covered for months. I was all ready last week, and I tried. I really tried. But I couldn't do it. And then, my birthday came, and I just felt so stupid. Twenty-one, and still waiting."

"You should wait," he said. "You should wait for someone you love."

"I don't think I'll ever love anyone but you," she admitted. "Rye, have you ever loved anyone?"

"Yes," he said, slowly as if he didn't want to admit to it.

She was afraid to ask, but made herself. "What happened?"

"It didn't work out."

"But you got over it, right?" She asked. He certainly seemed to be making the most of his life with the opposite sex.

"No, I don't think I'll ever get over her."

"Oh." Something inside her died right then and there, and maybe this was just what she needed to hear to finally be done with him. He was in love with someone else.

What a fool she'd been.

"I have to go," she said, pulling herself away from him.

He kept his arm around her, pulling her back down to him. "What are you going to do, Emma? Find someone else and crawl into bed with him?"

"What if I do?"

"I can't let you do that," he said.

"And just how do you think you're going to stop me?"

Chapter 17

"Like this."

His mouth came down on hers. His warm breath, and then his lips, his tongue, his touch exquisitely gentle and slow. Her tears started falling once again, because it was so sweet, bitter, bittersweet. This was what she'd wanted so badly for more than two endless years, what she thought she'd never have.

"What are you doing?" she whispered.

He drew back a fraction of an inch. "Kissing you."

"Why?"

"Because it's usually a really good place to start."

"Start what?"

"Making love to a woman."

She froze. "You're not going to do that."

"Not if you don't want me to. But there's no way I'm going to let you have another night like tonight. No way I'm turning you loose on the world determined to find some man—any damned man—to have sex with you."

Before she could say anything to that, she got his mouth again, warm and sure, moving over hers. No one kissed quite like he did. She should know. She'd kissed a lot of guys trying to find someone who did, someone who could bring her body alive the way he did.

It was like an infusion of heat, of need. It blossomed deep inside of her, maybe in her heart, eventually settling lower, deep in her belly, and spreading all the way to her fingertips and her toes. Her whole body started tingling. It was like every inch of her skin was on edge, begging for his hands, his mouth.

Her breasts were full and heavy, her nipples hardening. He drank from her mouth, taking and taking and taking until he made her head spin. He turned her in his arms until she was facing him, lying on top of him, and then he shifted his legs, spreading them to either side of hers, and he was . . .

Oh, he wanted her.

She could feel him, hard and swollen and throbbing against her.

She gasped. Couldn't help it. He honestly wanted her?

"You're going to have to say it," he said. "We're not having any mistakes about this, and you've got to swear to me you're not still drunk."

"I'm not," she said. She thought she must be dreaming, but she wasn't drunk anymore.

"And this is what you want?"

"Yes."

"Emma, I don't want you to regret this in the morning."

"I could never regret this."

"Because there's no going back from this."

"I know that, Rye."

"And you're safe? Right now? That shot you were talking about—I'm not going to make you pregnant?"

"I'm safe," she said, still not quite believing he was

going to do this, that the two of them were. "What made you change your mind?"

He sighed, his hand at the side of her face, his forehead coming down to rest against hers. "I think you'd honestly go through with it, that sooner or later you'd find someone and make yourself do this for all the wrong reasons. You might get hurt, Emma. There's no telling what someone would do to you."

So this was a favor?

He kissed the tip of her nose, and she noticed that his breathing was labored and not quite steady. "I'll be gentle."

"I know you will."

He kissed her cheek then, a butterfly kiss. "I'll be thorough."

Emma shivered, about a thousand highly erotic pictures rushing through her head.

"I'll make it very, very good for you."

Oh, he would.

He kissed her mouth again finally, hungrily, completely, just as he'd promised. It was like her body had turned liquid and molded itself to his. He buried his face in the tender skin at the side of her neck, and she shivered and clung to him, trying to get closer, desperate to hang on so tight he couldn't get away. Little moaning sounds were coming from her throat. She couldn't help it. It was like her whole body was crying out.

With trembling hands, she undid the buttons on his shirt, wanting skin beneath her fingertips, against her palms, wanting to see him and taste him, wanting to love him.

It did seem much like a dream. She'd had so many of him over the years. The sureness of his touch, the feel of him, and the way his body just seemed to fit against hers. None of this closing her eyes and trying to pretend to feel something, when she really felt nothing. No more wondering what was wrong with her that she couldn't respond to anyone but him.

He was beautiful. Honestly, he got more attractive every year. His body, though still familiar, seemed even leaner and harder than ever, and it was wonderful to touch him, to have the freedom to indulge herself with him.

She got the last button of his shirt free and stroked a hand across his chest, all those intriguing dips and swells, those little golden hairs feeling slightly rough against her fingertips, and his nipples bunched in knots.

She tilted her head and covered one with her mouth, licking, sucking.

He groaned and his body bucked against hers.

Emma lifted her head, dazed and very, very happy. She'd made him want her?

Or was she going to be like all those other women he brought here to this very bed? What had he said? *Just women. No one special.*

Emma lifted her head, and he did, too. They stared at each other.

"What's wrong?" he asked. "Change your mind?"

"No." No way she was giving up this night, this chance with him.

"Too fast?"

"No." It was perfect. Everything except when she couldn't shut her mind to traitorous thoughts like that. *No one special.*

He took her face between both his hands, leaning down until they were eye to eye. "You can call this off anytime you want. Just say the word. That's all you have to do."

"I will not change my mind," she said, and she wasn't about to let him change his, either.

She took his mouth, took his tongue, and when she had it deep inside of her, she imagined him lying heavily on top of her, pushing his way inside, thrusting in and out, and her grabbing on to him and not letting go.

That's what she wanted.

Everything.

He groaned again, and he was hot to the touch. They'd slid down in the bed until they were lying face-to-face on their sides, and she let her hand slip between them, reaching for the hard ridge of his that pressed against her belly.

She found him, her fingers stretching over the length of him, and then pressing her palm against him.

He was so big. She'd never understood how this could work. She knew her own body. There was no space inside of her that was big enough to accommodate him, although the thought of trying was enough to set her blood throbbing.

She rubbed up and down with her hand. He went still, sucking in a ragged breath. "Like this?" she asked.

"Just like that."

His voice was low and strained. He went to work with his hands. Roaming over her body through the clothes he'd given her to wear and then slipping beneath the shirt, his hand covering her bare breast, cupping it, taking the weight of it in his palm. He flicked a thumb back and forth across her nipple, and she came up off the bed, forgetting everything else but that for a moment.

He rolled her over onto her back, took the other nipple into his mouth through her shirt. She slid her hand into his hair, holding him to her, not about to let him go. She ached. Just ached. If he didn't take

her clothes off right this minute and come inside
her . . .

"I can't wait any longer," she said. "I can't."

"You will, and you'll be glad you did."

"Rye—"

"Emma, believe me, if I can wait, you can, too."

"You don't want to, either?"

"No," he said raggedly.

"I've been waiting forever," she complained, her
body practically humming with tension. It was like
those funny purring sounds a contented cat made, like
a little revving engine. Zoom, zoom, zoom, zoom,
zoom. "I can't," she said. "I can't."

"You can." But he slipped his hands inside her
sweatpants as he said it and pulled them down and
off, throwing them into the corner. Her shirt came
next, and then his, and then his jeans.

Her mouth went dry at the sight of him naked, that
tight, well-muscled body, the curling, rippling muscles
of his shoulders and his chest, the hard stomach, trim
hips, and . . .

Oh, my. She wasn't sure how he'd kept that confined for so long in those snug jeans. It sprang free
now, big and thick, from between his thighs. She followed the line down his chest and stomach, that fine
dusting of hair that narrowed into a straight line, lower
and lower, leading to this.

He'd stood up to yank off his jeans, and before
he could climb back into bed, she reached for him,
her hand touching him there. It felt oddly delicate
and soft, while what was beneath was amazingly
hard.

"Emma," he groaned, all the breath seeming to
leave his body.

"What?" She rubbed her palm along his length, loving the texture of this skin, imagining him pushing inside of her with this. She throbbed just thinking about it, and it seemed he did, too.

She took him more firmly in her hand, wrapping her fingers around him, thinking she wanted a taste of his skin, that the texture was so amazing. She imagined having him in her mouth.

There were girls she'd known who thought nothing of doing this for a guy, guys who thought it was somehow their due for simply existing and being a male of the species. But she'd never felt like that.

She'd never wanted to, until now.

She caught him by the side of the bed, while he was still standing, and kissed his right thigh. Her hand closed around his hip, and she nudged him with her nose, finding that even the scent of this part of him was sexy.

He groaned, and she rubbed her nose along the entire length of him and placed a kiss on that soft skin just below his belly button and then moved lower, excited and uneasy at the same time.

She knew people had sex all the time. People everywhere. But really, there was no way that could fit inside of her. She went back down the length of him with her tongue stroking, finding the skin just as delicate as she thought.

"Emma, I don't think this is a good idea right now."

"Why not?" She wanted to taste him, wanted him inside of her like this, and then later . . . Later she'd have him lying on top of her and taking this and . . .

"Emma!"

She opened her mouth wide and took him inside. His entire body went tight, his hand in her hair latching on to a handful of it, and she wasn't sure at first if he was going to hold her there or tear her mouth off of him.

He held her there, little ripples pulsing through him.

She would never have believed this could turn her on so completely, but it did. Like when he'd put his tongue in her mouth, thrusting smoothly in and out. She'd latched on to it and taken up the rhythm herself. That's what it must be like to have this inside of her. Like that kiss and her taking him this way. She didn't see how it could possibly be better, because this . . .

She could feel the power in his body, the strength, all those lovely muscles bunched together and him holding himself rigidly under control and just melting for her. The sounds he was making, the hold he had on her, like he might come apart at any minute.

It excited her, had her thinking he just couldn't get enough of her as she picked up the subtle thrusting rhythm he made now with his hips, taking him in and out and thinking about having him there in that other place.

"Enough." He groaned, took her by the shoulders, and pushed her firmly away.

He pushed her back onto the bed and followed her down. He nudged her legs apart, settled himself between them, and with a few little adjustments of his body against hers, he was there, right at the heart of her. He pushed inside just a bit, pausing there at the entrance to her body.

He was wet from her mouth, and she was wet, too, from everything he'd done and the things she'd done to him. Embarrassingly so, she thought, not that she really cared at the moment.

He felt so good on top of her, overwhelming, overpowering, overheated, and this was a kind of intimacy she couldn't imagine sharing with anyone but him. She couldn't imagine trusting anyone else the way she trusted him.

"Rye," she whispered into his ear, "I'm so glad it's you."

He kissed her, slowly, sweetly, hotly. "Are you ready for this?"

"Yes."

He arched his back slightly, thrusting smoothly, slowly, stretching her, filling her. She wanted him all the way inside, struggled to find a way to take him there, squirming and wriggling her hips and lifting her body up and to his.

"Careful," he said. "I don't want to hurt you."

"It doesn't hurt. Not exactly. It . . . Rye!" She needed him. Now.

"I'll get there, Em. All the way. I promise."

And he did.

Ever so slowly, until she thought she would scream. As it was, she feared she'd left the imprint of her fingernails in his shoulder, she'd held on so tightly. He'd rocked, little by little, coming deeper with each thrust. She'd nearly wept in frustration, and then there it was.

The barrier in the end seemed like nothing. One minute they were both straining against it, and with the next subtle thrust of his hips, it was gone. He pushed his way so deeply inside of her, they both gasped and went still.

He dipped his forehead down to hers, nuzzled her ear with his mouth. "Told you I'd get there."

She groaned, thinking maybe she just wouldn't ever have to move again. Not wanting to ever let him leave this spot.

He was inside of her, a part of her. They were

in that place where two people couldn't get any closer.

"You okay?"

"Yes," she said.

He eased back maybe an inch, and before she could protest, he came right back. "Hurt?"

"No."

Her body had a grip on his, and this sliding sensation . . . It was interesting. Better than interesting. He pulsed inside of her, throbbed. She could feel it. There was a rhythm to it, like the one beating inside of her.

"More," she said.

She could feel the grin come across his face, feel laughter rippling through his chest. He pulled back and came forward again. "Like that?"

"Yes. Like that."

Before it was done, she had her legs wrapped around his waist practically, at his urging, and her body was rocking back and forth against his. The rhythm built higher and higher. It was like someone else had taken over her body, her but not her. Like she'd become something of a madwoman, begging him to finish it, to take her harder and faster and higher. She held on to him as tightly as she could, until her arms ached, and her whole body ached, and tears seeped from her eyes.

He was a powerful man, and it was a beautiful thing, the way he moved against her, the way he seemed as out of control in the end as she did.

The way the waves rippled through her and her entire body went tight. The way she squeezed him in little waves, and the way he buried his face against her neck and his whole body shuddered as they strained to get one centimeter closer, because nothing could be close enough.

She felt him come inside of her, felt the heat and the moistness, felt what it did to him when it happened. He shuddered and then collapsed on top of her.

It seemed like nothing in the world moved in that first instant afterward. Like the whole world had spun down to a grinding halt.

And then she became aware of the fact that her body still throbbed joyously, as did his, with him buried deep inside of her.

They were both gasping for breath, and he kissed the side of her face next to her ear, and then strung kisses along her cheek, her jaw, finally her mouth.

He kissed her eyes, her nose. "You okay?"

"Yes. Thank you."

"You're welcome." He laughed again. "I must be crushing you."

"No." She wrapped her arms around him when he started to lift himself off of her. This could not end. "Stay. Stay right here."

And he did.

She slept like the dead, or maybe like someone who wished she was dead by the time she slowly came awake.

Her head hurt. There was light coming from somewhere. When she dared open her eyes just for an instant, she realized the light hurt, too. Her stomach felt hollow, like it might have been pulled from her body and stomped on by a herd of wild horses and then put back inside her. She felt feverish and oddly cold at the same time.

Somewhere in the very back of her throat was a faint taste of alcohol, and then she remembered. . . .

Emma groaned and rolled over, burying her face in her pillow.

No, not her pillow. Hers was big and thick. This one was flat, almost nothing. What was the point in having a pillow like this, like a pancake?

Then she remembered . . . She'd gotten drunk.

What a fool she'd been.

She'd gone to Brian's apartment.

She'd tried so hard to like it when he touched her, when he kissed her, which was so unlike the feeling of Rye touching her, Rye kissing her.

Emma's eyes jerked open at that.

She was in a bedroom, an oddly empty room.

There was a bed and nothing else.

Hardwood floors, sanded smooth, but unfinished.

She remembered that look . . . That unfinished look.

Then she heard the shower running.

She remembered that shower, didn't she?

She figured out at about the same time that she wasn't wearing anything at all, that she was oddly aware of every inch of bare skin pressed against the sheets, and she was a bit sore in a place that had never been sore before.

Then she remembered Rye.

"Oh, my God." She closed her eyes and begged, "Please, please, please don't let me have done this."

He'd found her. He'd come to get her when she'd called Sam. She could have sworn she'd called Sam, but Rye had come and brought her here and . . .

She'd yelled at him. She'd cried all over him and told him her stupid plan and why she hadn't been able to go through with it. She'd told him how miserable she'd been and how lonely and that she'd been waiting for him all these years.

She'd told him she loved him.

And then she'd done something almost as stupid as what she'd planned to do with Brian.

"Oh, my God," she said again.

She'd blackmailed her way into bed with him.

Surely she hadn't done that.

Begged? That wasn't any better, was it?

She had to get out of there, couldn't stand the idea of having to face him this morning, the memory of what they'd done together burned into her brain. An experience that had seemed so wonderful the night before, but so humiliating in the light of day.

As the sound of the water in the shower ceased, she threw back the sheet and pulled on the clothes he'd given her to wear. She ran downstairs. Her shoes and her coat were by the door, the coat pocket still held her wallet and keys.

If she could get back to campus, she could get into her room and hide.

She threw open the front door as she heard him call her name, and then she ran outside.

He couldn't believe she was gone.

He had no idea what he would have said to her this morning, how he could have explained, where they could possibly go from here. But he'd counted on at least having the opportunity to figure it all out and to say it.

God, he'd slept with her. She'd been a virgin, and he'd slept with her. How could he have done that? How could he have let himself? All these years, he'd stayed away, and now this . . .

First things first. He forced himself to try to calm down, think this through. He couldn't tell her anything until he could find her. After assuring himself that she was nowhere in the house, he got dressed and called Sam's. What he might have said if his brother answered, he couldn't imagine. Thankfully, he got Grace, and Grace would do anything for him.

"Is Emma there?" he asked.

"No, she went back to school last night. It was her birthday, and you missed it," Grace said accusingly. "If you ever missed my birthday—"

"I would never miss your birthday," he reassured her. And if he hadn't felt so bad about missing Emma's, so guilty . . . If he hadn't gone over there later, once he was sure the party was over, and hung around waiting for someone to tell him how she was, so he wouldn't have to ask, none of this would have happened. "I need a favor, Grace. I need Emma's phone number at school."

She gave it to him, and then, just in case, he got the name of Emma's dorm and her room number, telling himself she hadn't been drunk, and she had been sure of what she wanted. Not that it was any excuse.

He thanked Grace and hung up, dialed the number for an hour straight before Emma picked up the phone.

"Let me guess," he said. "You're having second thoughts this morning?"

She hung up on him. Didn't say a word. He just heard a click and then dead air. He called back. She didn't answer. Her answering machine picked up again, hers and some girl named Melanie's.

"Emma, I'm sorry. Okay? And I'm worried about you. Please talk to me."

She didn't. He waited so long without saying anything that the machine clicked off. He called back, again got the machine.

"Emma—"

She picked up the phone. Before he could say two words, she said, "I don't want to talk about it, and I don't want to talk to you. I'm turning off the machine. I'm taking the phone off the hook."

"Emma—"

Which was obviously what she did. Now when he called, all he got was a busy signal, until the phone company came on the line, helpfully offering to keep dialing for him for a nominal fee. He should let them. She couldn't keep the phone off the hook forever.

But he was in no mood to wait her out. He got into his truck and drove, still seething at the way he'd obviously botched things with her once again. He found the dorm without any problem, parked in a place that he feared would surely get him a ticket, but he just didn't give a damn.

She was going to talk to him, one way or another.

He got out of his truck, slammed the door, stalked up to the entrance, and found her two steps outside the front door going somewhere, probably to escape before he got there. She paled at the sight of him and backed up until she was against the wall.

"One way or another, you're going to talk to me. You owe me that." Her chin came up. She gave him a painfully sad look. "Oh, hell, Emma. I'm sorry. What was I supposed to do? Tell me that? What was I supposed to do?"

She was trying to say something, trying not to cry.

A woman in the most somber brown dress, one who looked like a prison matron opened the glass-front door and glared at him. "Is there a problem?"

"No. No problem," he claimed.

"Emma?" she asked, clearly unwilling to take his word for it.

"We're fine, Mrs. Grant. We're just going over here to talk."

The dragon lady gave him a look that would have felled lesser men, or at least men who'd never been in prison. He took Emma by the arm and stalked over to a park bench under a tree in the corner. It was cold out here. He hadn't realized before. He'd been too steamed. And she looked hurt, dammit.

Logically, he knew he hadn't hurt her. At least not physically. She'd been with him every inch of the way. But emotionally . . . He didn't know where to begin emotionally. He couldn't make sense of his own feelings right now, much less hers. He'd been blindsided by the whole thing. Terrified when he'd gotten her call, terrified in the truck on his way to find her and again once he'd seen her. Even more so when she'd explained her little lose-her-virginity plan to him. He'd been furious that she'd been drinking, that some little shit had torn her blouse, furious at what might have happened to her.

It seemed she'd been miserable for two solid years, and that was about to burn a hole in his gut, too. He had no idea where to even begin or where they went from here. The best he could do was, "Tell me what's wrong, Emma."

She shot him an incredulous look.

"Okay . . . You obviously regret what happened. . . ." Hadn't he known they would? Wasn't that why he'd tried so hard to resist her all this time? Logic went right out the window, and he had to ask, "Did I hurt you?"

"Just my pride."

Pride? Okay, it hadn't been one of her finer moments. But, hell, they all did stupid things every now and then. She was one of the most levelheaded, responsible people he'd ever met, except when it came to him. Not that he wouldn't rather cut off his right arm than ever hurt her. Which he'd done.

And God knew he should have found a way to keep from having her last night. He'd never thought he would, but he'd burned for her, and he could have sworn she had done the same for him. He'd been surprised the bed hadn't gone up in flames, despite the considerable restraint he thought he'd managed to use with her. Then she'd run away from him this morning.

"Okay, pretend I'm totally lost here. As clueless as any man can be, and explain it to me in little bitty words that maybe I can understand, Emma. Because I'm not leaving until I understand what I did that was so wrong."

"Oh, for God's sake, you didn't do anything wrong," she said. "It was nice of you to be so accommodating."

"Accommodating?" There was nothing accommodating about it. He'd been dying for her, and he'd finally let himself have her, and now she seemed to hate him for it? "Try it one more time, Em. Little bitty words, remember? I'm just not getting it."

She looked like she'd just as soon spit on him as anything else, but she said, "Don't you remember anything I said to you last night?"

"I remember everything you said."

"And how do you think you'd feel if you were me, and you'd said those things to someone?"

What? Back to her genius plan? Okay, it was bad, but hell, he'd had to admit to killing someone. The two really didn't compare, did they?

"You're embarrassed?" he guessed. But that didn't equal fury, did it? It didn't equal this kind of pain.

She looked even sadder. Tears were coming any minute. He had to stop them.

"Emma, it's not like I haven't ever done anything . . ." Not stupid. Her whole little plan was incredibly stupid, but he'd yelled that at her last night when he'd been scared for her and so mad he could hardly see straight. He wouldn't say that again. "It's not like I've never made a mistake. Not like I haven't done things I regret. It happens. Not that often to you, I know, but . . . Give yourself a break. So you're not perfect."

She didn't have to be, certainly not for him.

And he had to find a way to apologize for the past two years, for the fact that she'd been so unhappy. He'd never wanted that for her.

"A mistake?" Then she was crying. *Damn.* "I backed you into a corner until, out of a sense of fear over what I'd do next and maybe guilt, you took me to bed with you."

"Guilt?" No, he just couldn't stand it anymore. Couldn't stand the idea of anyone else touching her. Couldn't walk away from her one more time. Couldn't stand her looking so lost or being so sad. "It wasn't guilt, and I thought it's what you wanted. I sure wanted it."

"Oh, right. That's why all the other times I've thrown myself at you, you turned me down. The only reason you were even there last night was because I was drunk and in trouble and thought I'd called Sam. Didn't I call Sam?"

"Yes. I came by the house later, and I—"

"Felt some obligation to come save me from my own stupidity?"

"I was scared shitless about what had happened to you."

"That's what I said. You were scared, and then you felt guilty. That's all I had to do to have you, huh? Scare you and then turn on the guilt. If only I'd known, I could have had you years ago."

"Emma, it wasn't like that." Oh, hell, it had started like that, but . . .

"Please, just leave me alone," she said. "I'm sorry

I dragged you back into my pathetic little life. I'm sorry I scared you, and I'm sorry I played the sympathy card so well that we ended up in your bed."

"Sympathy? What the hell do you think sympathy had to do with it?"

"Oh, please. Are you going to make me say it?"

"Say what? I have to understand why you're so upset." He couldn't begin to fix it until he understood, and he had to fix this. He couldn't stand to see her this way.

"It's humiliating, Rye. What is it people call it, a pity fu—"

"Don't you dare," he said.

"You were afraid if you didn't, I'd find someone else. That I'd do another really stupid thing and maybe get hurt."

"Emma, there was no way I could have let you do that."

"That's what I mean. You bailed me out of another messy problem. I'm glad you didn't get thrown in jail for it this time, and I'm sorry. Really, I am. The next time I get into trouble, I promise I will not call you."

"Well, who the hell are you going to call, if not me?" He was screaming at her by then, and as baffled as he'd ever been by any situation he'd ever gotten himself into with a woman.

He had to get her out of here, someplace private where they could talk. He'd counted on them having a nice long talk this morning, and he supposed he should have taken the time for it last night, before he'd touched her. But he'd been so mad he could hardly see straight, and then he'd just let himself have her. No more pretending. No more waiting. How it had all gone so wrong this morning, he would never understand, and he really didn't want to have this conversation turn into a public shouting match.

"I have to go," she said, getting to her feet.

"No way," he said, rising, too.

She started to stalk off, and he grabbed her by the arm.

"Rye, let me go."

"So you can run away again? No."

"I think the lady's done talking," a deep, authoritative voice said.

Rye looked up and there was a cop. No . . . campus security.

Great.

That's what he got for getting involved with a college girl. The guy was looking at him like he had to be the scum of the earth, trolling college campuses for little girls.

Yeah, he could just imagine how this looked.

"Let her go," the officer said.

Rye let go. He didn't argue with cops or pseudo-cops or anyone like that.

"Anything I should know about?" the officer asked.

"No," Emma said. "I'm fine."

"You're sure?"

She nodded. The pseudo-cop looked at Rye. "That your truck?"

"Yes," he admitted.

"You need to come with me, so I can write you a little ticket. It's a permit-only zone, and I don't think you're a student, are you?"

"Not quite."

He was almost desperate enough to claim to be Emma's uncle. Had he really sunk to that level? To ever claim that relationship with her? If the cop had heard enough of their conversation, he'd really love that part. Rye was an ex-con sleeping with his brother's adopted daughter. Days just didn't get any better than this.

"Emma, please come with me," he said.

She shook her head.

"We're not done," he told her. Shit, he sounded just like her old friend Mark, who'd made a threat just like that.

"You gonna go? Or am I going to take you in?" the officer asked.

"I'm going."

Straight to hell, it seemed.

Straight to hell.

Chapter 18

He kept calling. She kept hanging up, when she answered the phone at all. Melanie talked to him several times and claimed he sounded honestly sorry, worried, and as baffled as any man could be. He left long, apologetic messages on her answering machine.

In her saddest moments, Emma worried that she was acting like the kid he'd accused her of being.

Then he started with the flowers. Tiny, pale, pale pink roses. They were so pretty, she couldn't resist. The card said simply *I'm sorry.*

Sorry about what? Because she'd humiliated herself in front of him? Or because he'd made love to her. Okay, he'd had sex with her, and she'd made love to him, and it had been . . . Oh, her whole body started trembling just thinking about it.

"That good, huh?" Melanie had said, when Emma had stumbled through her explanation of what had happened.

Yes, it had been that good, everything she'd ever dreamed it would be, except she'd blackmailed her way into his bed. If that wasn't bad enough, she'd told

him she loved him. She'd told him she'd been waiting
for him and even now, she couldn't get him out of
her head or her heart.

Thankfully, he finally stopped calling.

She sat in her room staring at her flowers. Four
days later, just as they'd started to wilt, she got more,
lavender colored this time. The card said, *Please talk
to me.*

She had terribly erotic dreams about him. If years
of wanting him were bad, wanting him now—knowing
what she was missing—was even worse. She relived
every moment, every touch of his hands and the feel
of him moving over her and inside of her. How was
she ever supposed to forget him now?

More flowers came, soft yellow. *Please don't do anything crazy.*

Like what? All she'd wanted to do was break his
hold on her, move on with her life. Going to bed with
someone seemed like a drastic step to take, but she'd
been desperate. All this time, she'd been saving herself for him. Having sex with someone else meant giving up on that dream, giving up on him, which she
had to do.

It had all made some kind of twisted sense to her
a few weeks ago.

Flowers kept coming. His cards got funnier.

Emma,

  *I hope you're finding this amusing, because the
clerks at the floral shop sure are. They know me
by name now, and they've got a pool going as to
what I did to make you so mad at me that even
all these flowers haven't gotten me out of the dog-
house. I need to see you. I need to talk to you.
My birthday's next week. Grace is making me a
cake with black icing (I think she's still mad at me*

for not coming to your party) and I know this isn't
a conversation to have with an audience, but
maybe we could go somewhere afterward. Please?

Emma folded the card and slipped it into the enve-
lope. It was ridiculously small. He'd put the message
in the tiniest print and scrawled it on both sides of
the card to make it fit.

She missed him like crazy.

She had a million things to do, papers to write, projects to finish. Finals were only six weeks away, and
she'd hardly done anything but fret.

"Doesn't look like he's going to give up anytime
soon," Mel said.

"He feels guilty. He has this whole protective thing
going with me, always has. But that's it."

"How do you know?"

"Mel, he's ignored me for more than two years."

"And now you've managed to get his attention."

"By doing something stupid."

"Emma, you've been feeling rotten for two years,
and if there was anything you could have possibly
done to get his attention, you would have. Well, you
finally did it. Maybe not in the way you'd have liked,
but he's paying attention. What are you going to do
about it?"

She couldn't decide. Like a coward, she caught a
ride with a friend who was going to Baxter the weekend of Rye's birthday, and then couldn't bring herself
to go to her own house that day. The whole charade
between them had turned into something like a divorce. They shared custody of the family. Today was
his day to have them.

She lingered outside, watching and waiting from a
house two doors down, and when the party broke up
around seven, he came walking down the street to his

truck, parked not far from her. She stepped out from her hiding place next to the shrubbery as he'd just finished loading up his stash of gifts.

He turned around and stared at her. "I thought I was going to have to hunt you down tonight."

"Hunt me down?"

He nodded. "I'm tired of being reasonable. I'm tired of trying to figure out what I did that was so wrong and begging you to talk to me."

"You didn't do anything wrong."

"I must have. You disappeared. I know you're not up on all the morning-after etiquette, but it's really rude to run out without saying a thing or giving the person you were with a chance to say anything. I had a lot I wanted to say."

"Sorry. I couldn't . . .," she said. "I just couldn't stand to face you."

"Well, you're going to face me now." He opened up the passenger-side door and said, "Get in the truck."

She got in. He took her back to his house. She studied it without the alcoholic haze that had hampered her view or her memory of the time before.

"The house looks nice. You're almost done, aren't you?"

"Almost," he said, taking her hand and helping her out of the truck. Almost like they were on a date.

Emma closed her eyes and tried to steel herself for what was to come. For more of his guilt and his outrage over her whole stupid plan.

He unlocked the front door and flicked on the lights. She stood there in the foyer looking all around. He still hadn't stained or varnished the floors or painted or papered the walls, and it had been more than six weeks.

"Having trouble making up your mind what you want?" she asked.

He'd shrugged off his coat and hung it on a peg on the wall, and now he was reaching for hers, drawing it off her shoulders and hanging it up as well. When he turned back to her, he was smiling.

"I know exactly what I want, Emma. I just haven't let myself have it." There was heat coming off his body and a world of possibilities in his eyes.

"I was talking about the house," she said.

"I wasn't."

Oh.

"And you know what?" he said. "I'm getting really tired of not letting myself have what I want."

Well . . . What was she supposed to say to that?

He was coming closer, too. Not that there was any-place to go, really. She took a step back, which brought her against the wall.

He turned off the lights he'd just turned on a mo-ment before, and she really didn't understand. Not until he put one of his hands on the wall just to the left of her head, the other by her right shoulder and leaned into her, until she could very nearly feel the imprint of his altogether impressive body against hers. It was just a breath away, a whisper.

What was he doing?

She'd expected to get lectured about her own safety and waiting until she was older and in love. With any-one *but* him. She hadn't expected him to touch her at all.

"Was that it, Emma? The wanting part? Could you possibly think I didn't want you that night?" He was smiling in the most understanding way.

She was near tears. "I didn't give you much choice in the matter."

"I can say no." He came nearly close enough to touch his lips to hers. "I do it all the time."

"Oh, right—"

"And the revolving door line? That really wasn't very nice."

"You have a different woman every six weeks," she reminded him.

"Not in my bed," he said.

"Okay, in theirs—"

"Nope."

"Rye—"

"I told you, I'm really tired of not getting what I want, especially now that I know what it's like. That my body knows. Now that I know you want me just as much. Tell me that, Emma. Tell me you want me half as much as I want you."

"More," she said. "I must want you more because—"

He shut off the words with a kiss, a ruthless, ravaging, wild kiss. It was like someone opening the door on a furnace—an instantaneous blast of pure heat. He brought his body fully into contact with hers, pressing her against the wall and attacking with lightning-fast hands.

They were everywhere, working furiously over the buttons of her blouse and tugging down the straps of her bra. Undoing the button at the back of her skirt and tugging the blouse up until he found skin, tunneling up under her skirt until he got his hands inside her panties and found even more skin.

It was like going from zero to sixty in about three seconds flat.

All of a sudden, she remembered everything she'd tried so hard to forget, that glorious, hard body of his, and his wicked mouth, the slight roughness to the skin of his hands, a working man's hands. He surged against her. She put her hand between his legs and rubbed the hard ridge nestled against her belly.

He groaned and ripped his mouth from hers long enough to say, "Help."

She unbuttoned his jeans and unzipped. He shoved them and his briefs down, pulled down her panties as well.

"Rye?"

"It's been six weeks, Emma."

It had been, and if she was any judge of the situation, he was desperate for her.

His hands went beneath her skirt once more. Palming her hips, he lifted her feet off the ground and urged her thighs apart. It left her completely open to him. He settled himself between her thighs, her firmly against the wall. She wrapped her legs around his waist, for balance in her precarious position at first, and then because it was the only real leverage she had to pull him closer.

She was wet, just like that. He teased her, letting the full length of his erection slide along her slick, wet heat. It was so very wicked, knowing one subtle little shift of his body and hers, and he'd be right there, right where she wanted him.

"Rye," she groaned.

"Does this feel like a man whose arm you had to twist to get him here?"

"No." She laughed.

"Tell me that little shot of yours is still working."

"Shot?"

"Birth control, Emma."

"Oh. Yes." She'd gotten a postcard last week to remind her it would be time to come in next month for another one, so she was still good. Still safe. And in just a minute, he would be inside of her.

"Rye," she said again.

"I'm coming. Promise." He grinned against her mouth. "Open up for me."

She thought he meant her mouth, but that wasn't it. He lifted her just a fraction of an inch higher and gave a little thrust of his hips. There he was. Right there. It was still a stretch. He still made her feel so full, overwhelmed almost. Like she just couldn't quite take him, but in the end, she did.

He slid home, gave a very contented-sounding sigh, his face right next to hers, his gaze locked on hers. For a second, they hung there together, time frozen around them, while they were as close as two people could be.

"This is how I want you," he said, rocking ever so slightly against her, and then harder and harder, until he was so deep inside of her she didn't think there could be so much as a molecule between them.

She wrapped her arms more tightly around him, her legs, closed her eyes and let her head drop to his shoulder. Tears were coming, and this wasn't the time, but . . . *He wants me.*

All she'd ever wanted was for him to want her and to love her, and she'd never believed that would happen.

He wasn't treating her like a silly, desperate girl. Not that she hadn't appreciated every bit of tenderness and patience he'd shown her that first night. But this . . . This was raw and intense and so powerful. It was desire, pure and simple, fast and hot, shattering every bit of reserve and control she had.

"Oh, Rye."

He thrust against her, her whole body shifting with each rush of his. She could feel him pulsing and swelling inside of her, could feel the grip her body had on him, could feel it all building and building until they simply exploded.

She shuddered against him, and he held her there,

pinned against the wall, leaning into her and nearly crushing her.

Not that she cared.

He wanted her.

Truly, desperately wanted her.

The way a man wants a woman.

Against the wall, barely inside his front door.

Oh, my, Emma thought.

How terribly grown up.

He eased back, giving her a lazy, satisfied grin and a slow, sweet kiss. "Did I mention that I missed you?"

"I missed you, too," she said. Not just in the last six weeks. There were more than two years that she'd spent desperately missing him.

He eased back, lowering her feet to the ground. She started trying to put her clothes into some order, but her panties were on the floor about five feet away. No way to get to them. She was going to button her blouse when Rye's hands stilled hers.

"I'm just going to take that right back off of you."

"But we just . . . I mean . . ." Of course, if he wanted to do this again, it wasn't like she was going to object. She was just surprised.

"Emma, that was just to take the edge off," he said, grinning at her.

Oh.

He took her to bed, and it was sweet and slow, a lesson in the rewards of patience. It was only as she was lying in his arms afterward that she thought of something. He hadn't used a condom. Not that she was at risk for getting pregnant, but she'd been raised in the safe-sex generation. It struck her as odd that he didn't use one.

"Rye?"

"Hmm?" he said lazily.

"I was thinking about what you said downstairs . . .
What I said . . . About the revolving door?" She really
wanted to know about that.

"Emma, there's no traffic going in and out of here."
She could hear a lazy brand of humor in his voice. "I
don't need a revolving door."

She frowned, not understanding. Not really wanting
to talk about anyone else who'd been with him,
but . . . "That night of my birthday? And tonight?
You didn't use a condom."

He slid down beside her until they were face-to-
face, side-by-side. "No, I didn't. We don't need one,
do we? You're not going to get pregnant, and you've
never done this before, so you don't have anything,
and neither do I. I made sure of that, Emma. I'd never
take a chance like that with you."

"I know, but—"

"Emma, I haven't been with anyone in more than
two years. Except you."

She didn't quite believe the words. They were floating
around in her head, but she couldn't arrange them in
any order that made sense. "But . . . all those women?"

"I told you I was capable of saying no. I turned 'em
all down."

She could barely breathe, barely get out the word.
"Why?"

He kissed her, lingering softly, smiling. "Why do
you think?"

"I don't know."

"Yes, you do," he whispered. "They weren't you,
Emma."

"But I saw you with them—"

"I'll admit, I tried to make some things work. Probably just like you did. I really tried, and I just couldn't
do it."

"I saw you laughing with them, and flirting with them, and I saw their hands all over you." She'd suffered unbelievably seeing him with all of them.

"That's all it was," he said. "Killing time. Trying to get on with my life. I sure didn't ever expect to end up here."

But he liked it here, didn't he? Sometimes life took people places they never expected to go. Like here. She would never be sorry for that.

"Sam asked you to stay away from me, didn't he?"

"I don't know if asked is the right word." He grinned. "He's your father. He had a right. Hell, he had an obligation to do what he thought was best for you. But I didn't stay away because he told me to. I stayed away because you were just turning nineteen and starting college—"

"And you didn't trust me to know my own mind? To know what I wanted, what I felt?"

He took a breath, looking truly worried now, truly sorry. "I felt like I had an obligation to give you that time."

"I've been miserable all this time." Miserable wanting him and thinking he just didn't care.

"I know that now. I'm sorry. I never wanted to hurt you, but I had to do what I thought was right."

"You could have told me. You could have said, 'Just grow up a little bit, and then we'll see.' "

"And what would you have done? Waited for me? That's not living, Emma. That's not taking time to be sure about what you want, what you need."

"So you're saying you did this for me?"

"I'm saying it seemed like an impossible situation, and I did the best I could. I'm sorry if that hurt you. I'm sorry if it makes you angry. I don't know what else I could have done. I wish you'd been happier, and sometimes I wish we hadn't met until later, when you were older, or that there weren't so many years between us in the first place. Hell, I wish I'd never stolen that car or killed anyone or gone to prison. But I can't change any of those things, just like I can't change this. I did the best I could for both of us."

She drifted off to sleep in his arms, thinking about what he'd said, thinking about where they went from here. When she woke up two hours later, rolled over, and reached for him, he wasn't there.

Emma sat up, listening and hearing nothing. The bathroom door was open, a faint light spilling out. He wasn't in there.

She wrapped herself up in a sheet and went downstairs, finding him in the living room. It was surprisingly chilly for April, and he'd built a fire, was sitting on the floor in front of it, his back against the sofa. His chest was bare, and he had an afghan wrapped around the lower half of his body.

She stood there waiting, not sure what to do. He took her hand and tugged her down to him. She sat facing him, letting him draw her head to his chest.

She wrapped her arms around his waist and wondered where they went from here. He wanted her, with a kind of desperate hunger that thrilled her, and he didn't want anyone else. But he'd just turned thirty-six to her twenty-one, and he was still Sam's brother. Some people would likely be shocked by that, regardless of the reality of the situation. Sam might still pitch a fit.

"Couldn't sleep?" he asked, his hand running lazily through her hair.

"You weren't there." She could get used to having him there, every time she reached for him deep in the night. She could get used to snuggling against his big, warm body and having him wrap his arms around her and waking up beside him every morning.

"I was just trying to figure out what I'm going to do with you," he said.

"What do you want to do?" she asked, stroking a hand down his chest, because if this was all she could have of him for now, she'd take it.

They could have a gloriously carnal affair, sneaking around in secret for as long as it lasted. It would give them a chance for the bond between them to grow, a chance to let him get used to the idea of them being together and maybe to let go of some of the guilt, of the sense that this was somehow wrong. Once it was out in the open, he'd have to make some decisions. She knew what she wanted, not just his body, but his heart, as well.

"What would you do, if you could do anything?" she asked.

"Wave a magic wand and make you about twenty-five. Of course, then I'd be forty, and you probably wouldn't want me anymore."

"Planning on falling apart when you hit forty, are you?" He'd be fabulous then. He'd always be that in her eyes. "Do you really think anything's going to change in a few years?"

If anything, the age gap would matter less and less.

"You have some things to do, Emma. Another year of college. You have career things to think about."

"No, I'm done in May," she said.

"What?"

"I haven't had anything else to do. I've been working as hard as you. The summers. The extra class load. It pays off. I'm graduating in May."

"As in . . . next month? That May?"

"Yes. I thought about getting my master's degree,

but I just don't think I can go right into that. I talked to a couple of people I trust, and they all said it was a good idea to get in a year or two of work experience first."

"Counseling, right?"

"Yes. There's a shelter about twenty minutes from here, on the outskirts of Cincinnati. For battered women and children. They were actually excited by the idea of having someone with firsthand experience. If it works out, I'll be working with the kids, mostly. And there's a counseling center on campus that's interested in having me part time. Lots of college girls get beat up by their boyfriends, you know."

He nodded. "I think I heard something about that."

"I've been volunteering there for about a year. It's been good for me. I tell them my story, and they listen to me, because I've been through it. And I like being able to help them."

"So, you're all set."

"Except for figuring out what I'm going to do with you," she said.

But she knew what she wanted. She reached up and kissed his jaw. It was rough and shadowed with stubble, and she loved just being able to touch him when she wanted. She loved being this close to him.

She wrapped her arms around his neck and kissed him more fully, rising up on her knees and pressing her body to his. The sheet was caught between them in front, but came untangled in the back, leaving that half of her bare, which seemed to interest him.

He stroked her back, up and down. "You have the most incredible skin, and the way you smell . . . It's vanilla, isn't it?"

"Yes." A lotion she'd been using for years.

"I remember. From the second time I ever saw you.

You walked into the kitchen straight from the bath. I smelled vanilla and wanted to nibble on you."

"You did?"

"Yes, right from the start."

"You did a pretty good job of hiding it," she complained.

"I didn't think I did."

"You kept me guessing."

And suffering. Oh, she'd suffered for him. But now she was in his arms. She kissed him, a soft, lingering, heated kiss, and ran her hands down his arms, down his sides, thinking to . . .

"What's this?" she asked. Her hand was on his right side, just above his hipbone. There was a raised ridge of skin she vaguely remembered finding earlier, when she'd been too interested in other things to ask.

He went still, staring into her eyes. "Old wounds."

She eased away to sit beside him, holding the sheet to her and looked. There was a ragged scar along his side just below his waistline, obviously old, but long, and she would have bet the cut had been deep.

She traced it with her fingertips. He was hardly breathing. "A knife?"

He nodded gravely.

"The guy who . . . the one you . . ."

"The one I killed." He said the words for her. "Did you forget, Emma? Forget who you were with? What I've done?"

"I know what you've done." She took his chin in her hand, making him look at her, when she knew he didn't want to. "I've always known. Do you?"

"Of course I do. There's not a day that goes by . . ."

"I'm not sure you do know. Joe told us the guy who jumped you had a knife. It looks like he used it on you. This is from him, isn't it?"

Rye nodded.

"It must have been bad." She turned her attention back to the scar, because it was easier to see this than the look on his face.

"Especially when they came into the treatment room in the infirmary and told me he was dead."

Emma shuddered at the thought of that awful day, mostly of what might have been. "And what do you think would have happened if you hadn't fought so hard that day? Do you ever think about that?"

"Morgan would still be alive. I wouldn't have spent years behind bars."

"Or you would have been dead," she said matter-of-factly.

Rye's gaze locked on to hers.

"Surely you've thought about that," she said, but she could see that he hadn't. "Rye, it's one of the first things they told us in the self-defense classes I took after that mess with Mark. If you're going to fight back, you've got to be willing to hurt the other person. You can't be squeamish about it, because if you go at it halfway, you're just going to make them madder. They're just going to hurt you even more. You have to hurt them enough to give yourself the time you need to get away."

He closed his eyes and looked away, pain etched across his face.

"Rye, it's me," she said. "Tell me. Please?"

"There was . . ." His voice broke, and he started again, struggling for air. "There was no way to get away."

Emma nodded. She'd guessed that part. "So it was either him or you. Did you think he would have let you go? Did you honestly think you had a choice?"

"I don't know what I had," he said. "He was a bad kid. A scary kid."

She glanced back down at that scar, thinking of the knife going a little deeper or slashing into him again. His heart. His lungs. Anywhere on his beautiful body. It would have been so easy.

"He attacked you, and you fought back," she said. "I know it must haunt you. But if only one of you was going to come out of that alive, I can't be sorry it was you. And after having someone come after me the way Mark did, after being that scared and feeling that vulnerable—"

"Don't," he said, taking her face in his hands, pressing his cheek to hers. "Don't think about that."

"No. I have to. We never talked about it, but I want you to know, because you might be the only one who really understands. I would have done anything to stop him, anything I could have. He knocked you out, and you didn't move for the longest time. I thought he'd killed you that day, and then I thought he was going to kill me. He was that out of control. If I'd had a gun, I would have shot him. If I'd had a knife, I would have used that. I would have done anything to keep him from hurting you or me any more than he already had. I should have told you this a long time ago, but you wouldn't talk to me, and you didn't want to see me."

"It wasn't that, Emma."

"Then what was it? This?" She touched the scar once again. "Everything you've done? Everyplace you've been?"

"All of that," he said.

And then she knew what to say, what he had to hear, and it was the truth, too. He couldn't argue this with her. He had to listen.

"If I'd fought back that day against Mark. If, in the end, he was dead, would you have blamed me for that? Would you have thought less of me?"

"No."

"If I'd gone to prison for it?"

"No," he insisted.

"And how is that different from what happened to you?" she asked.

He didn't say anything to that, looked dazed and sad and very much alone.

"You wouldn't have blamed me. I know that," she said. "I know what you went through must have been awful. I know it changed you. I know you lost years of your life. But it's over. Let it be over, Rye. Let me love you." *And love me back,* she thought. *Please love me back.* "It's time you forgave yourself. It's time to get on with your life, time for you and me. It's our turn. I know you want that."

"I've wanted a lot of things," he said raggedly.

"Well, this is one thing you can have. You can have me. And all of my love. For all of your life. I'm right here. I've always been here. All you have to do is reach out and take me."

She didn't think he'd do it, because she didn't think the words had sunk in yet. She knew forgiveness—especially of one's self—was a long, lonely road. But there was nothing to keep her from reaching for him. He was here, after all, and so was she. Tonight was theirs.

She turned to him, raised up on her knees, and then straddled him, the sheet caught between them for a moment, his arms hanging by his side. She wound hers around his shoulders, pressed her entire body to his, and kissed him deeply.

"I know you want me. And I'm right here."

She kissed his closed eyes, his forehead, the roughness of his jaw. His hands came up slowly, along her calves, her thighs, tugging on the sheet, bunching it together in his hands until he pulled it from between them, the afghan coming after it. He flung them toward the corner, and then she was naked in front of the fire with him.

His hands cupped her bare bottom, pulled her thighs apart, and settled her over his lap. "I don't know how you can stand to have my hands on you."

"I love having your hands on me."

She wriggled against him, heat to glorious heat. He was hard again, and in this position, she was totally open to him, could rub up and down along the length of him.

He groaned. "Like that, Emma. Just like that."

He kissed her deeply, hungrily, and then he lifted her up a bit and shifted beneath her until he was pushing inside of her once again, showing her with his hands on her hips what he wanted her to do. This way . . . This way it was up to her to set the rhythm, to tease him by rising up until he was barely inside of her and then wriggling her hips until he pulled her back down. She liked teasing him, liked pushing him to the point where he demanded more.

Her body fell into a natural rhythm, long, smooth strokes, rocking against him. She didn't intend to show him any mercy at all, not after how long he'd made her wait for this, for how much he'd made her suffer.

"That's it," he said. "Take me."

She didn't. She made him wait. His jaw tightened, and she knew she only had as much control here as he was willing to give her. She sank down upon him once more, taking him so deep. His hands tightened on her hips, gripping them in a way that spoke to the kind of tension filling his body.

"I'm done, Emma. I'll beg. Right now. Take me."

He urged her into a fast, hard rhythm, pulled her down and wouldn't let her pull back. He thrust up into her as best he could, and then she felt it one

more time, that glorious pulsing sensation, taking over
her body and his.

She buried her head against his neck and put her
arms around his shoulder and just held on. He cried
out and filled her completely, left her weak and spent
in his arms.

She kept thinking it had to feel less overwhelming,
that surely sooner or later she wouldn't feel like just
for a moment she'd absolutely died or ceased to exist
or left the planet. But this was power and intimacy on
a level she hadn't truly understood before.

It left her even more vulnerable than ever.

He'd always had her heart.

Now he had her body, as well.

Later, he took her back to his bed. She woke the
next morning curled up to his side. He was lying on
his back, her head against his chest. He was slowly
stroking her hair. It was so sweet, she didn't want to
let go.

"Do you have class this morning?" he asked drowsily.

"Yes, but not until ten."

"We need to get going, if you're going to make it."

She held him tighter. "But I don't want to move."

"All right. I'll get up. I'll get dressed, and while
you're in the shower, I'll make breakfast and then
take you back. How about that?"

"I don't want to go back."

He laughed. "You've only got a month. You can
stand it for a month, can't you?"

If, at the end of that month, she got him, she could.
Was that what he was saying?

And how did this work exactly? This morning-after
stuff. He'd told her it was terribly rude to just run out
without saying a word. He'd told her there were things
he wanted to say, and here it was, morning again.

"Emma?" he said, sitting up in the bed, leaning over her to kiss her softly.

"Yes. That's fine." For him to get up and fix her breakfast, then deliver her back to campus. Was she agreeing to that? Or to being away from him for another month?

He rolled out of bed and walked naked into the bathroom. She turned and watched him go in the glorious light of day, watched that subtle play of muscles in his thighs and hips as he walked, the narrowness of his waist and the width of his shoulders, the muscles in his arms.

It was an amazingly intimate moment, him leaving the bed, leaving her here, wrapped up in the covers and the warm spot he'd created for her. Her skin still tingled and she was so aware of the fact that she wasn't wearing a stitch. She loved stretching out beneath the sheets and curling up into the spot he'd just vacated. She thought she could still feel the imprint of his hands and his mouth on her body, and the altogether pleasant smell of sex clung to her and hung in the air.

So, did what happened last night make him hers now? She certainly felt like she was his. What would a grown woman do in this situation? One of those women he'd refused to take to his bed?

She still couldn't believe he hadn't. Not to say she doubted his word. Just that . . . Well, he was a man. As a group, they seemed quite able to divorce any true emotions from the whole process of sex. Certainly, the ones she'd met had been quite willing to bed her, all emotions aside. She was quite happy that he couldn't keep his emotions out of it, and that he hadn't wanted anyone but her.

He was out of the bathroom a moment later, a towel hanging precariously around his waist. "All right. Up," he ordered. "I'll see if I can find all your clothes and bring them to you."

She blushed at that. They were littered across the hall by the front door. She got into the bathroom and showered quickly, trying not to lose herself in the lingering scent of him, his soap, his shaving cream, his cologne. The whole place smelled of him.

Her body felt different beneath her own hands, her skin sensitized all over, and she was a bit sore. He'd warned her about that, but she hadn't cared at the time.

She got out of the shower, found her clothes in a stack outside the bathroom door, and hurriedly dressed. He was downstairs dishing out scrambled eggs and bacon, and it made her think of the meals they'd shared when she'd first met him.

She'd worried that they'd never again share even the small intimacy of a meal together, and now here she was, fresh from his bed, from the most incredible night.

She ate her breakfast, enjoying the quiet sense of companionship, enjoying just being in his presence. She had missed him terribly over the years.

They finished the meal, cleared the table, and then she stood in his kitchen, looking here and there while she tried to figure out what to say.

"What do you think?" he asked, leaning casually against the counter, his hands behind him propped up on the wood trim at the edge of the ceramic top.

"Hmm?"

"About the kitchen?"

"Oh. It's . . . What are you going to do in here?" It was much like the rest of the house. Everything was in place, but he hadn't chosen any colors or patterns, except for the dark green tile flooring with a marblelike pattern in it.

"Rachel has some smoked green glass. She's trying

to talk me into glass-front doors on some of the cabinets, and she thinks I should forget the backsplash or
any kind of wallpaper, tile instead on the walls between the upper and lower cabinets, patterned or even
hand painted. What do you think?"

"That sounds nice. She did a scrolling vine pattern
in a kitchen for some people who live out River Road.
It was pretty." Not too feminine. He wouldn't like
that, and he was good in the kitchen. He'd want a
place where he felt comfortable. And if he cared to,
he could go with some greenery, either real or fake,
on top of the cabinets, in keeping with the design on
the tile.

"She mentioned something about that," Rye said.
"I'll have to look at it."

"And the cabinets? What kind of finish?"

"I'm thinking cherry?"

He said it like he could be swayed one way or another. "I like cherry. It has a warm feel to it, but it's
not too dark."

He nodded. "Cherry it is."

Emma's foolish heart started beating faster. Surely,
she'd read too much into the casual exchange. She'd
teased him about having trouble figuring out what he
wanted for this house, about whether he was ever
going to finish it, and honestly, it looked like he hadn't
done anything since she was last here.

Sam was always talking about how hard he worked.
There'd been a time when every spare moment went
into this house. As busy as he might have been, he
could have found time to finish some things here over
the past six weeks.

Unless he didn't want to finish them on his own.

She'd always been afraid he'd bought this house for
someone else—for another woman—but it was obvious now that he hadn't.

And he wanted to know what she'd do to finish out the kitchen. . . .

"We've got to go, or you're going to be late," he said.

She frowned at that, but followed him to the front door. He took her coat and helped her into it, even going so far as to button all the buttons, grinning as he did. He helped her into the truck and drove her back to school. She slipped her hand into his, and he held it the whole way. When he parked beside her door, he walked her to the front door and kissed her once, then again, lingering there, his nose nuzzling against hers.

"I'd better go before my friend with campus security finds me."

"Rye, I'm so sorry about that."

"It's all right," he said, pulling back finally. "So . . . A month, huh? I guess you're going to be busy, tests, papers, getting ready for graduation?"

"Yes."

He looked serious for a moment. "I've got some stuff I have to do, too."

"Okay." With Sam? Was that what he meant? He had to talk to Sam? Or was it something else?

"What's the date?" he asked.

"Hmm?"

"Graduation? The date?"

She told him.

He kissed her one more time, and said, "I'll be there."

Chapter 19

She was afraid it would be one of the longest months of her life, but the time flew by. She had so much to do, and she had hope for the first time in so long. She studied like crazy and firmed up her job offer, and she kept waiting for a call or a visit from Sam about her and Rye, but that never happened.

Graduation day was chaotic, crowded, and kind of frenzied. She just wanted it to be over. She'd never regret coming here and getting her degree, and she had needed to be on her own for a while, to learn to trust herself again. But at the same time, she just wanted to get on with her life.

And she wanted Rye.

Sam, Rachel, Zach, Grace, and her grandfather came together for the graduation ceremonies, and she'd arranged to meet them in front of her dorm afterward.

Zach, who was taller than she was, gave her a big squeeze and lifted her off the ground. "You did it."

"Finally," she said.

Grace brought her a small bouquet of flowers that

had likely been swiped from someone's garden. She'd charmed all the neighbors. They never complained.

Emma took the flowers and said, "Thanks, Grace. They're beautiful."

"We should put one in your hair," Grace said quite seriously. She was into all sorts of ornamentation and decoration, hair included.

Rachel was crying and smiling at the same time. "We just haven't had enough time," she said, which was the same thing she'd said when Emma went off to college. "How are we supposed to let you go?"

"We're not going to," Sam said, giving her a big hug himself. "You'll always be our daughter."

And then she started to cry. "I know that."

Sam let her go and looked over his shoulder toward the circular drive out front. "I think someone's waiting for you back there."

Emma closed her eyes for a moment, one last chance to wish it would all come true, and when she looked over Sam's shoulder, there was Rye.

He was leaning casually against the side of his truck, looking so sexy in his jeans and a dark brown sweater. He had a big bouquet of roses in his hand, hanging down by his side, and he stood up straight when he saw her and gave her a big smile.

She took off running, not caring what anybody thought anymore. He came toward her, catching her and lifting her into his arms, twirling her around until she was laughing more than crying, pure joy sweeping through her.

She wrapped her arms around him, and he finally lowered her to the ground to where she could stand.

"Told you I'd be here," he said, kissing her wet cheek.

"Sam asked you to wait until I graduated from college, didn't he?"

Rye hesitated. "He told me he wanted you to have this time for yourself, without thinking about getting serious about anybody."

"And now I'm done," she said, beaming up at him. "I'm afraid to even turn around and look. Does that mean he's okay with this?"

"He's a father. I don't think any father is crazy about any guy who comes after his daughter at any age. He's also wondering what we've been doing behind his back—"

"I'll tell him."

"That would not help," Rye said, laughing.

"I mean, I'll tell him it was me. That I went to you and . . . You know. That I blackmailed you."

"That is not the way it happened, Emma, and I don't think any kind of details are going to help. What he's imagined already has been hard enough for him to take. I told him I managed to stay away from you until your birthday, and left it at that."

"Oh," she said. "And he's okay with that?"

"I'm still standing," Rye said. "I figure that means he's taking it well. I also told him I was done hiding how I feel about you."

"Wow," she said, smiling and taking a breath. It was happening. Really happening. "And . . . What does that mean?"

"Well, I've been thinking. . . . We could do this two different ways."

"Okay."

He handed her the flowers, a big bunch of roses in a rich, ivory color. "We never really did the dating thing."

"Dating?"

"You know . . . movies, dinner, dancing, picnics."

"I've been on dates," she said. "Lots of dates." That wasn't what she was looking for here.

"Or we could skip that part and go straight to the good stuff."

"Which would have something to do with me in your bed again?"

He grinned. "That works for me. But it's really not going to go over well with Sam. Besides, I told you, I'm through hiding the way I feel. And I'm sure of myself. Absolutely sure, but I want you to be sure, too. I'm in love with you."

More tears came, falling faster this time, blurring her vision, but she managed to get out the words, "I love you, too. I always have."

He pulled her to him and held on tight for the longest time, and then he laughed a bit and wiped away a few of her tears. "I guess we don't really need the dating part."

She shook her head.

"Did I tell you I bought a house last year?"

"I think I heard something about that."

"I know exactly what I want for it, but you know, the whole place seemed so big when it was just me, so empty. I got so far with it, and then I couldn't seem to make myself go any further. It's been sitting there, not quite finished for a while now. There's a nasty rumor going around town that I just can't make up my mind about anything."

"Really?"

He nodded. "I was lying to myself all along. Told myself it made sense to buy it as an investment and that it would give me something to do to maybe keep my mind off you. I told myself I did it because it seemed like Sam actually wanted me to—"

"He did," she said.

"Which I took to mean that he wants me around."

She grinned. "He does. Almost as much as I do."

"But I really bought it for you. I bought it because

somewhere deep down inside, I imagined that someday I might be able to share it with you. It won't
mean anything to me without you," he said, kissing
her softly. "So . . . I hope you like the house."

"I love the house."

"I wanted to ask, but then I would have had to be
honest with myself about what I wanted in the first
place, and I wasn't quite there yet. Sorry."

"It's okay." Everything was just fine today.

"There's one more thing you need to think about.
Think carefully, Emma," he said, looking uncertain
for the first time. "One day, I'm betting you're going
to want children—"

"I will."

"I'm going to want that, too, but if I'm their father,
they're going to find out someday where I've been,
what I've done."

"Then we'll just have to tell them," she said.

"Have you really thought about that? Your children. Telling them their father killed someone.
That's . . ." He swore softly and looked away. "That's
something I'll never be able to escape. I won't be able
to hide it, either."

"Then we'll deal with it." She could deal with anything with him.

"You don't have to deal with it, you know."

"Rye, I'm not having children with anyone but
you."

"You're sure?"

"I'm sure. I told you the night of my birthday and
yours, and I meant it. I love you, and I understand
everything. I don't blame you. I'm so grateful that, as
awful as all that was, you came through it. I'm grateful
you're still in this world and incredibly grateful that
right now, you're with me."

"And I'm grateful for all those same things," he

said. "I don't think I ever would have managed to let
it go on my own. I've been living like a man half alive
for so long. That's why I came here in the first place.
A buddy of mine from prison got sick with cancer,
and right before he died, I went to see him. He said
he'd been living the whole time he'd been out of
prison like he was still inside. Living like a man still
locked up, and after he was gone, I thought I was
doing the same thing, thinking it was better not to
have anything, because you don't have anything to
lose that way. No one can take anything away from
you. It wasn't enough for me anymore, and Sam was
the only thing I had left. So I came to find him. And
there you were."

She blinked back tears, thinking she was awfully
glad she was there.

"I love you, Emma. I love you for dragging me back
into the world, dragging me into the middle of your
family and sharing them with me, and making me feel
like a human being again. Making me believe in all
the possibilities between us. That I could have a place
here, a home, a family, and you. That's all because
of you."

She just held on to him then. There was nothing else
she could do. She'd always seen all the good inside of
him, all the strength, all the love.

He was wiping away her tears when Grace ran up
to them and grinned at Rye. "You're here!"

"Yeah," he stepped back from Emma and ruffled
Grace's hair. "I'm here. I heard there was a party
today, and no way was I going to miss it."

She looked from him to Emma, unsure what to
make of the smile and the tears on Emma's face.

"Don't worry," Rye said. "I'm not going to make
her cry any more."

"Promise?" Grace asked, obviously torn between her loyalty to her sister and the crush she had on him.

"Promise."

She grinned again. "Can I ride back to the house with you?"

"Sure," Rye said.

Grace took him by the hand and tugged, getting him to follow her back to where the rest of the family was. He grabbed Emma's hand and pulled her along with them.

She braced herself for Sam's reaction most of all. He stood straight and tall, not smiling, but not arguing, either. They all just kind of looked at each other, not knowing what to say. Rachel finally stepped in, saying they needed to get back to the house. There were more and more people coming for Emma's party. She managed to talk Grace out of riding with Rye by saying she needed her home right away, so she could help arrange things for the party. Grace loved throwing a party.

Rachel turned to Emma. "Don't you have things to clear out of your room? Big, heavy things?"

"Yes," Emma said.

"You probably need a couple of men to haul all of it downstairs," she said, looking at Sam and Rye. "Why don't you show them where your things are, and then we'll head home."

Emma wasn't sure it was a good idea to throw the two men together at the moment. She risked a quick glance at Sam, who still hadn't said anything, and at Rye, who looked resigned to whatever was coming. She wondered just what their conversation had been like when Rye had told Sam he would be here today. And how had he put it? That he was through hiding his feelings for her. How had that gone over?

She was about to find out.

"Come with me," she told them, heading into the dorm and up the stairs.

They followed, not saying a word. She unlocked her room, where her things were all packed and boxed up, ready to be hauled away. She showed them everything that was hers, thinking of the day she'd almost gotten Rye arrested by campus security, hoping he and Sam wouldn't attract that kind of attention today.

"I'll see you downstairs," she said, grabbing one of the smallest boxes and going, against her better judgment.

Neither one of them followed. Outside, Rachel gave her a big hug. "I'm so happy for you. I know how long you've been waiting for him."

"I didn't think this day would ever come," she said, glancing back at the front of the dorm. "I'm still not sure it has."

"It's going to be fine," Rachel told her. "Sam and Rye have come a long way in the past two and a half years."

"Still . . . I think I'd better get back up there."

She held her breath the whole way, walked so slowly down the hall to her room, pausing just outside the door, her back against the wall, ready to start praying. But there was no argument going on inside. They were just talking.

"I can imagine the kind of man you wanted for her," Rye said. "I know I'm not that man. But I love her, and I need her. And she loves me, Sam. I spent more than two years telling myself there was no way I deserved her, and she spent the same time being miserable thinking I didn't want her. I'm not going to do that to her anymore."

She waited, as did he. Emma closed her eyes thinking, *Come on, Sam.*

"There may be a better man than I am out there somewhere for her," Rye said. "But there's no one who's ever going to love her as much as I do. No one could ever need her the way I do. I know all about the age thing. I know some people won't understand about the whole family thing, either. But do you really give a damn what anybody else thinks? She's it for me. The only woman I will ever love, and I can make her happy, Sam. I promise you that."

Long, tense moments of silence followed. Finally, she heard Sam say, "She'd better be happy. Or you'll answer to me."

"Guess this isn't what you had in mind when you wanted me to be part of the family, huh?" Rye said easily. She could hear the smile in his voice, and then the conversation took on a more serious tone. "You know, the last thing I expected when I came here was for you to treat me like a brother. But that's what you did. I'm not sure if I've done the same in return. I'm sorry about that, about everything I thought about you before I ever knew you."

"I'm just glad you finally came. Glad you're still here." Sam cleared his throat, his voice more gruff than ever when he continued. "And you'd better not ever take my daughter away from here."

Emma didn't hear anything for a long time. When she peeked inside the room, they were embracing. Rye was laughing. She sneaked away and went back outside, knowing everything was going to be okay.

They got her stuff loaded eventually and drove back to the house. It was full of people that afternoon. They spilled out onto the front porch and the backyard, laughing and talking, more than a few people raising an eyebrow at seeing her and Rye together.

Oh, well.

After seeing her chasing after him for years, she

couldn't think it came as a big surprise to anyone how she felt about him.

They'd just have to get used to it.

Night was falling by the time she finally found herself alone with Rye. They walked into the backyard under one of the big trees, and Emma took a moment to look back at the house that seemed to glow in the darkened night, warmth and laughter and all the sounds of home spilling out.

She loved it here, loved her life. She loved Rye and turned around to tell him so, only to find him pulling a little jewelry box out of his pocket.

"You know . . ." He grinned at her. "I had a feeling that whole dating plan we were talking about might not go over so well. And just in case, I picked up a little something. . . ."

He put the box into her trembling hands. She just stood there staring at it. It seemed all her dreams really were going to come true.

"It helps if you open it, Em," he said softly. "Otherwise, you can't see what's inside."

She still couldn't do anything. He took it from her trembling hands and lifted the lid, pulling out a diamond, an emerald-cut diamond solitaire, flawless and dazzling, which he slipped onto her finger. Kept hold of her hand, brought it to his lips, and kissed it, right above the ring.

"I was really hoping you'd marry me," he said.

She nodded, crying so hard now.

"You're sure?"

"There is nothing in the world I would love more than marrying you."

He pulled her to him then, lifted her again, and swung her around. When she landed on her feet once more, she had her face pressed against his chest and then heard voices coming from the house, Grace's mostly.

"Where did they go?" she asked.

"Outside," Rachel said. "And don't go back there."

"But I want to see Rye."

"Come on, Grace. Give 'em a minute," Zach said.

Was everyone there?

Emma started to laugh. Rye did, too. She loved it when he laughed.

They both turned around and there on the back porch was Grace, staring at them. Zach was tugging on her arm. Sam was standing in back with his arm around Rachel. He didn't look upset.

Rachel was crying. Zach was grinning, and Grace . . .

"Oh, no," Emma said.

"What?"

"Grace looks upset."

"Yeah," Rye said matter-of-factly. "She has this crazy idea that she's in love with me, that I was going to wait for her."

"Crazy, huh?"

He nodded, then kissed her softly. "I'd have waited forever for you. Although I'm really glad it didn't come down to that."

"Me, too."

He looked at Grace and shook his head. "I have this effect on younger women, you know."

"Really? We're going to have to do something about that," Emma said.

"What are we going to do with her?" He nodded toward Grace. "I think Zach just guessed what's going on and told her. She really does look upset."

"We'll make her the flower girl at the wedding."

"That makes up for losing a guy? Being a flower girl?"

"When you're ten and love pretty dresses and getting your hair done and being the center of attention, yes, it does. And even if it didn't, she can't have you. You're mine."

"Yes, ma'am," he said. "Come on. Let's go break the news to them and then, I guess, to everybody else. Geez, we'll probably have a couple hundred people at the wedding, won't we? Even if we just invite the family and close friends alone."

"At least," Emma said.

"I guess I'd better get used to it. We're always going to be surrounded."

She nodded. "It gets a little intense at times, and they can be nosy and kind of pushy, but they mean well. And they're family."

"I can handle a big family," he said, putting his arm around her.

Together, they headed toward their big, happy family.

"Count on Catherine Anderson
for intense emotion and deeply
felt relationship."
—Jayne Anne Krentz

PHANTOM WALTZ

Catherine Anderson

"A MAJOR VOICE IN THE ROMANCE GENRE".
—*(Publishers Weekly)*

A long-ago accident has left lovely Bethany
Coulter confined to a wheelchair—and vulnerable
to betrayal and heartbreak. She's vowed never to
open her heart to a man again. But there's something about Ryan McKendrick, the handsome
rancher who's so sweetly courting her. Something
that makes her believe she can overcome every
obstacle—and rediscover lifelong, lasting love...

0-451-40989-2

To order call: 1-800-788-6262

Anderson/Phantom O383

Stephanie Gertler

JIMMY'S GIRL   (205162)

Ever wonder about lost first loves? Emily, an artist and stay-at-home mom with nearly grown children, does, for she is stuck in a troubled marriage. Memories of a sweet, rebellious boy named Jimmy, who kissed her under her pool table when she was 16, haunt her. Without knowing why or what she hopes to gain, she tracks him down. Jimmy is now a middle-aged Vietnam vet, living out a passionless marriage. Once they connect, it is as if they had never parted. Despite the physical distance and marital entanglements that separate them, they decide to meet.

PRAISE FOR *JIMMY'S GIRL:*

"A tender evocation of lost love, and what it means to find it again."   —*Kirkus Reviews*

"A sweet response to one of life's constant what-if questions."
                                          —*Booklist*, starred review

To order call: 1-800-788-6262

Bestselling Author

ISABEL WOLFF

The Trials of Tiffany Trott

Tiffany Trott has had her share of dates from hell, but she's not one to give up. So, she's holding her nose and plunging right back into the mating pool in this hilarious novel of dates and disasters, friendships and fix-ups. She's determined to find her knight in shining armor—or at least a guy in <u>men's</u> underwear.

"A delightful read!" —*Literary Review*

"Wonderfully comic...Will appeal [to] anyone who is longing to laughout loud at life." —*You* Magazine

0-451-40888-8

To order call: 1-800-788-6262

ONYX

CYNTHIA VICTOR

"Cynthia Victor tells a riveting story!"
—Julie Garwood

"Excitement and emotion on every page."
—Sandra Brown

CONSEQUENCES   0-451-40901-9
Page and Liza. Strangers raised a continent
apart....Rivals for love, money, and success...Sisters
bound by a betrayal no woman could ever forgive.
Or forget.

Also Available:
THE SISTERS   0-451-40866-7

To order call: 1-800-788-6262